CONTENTS

ADAM 315

#0 - A Stealing Fire novel

by Dani Lebeaux

DEDICATION

To all of those who loved me, even at my most unloveable, and to all of those who have caused me pain. As I have struggled, as I have triumphed, as I have found meaning and I have found myself, for all of the things that make us what we are, I am thankful.

EDITORS NOTES

This reprint as authorized by it's original Authors, represents the first unabridged edition Of "Adam 315" since it's original publication in 2026 PT.

Special Thanks extend to

Councilwoman Cassandra Reynolds - Olympus Protectorate; Earth Allied Forces

Councilman Dr. Steven Malcom - Olympus Protectorate; Earth Allied Forces

Councilman Adam Godwin - Olympus Protectorate; Earth Allied Forces

and to those loved ones both present and past who have played their part in this incredible journey.

All documents and recordings curated courtesy of the Council for Historical Preservation: Earth Allied Forces.

-01 N.E.A.- (New Earth Alliance).

PROLOGUE

It should have come as no surprise that the man in front of me bore little resemblance to anything that I had expected. No matter how objective I might strive to be, anticipation has a way of making the mind wander for most people, and I was no different. However now at the moment of introduction, I could scarcely see a single feature more monstrous in him than his sheer size. Admittedly that in itself impressed notably upon me at the reality of his arrival.

The buzz at my door had come only moments earlier, after which I had paged him in without a word between us. Normally I would have peeked at my screen to view the camera feed, but by request, I had disabled the system for the night in preparation for my subjects arrival. I had also asked him if I should leave the lights on at the very least, but the offer was declined politely without explanation. So while I heard the freight elevator bringing my soon to be subject up through the dark, even from where I sat, I could only imagine my guest navigating the strangely haunting space below.

The truth is that I had recently put the first 2 floors up for lease after the previous tenants decided to retire. I was happy for them, naturally,. They were a lovely couple, but it was going to be difficult to find anyone to fill the space who could in my mind, possibly replace the charm they brought into my world. There was just something quaint and cozy about living above an antiques warehouse. Luckily, this nostalgia of my heart meant that the sign reading "Joe and Franks Vintage Surplus" still hung above the door by the sidewalk entrance, marking my building most readily evident for those inquiring of directions. Admittedly it also served as the right type of comforting icebreaker for those seeking anonymity within the boundaries of my profession and I will miss it when the time comes.

That being said, I was alone for the night as the sole occupant of the top floor, with all the privacy in the world in order to conduct my business, a consideration that suited my mysterious subject just fine. Even having been paged in and fully announced just moments earlier, he still knocked at my door before entering, which seeemed amusing to me given the circumstance, but I called out for him to come without chuckling to myself. I had watched him duck forward and to one side simply to enter my office, but that was enough to establish at least a baseline of why he might fabricate such claims as he had made in his messages.

For safety sake, as always with these types of things, I would be cautious to approach until I had a clearer impression of the subject himself, especially with my main security measures disabled. If needed, the emergency call button was still active below the corner of my desk, but in all my years here, Ive never actually used it. It wasn't that I feared what the man claimed to be. Quite the opposite in this case I admit. He seemed not only friendly, but polite, courteous and old fashioned throughout our correspondence to this point. My hesitance stemmed simply from experience. I knew any claim of such nature as those which he had made, typically accompanied some level of mental issue which could either be benign... or not. I only wanted to be prepared.

So I remained behind my desk as I stood to acknowledge his entrance in greeting, partly hoping that the gentleness and calm projected by this choice, would promote comfort and ease for his initial impressions. However I was also making conscious attempts to accomodate what little I knew that he believed of himself. After all, whether legitimate or legitimately delusional, the last thing I should want was to spook this man, especially now that I saw his size.

At this point I could see little else by his silhouette, but I could tell from a distance that he wore a long black coat, and an oversized blue gray scarf whose fabric was worn thin with age. Even after he had made his way inside and gently closed the door behind himself, his details remained obscured over the distance as the only illumination within the hall outside belonged to the soft glow of the emergency lights nearest the lift, leaving my eyes to adjust once more to the dim of my desklamps' warm but limited glow within the room, while the blinds hung closed behind me.

Perhaps if I'd chosen a smaller office for myself we might have seen one another better, but I'd picked this one for good reasons. Despite my apartment being just down the hall, the fact was that a lot of nights, more than I should rightly admit, I slept here on the sofa, and it was far more common for me to hosts guests in a professional capacity, than for me to invite anyone over for social reasons. Besides all of that, the view was amazing at sunset as the rear of the building faced due west with no other structures between myself and the city park nearby. I also liked that the space allowed me to frame my old articles in a single line along the wall, rather than jumbling them over and under each other around the room.

In contrast to all of this, the distance between us, the dim light and so on, the big mans movements were clear. He silently looked my way with a slight gesture of inquiry towards the teapot and glasses which I had prepared upon the rooms' side table. I nodded without a word, and he also in silence, stepped towards them with nary a rustle of his clothes while I remained seated.

I watched him stoop once more to pour himself a glass and my eyes widened in strain to make out what detail I could of the interaction. The mug itself nearly seemed like a childs plaything in his overly large hands, vanishing as they wrapped round its curve with only one finger able to fit through the handle. Even though I knew the size were standard mugs, not in fact some toy tea set, I imagined much of the world must look like that to him, and it made the whole scene oddly charming somehow.

All the while the silence echoed off the walls as if we stood amongst a field of graves, with every sound of movement or contact, being amplified in the stillness. I looked down to my laptop momentarily and listened with no rush to advance the proceedings beyond whatever pace he might choose. I heard 2 cubes of sugar being first dropped and then stirred into his tea, followed by the light clink of the spoon being set down once more, and the low slurp of liquid thru his lips followed by a deep and resonant breath.

I knew that he could hear the tapping of keys as I took notes. The camera of my laptop was on during all of this I might add, facing forward to see him as I did. This too was no secret. He expected me to be watching. By contacting me, he had asked for the scrutiny. He knew what his appearance was, and he knew that the story which he was telling would demand skeptical review, but that doesn't mean professionalism takes a back seat. He may have asked for the outside cameras to remain inactive, but it was ok to stare. It was expected to type. It was even expected to record these sessions, but discretion still mattered. So when I looked up from my screen, I did not stop typing.

What's funny is that even then, first impression, no view of his face or expressions, no sound of his voice, while he was busy dwarfing all else in the room, dressed in dark and coming to my office after hours to expand on a claim which was as wild an assertion as I'd ever entertained professionally, his gentleness was apparent.

I saw a man of great height and broad shoulder yes, standing with his dark black hair pulled back into a loose pony tail above a still shadowed face, drinking quietly from a small cup of tea which was clearly not produced for any person of his size, and I watched as he politely and cautiously walked forward with the same nervous apprehension which I had seen dozens or more times before an interview. I watched his body language and demeanor as he made sure not to stumble on the edge of the rug, and with careful assessment, I made each judgement as if my life depended on them. If there was any violent intention within him, it was not visible at present, nor did I feel it might suddenly appear from a lack of restraint or control, but I had interviewed murderers before who held such calm.

With each advancing step, this man, this vitruvian behemoth, only served to illustrate more the meter of a measured individual, both considerate and careful in his ways. His footsteps did not stomp, stumble or shake the floor beneath us, which I tell you honestly they should have, however he continued to lean slightly forward as he walked and I observed what appeared to be a favorance toward one leg over the other. His lean seemed not out of timidity so much as an attempt to bring himself closer to the level of an average height, as if it were thru habit more so than situational accomodation... however I have seen the favorance of his movements before as well, and I determined a very high likelihood that he had overcome some previous injury long ago to the opposing leg. This happens sometimes where in these instances one never entirely loses the mental inclination to limp once it has healed. This I felt, but could not yet verify, seemed by observation, to be be such a case.

While the light exposed more of him with each step, I could see now that his features were that of a man somewhere in his mid thirties. His hair was stylishly aquitted and his clothing tidy if not a bit timeless. The woolen coat, the scarf, the plain black pants, shirt and boots all but vanishing as shadows. He wore no beard or scruff and he had a pronounced structure that I myself might even call handsome after an affect. His lips were a bit thin for my personal taste, but yes I could see this man being the envy of many others, and desire of more than that.

However all of it seemed tailored toward the impossible. No matter how quiet, how clean, or how polite, gray, dark, shadowy, or otherwise that this man might make himself, there was no way possible that he could ever hide on the street or in a crowd. As he closed the distance between us to set himself into a chair nearer the light, that truth became clear to me. There in those awaited but revealing seconds, I bore witness to what was a stark difference of the man himself so far beyond his uncommon proportions, that description proves difficult even from my original notes. It was something only visible now in the close proximity, but would have been remarkable in any light at this distance, even if not at any distance in full light.

People despise the concept of judgement, especially in reference to journalism, which strives to be unbias and truthful, but they neglect to realize that judgement is in fact an integral part of this job, to judge attributes, draw conclusions, investigate fully when possible and report descriptively among other duties. I am appropriately expected to observe, note and inspect anything which may be of relevance to a stories' credibility or motivation... and this mans' physical appearance was certainly a part of that.

So, as is the task, I will attempt to describe the subject now as he appeared to me then, complete with perspective and questioning notation as they occurred in the beginning, without omission or exageration on my part, for these matters are relevent to every single word that might follow in the story he claimed.

To begin beyond what I have already stated, I could make out a faint scar that ran the length of his scalp, only jutting sharply downward above the edge of his right brow. This was dismissable unless you focused directly on him face to face, but not for lack of presence. Surely it was a large scar, but it was not glaring or distracting to his shape or features. Truthfully I would say with conviction that in relation to his most striking trait, a trait all its own in uniqueness, the scar was nearer to nothing than it should have been had it appeared on another.

No, this other characteristic was much more evident and intriguing all at once. It sparked immediate unease to see, even while it filled my mind racing with questions to what in fact it was that I was seeing, and all of this is to say that what it was, is, and was then, would be described as an entirely strange and alienating quality about his skin itself. I do not mean to defame or demean the medical conditions of any individual, but this was not a matter of some dermatological condition, injury, or disfigurement.

Especially in light of his claims, I tried my best to act unsurprised, to look calmly and easily toward him in a controlled manner as an outward form of healthy skepticism, rather than shock or fear which might serve in his mind as premature vindication, but this quality to his skin simply cannot be overstated in the visceral reaction produced by its sight.

Perhaps it makes me seem bias, eager to validate, or even bad at my job to say this, but being as alert as ever and believing myself prepared before his actual arrival, I now found myself feeling as if I had just stepped into the fog of a dream while the world had become hazy around me, blurring the lines between reality and the stuff of fevered hallucinations. There was cognitive dissonance forming in real time as I tried to restructure my basic definitions of human physiology in order to proceed.

His skin as I said, that was the thing. It was unnatural and foreign, but not entirely. There was familiarity of a sort. It looked thin, but only in the way that you would expect of the elderly perhaps, or maybe more so a section of plucked poultry, patted dry and stretched like cling film over something larger than its rightful measurements... but no, that wasn't close enough either... cling film itself? perhaps layers of it? Elastic wax paper? Or parchment?

It was pulled over those measurements, happening to be the face of a handsome and agreeable man, but barring some severe medical malady that I'd never witnessed before, he didn't appear fully human, which for those who familiarize themselves with bad CGI or the uncanny valley, may be well aware, can produce a shock to the baser part of ones mind as it struggles to either rewrite the definition of what people look like in general terms, or to reject the image for simply looking wrong in the first place.

So here he was, in the flesh, real as could be, which made everything else seem a bit less real by proximity, and therefore easier to accept. But about that flesh, all at once appearing both leathery and yet so papery frail that I couldn't quite tell if what I saw was opaque or indeed translucent without staring straight into it; I remember thinking at that point, that "There's no way to fake this" when I had finally zeroed in on its cause.

It had taken me a few seconds in my surprise... but I finally had it. That was it. Yes, his skin was truly translucent, not entirely transparent mind you, but clearly see thru in several places, which are abnormal enough on their own. Beyond this, it was tinted with a slight golden hue which seemed to visibly pulsate in measured time...

At this point I must clarify, this was not an added golden hue atop of some red, pink, white, or brown tones as would be expected, This was no issue of melanin abnormality, nor even extreme albinism alone, as one might think at first description. I truly mean that there was no redness to be seen anywhere on him at all. Neither blush of the cheek nor vein of the eye, not even pink of the lips, but instead... Only that slight yellowness just beneath the surface, broken with darker, hints of greenish black to the lips, gums, and areas surrounding his eyes, which still showed thru with the capillary action of that yellow pulsation within, as if I were watching the blood of his veins being pumped just beneath the form of it all.

So the texture wasn't the issue after all where his skin was concerned. Able to now to observe that more objectively, I could finally conclude that it was not overly dry, nor cracked, nor as I could actually see the measure of it's thickness, even thin or overstretched. It was just somehow inhuman due to something unfathomable in the series of inevitable conclusions.

I picked up my own tea and began to stir it... As we silently awaited the third member of our endeavor. My subject looked down towards my seated position across the desk and offered a gentle smile, raising his glass as if in salute. His teeth were as perfect as any I had ever seen, frighteningly white and straight against the outline of his dark lips and yellowed skin, yet the expression seemed practiced and without ease. Could he truly be as unnerved by my presence as I felt by the oddity of his?

From what I could see behind his teeth, his mouth was equally devoid of the red and pink hues considered natural to the common man. I couldnt quite make it out, but his tounge and inner mouth, as best I could tell, resembled the same dark, blackish-green tint of his lips. My heart raced as the reality of my agreement set in. I could no longer deny in the back of my mind that I was beginning to believe who this man claimed that he was, or what this interview would potentially mean to the world, nor to the man sitting across from me. Seeing was believing, and for the first time in my experience of extravagant claims, I wasnt headed towards debunking the latest urban legend or uncovering a hoax. Here he sat, in the confines of my own office... and he was real.

Nervously, I breathed in deep and leaned back in my chair

returning a smile before glancing at the time on my laptop. I hoped the smile would not give away my apprehension as his had already shown, or my pure wonder.

"He should be here shortly." I assured my guest as I looked up for a reaction. There was a slight pause while I curiously awaited his response.

"Have you told him anything about who I am?" He asked.

I was somewhat broken from my admitted trance at the sound of his words. This was the first time that I had actually heard him speak. Our correspondence having been previously through email alone, I found that his voice, soft and low, brought crisp clarity to the formation of those words. They were evenly and gently paced with an articulation that seemed as if he had grown up in the American midwest. There was no accent to speak of, and no slur nor drawl to his pronunciations, nothing in fact to hint at what I had been told to be his foreign origins.

He sat in my mind firmly as the consumate nervous gentleman whom I had seen just moments ago stirring his tea from across the room. I imagined now how difficult typing must have been in our earlier contact. I pictured his large fingers meticulously hitting each key with the faintest of touches in order not to press 2 or even 3 letters at once. I could not help but to laugh slightly at myself, partly for the mental image, but also partly in surprise at my own expectations. This thought relaxed me further and I responded congenially while I slightly rubbed one hand above my brow.

"Actually, no. I wasnt quite sure how to explaint he idea to anyone without being hung up on to be honest. The doctor seemed quite intent with the promise that you would be able to answer his questions about the sample I sent him." I looked back up and met the subjects gaze, still wearing a genuine smile on my face.

"I see... So he believes he will be meeting with another scientist then?" he asked. His face looked nervous as he leaned forward,

shifting uneasily in his chair. I could see him holding his tea now with both hands on his lap. My answer was not intended to sound flippant or insensitive, but I found it falling from my lips before a second thought. Part of me questioned if perhaps I was losing my touch.

"Well, you are." I said. "A scientist that is... From what I can tell from our discussions, I think you are probably one of the most uniquely equipped individuals to have first hand knowledge in this particular field..." I continued.

His discomfort could be seen clearly as his eyes darted towards the door. I had to put him at ease before he tried to leave. I could not let the story of a lifetime walk out on me over a stupid mistake.

"He does know to expect something remarkable... and he is known to be very open minded. I assumed that was part of why you requested him in particular." I chimed, while twisting in my chair playfully, hoping that the open display of innocent "femininity" might somehow convince him of his safety. It is not something I have used many times before, but knowing the importance of this fact in many cultures, I gambled the chance.

He seemed to relax a bit back into his seat as he brought his left hand upward towards his face and placed its' thumb gently upon the crease of his chin. I knew that I had him thinking then. So I continued to speak. "I met him once in Geneva" I added

My last sentence paid off. I watched as my subjects' train of thought changed. He reached again for his tea as his eyes looked deep at the glass, picking it up slowly.

"Geneva..." He breathed longingly.

It was as if he had drifted to another place, speaking more to himself and under his breath than to me. I took note during this open stare, to study of his eyes themselves. They were pale and colorless, reflective of whatever came near to them, watery even in their vastness, shimmering like mirrors of the world.

My following comment attempted to draw his mind back to the present. A reminder of why we were meeting this night.

"He was attending the genetics conference." I continued. "I was there for a story." I offered further, allowing my words to trail off... A slight but silent laugh escaped from his mouth as he smiled genuinely at last. There was simply the sound of air escaping his lungs before he spoke.

"Same hotel I might guess?" He questioned with bemusement, but his chuckle was cut short as he turned his head sharply toward the right, the smile dropping from his face.

"He is here." He sighed as he turned, entirely facing his back to the door. I watched the giant lean slightly, as if to intentionally hunch forward before placing his hands onto the arm rest of the chair where he sat. He prepared to rise to his feet.

"Did you leave the door unlocked after paging me in?" He asked me nervously.

"I did." I told him as I too stood, finally hearing the familiar sound of the elevators motions outside.

I wondered how he had known.

PREFACE

The following is a full and complete documentation of my interview sessions with the individual that the media have since dubbed Adam 315.

My personal notes, as well as accounts of the days following the interviews, have been interspersed after the fact and reformatted within appropriate placement of the records taken by the autodictation of each recorded session, in order to best relay an account of these historic events.

~Cassandra Reynolds~

> *"I have resolved every night, when I am not imperatively occupied by my duties, to record, as nearly as possible in his own words, what he has related during the day. If I should be engaged, I will at least make notes. This manuscript will doubtless afford you the greatest pleasure; but to me, who know him and who hear it from his own lips - with what interest and sympathy shall I read it in some future day! Even now, as I commence my task, his fulltoned voice swells in my ears; his lustrous eyes dwell on me with all their melancholy sweetness; I see his thin hand raised in animation, while the lineaments of his face are irradiated by the soul within. Strange and Harrowing must be his story, frightful the storm which embraced the gallant vessel on its course and wrecked it - thus!*
>
> *-Mary Shelley-*
>
> *"The Modern Prometheus"*

SESSION ONE

Interviewer Name:

Cassandra Reynolds: Journalist for "Washington Post" newspaper and special columnist for Al-Jazeera International.

Second Interviewer and Consultant:

Dr. Steven Malcom of the Boston College Institute for Scientific Research and Advancement: Specialization in structural biochemistry. Published author and Nobel laureate

Interview Subject : Adam

The time is 11:47 pm. March the 21st, 2024

Location: Personal offices of Cassandra Reynolds, Washington D.C.

CR = Cassandra Reynolds

DM= Dr. Steven Malcom

AG = Subject - Adam

Personal notes Italicized.

◆ ◆ ◆

A GLIMMER IN THE VEINS

Several weeks ago, I was contacted via email message by a man calling himself Adam. After some degree of correspondence and initial questioning I have decided that his case is worth further investigation if only for the story behind why a man would make such claims. Five days ago as agreed between the subject and myself, after many precautions and assurances, I received a package containing two small vials with instruction to forward one of them to a Dr. Steven Malcom of Boston College, with explicit intent for their study. Following further instruction, I extended my personal invitation to the former, that after he had taken time to evaluate the properties of this substance, he might participate with my investigation into its origins. The day after delivery confirmation of said package reached my email, the doctor agreed.

This documentation begins at the arrival of Dr. Steven Malcom. Subject Adam formerly present.

Our latest arrival had knocked briefly before I called for him to enter the room from behind my desk. The raise in my voice made my subject wince in surprise and I felt somewhat guilty for my lack of professional courtesy.

As Dr. Malcom entered the room Adam was already out of his chair, still facing me, but standing all the same. For the first time since his arrival, I was able to accurately gauge the height difference between me and my new acquaintance. With no exaggeration he easily stood above me by at least 70 centimeters. I watched anxiously for the Doctors reaction as Adam turned to face him. However at first he paid no mind to us aside from to halfway acknowledge that we were in fact present at all, proceeding instead to close the door behind him and turn the lock without asking.

It was quite interesting to see a renowned scientist walking into the room in a baseball cap, but it matched his outfit of shorts and a tee shirt, which I found odd for a chilly day in March, however I considered that the nights had felt warm as of late, especially more so I assumed by comparison to Boston itself, as I recalled from online, that they were still experiencing snow just days before.

The doctor removed his hat to hang upon the coat rack by the door before finally turning in our direction, yet he still did not look at us directly, instead busying himself with his head downward as he approached quickly, tussling his medium brown hair to remove any trace of "hat head".

Doctor Steven Malcom... He was every bit the individual I remembered meeting in Geneva. An athletic and somewhat boyish man for his age, who looked equally the part of baseball coach as he might a scientist. Possibly a bit aloof, and perpetually casual, he was also quite kind and approachable, even while discussing matters of technicality that most would find boring or impenetrable coming from anyone else. I recalled his mention that he had originally studied to be a physician before research turned his head, and felt that it might have suited him well if for no reason aside from what seeemd to me a natural way about him which might have been the perfection of bedside manner.

His hasty and single minded entrance were not out of character I thought, but locking the door seemed a bit presumptuous. It wasn't until he nearly bumped into Adam's chest that he finally looked up to greet us. His head leaned back as he craned to look towards Adam's face. Startled, he stepped backward, at once offering his apologies as he extended his hand in introduction. In my head I had to laugh when he stopped short to do a double take. That was the reaction I had been waiting for. Desperately I needed to see how someone else responded to the giant figure that stood before us.

To my chagrin as well as admiration, he paused only for a moment with his eyes wide and mouth open before he advanced his arm the rest of the way with quick but unquestioned recovery, even though his words came out in clear surprise to even himself.

DM : Um.. Doctor Steven Malcom.

Adam took the doctors hand in both of his own, engulfing it as if it were the extremity of a young child. He also bowed slightly as he gave the doctor a gentle yet firm shake... a gesture which we had bypassed upon first greeting, I now felt regret for skipping this, as it seemed to mean a great deal to the large man.

AG: Thank you doctor for agreeing to meet this evening. I am Adam.

Steven leaned slightly to his right to look towards me with obvious confusion. I removed my hand from my mouth only long enough to give a quick wave, but had to place it back near immediately to prevent actually laughing aloud.

CR: Hi Steven.

As Adam released his hands from around Stevens' and stepped to one side, I decided to correct my previous error, and reached over my desk to shake his hand myself.

The feel of his skin was warm and soft, dry but uncalloused, and the shake it gave was both firm and heavy without tightness.

CR: So now that we are all here, Steven there is tea over there on the table if you'd like some, and you have your pick of seats.

He chose to skip the tea as he headed towards the small leather sofa to my left of the room. It put him ever so slightly behind Adam in relation to myself, but it seemed an appropriate placement. However neither him nor Adam seemed ready to be seated just yet. Steven turned back towards us slightly rocking on his heels, hands in pocket.

DM: So... you are the man responsible for the liquid gold?

He smiled jokingly.

DM: I gotta tell ya, I am incredibly curious to find out the story behind this stuff. I don't know how much Cassandra has told you, but I've been running it through at the lab and it's absolutely amazing. No one has ever heard of anything like it. We can't even identify the suspension fluid, but the contents, on a cellular level its mind blowing!

It was at this point in the conversation where Steven Stopped short and became serious... His demeanor changed from excited to suspicious.

DM: Just who are you Adam? And how is it that someone I have never heard of, has come up with this? Surely if you produced it then Cassandra wouldn't have approached me.

I turned towards Steven. My own expression dropping into the weight of the questions inference without balking at the seeming absurdity of the obvious omission to the conclusions to be drawn by Adam's very appearance.

CR: Before we actually start with the rest of the questions... I think you may want to prepare yourself Steven.

I decided it was the right time. Dr. Malcoms insistence on objectivity without assumption called for directly demonstrative evidence to confirm Adam's claims about the strange liquid contained within the vials... Adam and I had previously agreed upon this course of action after my first response from the Doctor had come thru, but admittedly up until actually meeting him in person just moment ago, I had reserved for myself the right to back out of this plan.

Despite all of our correspondence and my willingness to conduct this meeting, it was still far more likely that he was delusional than it had seemed that this action might come to pass. However now as the time had come, it was my confidence and trust in my subjects authenticity that compelled me to follow through. Adam, I was certain at this point was if not entirely sane, then at the least likely honest about the contents of the vials he had sent, and the actions to follow were important. We had to show the Doctor firsthand if we expected even the slightest benefit of the doubt.

I walked to the side of my desk and removed a letter opener from the top drawer. I looked Adam in the eyes, handed it over and nodded. He understood.

Dr. Malcom seemed very evidently concerned to see the large man now holding a sharp object, and he looked worriedly towards me in object confusion. However I believed that this show of trust was necessary. We proceeded.

I rolled up my right sleeve and extended my arm palm up, towards the giant in front of me. We met eyes once more as he took my arm in one hand. Adam was entirely gentle as expected, but I braced myself none the less. We shared a silent confirmation with one another as the doctor looked on. I did not close my eyes, nor wince as he sharply stabbed into my forearm.

I felt the letter opener pierce my skin deeply. It was no worse than an immunization round, but I thought for a moment that Dr. Malcom was going to lunge at Adam if I did not gesture otherwise. It was such a protective stance that I determined this to be merely the doctors nature rather than any personal feeling for me. So I turned towards him with assurance as Adam removed the small blade, and the Doctor stood down.

I folded my other arm over in order to place two fingers over my fresh wound as Adam turned his palm outward towards Dr. Malcom as if he were a stage magician demonstrating the emptiness of his sleeves. I could swear a small smirk played across his face. However, he seemed entirely professional about the ordeal, much more collected in fact than the scientist whom I was certain would object at any moment.

After this, Adam brought his hand back towards his own body and closed it around the blade of the letter opener. It was a swift motion that I am sure cut him much deeper than it had myself. He quickly reached behind me to lay the letter opener once again on my desk and I turned my body to allow him easier access to me while motioning with my head for Dr. Malcom to come closer.

CR : It's quite alright Steven. You will want to see this.

His inquisitiveness as a scientist seemed to take the lead and he walked towards us. I held out my arm once more and removed my fingers as he leaned in to inspect. Blood flowed from the wound slowly as the pressure was released. He looked up towards me.

DM : Why?

His questioning was cut short as Adam opened his palm revealing the yellow liquid that was his blood. The doctor looked up at him and then back towards me in disbelief, but we spared no time in proceeding before he could ask a word. Again Adam gently took my arm in hand. I nodded approval once more and with that, he moved his gashed palm to me and lightly pressed it over my open cut until I felt the wetness of his blood mixing with my own. As he slowly removed it once more, even I was in awe to witness what I felt confident would happen next.

It was not like a scene from a movie. There was no retraction of my blood or instant cleaning of the wound. Instead, what transpired was like watching a construction in time lapse. The cut didn't just close, but rather seemed to stitch itself back together with the growth of new skin. It didn't burn. It was not truthfully painful at all, just a slight itch that quickly dissipated.

Something else did take place that I could not explain however. Adam no longer looked as a stranger to me, but as a friend. My worries had melted off and somehow I felt different than I had before, like I had known him for years. It was all like this was the most natural thing in the world and I had been crazy to have ever doubted the giant who offered such a gift to my person.

Within seconds the wound was gone, healed over without scar as if it had never happened. Adam opened his palm upward to reveal that the same had occurred on his own hand in equal or less time.

Dr. Malcom's jaw dropped. His eyes wide with an expression I have found usually reserved for children. He spoke with a quieted sense of awe.

DM : No offense intended but what the fuck did I just watch? How is that possible? It's *in* you? It's your blood?...

AG : If you would be seated Doctor, I will answer all of your questions.

I smiled and leaned my waist back onto my desk as I gestured for the doctor to return to his seat before standing again to walk round and pull out my own chair. Adam and I took our previous seats as Dr. Malcom returned to the sofa by the wall. He staggered a bit as he walked, turning around partially at least three times as if to ask a question, before turning back quickly to continue towards his intended place of rest...

It reminded me of watching my grandfather forgetfully shuffling from room to room trying to remember what he was looking for when I was younger. I did not actually know what was going through the Doctor's mind, but while I felt he may be momentarily suspended in his amazement and disbelief, I also knew all the more to expect heavily, a remaining skepticism once we began.

AN UNEXPECTED SYMPATHY

After Dr. Malcom retook his seat and we settled back in for what we all knew to be the long endeavor to follow, I felt it my responsibility to begin the dialogue. My recorder had been on since Adam's first entrance, but I stopped briefly to adjust my settings before moving forward. I double checked to be sure that the autodictation program had correctly transcribed our words so far and I hit save on my notes just in case. After affirming in the positive that all was in order, I pulled closer to my laptop and positioned the camera to face only Adam as he sat before me.

CR: Ready?

Adam nodded politely before looking towards Steven, who it seemed at least for the moment, could barely keep up with his own words.

DM: Umm uhh, Yes. Hell yes! By all means yes. Let's kick this pig.

Adam looked at me quizzically.

AG: I've not heard that one before.

He chuckled again, the same visible yet silent laugh I had observed previously in the evening.

CR: Alright then, let's begin.

I addressed Adam directly.

CR: For the record, would you state your full name followed by your age?

AG: My name is Adam Godwin. I am three hundred and fifteen years of age.

I looked sharply towards Steven as he prepared to call out in protest. He closed his mouth immediately and leaned back into his seat.

CR: No middle name?

AG: No

CR: So you are telling us that you were born in...

DM: 1709

Steven Mumbled skeptically under his breath and I turned again to glare briefly in his direction.

CR: Dr. Malcom you will have your turn.

AG: He is correct Mrs. Reynolds. I have been alive since 1709.

CR: It's Ms. Actually, but please, call me Cassandra.

AG: Yes miss. Quick math by the way Doctor Malcom.

CR: Before you explain to us how that is possible, I would like to ask... You seem to have corrected me when I said "born". Do you have an aversion to that term?

His tone was still formal and with no hint of offense however he spoke the following as if to make himself intensely clear to all present.

AG: I only strive for the accuracy due... I know your trepidation towards the opening of the topic too swiftly for Dr. Malcom's sake, but as for the reasons I have come, I do feel compelled to be as open and honest from the beginning as humanly possible under the circumstance. He has seen enough to afford me the same benefit with which you have so graciously given. I do not open my veins lightly or without purpose and I believe an equal show of good faith is in order.

CR: Doctor Malcom, do you agree to this?

He seemed calmer now as he nodded his head in agreement.

DM: I do. I apologize... It's just a lot to take in Cass... I mean Ms. Reynolds. Adam, you sound completely genuine, and *obviously* you are very special in some way I truly hope to understand. I just... are you an alien?

Adam laughed at the suggestion. I might add that this was the first time I had heard an audible laugh from him unrestrained. I was a bit surprised to hear the sound of it as it resembled the giggles of a young child rather one might expect from a man of his physical stature. Adam continued to smile in bemusement. He lightly rubbed his chin and turned to face Dr. Malcom.

AG: I assure you Doctor, I am more of this earth than you may believe.

Although my pity was now with Steven as I watched the wheels turn in his mind, I too found myself smiling as I covertly shifted the camera so that the doctor too would be in frame as we continued.

AG: I apologize for my laughter. It is simply an assumption I have never faced before. Please Doctor, continue.

DM: Interesting sense of humor for someone your age.

Again his sarcasm was noted yet ignored by Adam. I may have been accustomed to accomodating the claims of others without allowing myself the luxury of outwardly expressing personal judgements during an interview, but it was clear that Steven was not, and the lightly adversarial edge to his statements made for a frustrating, if not entertaining start from my side of the desk.

AG: Would you assume me to be without humor due to my age?

Adam continued to smile without apology, but spoke now in a friendly nature without allowing Steven chance to reply.

AG: Young man, when you have remained on this world so long as myself, you discover the importance of finding the humor in all possible.

Dr. Malcom now cracked a smile of his own as he leaned his elbows onto his knees and tilted to briefly rub his forehead before sitting back up.

DM: Three hundred and fifteen huh? I have gotta say, you don't look a day over ninety Mr. Godwin. Though I must confess that you could use some work on your complexion. How do you do it?

Though Dr. Malcom was now laughing, the joke seemed to pause Adam's levity and his face became mildly more serious. He looked Dr. Malcom directly in the eye.

AG: That answer doctor, is actually the precise reason I requested to meet with *you.*

Adam's countenance was now entirely serious. There was a brief pause and his tone darkened with the slow and precise direction of his following words.

AG: It is something I too desire to know.

Dr. Malcom composed himself almost immediately.

DM: That fluid... It IS your blood, isnt it?

AG: Yes... it is.

DM: You have my full attention then sir.

After breaking eye contact with one another, The room went quiet for well over a minute as we all seemed to breathe a heavy breath. They both looked to me with gravity before the doctor spoke one final sentence.

DM: Alright Cassandra... it's your interview.

The interruption over, I briefly offered a smile of courtesy as I composed myself once again.

CR: Well. Since your blood is obviously the first interest and largest part of this present discussions' catalyst... Let's begin there. You made mention of something in your earlier correspondence that referred to your appearance. I didn't understand it at first but I think since meeting you it makes much more sense. You told me that you had to quit "dying your blood" before we met.

AG: Yes, actually that is likely a good place to begin. Obviously you can see what I look like today since I have ceased my weekly injections.

CR: And from what you have mentioned previously, you did just that, so that we would see you as you are.

AG: I assumed it would be more appropriate. This is the first time in over 120 yrs that I have gone anywhere without altering my natural appearance.

CR: That is a long time.

AG: It has been necessary.

CR: Please, elaborate.

AG: Well perhaps we should begin with a bit of history concerning my appearance in general.

CR: That would be fine. The topic is not too sensitive for you is it?

AG: Ms. Reynolds, the topics which I am here to discuss will all be sensitive in nature to myself. I have come prepared.

I wish all my subjects were like that.

CR: I just wanted to be sure. Continue.

AG: I have made you aware of my age, and you personally have been partially informed of my origins. Now if you will, I would like you to think of my appearance in a different context.

Remove yourself from the preparations you were given and the age in which we presently live. Imagine the reactions of a less enlightened time.

While you may see my scars and think little of them, that simply was not always so. Even today I saw the surprise on the doctors face at his realization of my size.

My skin however... the colors beneath it. The movement I am sure you have noticed... has always been the greatest obstacle for my ability to blend in.

CR: Hence the dye?

AG: Hence the dye.

CR: Why only 120 years ago?

AG: Truthfully? because the option was not available before that time. The required breakthroughs in synthetic pigmentation that allow me to dye my blood without negative consequence were non existent to my knowledge, and to be honest, until they were, the thought had never occurred to me.

CR: So exactly what does it do? What dye do you use and how does it affect your appearance?

AG: Well to begin with, I tried to use purely red, to ghastly result. My appearance became orange obviously, but it also did no assistance to disguise the the translucency of my skin itself. To be frank, I appeared as a skinned corpse that someone had carved from all too many pumpkins, and it took over 5 weeks to leave my body. I was fortunate to be living on a well stocked and grown subsistence farm at the time with no need to purchase my food or venture out for provisions... else it might have been more difficult upon me as I experimented.

Eventually through trial and error, with many bouts of temporary sickness brought on by self inflicted blood poisoning, I was able to discover a mix of reds, and blues of an opaque nature, which at last allowed me to gain a more common appearance. The resulting difference astounded me immediately for it was the first time I had smiled in 15 years. Although it also broke my heart to do so.

It was a very tumultuous time for me...

I watched as tears began to well in his eyes and I felt my heart go out to him. I would not realize until later, exactly how far this question had touched into a subject so entirely devastating to his very being.

CR: Would you like to stop for a moment Adam?

He looked again to my eyes, making no attempt to wipe the single tear that rolled down his left cheek. I could see determination and strength within him but I had no idea just how much. He swallowed hard, seemingly swallowing his pain in turn before taking a deep breath.

AG: I should like to continue. It's only that with exception to a handful of incredibly special people.... You must understand Miss Reynolds... I was a monster before. As far as anyone knew, what they saw *was* a monster. I wasn't human. In the most fundamental capacity of life, I could nary walk down a street without being chased from town or someone attempting to take my life... I had even begun to believe for some time that I was destined to become the monster others believed me to be... In earnest admission I confess to you that I did not see myself with forgiveness to these sins of nature any more than those who feared me.

But when the dye worked at last, after getting it right... It had taken me three years, but I could tell by my hands that my skin was no longer translucent, my color was a slight tan... and I looked into the mirror for the first time... Nothing could have prepared me. What I saw was a man. I *was* a man. For the only time in my entire life to that point, after two hundred years I saw myself. I saw what I knew she had always seen.

Tears again began to flow, not one or two, but a torrent of liquid that began from his eyes, swelling as they rained down his glittering face. I felt a near irresistible urge to take him into my arms and hold him close. In a manner I had never felt for a subject ever before, I could not restrain my sympathy for this man... This beautiful, ancient, man that was openly crying in front of me... and again I knew that on the deepest level I had bought into what he was saying. I believed him despite of myself. It was but for the sake of professionalism that I offered only the outreach of my hands for him to grasp, and my eyes nearly welled up themselves as he silently took them and allowed himself to cry .

AG: I *was* a man...

He breathed painfully

AG: ... and she never got to see.

His tears were now sobs; As if I were watching him relive the very moment of his life that he felt those emotions, over one hundred years past, and here I was sharing in his pain not even knowing of whom he spoke or what loss could affect a man so deeply after such time.

It was then to my utter surprise that I looked up to see Steven having quietly made his way from his seat. He was kneeling before Adam's chair as he gently placed a hand upon his knee... However more so to my astonishment, I could see the tears in his own eyes as he gently spoke in comfort to the man he had barely just met.

DM: You're not alone Adam...

I heard Stevens own voice crack as he spoke in barely above a whisper.

DM: You're not alone.

It was only then I noticed for the first time the empty impression of a wedding band on Stevens finger.

I stopped my recording.

A LIVING LEGEND

Time : 1:06 AM, March 22nd

After a brief recess and refills of tea mixed with the comforting of tears. Each of us was reseated, and our interview began again as I resumed recording. Adam especially seemed steeled with new resolve towards telling us his story. He spoke now to Dr. Malcom.

AG: I don't mean to require too much of your recollection of history Steven, but what can you tell me concerning your personal knowledge of medicine between the seventeenth and eighteenth century?

DM: Um, sure, well originally as you likely know, a lot of the earlier studies were dictated by the church. There was a lot of bleeding based on the ancient Greek idea of humors controlling sickness vs well being. I know that Vesalius and Da Vinci participated in some of the earliest known dissection of human cadavers in order to map out many of our first anatomical drawings, and notably that Da Vinci's in particular wound up being crucial to later studies.

I think I remember something about the church only dissecting the bodies of criminals, sometimes starting out with a living person and basically going full autopsy...

I *do* know that it all kind of started speeding up after William Harvey. Once he put the whole circulatory system together into an idea that people could wrap their heads around, it kind of changed the game. That was somewhere in the early sixteen hundreds. Right?.. People started realizing that the body was a set of cooperative systems around then.

Is this the kind of thing you're after?

AG: Precisely. The recall memory of your schooling is very impressive. Please go on.

DM: Ooook... Well, my field, biochemistry... Essentially started with basic medicines. There was a lot of researching into texts from the middle east. The more the world was explored, the more ideas they brought back and experimented with... It had a lot of crossover with alchemy actually which is kind of cool despite its very poor reputation.

Um, meanwhile medical colleges started popping up and some surgeries of a sort were being practiced, particularly brutal ones of course, but progress after a fashion... Except you pretty much had to be rich to go to a "hospital". So that was the same I guess.

Steven looked at me and smiled before turning back towards Adam.

DM: I don't know. I mean what are you getting at? Are you saying that the way you are was something done to you?

AG: Not in so many words. I simply wish for Cassandra to hear some perspective from a medical professionals knowledge so that it might go on record, also a slight refresher for yourself as well before we continue.

DM: Ok so by the mid 1600's a guy named Wren figured out how to do blood transfusions using dogs for experimentation... Which yeah kind of sucks, but was really impressive for the time. In the very early 1700's another guy named Dippel claimed he had found the "Elixir of Life" while trying to chase down the path of Nick Flamel..

Adam raised his hand interrupting Steven before his next sentence could begin. He gestured with two fingers and lowered his arm.

AG: Stop there please...

Stevens eyes went wide.

DM: No...

This was whispered in disbelief rather than refusal.

CR: What?! What am I missing?

Steven was obviously very excited as he spoke in a quickened pace.

DM: Flamel, he was an old alchemist. Legend went that he found a way to make himself immortal with something called the philosopher stone. It was a mix though. A formula, some say it wasn't even a stone at all, it was a *yellow* liquid...

CR: So... Do you think Adam is Nicholas Flamel?

DM: No, no. He's much too young, but this guy Dippel was trying to recreate that right around the time...

Stephen looked at Adam.

DM: He claimed to have remade it didn't he? Called it "Dippel's oil", tried to sell the stuff the rest of his life... Right around the same time you would have been born...

Adam stood up and walked towards the table to refill his tea. After pouring another cup full and adding the customary sugar, he turned back to face us from across the room.

AG: And now we have reached the point where I am able to link the bridge between what each of you have either discovered or has been revealed to you.

Yes. Steven, I appreciate your knowledge of history. I knew you were the right man for this. In the past I made the mistake of choosing incorrectly, put myself in poor situations for hopes' sake which ended badly, but I've read all of your work, followed your career, waited for the right time. I couldn't afford a repeat of what's come before with individuals such as Doctor Black.

DM: Spencer Black?

Adam shook his head and Setevn blushed at his blunder.

AG: A creation of modern fiction. There was another without such infamy. Johann Conrad Dippel on the other hand, *was* actually a man that I came to know very well. In fact, he was the closest person I would consider calling a father. I assume Doctor that you are aware of many other rumors surrounding him, the accusations and mythos that shadow his name... Well then, I intend to clarify the truth within those rumors.

Steven was sitting on the edge of his seat in the most literal fashion, now enthralled rather than skeptical, he looked like a small child awaiting some confirmation of magic, his eyes wide and mouth hanging slightly agape in anticipation.

AG: Conrad, was of Geneva much as myself, a place known as castle Frankenstein to be precise. He was a theologian... But it was his disagreements with the church which brought him the very type of infamy which assured his name would live on. As you mentioned earlier Dr. Malcom... the church at the time, were the purveying influence when it came to medical study.

Father, was a deeply passionate man, and sometime before my "birth" he had taken to voicing his beliefs concerning not just his theories on the faith, but on the topics which we have been discussing here this evening. He essentially became obsessed with anatomy and alchemy together. The church branded him a heretic.

In this time, he began performing his own studies ranging from cadaver inspection, into theorizing on the bodily origin of the human soul. He *did* perform autopsies and procure the bodies of several deceased through various means in order to do this, but Conrad himself never took to extremes with anything more than his theories and his thirst for knowledge.

Steven felt the need to chime in giddily.

DM: He did create the pigment prussian blue though.

CR: Really? That's such a pretty color.

AG: Yes he did do that. He also did in fact claim to have recreated Flamels formula, but the reputation he has been labeled with as a grave robber, as some sinister ghoul... That was *not* the man I knew.

He had truthfully come so incredibly *close* to a formula that he *did* hastily, yet prematurely announce his discovery out of sheer excitement. He proudly proclaimed he had discovered the elixir of life and while in his paper he named it Dippel's oil... He never actually intended to complete a single vial.

It was a theory. That is what he did. That is the man he was. What he discovered would have changed the world and he knew it. He had found the secret to a miracle, but what stayed him was rational thought. He feared the consequences of a man taking such control into their own hands. He wouldn't even put the final steps down on paper.

However it was too late to go back on his word....Even with the robust ego that Conrad often had, he told me that he would rather have been remembered a fool for all time, than to be the man who destroyed the faith of humanity.

He voluntarily discredited himself until his death by selling a mixture of fluids and oils combined with the charred bones of animals and cadavers which served no purpose beyond that of a slight stimulant, with the claim that this *was* the formula he had created.

Regrettably though with bittersweet connotations for my own existence; it was somewhere amongst all of this, during which time Father was approached by a man named Emanuel Swedenborg who claimed agreement in nearly all of his theories. They became friends for a time and It was he who introduced Conrad to an equally empassioned young student called Edmund Breda.

Conrad saw brilliant potential in Edmund as well as danger, but he secretly accepted the young man as an assistant and apprentice.

Socially they were never seen together. Conrad feared that his association would drive the church after Breda as well, and his worry was chiefly concerned that such events might lead him down the dark path that he himself feared.

Adam began to make his way towards the wall to the left of the room. His face looked sullen. He leaned against the wall and slowly lowered himself to the floor careful to keep his long coat behind him rather than sit on it. Placing his tea in front of himself he sat with his legs crossed and stared down at his cup momentarily. It was as if he had somehow regressed from a wise gentlemanly man to someone much younger, a teenager almost. A teenager who felt shame or guilt of some kind.

Edmund Breda was a much less scrupulous individual from my Father... He constantly pushed boundaries in experimentation that made his mentor nervous. Conrad attempted to steer the young man away from pursuing the theories he had put forth, but Breda would not be deterred.

He took on regularly acquired debts using the name of of his teacher, my father, Conrad Dippel. After a time those debts nearly cost Conrad his home and reputation. On more than one occasion, this behavior would show itself... In my mind, this would have been enough to justify a personal disdain and distrust of him. Father on the other hand, held faith that he could save Breda from himself.

However it was also Breda's most detestable habit, to spread false word of my father's actions and claims. Passing off many of his own traits onto a man that had showed him alone, nothing but the kindest side of himself.

Adam reached to run his finger through his long black hair only to remember that it was in a ponytail. That was when he took it down and let it fall to his shoulders while he breathed a frustrated sigh.

AG: I am not going to sit here and claim that Conrad was entirely innocent. He was a bit of an egotist. He believed strongly in what he preached and would not be convinced otherwise, but it was the words and actions of Edmund Breda that led to the downfall and eventual imprisonment of Johann Conrad Dippel... He was charged with heresy at a time that such things came with a steep price.

His friend Swedenborg abandoned his faith in him and even began to publicly speak against him. While Conrad sat in prison for seven years... Edmund Breda continued to experiment out of Castle Frankenstein. He used Conrad's theoretical notes as a basis for conducting physical acts... He dug up corpses. He murdered more than one person, including what I know to have been at least one woman with child. He used Conrad's research which included the partial proportions for the real elixir of life and thru experimentation of his own, managed to replicate the true formulation.

From what I have gleaned over the years through much struggle... I know that it was approximately 1709 in which his experimentation reached its ultimate result. It was in 1709, that he created the abomination which Conrad had feared. And in 1709, Over a century before the woman I loved would relay a fictionalized account of my creation, I was wrenched to life without choice or consideration, in the tower of the castle Frankenstein.

A HIDEOUS AFTERBIRTH

The room sat quietly for only a moment while Adam allowed his words to sink in. We both awaited the response of Dr. Malcom who I could see marinating in his thoughts. We did not have to wait long. He spoke earnestly with no hint of disbelief or sarcasm.

DM: You are Frankenstein?

AG: No Doctor, I am Adam.

His voice cracked and he straightened himself with a deep draw of breath before the following words. They punched their way thru the stiffness in his voice as if he feared otherwise choking on his pain.

AG: Simply Adam... Godwin was a name gifted later, but Adam is that which I *took*. That which was intended and denied by my creator.

Doctor Victor Frankenstein was a creation of fiction born from collaboration and necessity in an effort to reach out for scientific minds who might be able to answer questions left unfulfilled concerning my existence. Every bit as much however, he was designed in thought and action to service a warning to any who might pursue a similar path of pain or misery as Mary saw them. He and in turn his *creature* were made to be monstrous from the beginning, a terrible lesson but not for evil intention on their parts so much as unrestrained obsession at the expense of others. I should like to believe that I was not, nor have I ever truly been the character of either, be it creator or otherwise, and yet I know wherein their persons were born and must confess to some degree that in fact at times, I have been both throughout my long and troubled years.

After all, who of us would choose to be made in that mold? I hoped that in such words, we might stave the ambitious drives of thoughtless persons who might otherwise cast ruin to life around them, and yet I know the sword of Mary's pen came with edges we had not imagined. So multifaceted were the degrees of her prose, that many could not help but seek inspiration from them.

DM: Well yeah, but... I mean you're saying that you are *essentially* him. I don't mean to sound like a dick given your feelings about it, or for you to think less of me, but you're basically claiming to be the reason I got into this profession.

Adam stretched his back and looked down again into his now cold tea.

AG: If I knew less of you Doctor, the words you say would pain me to hear, however I suppose in that perspective then yes... by your intended insinuation, I am... and *you* the result in hopeful best form of a terrible inspiration...

Yet by marvels of time and progress, a wondrous and caring result for which we never dared to dream, inspired by the monster to create, yet compassioned by his creation to feel and act with responsible goals and temperance.

As I said Doctor, I have read *all* of your work and I have seen these words to know that you were the man I must meet, perhaps the only who might finally help me to fulfill that which I long for so terribly.

To quote the novel which you so ardently admire, "When I reflect that you are pursuing the same course, exposing yourself to the same dangers which have rendered me what I am, I imagine that you may deduce an apt moral from my tale."

DM: This is remarkable. I know I should be more cynical and be calling you crazy right now, demanding tests, insulted that anyone would prey on my personal intrigue and passion for the story itself, but I mean here you are.

I know the story of Johann Dippel. I *know* the story of Frankenstein... Even to the point that yes when I was a kid, I was obsessed with it. I own a second edition copy that I keep locked in a glass case above my fucking work desk. I even referenced it in my acceptance speech for the Nobel, which now that I say it aloud, I'm sure you are well aware of...

So yes, Swedenborg was a friend to Dippel, and the events you describe fit with everything we know about his life, the time, the claims, the legends... And Breda too. Carl Fredrick Von Breda of course painted a famous portrait of Swedenborg. It's undeniable that the families knew each other at least to some degree... Telling me he made introductions between contemporaries, not only tracks, it's quite frankly likely, a detail that anyone could determine with minor research.

Yet, what I'm trying to say is that Adam, I might doubt your intentions if I simply heard the story you're telling, even with the sample you sent, but given the whole of it together... If it weren't evident in what I have already seen to bring me here; The fact that it flows through your veins clearly to the naked eye in place of blood, and what the two of you pulled with that letter opener, I mean good god man! It's as believable as anything else I could have posited from all of that, and I'm almost angry to feel so torn right now.

You are telling me that my childhood dreams have come to life and I'm sitting here talking to you, looking at you, humbled by an honor that I'm even involved while every scientific inclination of my mind screams that this can't be real.

Tell me that you are confirmation to the bias I wish to believe and yes I jump at the chance to indulge my fantasy, but I'm still looking at you wondering how the trick is pulled with absolutely zero answers to satisfy any alternative option *but* to believe!

Stevens words were breathless in astonishment, nearly tearful in their own confession and I almost hated to interrupt, but my job required a different sort of answers. I gave the doctor a moment but no more. I spoke timidly.

CR: Adam... Why do you call Dippel your father?

There was another deep breath.

AG: If I may respond first to Doctor Malcom.

They looked at each other.

AG: Your benefit of the doubt is gracious young man, and yes I knew these things you mention about yourself. However I do not intend to simply tell the tale as it were and leave some stone unturned that others might deny or question the validity of these claims. I open myself to this inquiry, these meetings for earnest purpose and before all is thru, you will have the greatest body of proof the world might require, if only you will bear with the time it takes to relay to you each import of topic as we progress.

Calm yourself good doctor and take comfort. I will not vanish. I will not pull the rug from beneath you. This is no trick, and in time I promise to satisfy your questions and lay all doubt to rest... but first we must journey together in order to satisfy that which is more than measurement and proof. For you were requested for one purpose of clarity, but our dear host here for another, and it is of my mind and my choice to say that understanding, comes from both.

Adam turned to me with deference.

As for your inquiry Ms Reynolds, I call him father because he was there for me... Breda left me abandoned and alone with no thought to the consequences or the life he had created, but Conrad took me in, taught me, partly made me the man I am for good or ill, and offered me counsel to shape my minds edge while I was little more than flesh and sinew heaped upon a world I did not understand.

DM: The old man and the family from the novel... That was Dippel wasn't it?

AG: Large parts that were.

DM: But it went deeper...

AG: Yes.

Dr. Malcom seemed to consider his next question carefully.

DM: Mr. Godwin... Respectfully I accept your offer, and I feel for you if this all proves true, but having read the book so many times, you must know there are questions I have to ask beyond the scientific. You tell us that there was intent behind the writing, but also that there was truth within it, knowing that I am versed in its pages...

So upon first thought in playing devils advocate, I must question how much of Breda went into the character of Victor or the events described. Because if Victor was Breda and you the creation, then there are things that have to be asked, cannot be ignored... Such as did you kill Breda's wife? Brother? Friend? Someone else? Many others? Are you confessing to us that you are a murderer Mr Godwin? How much would you tell us if it were true? And if not truth, would you really confess to such crimes in pursuit of a hoax?

What happened Adam? If you are who you say you are, then what is the truth? Are we sipping tea with a killer?

Adam looked up with shame in his eyes and turned towards me. I knew that Steven was right to ask such questions, and I supported them in theory, but so early in the evening was unexpected. Still I nodded to Adam that he should answer all the same. He looked away, continued to sit there for a moment, motionless as the words began to fall from his lips. His eyes pleading for forgiveness as they stared at the wall as if he were looking thru it into the middle distance...

AG: Yes... I must answer these. I knew they would come. Firstly Doctor, you have to understand as I have said and now reiterate, that Victor was as much a creation of fiction as he was multiple inspirations...

It would not serve our purposes, mine nor Mary's to simply create a villain nor a hero as none of us seem to be either in full. He and several others described by her work, were taken from the personalities of our friends and acquaintances including the rogue known to history as Byron, as well as his physician John Polidori. Even more of him was the countenance of Percy, or the questions of her own mind.

There was inspiration taken from my life to be certain, but Mary was an artist with goals and thoughts all her own that bent toward a drive to humanize the lead character of her work for personal reasons every bit as much as my insistence to demonize my creation had come from emotional bonds to myself. So I will answer your question in time, but there is much to know before that so that you might seperate and understand the differences in this one case between life and art.

CR: That seems fair. Where would you like to begin?

AG: My first memories seem apt in this case. Relevance extends to these... Doctor Malcom, It may surprise you that I do not recall being brought to life as an action. I have no memory of a laboratory, or afterbirth as it were, and though I know now that I was born within the tower of the castle, I did not awaken there. So you see from my very beginnings, the brush of life was embellished for agenda between realities thoughtlessness and fictions focused constructions.

My first memories in this stead, were of waking in a lightless cold space, I could see nothing, naked on a floor of unevenly cracked stone, though I would not have known these words until some time later. I was born to consciousness locked in a dark room, alone, wretched in tormented confusion, barely able to stand without falling over, and I did so repeatedly, blunting my body against the grit covered rock that bordered me on all sides. I could feel. I could hear. I could smell, and I could taste the damp, mildewed, and rancid slick of my surroundings but I don't know how much of that disgust came from what else had occupied the space before me, or from the rotting smell of my own birth.

I couldn't speak, but I made sounds, indefinite groaning howls of fear and pain brought on by ceaseless awakening to each sensation. It was only when I was able to look back afterward, that I could make any sense of it at all. I don't know how long I was confined, fading in and out of consciousness as I did. I don't know if I was even expected to live, but I suspect to the degree of personal belief that the answers to this was no. Without the processes of language I can only define my thoughts thru looking backward through the lens of time with more informed notion than I was at first capable, but in years to come and thru interactions with my creator, I feel certain that this state of imprisonment had been intended to be my death.

It was after this, after such indeterminable times that I recall at last the first touch of light to my eyes when Breda opened the door holding a torch in his hand only to throw a sheet at me. I know he spoke, but I had no recognition of words then, and so in memory cannot decipher their intention. He shouted, and he began to strike me with the torch, pushing me further into the corner with violent fury.

I felt pain, and I know that I suffered burns, but all I could do was to react. The sheet caught fire, and I threw Breda off of me. I lurched towards the door over his body not recognizing what I know now was an unconscious man in any way more than a fish who knew only water would recognize the difference between a roaring lion or a sleeping one.

It was the first look at my creator and it lasted only moments as he beat me without explanation, yet being my first sight, his image burned into my mind for every day since. The furious and unforgiving look of disgust and malice that he bore me, have haunted my nights as the stuff of terror and self doubt, even in times when I felt I'd recovered or moved past these things.

I had learned to stand in my darkened prison, learned to take steps forward, but never with the room to walk before. So at my unintended release I struggled to put one foot in front of the other, scrambling my form to and fro, until I tumbled uncontrollably down a tall and winding stair, striking my bones and flesh against its sharp corners with cracking moist sounds of a body being broken under its own weight until I came to rest, heaped at the bottom of these steps. Filled with horror and bewilderment, I forced my limbs to move once more, driven by a need to flee that meant only to escape the present conditions as if running away from the place, would somehow ease the pains of the moment.

From edge to edge of the hallway I'd found myself, I stumbled until the tangle of limbs and mass which comprised me, forced themselves upright while dragging my flesh over the coarseness of each new step. There was stone floor, stone ground, stone along the corridor to which I'd fled, and light which I followed into the brightness of a grey day cold with rain.

Somehow I found my way out of the castle into the woods where I continued with stumbling amblance. The light rains which might have chilled another form, over time turned to storm, and thunder assaulted my ears, filling my head with such turbulent commotion that I could not take even a moment to focus on or choose a path. Lightning flashed above me and I lost my footing over a log sometime after darkness had erased the light from the sky.

Without clothing or protection from the elements I curled my body close to the very log whose surface had stumbled my step and I stretched my arms over my head to hide in shaking misery. I remained there until morning, when almost lifeless in body, and without the sounds of thunder to distract my senses, my eyes took in attentive recognition the surrounding world for the first time.

Bugs crawled over my skin and I did not move. I felt the pain as they bit into me, but it was indifferent to the pain that filled my body otherwise. The itching and the soreness were nothing compared to the mystery of their motion and form and I knew somehow that these things were different from stone, or wood. That they like me, lived...

When the light came through the trees, and the sun began to warm the air, I rose again to motions with no direction of intent, falling over the uneven terrain to catch myself from tree to tree lest I collapse into the leaf covered ground, which happened often. I continued without knowledge of why, sometimes crawling upon the mud without decisive control over my limbs as I struggled to learn the basics of bodily choice.

How I made it anywhere is a marvel of it's own but for all I might have struggled, there is chance that this time covered less distance than to merely exit the castles grounds. It could have also been leagues without me realizing even in recollection, but I continued over hill and ravine, thru rivlet streams and forest until I heard the sound of voices and saw people thru the trees.

They were walking down a path nearby. I didn't know what they were of course, but I didn't know what *I* was either. They looked like the man who had beaten me, and yet different, each of them as different as the bugs which crawled my body, and yet the bugs still too were different from the people. I seemed closer to one than the other in some way. Not knowing my shape by sight, or size, nor numbers by which to count limbs, I only identified that I felt a kinship to their existence in proximity to what I felt of myself.

And so still unsteady on my feet, I braced my body on a nearby tree at the edge of the roadside just before stepping forward into their view. I remember my continued terror and confusion when screams escaped their mouths and they ran away, leaving me to fall once more into the grit of mud and grime as I reached outward...

Very soon, I tried to walk again with more speed but with no hope of following the mysterious figures which had entranced my urges, and no reason at present to flee, I took the now empty road as a place to practice walking without realizing the ideas of practice or why I persisted there, rather than return to the forest on either side.

Time held no meaning for me, and even as I rose and fell, I looked wide eyed at the world around me. There were colors to which I assigned no name, forms from which I felt no threat as well as those otherwise which surprised me from seeming nowhere, the sensations of breeze and sun, even the sight of birds above which alarmed me with their sudden honks all sang to me in wonderous terrible awe.

Falling into a ditch I had grabbed at a stick to raise my body more easily and I discovered that to lean on it aided in my movement going forward. I saw no others along the road that day and as best as I can now tell you, it was some time near sunset that I was finally able to balance and move forward with effectiveness enough to choose my path beyond. All the while, my entirety ached in intense pain both internally and on the surface of my skin. My eyes burned, every sound and sight was a shock to my senses even as my bones pulsed with pain and every patch of me itched both inside and out.

By nightfall I had retreated again to the forrest, feeling safer to surround myself with solid masses such as tree trunks and cover of canopy as much as possible rather than remain exposed along the road. Though the light fell from the sky, I could see all the same in each directions as animals began to stir, but they kept their distance from me while I sidled my body against an upright stone and brought my knees to my chest. I looked up at the stars without sight of the moon and I believe that I cried, for all reasons possible, not over my pain or solitude, but to feel overwhelmed by the beauty of the worlds very existence.

The following morning I moved forward once more but with growing efficiency. Spotting structures beyond the wood, I made my way into a small town before anyone else occupied the street, and there I found a piece of bread amongst a heap of refuse. Instinctively I brought it to my mouth and began to eat. I swallowed in large chunks before determining just how to chew, and I continued to walk...

I saw the form of a man hanging. I noticed the clothing that covered his body with absolute confusion. Knowing nothing of life or death beyond the recognition of animation, I worried that he might scream and run as the others had, but I continued to walk, pushing beyond my dread only to watch as a crow landed upon him and plucked a part of his form away. The bird swallowed and consumed the part of the man as I had consumed the bread and I marvelled too at this in fearful amazement.

For days, maybe weeks it was like that. Staying away from any contact, eating what I could find, guessing at that fact merely by instinct or some innate knowledge. I had no need to make movement of my bowels nor release my bladder and today I believe the confusion of such a thing would likely have terrified me even more than I already was. As for the most part it was only sleep that I required, but that need lessened with the passing of days as my body grew stronger.

Then one day, shortly after the sun had passed its peak in the sky, I was seen near the edge of a town as I crossed the road. Some people pointed, others ran... but it was the ones that came towards me that I tried to focus on. There was the racket of voices which echoed in my head like thunder. At first I was hit with one stone. Then came another and another, until I felt something from behind pierce my back while angry people surrounded me with violently, unremitting, attacks to my person. I know now that it was a mattock which pierced my side and deeply it tore thru my midsection in a blow that would kill most men.

I made my best attempt to run for the first time, but I stumbled in disorientation as I was continually struck, stabbed and beaten to the edge of a bridge. By luck I fell over and into the water, dislodging the mattock from my flesh, but the water was deep and the current strong. Instinctively I must have held my breath, but I know that I must have also lost consciousness, because I washed into a nearby lake without any recognition of how I had come to escape the townspeople, and soon after I awoke on its shore with sputtering coughs, crawling my way out not from the depths, but from where I lay to one side on sandy shallows which rippled at each edge of my lips.

To my gladness I found that my injuries were nearly gone, though the pain in my twisted form remained. I turned to raise myself upon my arms so that I might move to stand.

It was then when I glimpsed my reflection for the first time. Without knowing that the image staring back at me was in fact myself, I tried to strike it before falling back into the lake. It horrified me. I had seen men and I had seen animals, but none had looked so gruesome as this, save for the hanged figure who was partly devoured by the crow.

Eventually, as my reflection copied my gestures, I understood that I was seeing what the people had seen and I found an awareness of self which had previously been undefined. Being an individual and separate thing from my surroundings had not occured as a thought, despite seeing others and taking actions of my own, for I had not closed myself from the rest of the world in that way, and did not know until then, that I was not a part of other living things as I felt drawn to their presence.

It's odd to think of those days now. How my mind processed such simple definitions and concepts as object permanence or reflection, sense of self and distinction from the world around me... In some ways it came like memory. Though I knew nothing of who or what I was. In others it was entirely foreign, a new set of discoveries with each moment, magical in its ability to amaze, and like magic, a fearful mystery all the same.

Having seen my figure in reflection I took for the first time to observe myself with recognition of what it meant to see the limbs I felt and urged to motion. I walked from the waters edge and looked down at my arms, at my legs, my body.

I saw the substance beneath my skin. I saw the thick lines where I was put together, laden with stitches unraveled partly in my movements while others held themselves puckered against my flesh, holding pieces of me to one another in assembly not understood, knowing somehow that they did not belong to the same growth, yet had become a part of me thru other means. One of my legs stood out as being grossly more separated from the rest of my body than the other. Two jagged lines were present on its shin where the skin changed from soft, to thick and hard, and I recognized that they had been composited from distinctly different materials even while the borders of them tried their best to grow into one.

One of my arms was much the same, attached at the shoulder, still cleaved in part where the skin had not grown beyond the original stitching... I touched the areas to discover even greater pain before deciding to leave them alone.

DM: So that part is true? You were assembled from the bodies of the dead, not simply revived?

Adam's shame lost, he looked at Doctor Malcom matter of factly.

AG: Yes. I am, though how recently dead we chose never to address.

Adam descended into his memories once more placing Dr. Malcom's obvious curiosities onto the back burner for the time being

DM: So then you have always been this way?

AG: That is unfortunately a trick question I believe. I was assembled from the cadavers of men I never knew. I have no conscious memory of life before waking in the darkness, however this face surely smiled and cried long before I was born. Some remnants of what came before me, existed within and remain to this day. Would you ask if I am defined by this body? Was the ship of Theseus still the same ship by the time in which every part of it had been replaced between its departure from the first shore and arrival on its last? Or was the ship defined by its name and crew as they bore the burden of its direction and duty?

If I were to make a chair of leather and bone once belonging to a bull, to stitch it together using only leather chord, would that chair be a bull itself? And what if it sprang to life with a hunger for grass or inclination to moo? Would it then be a bull? Was the chair always as it was? Or was the chair once a bull?

These are questions I still cannot answer beyond my own feelings and beliefs. There is no objective logic which can satisfy every facet of their complexity, and so I can only tell you mine as perspective and experience might allow within the conflict of emotion and sense of self.

I was as this, but this was of what? A sum of its parts? Defined by my thoughts? given definition by others or by the man who created me? Was a greater deity or force of life at work in my inception? I prefer the words of Descarte as removed from such greater speculations of fate or faith. "Cogito, ergo sum". I am thinking, therefore I exist. All else is but a conclusion with cause for doubt and possibility of falsehood.

Regardless of these things at present, I had no advanced reasoning as of yet upon the past I recount. For some motive, after recognizing my own form I had chosen to retrace my steps, though I could not tell you how I knew to follow the waters upstream, or to return by landmark and vision recognized from before. I simply did so.

By the time that I had found my way back to the place where I had spent my first night, I was beginning to comprehend more and more at what I today know to have been an exponential rate. I still had no language to refer to, but my memories of images and experience gave me cohesion after a fashion, and the sounds of animals and birds held their own familiarity.

Was this the work of Breda? The memory of the pieces by which I was comprised, or the birth of a consciousness all its own which I might call mine?

Steven shifted uneasily.

CR: but you made your way back to the castle itself?

AG: Yes... In time I did. Breda was no where to be found. I ambled it's empty halls, looked for places I might recognize, touched the frames of furnishing which I did not understand. Even by darkness I could see within the confines of the rooms abandoned echoes, and found even more questions. In the forest I had touched wood both living and fallen, but now I found carved into mysterious things which were not trees. I saw my reflection in hardened surfaces that were not water, and I did not understand.

Even climbing my way to the tower where I found the closet which had held me, I scarcely contextualized the work of blood and bile which covered its surfaces. At the place of Breda's laboratory further down that hall, I found nothing remained but stain and, and I was sickened by the sense of familiarity.

Near morning but still within darkness, I heard movement from a room I had previously searched and I carefully followed its sound, hiding behind a corner to peer inside. There was a man, but not Breda. He carried a large dust covered trunk that he struggled with the weight of. I followed him out of the castle into a pre-dawn air for some time, taking care to stay hidden from view. I watched him as he met with a carriage shortly down the road and climbed aboard.

Crossing quickly and into the woods by the roadside, I kept speed by it's sight as much as possible and followed the man in hopes of some connection with the one I had seen upon first opening my eyes.

You have to comprehend I reiterate, that I had no way of knowing the difference between one person and another beyond the innate senses within me. I did not know the names of things or of places, but I understood the base concepts which compelled me to act upon my intuitions and questioning that I could discern the difference of sight to their characteristics and manner.

Occasionally the carriage would pass by or through a populated area and I was forced to make detours. Though I kept them in my sight to meet up with them by other means. But again even my directional sense seemed to be entirely instinctual and held surprising accuracy. There was no stopping for the duration of the journey. Eventually the object of my pursuit arrived at his destination where he unloaded the trunk and entered a building near what I now know to have been in the county of Grafschaft, or Wittgenstein.

DM: You were following Dippel weren't you?

AG: Yes. I would later know the man I followed that day as Conrad.

DM: So in the time you wandered, Dippel had been released from prison?

AG: Yes.

DM: I assume you made contact?

AG: No, I dared not... People had become in short order, a great source of fear to me. It was only somewhere in my primitive thoughts which I knew that he was somehow connected to where I had come from, and because of that I was irresistibly drawn to stay near him.

DM: So you hid. Like in the book?

AG: Yes. Originally I found an attached storage where I could watch and hear him. I had only intended the one night but my curiosity kept me. The chance to watch another living man in observation was too strong a draw for my ever expanding consciousness.

It was fortunate that he held such a strong affection for his own voice, as he read aloud most days which gave me the opportunity to hear the language as I watched him through his walls, rather than simply observe by sight.

CR: What about food?

AG: In my time wandering I had learned that I could eat several plants. I remembered the ones that made me feel ill as well as the ones that sustained me.

DM: Ill? So you could distinguish the difference of illness versus wellness even that early on?

AG: I could distinguish one discomfort from the sort of another yes.

DM: You didn't hunt?

AG: I had no concept at the time of consuming something that was once alive in some ambulatory fashion, much as I had no understanding of how a tree could become a table or tool. My context for the consumption of flesh was the bird which had dined upon the hanged man and the thought filled me with existential dread.

In fact I have often wondered to myself how humanity discovered such a thing in the first place, but feel rather confidently that if it were not in nature to do so, then such a thing would have been some type of madness or compulsion to even consider. A dog hunts out of instinct. A wolf knows without instruction that it must kill and consume the flesh of another type of animal to live. I did not have these urges within as of yet.

Also it was a strong awareness that the building I observed was not terribly distant from a township and though there was a nearby wood where I foraged. I feared any significant action or noise which might draw unwanted attention.

DM: That makes sense.

CR: So you lived in secret right next to his home and he never noticed.

AG: I actually would find out later that he had indeed noticed my presence, but believed me to be a disembodied spirit.

CR: Which didn't bother him?

AG: As mentioned before, his beliefs were very radical at the time. Much of his speaking was actually intended to my benefit, ghostly or otherwise. Conrad at this point in his life, was a lonely man. It was regular for him to make his way to and from what I would later discover was his new laboratory alone. Some days he had visits from others. However it was normative that such contact often ended in argument or on the rare occasion threat.

Other times he would travel away, and in his absence I often investigated the books, and devices present within his laboratory.

CR: And when did you first approach him?

AG: It was at the third change of season.

CR: So almost a year.

AG: Well, you have to understand the weather in the area... You have been to Germany. For all I know with clarity, it could have well been three years or less than one. I was in no habit of counting days, merely observable changes around me.

DM: Did you actually have a concept of counting by then?

AG: I did. By the time that Conrad and I met face to face, I had learned many things from watching him. The least of these included the spoken forms of Latin and German, as well as a significant deal of mathematics... By the time that we finally interacted, I was quite able to carry on in several philosophical debates as well as assist him with his formulas.

DM: That is astounding.

AG: He would agree with you.

Adam chuckled.

AG: The day our friendship actually began, a visitor had come by the home, demanding the collection of a debt which Conrad owed. They argued outside for a time and it continued up unto the point that the man drew back in order to strike Conrad with his cane. This action seen and understood in fashion of ill intent upon another would strike my heart like the flash of a smiths' hammer, and motivate what followed.

A feeling overwhelmed me which I did not have experience with until that moment. I had come to understand ideas of things such as loyalty, care, life, death, harm, and even violence in theory, but I had never moved to express these before the day I saw another human being under threat. It was then that I openly charged from the shed, accidentally tearing the door off the hinges in the process.

I quickly stepped between the two men, and grasped the strangers cane in my hand, breaking its handle in the process. He staggered backward several steps and looked at me with a blend of terror and disgust but undeterred, I shouted at him with the first words I had ever spoken aloud in the presence of another... "Er geschützt ist!"

I was startled by Adam's sudden shout but not merely due to its volume. Admittedly the tone and sound of his words were in fact terrifying even in this setting, as it came out equal parts roar and growl. Though Dr. Malcom seemed to be too enraptured by the tale to show any sign of surprise. He clapped his hands on his knees in excitement and quickly stood to mimic Adam's shout as he raised his arms in the air.

DM: "He is protected!" Seriously? Those were your first words?! Also, kind of badass that you remember your first words, but Oh my god dude that's epic!

Steven laughed wildly as he crashed back down into his seat. Adam however only offered a small saddened smile.

DM: And this was all from listening to him reading to himself for the most part?

AG: Not exactly...

Adam waited for Steven to calm down before continuing.

AG: As I mentioned about some of his more performative habits being for my benefit, the thing was, that Conrad almost always seemed as if he were rehearsing for a debate. Learning from him, even at a distance, came much easier than you might think.

CR: Still, to be able to soak in abstract concept from observation of a single individual is astounding. What did Dippel do when all this went down?

AG: My back was actually turned to him for the moment but the other man tripped over his coat in his attempt to flee, and as soon as he had regained his footing he *did* make a hasty retreat.

CR: Oh no! Did he run to the town?

AG: Actually no, he ran into the woods... I made no attempt to pursue. At the realization of what I had just done I was actually shaking between fear and anger. I was terrified of the consequences to both of us, but furious at the impudence of a man threatening violence over an offense which caused him no actual injury.

No matter what I had heard or how much I had absorbed of story or words, I simply could not grasp the willingness this stranger had held to hurt another person who for my sights had done him no harm.

When I finally turned to face Conrad for the first time, he

looked at me as if he himself were frozen between an equal sense of fear and reverence. I nearly ran for the woods myself... But not Conrad. He did not run, nor strike towards me... He stood there and we looked nervously at each other for what felt like eternity.

Then... Father... He slowly reached his hand towards my face. He touched my cheek with his shaking palm the way that you might approach a wild animal, and I could see tears forming in his eyes as he spoke the words that I recall with the greatest of pity in their tones.

"Oh, spectre... spare my wretched soul. It is true."

Adam looked back at his tea and made a motion towards his spoon to give it a quiet stir. He continued this for a few seconds. My instincts were gone at this point. My journalistic training had entirely failed me as I looked at Adam. I knew I should question. I should be leading a dialogue, but I like Steven, was too entranced in his tale to make demand or change to wherever he wished to take us. I wanted only for him to continue.

CR: Wow...

It was Dr. Malcom who had the sense to pull us both from the moment.

DM: Would you mind terribly if we take an aside for right now? Several of the things you just said have me wondering about quite a bit.

AG: No, I consider this a fine place to come back to at a later time. Continue Doctor.

DM: Thank you.

Doctor Malcom's mouth opened in the start of a question only to quickly shut again in an apparent decision to reword his thoughts before he finally asked.

DM: There's just so much. Ok, so I have some thoughts of my own on this, but I think its kind of obvious that you have had much more time to consider it and given the type of man you seem to be, I am fairly certain that you have mulled this over in great detail.

I would like to know just what your theories are on how you were able to advance so quickly... Cognitively that is.

AG: I think that is an excellent question and I am pleased to answer, though Im surprised you arent focusing on the healing first. You're right though, it is something that I have given a fair amount of my time to in order to come to a personal theory. I must confess that I've wanted someone to discuss this with for the past 25 to 30 yrs.

Though I have been a long time proponent that most of the base cognitive ability must have previously existed in my mind somewhere, It has only been since science has begun studying and applying definition of the brains inner workings that I was able to properly express this in the way which I desire.

It is my belief, that the physical formation of neural pathways within the brain itself may have been responsible for easing the capability of my synapses to fire in recognition of experiences that the individual donor would have found directly familiar perimortem.

I watched Doctor Malcom fold his hands together in front of himself as he continued to lean forward once again, resting his elbows onto his knees.

AG: Hence as the components of my body healed themselves into one, these connections became strengthened, awakening everything from muscle memory to subconscious associations between stimuli.

I was not sure that I understood what Adam was talking about.

CR: So *are* you saying that you are basically just a revived version of whoever your brain previously belonged to?

AG: Actually not at all. Although I believe that most of *what* we are, does exist within the brain, I am a strong believer that *who* we are, comes from something else.

An amnesia patient who regains their memory is still going to be the same individual after all, but may develop an entirely new personality in order to reorganize the remnants of pathways formed by past experience in relation to how they translate them according to new memory.

I was now feeling a bit foolish as the conversation continued to touch on subjects I knew practically nothing about.

DM: I see what you're getting at here. Most of what we consider personal memory is stored in the hippocampus... Those memories are formed in conjunction with the chemical neurotransmitters that convey the signals between neurons. If something occurs such as absolute brain death, then those chemicals no longer hold onto the things which made that person who they were as the chemicals stop receiving signals to produce and interact in the same way. But we don't know where that original energy and direction comes from to begin with. When you try to apply ordinary current to disembodied brain matter it only fires along the pre-established pathway, it doesn't come back to life with full true memory.

In your case the brain in question would have suffered literal death... So in theory that mixture of neurotransmitters was essentially wiped, like reformatting a disk...

AG: Precisely, and just like your disk analogy, the removal of the software in no way renders the hardware disabled.

Which is why it is my current theory that the structural maturation left present in fiber tracts on the cerebellum and cerebral cortex such as the diameter and myelination of axons remained viable neural mechanical pathways post mortem, despite the reset of neural chemical direction.

DM: Allowing for your healing to re-enable the synaptic connections that had been previously been the most frequently used once you began to stimulate each area...

Your memory is eidetic isn't it?

AG: Yes it is.

DM: I'm willing to bet that due to your bodies healing capabilities, 100 yrs ago barely feels like a week to you doesn't it?

AG: Well both yes and no. If 1730 per say were as close as last week then I would never be able to move on... I have spent a lot of time compartmentalizing my memories to the back of my mind in order to live in the present as much as possible, but when I do actually replay a memory... it does feel like I have actually just relived the moment on a smaller scale, that is unless I detach myself emotionally, in which case it all seems like a story happening to someone else.

I was still wrapping my head around Adam being able to essentially speak of his brain formerly belonging to an entirely different human being without suffering from an existential break down on the spot, but I did feel his last statement to be quite revealing. He did his best to not think of the past, but when he did, he had found a way to largely detach from emotional investment... I had heard that from subjects before. Soldiers, survivors... People whom suffered from extreme post traumatic stress.

Even though on the outside he seemed to be ok for the moment. I couldn't help but listen to my gut when it told me that the calm of the surface did not match the torrent beneath.

DM: But that still doesn't cover how Breda managed to reactivate your higher functions into what you are, or even the potential for who you would become. That's like wiping the disk and then replacing it with basic commands, that can create a rudimentary A.I. but it wouldn't result in a real consciousness.

AG: Conrad believed that what made that difference was something customarily removed from scientific thought.

DM: The 21 grams?

AG: The soul. As you know the common misnomer of 21 grams bears very little scientific merit in closer inspection, however the concept of a soul has never definitively been measurable or disproven.

CR: Wow guys, ok I need this in laymen terms for the record. Your'e bringing up souls and brainwaves and stuff. It's all very interesting, but you want average people to relate right?

DM: That *was* laymen Ms Reynolds. We even used computers as a reference.

CR: Steven, I have an I.T. guy for a reason. Besides, I have to make this simple enough for an article some day.

Dr. Malcom rolled his eyes at me and laughed as he turned back towards Adam, who was now rising from his seat on my office floor to approach me. He took my hand into his and looked into my eyes.

AG: Mary explained it to Claire like this. Close your eyes.

Just at the mention of those names his whole essence changed for an instant. But in that instant I could see his eyes fill with unfathomable joy... A joy that was only equaled with a sense of unbearable pain. I knew that my gut was right. He truly did relive the moments... even at the briefest of reminder. I closed my eyes as he asked.

AG: Now Imagine the stars... "We may know the constellations, but someday people will forget their names and even though the stars will remain, they will ever be ready for new ones to be drawn... it will always be up to us to give them their stories"

CR: Wow... Ok, see, now that, I can use.

Adam smiled, but my heart broke for him. He turned away and I heard him quietly drawing in a deep breath to disguise a somber sigh.

Dr. Malcom had become energized. He was wasting no time now as he laid in his follow ups into order.

DM: Alright well that covers the questions of the mind. I am perfectly content to call that theory a working solution for the time being. We can't prove or disprove the soul concept, as the whole 21 grams thing is debateable at best. That assertion has not actually been proven true beyond anecdotal persistence in pop culture despite massive failings in the scientific claim, but the rest holds water.

Would you mind if we went ahead and discussed your body though? I mean obviously we can skip the questions concerning physical strength. Just damn, I think that's going to have to be tested in a laboratory setting for sure. Anyway, I know I'm just jumping in here and that this is all personal, but you are here with obvious scientific mind and well... you know I have to ask.

AG: Yes Doctor, and you needn't concern yourself with standing too solidly on conciliatory propitiation. Straightforward discourse is best. It is what I had expected and hoped for, otherwise I could have simply invited someone of another profession. It is not as if there is any intention towards crudeness.

DM: Ok then, I'll look those words up later, but I get your point. That's great though, It will make things much easier from my side. Ok so, I imagine that it must have been very difficult given your size to actually .... "construct" you? Is construct a good word choice?

Anyway, to make you into what you are. I don't mean to in any way attempt to cast appreciation towards Mr. Breda given the actions you described him as following, but you are anything but haphazardly assembled Adam. To consider the idea that you came from multiple sources is unbelievable. I have to appreciate you as a whole, as a specimen of something never before seen. I'm sorry.

AG: It is alright doctor. The further I have gone to find answers, the more I have for the most part to admit my own admiration and appreciation for what my creator was able to accomplish. Especially with consideration towards the difficulty I have had in discovering even portions of the methods utilized.

And yes, "constructed" is fine. It is accurate to say the least.

DM: Sweet. So you do know how some of it was done?

AG: I do know a small array of details.

CR: Slow down Steven.

I don't know why I was so protective, but I shot a warning glance at Dr. Malcom.

AG: No, it is fine Cassandra. As I explained, this is part of why I am here.

CR: I know, but we don't have to cover everything tonight. Its already nearly 4 am. You don't have to go through all of this at once.

AG: Cassandra... I would like to answer these tonight as much as possible. There is much more to relate that will require its own time and for which Dr. Malcom may find less related to his field of expertise. His time is equally as valuable as yours or my own.

I reluctantly gave in. Adam looked towards Dr. Malcom again as he walked back to be seated upon the floor as before. Finally he slowly exhaled and began to speak.

AG: I am aware from my external self of only 2 individual bodies that comprise that portion of my makeup, neither of which were in life as large as I. However because of some unfortunate circumstances which will be talked on later, most of Breda's notes were destroyed, but not before I was able to glimpse several pages. As for what was lost before I could surmise further answers, it leaves me with no idea how many bits and pieces were used beneath the surface. I don't know for certain which organs he left out, or how many of them are ultimately human as opposed to animal or even mechanical...

Adam sighed and briefly shifted his weight from one side to the other.

I do know from I read, that due to the nature of the work involved, my body was intentionally enlarged by artificial means. My leg for instance... I mentioned earlier the lines present on my shin... They are several centimeters apart from one another.

He began to gesture with his hands as he spoke.

I later found the reason in a set of schematics and notations wherein the process described how one leg was sawed into 2 pieces at mid shin. A framework made from an unmentioned material, was then fastened between these pieces where afterward they were submerged in an airtight tank, which had been entirely filled with Dippel's recipe for the elixir of life, which for ease of our purposes going forward I'd like to simply call Dippel's oil.

Unfortunately the recipe itself was not present on the page. However being aware of at least the base ingredients... Breda made use of a minimum of one woman with child which I know of, whome he kept alive in order to regularly draw the fresh amniotic fluid necessary for such quantities. His distance from a hospital was too great for him to have collected it from afterbirth and transport it back to the castle as he might have the placental tissues.

DM: Wait, he kept a pregnant woman in the castle just in order to extract fluids? How much? and what happened to her afterward? What about the child?

AG: Unfortunately Doctor, that type of thing was not unusual for his research, and yes I know of at least one such case where it was affirmed that neither her nor the child survived to term, as he referred to the harvesting of raw material from them both post mortem. I suspect she was not the only casualty in this pursuit, as his specificity referred to quantities which would have required more than one human body can feasibly produce, even in peak health over a nine month gestation. However this does not necessarily conclude that all such material came from human sources, and there is an outside chance that she was the only one.

Regardless of this amoral morbidity... It was by such means of suspending harvested parts in dippel's oil, kept at a constantly controlled temperature, stimulated by the intermittent flow of current provided by the rudimentary generator which I know to have been Conrad's design, that my leg was allowed to incubate until new bone and sinew had grown to connect the segments.

After the new leg had formed in the basic under structure, Breda applied boiled sheepskin over the area using sutures he had cultivated from the primary bodies own intestinal tissues.

A similar method was used in the construction on most of the individual parts of my bodies construction. That is of course with exception to the sheepskin.

The central mass was allowed to incubate long enough to regrow the dermal tissue in its entirety. It was only for the right arm, left leg and scalp with which he seems to have improvised.

I assume that some apparent urgency led him to take the shortcuts which he did for these areas. As you can visibly notice, the top of my forehead seems less like it was sewn by a medical professional and more as if it were ripped apart and simply put back together in place... leaving the scar that you see today. Since the tissue extending up from my temple seemed once to be made of rawhide, I can only assume that either some unplanned circumstance arose, or this damage was inflicted some time near the death of the original donor and the surrounding cell structures were left non viable.

From his notes and the interactions I will describe later, I know that the choices to enlarge my proportions came from a need to work on scale with the limits of his own dexterity. In order to reconstruct arteries, attach nerve tissues from one seperate source to another, he first had to craft the means by which to handle them as well as see them clearly, and this required that my body be what it became.

Dr. Malcom sat for a moment seemingly concerned as he began whispering to himself and shaking his head in an occasional indecipherable fashion.

DM: So he created a giant because it was easier for him to sew together... and what he couldn't sew, he grew together in an incubator filled with the same fluid he would use to fill your veins... Which explains your healing...

The sample you sent was so rich with unassigned stem cells that I can easily imagine how it could have practically been used as amniotic fluid on its own, but the other components don't make sense and even stem cells on their own don't account for the rate of healing that you've described or what I witnessed with Cassandras arm.

Why again haven't you been able to find out what's inside of you after all these years? You have been curious. There *has* been non-invasive technology that could have at least partially answered some of these. Hell, even invasive surgery would seem like an option given your rate of healing. I'm surprised that with the pain tolerance you must have, that you've never tried to vivisect even part of yourself to look inside.

AG: Truthfully, It is because I have known that the medical or scientific community at large would neither leave me alone nor allow me to go on living if I were revealed. Non-invasive technology does exist for *some* of the answers, but not all... and yes I *have* attempted more than once to conduct my own first hand procedures, but there is never enough time before I lose consciousness from the sensation of doing so. By the duration of unconsciousness caused, I awaken to find myself too healed to continue.

Steven looked back at him with overt worry...

DM: But you're here now Adam, what brought all this on? I know you have mentioned me being able to find answers for you, but more so, you have seemed focused on the answers and proof you insist can be provided to me. You have lived three hundred and fifteen years without these things. You have had a life it seems, a woman you loved, a man you call your father... to tell the truth I don't understand how you expect me to do this without involving my team or somehow to avoid the same things you just mentioned. You're here telling a journalist, speaking with a physical biochemist. You have to know that you will not only be exposing yourself to the world, but that you may not survive their demand for answers.

Adam blinked one slow time and continued.

AG: Because Steven... The answers to all of your searching are here within my body... and I believe that with it, you can change the world. A cure for cancer, a way to prevent alzheimers disease, maybe even practical immortality. Children need not die from disease, mothers need not lose their sons and daughters in war... I expect your team to do exactly what is required... That which Frankenstein sought, that which inspired you to seek in turn, is within your grasp. Edmund Breda be damned Steven Malcom, *you* will be the savior of humanity.

As you mentioned, I have lived for over three hundred years. I have seen the world march forward with both promise and devastation, and I have loved deeply with all of my soul, but more than anything Doctor... I have lost. I have lost more than I ever thought a monster like me could imaginably be blessed to hold even for a moment. Such loss I know you may imagine as I see the naked remnants of a wedding band upon your hand, but even still, you do not know the pains and solitude I have endured.

I am here Steven... *You* are here, because I have decided that it is time for me to die... and I wish for it to mean something.

My hand went over my mouth in shock as I suddenly struggled to find breath. Adam turned to look at me in an attempt to offer comfort, but his words offered none, only more confusion. He spoke with calm resolution and assurance.

AG: And you Cassandra, my only living descendant... You will tell my story to the world.

I closed my laptop.

SESSION TWO

After the disturbance of Adam's announcement during our last interview, I stopped recording entirely. What I recount now is of memory only and I apologize in advance for the personal nature with which it has been written.

At first, I stood there in pure shock for what seemed like an eternity while I watched Steven argue his best to talk Adam out of his plan. He told him that he refused to go through with it, that he was a doctor, and it went against everything he stood for. Adam countered with an argument for the greater good and quality of life, reminding us of his advanced age with insistance that any level of quantity by comparison to others had already been fulfilled long ago.

When I finally jumped in, I had to temporarily put aside the idea of what he had said about us being related and I joined Steven's side by trying to convince him together that this didn't need to happen. We told him, we would keep it all a secret, that we could conduct other tests and find his answers without any cause for death... We tried to change his mind, but it was obvious he had thought out every reason and possible reaction with a logical counter in advance.

We kept trying to persuade him well after sun up and into mid day as our tempers and emotions ran wild, but he calmly sat there the whole time. He never raised his voice or resorted to anything other than a simple weighing of the facts to try and dissolve our objection, until in the end he had backed us into a corner where we found ourselves forced to give in to the simple questions he posed in return. If we didn't go through with it, then he would find someone else, someone who we knew would not care. He was going to proceed with this no matter what, and the only way that we could help if we truly cared about him or the rest of the world in regard to how the discovery was treated and the science conducted, was if we played our part.

So there I was being told that I had a relative I had never known... making him my only living family, and in virtually the same breath being told that I was going to help him to essentially end his life. I chose to deny it. I called him insane. I tried to deny everything he had said until I lost my composure. I lost my professionalism. I yelled at him. I tried to convince myself that I didn't believe he was who he said he was. I tried to convince him of that, but nothing worked.

Eventually, feeling like he had caused too much distress and hoping that time to think would bring us around, he left... but not before he had convinced Steven to fast track a DNA test between samples from each of us. I begrudgingly agreed to it, but I was terrified. I'd only known him face to face for a single day, and somehow over that time I already felt as close to him as any other person I'd met since I was a teenager. I felt heartbroken and defeated.

Steven stayed with me in the office the rest of that day and into the next morning before returning quickly to Boston so he could personally perform the testing.

Yesterday I got the call from the lab confirming Adam's claim. Steven was already on his way here. He stayed with me again last night in my apartment's guest room.

March 29th 5:35 pm

Interviewer Name:

Cassandra Reynolds: Journalist for "Washington Post" newspaper and special columnist for Al-Jazeera International.

Second Interviewer and Consultant:

Dr. Steven Malcom of the Boston College Institute for Scientific Research and Advancement: Specialization in structural biochemistry. Published author and Nobel laureate

Interview Subject : Adam

The time is 8:16 pm. March the 29th, 2024

Location: Personal offices of Cassandra Reynolds, Washington D.C.

CR = Cassandra Reynolds
DM= Dr. Steven Malcom
AG = Subject - Adam

Personal notes Italicized.

A LOST TIME

Steven and I stayed up late last night just talking everything through. Part of me feels like we've almost become nocturnal at this point, since for several nights now I find myself awake throughout, only to bed down in the early hours of the morning. I know he has too since we've been texting most of that time, but it was nice to vent face to face with someone who understood, since no one else really knows about all this yet.

When I woke up, I peeked into the guest room and saw that Steven was still asleep but the time had already passed 5 pm. Taking advantage of this opportunity I composed myself quietly, brushed my hair, and walked down the hallway to the office where I took written record of recent events up to the end of my last entry. I'ts been a few hours now. I'm only jotting this down to catch up before I hit record on tonight's video but I don't want to skip anything important.

So, not expecting for Adam to arrive until sometime closer to nightfall, I locked up behind me and walked a couple of blocks to the small Italian place where I often buy my dinner when I'm working late. Knowing Adam's diet, I ordered a large vegetable supreme pie and bought for myself and again for Steven, both calzones and garlic bread in addition to two gallons of their homemade lemonade. It was still early for their regular crowd and I had to wait for the oven to warm, but it's always worth it. I sat and waited for the order until it was done, while I watched the Lobby television. Afterward I thanked Mr. Parcini and headed back with my hands full.

By my arrival I was somewhat surprised to find both men standing in wait outside of the office door, but I don't know whether Adam woke Steven, or if he had already made his way out looking for me. I find it highly likely that he woke up on his own and was just uncomfortable in my apartment by himself. All the same, I wonder how close I got before Adam heard me and informed him of my arrival downstairs. He probably already knew about the pizza before I even got into the elevator, but not likely the lemonade or he'd have met me at the sidewalk entrance instead. I'm sure Steven and I will discuss it later.

I handed Steven the food boxes and Adam took the lemonade from me while I opened the door for them before heading straight here to my desk. They've entered the office now and Steven has set the food on the coffee table. Some of the small talk they've been engaged in will have to be omitted, but it seems as if all I've missed is something to do with the weather in Geneva.

Recording begins, March 29th, 8:16 pm

CR: Ok guys, rolling.

DM: This smells delicious... But yeah I'll have to check that out next time I'm there. It sounds beautiful.

Steven yawned and turned toward me.

DM: How long was I out?

CR: It's a little after eight.

DM: And when did you get up?

CR: Little after five... This place is just down the block. You?

DM: Ten minutes or so. Big man showed up not long after.

CR: You were already waiting in the hallway weren't you?

DM: Well yeah, I mean I didnt know where you were.

CR: Figured as much. I brought dinner obviously.

AG: You didn't have to...

DM: Obviously. Wait, did you say rolling?

CR: Don't worry short stuff, yours is veggie. Yes, we're active.

AW: Oh you dear angel... you *really* didn't have to.

DM: Damn you type fast. Is it just me or was the laptop open when we walked in?

CR: Comes with the job. Yeah I took down some notes before heading out while ago.

Adam laughed as they each grabbed mugs from the side table on their way across the room. They poured themselves lemonade and began to sift through the boxes on the makeshift buffet where they'd set the food.

Adam retrieved the entire box of his pizza and found a seat on the floor where he could lean back against the wall. Following suit, Steven as well carried his calzone, box and all, to where he planned to sit. I thought to offer them plates for a moment but by the time I looked up Adam was midway into his first slice and Steven was cutting into his meal with the plastic cutlery provided.

All in all, I felt like the mood of the room was one of a false happiness and polite pretense while anxiety hung over all of us concerning the expected continuation of our previous discussions. For the time being, we tried our best to ignore the elephant in the room as one often does during meal time.

AG: Oh god, that is good. Later on you should remind me to tell you about this little woman in Italy. Absolutely amazing food. Though of course more in the traditional vein where ingredients are concerned... This is also delicious. I always love to see a brick oven still in use. Truth be told I could *live* off of olives and peppers alone mind you, but cheese, cheese is the delicacy every time.

I find Adam's fluctuations of manner and speech intriguing because while he tries so hard to hide it, small tells of his age seem to pop up without his notice. This was something I had taken note of before, but at times he seems so average and informal that it can be easy to forget the claims of his origin until he is allowed to speak at length. However it's not just things like his recognition of brick oven pizza by taste alone. I know plenty of normal people who can do that just from being food snobs. It's more that the longer he talks without interruption, the more inevitable it becomes that his words themselves give way to what I can only describe as anachronistic patterns that echo to me the composures of classical prose.

It seems more to my understanding so far like an old habit rather than anything intentional. I've seen it before with subjects accents, but never so much with their entire sentence structure. Even while he continued in this way very informally, I have paid close enough attention to conclude in earnest that the occasional use of modern syntax and vocabulary are not some failing to uphold a fictitious imagery, but rather the opposite. It's called code switching.

He tries very hard to sound like other people, but that mask slips the longer that he goes on, and given enough time uninterrupted, he reverts to what is most comfortable for him in that older form which on occasion includes a variety of accents different from the plainness of english he will begin with each time.

AG: However I think I might have given the wrong impression last I was here. It was very sweet of you to buy the vegeterian pizza, but I do actually eat meat these days. Most of my diet is restricted to large predators where I currently live, and though the urge to hunt did not occur naturally in the beginning, I do by neccesity and enjoyment consume quite a bit of preserved and prepared animal proteins. After all, if man as a whole did by nature have the instinct I lacked, then who was I to deny the tradition when my body hungered for it.

Adam smiled.

AG: Of course I acknowledge the fact that humanity thrives and feeds off of death, but I do not judge.

DM: Wait. What do you mean by that? Thrives and feeds off death? And why would you judge humanity? Do you really not consider yourself human?

AG: Oh, no offense is meant, simply the truth. From trees to leafy greens, that which man often utilizes, must surely die to become most useful to him. A stave must be cut or collected from the ground. A fence must come from either the wooden bones of life or the elements of the earth.

Even with all of the synthetics of the modern world, everything from the glue that holds your book bindings, to the leather of your shoes, even the polishes used on your dry goods or components within your shampoos, come from the products of an animal's death. Not to mention the need of any product that is made from plants which even of themselves require death of all types in order to create the most abundant soil from which they may grow.

Life itself requires death in order to persist, therefore I choose to let it not be wasted. I may refrain from causing death unduly, but by no means could I feign innocent ignorance of denial to these facts around me that by some means it will occur, and I will thrive or feed off of its action. I exist because of death in an obvious fashion, but so does everyone else in their own way.

I fault no person for choosing to not consume meat for personal reasons of their own choices, but for myself I feel that if my existence is one born at the offerings of death, then the greatest way to pay thanks to that, is to be sure I make myself worthy of those contributions in honor to the life that was taken.

DM: Circle of life then?

AG: Brilliant song, better film. Actually a huge fan of several from that era... but essentially yes. Have you never looked at it that way? I would challenge you to find any single item in this room that did not require the death of another lifeform.

DM: Well yeah but its not like the mug here is made of bone.

AG: You think not? Let's inspect. Ceramic, glazed... Glaze which commonly utilizes heavy metals which leach into the water supply causing eventual death of minor ecosystems. Ceramic which is made from clays which consist of eons of mixed elements to a soil comprised of decayed plant and animal components broken down until they become useful in a new form altogether? Not to mention the source of pigments chosen such as the bone ash used to whiten the ceramic into china, or the land utilized to build the factory where the product was made. Even the trucks which carry the product to the shelf run off of *fossil* fuels which by definition came indirectly from the remnants of what was once living long ago. From dust to dust Doctor. There is no removal from it, no avoidance of its weight upon us. We are consumers of death and there is no alternative within physical life.

DM: Quite a perspective over pizza and lemonade old man. Is that why you want to die? To become useful to the world as you put it?

I was glad I had hit record before we started eating or else I might have missed the turn in topic as previous issues were suddenly forced from the small talk. Steven and I returned our gaze upon Adam and I approached to be seated in front of him on the floor. Adam however, still presently engaged in devouring his pizza looked up in surprise of our expectation.

AG: Oh? Well then I suppose it's time. Doctor, would you please bring me that last gallon of lemonade before we begin?

Steven stood and grabbed the plastic jug from my desk bringing it to set between us as he retook his former position.

DM: Speaking of fully synthetic...

Adam reached for the jug as he joked once more with the doctor.

AW: Stearic acid used on the plastic, derived from cattle fat... So I left off?

DM: oh ya know, you want me to kill you. You'd just met your father, and oh yeah, Cassandra is one of your descendants. Start where you want.

I reached to calm Steven, realizing that his passive agressive demeanor was agitated over the pain of the last days, but I did not know which injury hurt him most.

AG: Right then, straight to business. How different from Breda you truly are doctor... Though I may change your mind before the time comes.

Adam took a large swig of lemonade from the jug.

AG: I suppose we should begin with a continuation of my time with Conrad. I will tell the tale.

By our first meeting, he had already retreated to Geissen after killing a man in a duel some time prior, but returned to Wittgenstein where I found him. Contrary to popular belief however he did not reside in the castle itself, but a small cottage elsewhere on the grounds. He preferred the solitude of nature beyond the more extravagent trappings of life, and lived simply despite his reputation. The words of his former friends and acquaintances had thoroughly ruined any reputable impressions that others once held to his name and he found solace in living according to his own principles.

Of course upon meeting me for the first time, he was overwhelmed with guilts of his past which felt to him as punishment for the hubris he described as occupying much of his life, but he took great care to atone for those sins of that past, and in his way, I believe that his treatment of me gave him a sense of peace rather than the weight of pennance.

And there it was. His speech was already shifting. Even in his attempts at levity he turned back toward that older way that he struggled to hide without even realizing it.

In all the world it must be known to each of us that our motivations are our own, driven by what we hold inside, and the best we may do where it concerns us as to the drives of others, is to guess or draw conclusion based upon our own experiences.

Conrad would show me many things about himself in our time, but on the day that we met, I moved to protect him not for some great bond which I wished to be so, but for the need within me to prevent what I saw as another living being being faced with a type of treatment I knew all too well myself... and in this I learned greater that I hated not the stranger moved to violence, so much as I burned with anger at my own creator for his actions against me. I found in my way, the base for empathy being rooted in my own understanding of pain and confusion and the wish to prevent these befalling another.

In years to come I would struggle to understand my creator, to justify in my mind Breda's actions against me from my beginnings to his end, even feeling as though at some point, I might be freed from these after he had passed from the earth, but whatever good might have come from that, ultimately proved lacking.

It did not truly matter what he thought of me or what he believed. Whatever motivations moved him to do the things he did, died along with his body, and still I would remain, foolishly carrying out the motions of life which might prove myself better than he had articulated. Whether to prove them to myself, to others, or to his wandering soul, it did not matter. What good was any proof to a corpse? What good would it have done me to understand this sooner? None, I fear to confess. For the needs that drove my actions had to be understood from within a perspective not born of the pains he had caused, but of this empathy and care outside of myself which I first discovered from my true father... and though Conrad also would pass too soon from my world, this lesson would stay within me for the centuries to come.

As to Conrad of course, his first gaze upon me was one of piteous empathy for me as I had felt for him, which had motivated me beyond fear to expose myself to the threat of man. Yet his words were not of shock so much as disappointment in lifes cruelty. He was not disappointed in me to be clear, but in my creator, who had followed thru along a path which had been warned against by his mentor, the betrayed, the off cast, the disrepudiated, Johann Conrad Dippel.

I have mentioned before some sources of inspiration concerning the fictitious personage of Victor Frankenstein as a whole, however in this moment I must expound that the accounts of that characters charmed youth came mostly from Mary's own mind, as his words at the books beginnings poured out such pleasant circumstance and inspiration to create of perception a man both admirable and driven by which to hang the tragic trappings of the story that would follow.

However within these framings she also found suitable to enfold the tales which I had relayed to her concerning my time spent with Conrad himself, as well as many others, not only in my own education, but also the mentorship and subsequent pursuits of my creator and father as they had come to their actions and acquittals toward one another's company.

You asked during our last conference if Conrad were the inspiration for the old man in the story, and I answered truthfully to tell you in part. However as better instance might relay, it was my time with Father that inspired thoughts which would direct Mary to draw such bold contrast to the tendancies of Victor's own parentage, in opposition to the directives he would later take toward his creation.

To quote her written words as example. "With this deep consciousness of what they owed towards the being to which they had given life, added to the active spirit of tenderness that animated both, it may be imagined that while during every hour of my infant life I received a lesson of patience, of charity, and of self control, I was so guided by a silken cord that all seemed but one train of enjoyment to me."

DM: Stop. You actually know the entire work by heart don't you?

AG: I do... Yes. Yet it *is* relevant. By this type of contextual account, Mary divided the personages and character of the creator and his counter, as if to preemptively condemn the actions of Breda my creator, while exalting those of Conrad who I called father, by crafting his being as figurative grandfather to the progeny of creation that would ultimately result.

"Victor must be blessed undoubtedly and in abundance with that which he would deny" She insisted, an expression that found form in what would serve as her great admonition and refusal to excuse his latter actions. In my own mind it is this complexity of hatred for Breda, but temperance of quality given to Victor that fuel the intonement of her works entirety.

And so with Conrad, it was indeed a "deep consciousness" of what he "owed" to me due to his part in my creation that he taught me in secret and care for his remaining years and acted upon me as he did.

Still Mary could not resist the expressions of her own life and loves as she birthed her patchwork creation within the fictions of truth she bestowed with her every line. Her father, mother, love of a sister, her eager and earnest friendships and loyalties, all bled their way into her creation until even the lines of protagonist or adversary blurred to seperate themselves from where any of us punctuated individually for the others to begin...

But I digress... to tell solely of my years with father else I might lose myself in analysis of my dear loves artistry...

DM: Wait just a moment.... so the character of Elizabeth in the novel... Not really inspired by Breda's wife then?

AG: Only in part of her tragedy. I know very little of the woman my creator married bar the limited interactions which led to her end, and as we approach such times I shall tell you of her in full to what I am aware. Yet, no, Elizabeth was primarily in my feelings, an expression for Mary to speak of the forbidden love between herself and her own version of a gifted sister unborn by blood.

It was clear from the beginnings her homages to Claire in covert declaration to posterity, however that understanding will become clearer when I reach such portions of time in which I encountered them. Patience is neccesity good Doctor. Trust that I will answer all as I continue, and if I have not, then you may ask afterward and I will disguise nothing from my response.

CR: Please Steven, if you interrupt him again before he tells us about his father, Im going to make you read the transcripts from us finishing these interviews without you.

DM: I'm not the only one taking the asides here. The big man is stalling.

Adam sighed.

AG: It's not his fault Ms. Reynolds... Truly, relaying the events of ones life in retrospect is difficult without some measure of context which lands often non sequitur in the mind.

Obviously the nature of mine having been previously relayed in part through fictions familliar to the good Doctor, affects my thoughts a great deal.

I shall strive to move better forward in narration to the events as they occurred.

DM: I think he may have attention deficit disorder of some sort Cassandra.

Steven added this sarcastically but Adam, not willing to be baited into confrontational attitude, responded with playfulness and moved ahead unbothered.

AG: Ahh, yes well if you would forgive it, I think I am simply old and privy to tangents, not so unlike father as it were.

Perhaps I *am* avoiding the progress which came next however. Remembering the good times can bring a pain all its own to bare, and despite the curtain of weight which surrounded us, I do greatly regret that such beautiful and gracious times were both short and underappreciated during their stay. In some way perhaps I wish to prolong them by extending the wait for their telling, but you are right... I must press on.

As fortunes would prove through fates fickle delivery, Conrad surmised near instantly the nature of my being. He had listened with heavy heart and boundless concern of the rumors toward the activity of his former protege during his time incarcerate, and fearing just such an occurrence, made haste at first opportunity to retrieve what remained of his works from the abode that Breda had usurped from him.

"He rejected then the product of his own arrogance... and you by wandering nakedness expelled untethered into the wilds?" He'd spoken. He said these words with such sadness and pain while still holding gentle hand upon my face, but even then I could detect amongst his tones a bitter disappointment in his former protege.

I had not considered before the truth in his words concerning my unclothed appearance however, yet I stood before him as he described, naked and exposed in every respect, obvious in my malformity and makeup.

Silently I cried in shame, his would be attacker long beyond sight by then. The mysterious man draped me beneath his coat with gentleness and ushered me into his home without fear or revulsion. There in those moments seated by the hearth within, my first taste of humanity partly unmade the wretchedness of my heart and my first steps toward *true* humanity were born. Though I would forever and still stand apart in my own interpretations of definition as you have questioned of me.

I had attempted over the course of my seclusionary months to pull what remaining sinew held together my original stitching as all of my separations had by thus time healed to oneness. However what I had missed, my host proceeded to tend as he gently washed my form with cloth and water, lightly tracing the lines of my construction in pity and awe.

"Weep as you must." he told me quietly... and there we sat for some time while he tended my body and comforted my thoughts.

"You spoke at the other who was here... Do you know words other than these?" He asked me after some time, rising to pour himself drink from a nearby kettle.

"Only that which I have heard from your voice." I responded.

His face looked grave at this.

"Intelligence then... What horror that imposter has done to you..." He muttered in saddened anger.

That was the start for us of a long inquiry in which I relayed best I could then, the same story in which I have passed now to you of my awakening and subsequent days up until the meeting of our persons.

"Then as product of my mind as much as his hands, I will fasten myself the duties to give what he would not. Have you a name dear creature?" He asked.

I did not understand at first the claim he made on me, but informed him of my namelessness.

"What wretched foulness that is your creator, not even a name afforded to his own work, the very Adam of his make, and not even the decency of virtue to proclaim you." He swore.

It was then that Conrad explained to me through my limited comprehension, that of his relationship to my maker and all that came of it, leading to the argument which splintered their bond. They had been introduced by mutual acquaintances, found in one another a shared interest in several avenues of knowledge, and formed a true bond it seemed for several years. Conrad at the time was very much brash and outspoken yet prideful as well and in his descriptions truly felt himself akin to the young man whom he had taken beneath his wing.

However at some length, an altercation of controversy arose that divided their tenderness for each other. In fact, this would arise over the concept and very possibility of creating life such as myself and whether or not to act on such theory was within the rights of any man to follow through at the cost required. Breda felt justified and entitled that the likelihood of success demanded action to follow through in more than thought. Conrad however considered the steps required to be evil and would not indulge a partnership in those deeds... And so this, his beloved protege betrayed their trust and thru deception and lies, made possible Conrad's forced removal from his company in literal imprisonment, so that he could move forward unchallenged.

This cost Conrad dearly, and he suffered long by Breda's actions against him, until at last freed, he had through winding ways of lifes adventures, found himself there in his cottage on the bordering grounds of Wittgenstein, where I had followed. No further contact had come between the two men, and though bitter in his animosity over the ordeal, Father was glad to be absent from the man for fear of his actions were he to cross path once more.

It is strange how time itself may soften or harden these views. In fact years later, upon his deathbed, my father would beg of me not to curse the name of my creator as he so often had, beseeching me to make peace with him for the betterment of my soul, that I might not be alone upon the earth, but from the start of our time, this had not been his way, and I dare report his hatred of Edmund Breda would rival that of even Mary or Percy on my behalf.

However that was some time later. For the most of it, Conrad and I lived together for the next several decades without significant incident. He tended to his business per usual, and rumors circulated around his isolation. He would go into town as needed and I would keep to the cottage. We lived as father and son.

He taught me as much as he could about the world outside of our domain. We discussed philosophy, spirituality, literature and science. At times his temperment would swing wildly, and he would rave in anger at the goings on of the world. Other times his quiet way would seem at peace within the shade of the forests nearby.

As for myself, the questions of my nature occupied my mind intensely. After a reading of Paradise Lost, I found myself one day engaged in debate over the questions of my being that escalated to heated argument at fathers insistence that I was something other than what I felt at that time.

I argued at the meaning of my existence. If I were destined by some greater god in the heavens then why should my life be secreted away? Like the anger of the Morningstar, I felt wrath grow within me at the favoritism of man, and part of me wondered aloud if I was in fact the great beast spoken of in Revelations, but father would have none of this talk.

He believed that I was a man, and like all men, beloved by the creator of earth. I was less certain. Was I a man after all? Was I born of God? A resurrected soul like Lazarus or dare I say Jeshua himself? Or was I merely a crafting of man? A sin incarnate, birthed by the hubris of my creator in demonic form? Had I lived before though I did not remember? Was I the same person or persons by which I was composed somehow? Or was I a life all the new in its own? If I were a new life, then where from had come the soul if I indeed had one? From some ethereal plane I could scarcely fathom? Beyond the ether? Was I even truly alive or simply a mimicry of actions which seemed as life?

Even and ever the nature of God and life itself would be the questions I pondered at endless length many a time. Father passioned his reply to these arguments with the breath and conviction of a man desperate to save that which he claimed as his son, to save my soul as he saw it...

But especially that became my chief dispute. How could I, a creature wrenched to life from death, contain a soul? By the sciences that had given me breath, what proof was there of such an ephemeral quality?

Within the dim of his laboratory, we tested the limits of my capacities for many years. My strength which proved greater than that of ten men, gave to me a sense of monstrousness that I should stand apart so uniquely equipped beyond the limits of man, but also within this, the abilities of my body to heal from any and all injury inflicted, no matter its severity, imbued in me a pride that I might become a beacon of hope to the troubled world; If only we could replicate the mechanisms of those abilities to share with the ill or less fortuned.

Where father was most intrigued, seemed more in truth to the limits of my mind. He celebrated me privately in my depths of curiosity and determination of truth, which he claimed uncommon amongst the masses of man, despite so far as I could tell, the exposure of such words written by many who I felt far superior to any thoughts or questions to which I had yet asked or reconciled within myself. How I inquired, could I be so unique and worthy of his praises when I compared nor contributed nothing on equal to the works which we read night after night? I was no Milton, no Shakespeare, no Plato nor Agrippa. I had solved no lasting question or formed any great work of art or meaning to the world around us. I had merely read their words and asked aloud that which they stirred within me. Over thirty years of isolation with little but Father's tutelage and the odd inspection of his dealings with others, had left me filled only with more mystery which I questioned, than that which I had resolved for myself or others.

When visitors attended the home, I would hide, and upon their departure I cursed the freedoms which they enjoyed, but Father insisted that this must be the way. He dreamed for me a day that these ways would no longer be neccesary, but as age took his body year by year, he knew I would persist beyond, without home, without companionship, and without the shelter of his protection.

This is why upon his final written words, he would plead with me that I might find my creator and make plain the request for amity between us... For the hope that Breda might after such years, have found it within himself to embrace and care for that which he had brought into the world, But I was a tempestuous child, mercurial and proud despite the knowledge of my failing and malformity.

I hated the sight of myself even as I convinced some part of my minds determinings that I was somehow superior to mankind, deserving of better within the world, worthy of elevation for the praises which father had filled my heart... and still I could scarcely stand the fleeting visions of my own reflection.

In the end of it, I woke one night quite by chance to a restlessness that provoked me toward the reading of poetry to calm my emotions, a habit of distraction which I found settling at such times... but walking toward the modest library to read, I noted a light emanating from the chambers of fathers room.

I found him cold... His body stiffened and eyes fixed with his jaw open, sprawled naked upon the floor of his bedside...

Kneeling to rouse him, I knew before touch that he had perished. I am unsure how it is even to this day and after many sights of this nature, just what device within the living, death is so recognized, but that part within me that I believe exists in all of us, did not stir a single question as to whether he would wake. I knew with certainty that to hold such would be a gross form of denial brought on by shock, but still it is hard to reconcile the sudden absence of one so accustomed to presence within your own existence.

His life I knew was gone however. Whatever exists within the form of man which gives animation and vitality, had departed from the remains before me, and I knew with absolute certainty this truth even as my mind reeled to reject the shock and horror of its clarity.

What I saw and touched was not Conrad. It was a body, mere physical remains which had housed once the most caring and inspired personage I had yet known since my creation... and yet at last and for the first time, I saw a greater similarity in his form to my own than I had ever felt before.

He had prepared me for so much by that time that I knew what must follow. I was not to move him, nor attempt to contact another, but instead I must collect the necessities of my life alone, and depart forever from our home... This was my duty as his loyal son, though I simply could not force myself to leave his side.

I sat with his body for what felt like an age before the sun began to peek through the windows. Its light filtered in over his form in slow and uncaring motion as his remains upon the earth lay still and fixed. The sight of his open jaw troubled me, but I dared not touch it. His lifeless eyes stared without action at the distance of some unseen focus. A shaft of this light moved over his face, and like the shadows of a sun dial, I was aware of the passage of time. I watched it with deep sadness until nearly the noon of day before I rose.

No tears filled my eyes. No delerium took my body, but I was broken by the torrent of realizations that moved within... It was senseless to speak to his body as if he remained, but I rose from its side as if, like he had done so many times, I were speaking to some unseen spirit that accompanied my presence. I made promises to do as he asked, even while I gathered the belongings I would require. I moved from room to room, collecting my clothing, my personal books, and all of the journals of my father which pertained to our life together.

No other form came toward the home that day. No visitors, no interruptions, and not a stray obstacle at all to my remaining task. The birds sang in the trees. The animals scurried in the wood, but I felt the weight of silence.

"I am not a man", I thought repeatedly. "I am death... and he has joined me at long last only to depart... Now you see father? Now you see the difference between you and I, that your body matches my own?! You have left this world and me in it! but remain here as I must leave... I know somehow that you hear me from whatever plane you have escaped to. Do you see me now?" I asked the air around me.

When I had loaded a trunk with that which I intended to carry, I strapped it upon my back like a bushel of wood, and opened the door to depart. The sun was setting as I recall... a most brilliant orange to be seen across the distant field toward the castle...

"Goodbye Father..." I spoke one last time...

and so it was that I left the grounds of Wittgenstein in the year of 1734... Turning toward the forest to make my way in secrecy, I left the door ajar and moved into the shade of wilderness without a soul to tell...

They would find his body some time later, the men of town who had troubled him so in life, but he would not be there to argue them whatever will or desires they had, not to begrudge their small mindedness or bear the weight of their judgements... He I felt, had found peace in the finality that I might never know... and I would strike forward to seek my own in solitude.

" You are protected."

Adam stared at the jug of lemonade on the floor as he whispered his final words. I did not ask if he needed a moment. It was given without question. At last after a time, he reached for the jug and took a sip before setting it down once more.

THE PRODIGAL

AG: So that was my *first* life as one might say... You should not worry over the difficulties of the telling. I know I delayed speaking on it for fear, but it was very long ago... The events to follow are much more difficult in truth I suppose, but my time with Father was ultimately happy, and I was allowed decades with him in peace before the end came.

The night after his death, I walked with no direction with which to aim my ambitions. I knew in my heart that I would be starting anew, and so I moved toward the rising of the sun. For another day after I walked this way until the late of night without hunger or rest, until at last I decided in the solitude of the wilderness to make camp along the height of a bald hilltop so that I might see the stars.

Starting a fire, I sat alone beside the trunk which contained all which I owned, an inheritence both meager and profound on which I leaned for many hours before opening to retrieve the contents within. Rifling through these I found the last journal which father had kept, and I read what he had written.

On it's final page, separated by many empty spaces where he had intended to write for days more, I found the message wherein he pleaded the case that I should find my creator. Along with this, he had included an address to which would set my course toward the last known inhabitance of the estranged architect of my being.

I thought long and hard that night about what should be done with the endless notes of research and musings which

Conrad had set to page concerning our endeavors over the years. I knew the extent of what secrets we had uncovered, but through all of our time, no secret formulation or epiphany had given answer to the missing components of Breda's work.

Still the danger of what did exist concerned his heart for the future of mankind and for my wellbeing, and yet I could not bring myself to burn the works of my fathers mind... Again I did not sleep.

Instead, by the light of dawn, I dug a hole within the ground large enough as a grave, and I buried the trunk within, keeping only a satchel by which to carry my chosen belongings with me as I set course for the country of what might be considered my *other* fathers home.

Doctor, I see on your face the question you wish to ask, and yes I have returned to the hilltop once more and retrieved these in years since, though it would be a long time after and with great effort as I was forced to break thru many levels of concrete beneath the floors of a coffee house which had been built atop the hill. If you wish to read from them, I will provide these for you after the conclusion of our works.

Steven nodded in appreciation at this.

DM: Thank you.

AG: I will be sure to also include the ciphers.

CR: He coded them?

AG: If you might have expected differently I fear I have illustrated poorly the extent of Father's concerns. History may recall of him boasts and false claims even into later life, but I assure you, Conrad the man, never wished for any other to know the full extent of things he had done or discovered. His discredit of repute was a creation of his own paranoia in earnest attempt to undo the potential damages to posterity and prevent his earlier work from birthing another who might follow it down the same path which had led Edmund to my own conception.

It was by the coding of his words that I knew precisely which volumes to leave versus the ones to take with me upon departure. Yes dear Doctor... he coded everything that truly mattered.

CR: Wow... I've never even encrypted a story before.

AG: You may wish to strike that from record afterward.

CR: Solid point...
It should be noted that this portion of conversation was in fact stricken from the original publication of these events, however given the facts of what has changed since then, I freely admit that in my professional days as a journalist, I was so careless as to not encrypt anything I wrote. I locked my laptop in a safe some nights, but never encrypted a single file, even the recordings transcribed from these interviews.

AG: After the burial of these things I must confess, I struggled greatly in decision as whether or not to honor Father's wishes, but alas did set my course toward the direction of my creators country and placement.

This path as it would turn, led me much along the same directions as my former journey from the castle where I had been awakened upon my first memories, and in fortune I was allowed to see the townships and passages along the way once more with new eyes and understanding.

I lingered on the periphery of these for days in observation of many habit and deed which held meaning in my sight for the first time. Despite all I had read and every bit of learnedness instilled in me by fathers tutelage, my life had been largely devoid of such sights and I marvelled at the strangeness of even the simplest human interactions. I saw families, friends, quarrels, and cooperation, especially though, I saw love.

Some food was stolen where I could manage it, and I hold no shame in that now as I held none then. For I took no more than I might require and from none who seemed of need more than myself. I had not known then how wretched a cook father had been in truth, but the experiences of taste and scent unfolded to my palette as only another form of beauty in this world.

The more I witnessed of these peoples along my way, I supposed even then, that I lingered less for curiosities own sake than by the great longing of solitude. I missed Father. I missed the companionship of another with whom I could share my thoughts and trials, but beyond this I missed a thing which I had never truly known at all, that which I might never know... to be a part of the world.

However I knew this was not possible. No matter what I held inside of myself, the curse of my own reflection forbade exposure to the simple folk of that country for I appeared as I knew, a demonic wretch to the eye and source of frightful perplexity, which spawns dangerous mistrust and violence from the simple minded.

I recalled the few times in my life which I had allowed myself to be seen and the sting of memory burned within my heart as a blazing pain that knew no relief. If only like Conrad, another might see beyond the deformities of my flesh and chance their perceptions to learn before casting judgment of some perceived evil, what might I give in return for such kindness?

If there was any other who might do this, it would surely be my creator who knew the truth of my being not as devil or foul spirit, but as his own crafting, merely another traveler along the roads of life, born to misfortunate visage by circumstance rather than supernatural evils of disposition. His earlier mistreatment of my form I had hoped perhaps to prove a regretable folly born of fear, for I lacked then the means to communicate or make known that I might be more than a beast or miscarriage of virtuous works.

Perhaps he had searched for me even in the years since. If my father, who had been so mistreated and maligned by this man, betrayed, imprisoned, pauperized, ruined by he in spirit and standing, could find in his heart to lend a second of chances for hope of my sake, then I too must be willing to look past the evils he had once done and seek to forgive, if only for the remotest of chance that I might find some place to belong once more.

It was with these thoughts that I carried forward in prospect and silence until at long last I reached the home once fled by all involved in such twisted fates of my creation. Only I did not find Breda at the castle, nor had I expected to, abandoned as it was, its tower since wrecked by some unknown catastrophe, I searched the grounds by nights deep shadows for any clues that might enlighten my path before continuation further to reach the address which had been written.

I suppose it was some deep and morbid part of myself that wished to stay, for it was the place of my birth yes, but also the birthplace of my father as well, and some connection felt due to its gifts upon me... Despite the pains of my experiences within. That same part of myself smiled internally to see the damage to the tower I admit, for I knew the cage of my early days held no true power save for that I allowed within myself...

and to see it now in destruction, was a lift to all weight of its fearful holds over me.

I breathed deep. The grounds as well as surrounding forest, truly were a beautiful sight. Father had told me once of a legend attributed to this place somewhere amongst the grounds... a fountain of youth it was said, where old women would test themselves on moonlit nights in hopes of regaining some lost vestige of earlier years. This he relayed had partly inspired his later endeavors in both science and alchemy to achieve on his own accord, and thus it seemed led to my eventual formation.

I found such stories both intriguing and fanciful to say the least, but after having found its location, hidden away behind an old garden, this was where I rested my frame in slumber for the remaining hours of night, as the memory of his stories held magic to me, and as I looked to the stars above, I almost felt as if he smiled down on my endeavor with pride.

The next morning, I stuck closely to the roadside, moving south along the route to Geneva with focused ears that I might by chance hear the name of Breda pass from the lips of some unsuspecting traveller. There was no such fortune as thus, yet I moved onward with vigorous step by each day, anxious at what I might find upon my arrival.

The rivers and streams were cold if I was forced to fjord them, and the drying of my belongings would have taken much time from my days. So upon each, I carefully timed the comings and goings of others so that I might cross unseen over the bridges available, until at long last I came to the borders of my destination near Plainpalais.

It was here as I approached the address concerned that I first saw at some distance, a party of townsfolk moving in procession from the grounds. Upon closer inspection from a nearby hill, I observed the presence of 2 carriages, the lead of which trailed an ornate cart fastened behind its frame, carrying a coffin. The last of which held inside, a party of grieving family.

I feared at once that the man I had come to see had perished. How odd that I should now find myself not only anxious to meet with my creator, but in fact concerned for his very wellbeing. Alas the coffin atop the trolley was not the size of a man at all, but the size instead of a child. Observing this, I felt instantly the pangs of pity within my heart. Had my creator lost a child? Could that by means of altered fate have been my own sibling who I now watched taken to be buried?

Moving as closely along the road as I could dare, without risk of sight, I followed the procession to their destination. I saw from my vantage at the edge of a wood, a wide plain and lake beyond, but upon the top of a nearby hill, at the base of an ancient tree, there sat a small collection of ornate stones designating the cemetary where the child would be laid to rest.

The plain, hilltop and the lake were surrounded on nearly every side by tall mountains, leaving only one entry or exit by which one could move aside from the lake itself. So from my vantage I watched at a distance as I listened to the words of the people while the child was lowered into the ground.

A sermon was given in latin, and I learned forthwit that the child held the last name of Breda, but was fathered not by Edmund but another... After this, I watched as grieving figures wept and departed. The carriage moved on once more back along the road it had first entered and past my view from the woods, but my creator was absent from it. Looking back to the hill, I discerned the reason.

And there he was... My creator, alone atop of the hill, filling dirt into a childs grave. I thought to move toward him, to rush and risk my very life as all anticipation peaked within my mind, but I did not. I knew the folly it would be to not only surprise one in such grief, but to look as I did, even to my creator, I knew that I must approach with caution.

After all else departed, I moved closer by slow increments. A storm began to thunder in the distance. It echoed thru the mountains into the valley and lightning began to flash between the peaks and summits. The light of day grew dim and the sun began to fade, but still upon the hill, the figure shoveled. I hid the best that my size would allow amongst smaller clumps of trees until with nary a furlong between us, I stood hidden behind the last blind available, to view the object purpose of my travels. However what I saw before me was not possible to behold. It was as if he had not changed a single bit, completely untouched by the age that should have shown on his face.

Had I not passed thirty years with father? watched him age and grow weary with the passing decades unto his death? Yet here was Breda, shoveling with a movement that further solidified the truth of it. He, like myself had somehow remained fixed and capable through times passage so that the Edmund which I watched on that day, looked identical to the man who had beaten me and locked me away.

My heart filled with panic and thundered in my chest like the distant storm. I had not anticipated the reaction within me to lay eyes on him once more, and in this state! In my mind I felt the memory of fear as I first saw his face, angry, brutal, and violent, while he assaulted my body. To any other, the man I looked at might have seemed a perfect gentleman, stricken by grief and responsible in his duty to take a servants role in the burial of his nephew... But I by contrast beheld the monster of my nightmares.

By nightfall he had lit a lantern to complete his work, and meant soon to move on from the valley before the rains set upon him. I thought once more to approach but wavered when a flash of lightning lit the night sky as broad day, and I saw in his eyes that he had seen me. Fixed and terrified, I stood for only a moment before turning to flee. He had certainly witnessed my presence. My eyes had met his, and in them I saw such recognition that he knew me for what I was.

I bounded as fast as my legs could carry toward the mountains which had been behind me, but at the edge of the wood instead I found a cliff face of sheer stone. Such was my will to escape that I grabbed thoughtlessly upon this wall and scaled the heights as if one pursued, but looking back I saw that he had not followed. He stood as he was without motion, watching me from the distance. Still I did not stop. I saw him only this once more. Throwing myself over the last available edging and onto a wider path, I fled along the passage without looking back, until when I at long last had courage to do so, I could not see the field and lake below at all, and in truth had travelled some great distance.

He had seen me... He was aware of my continued life and presence. Was this not what I wished? Need I do any more to approach him or should I merely wait for him to seek me? Did I truly want him to pursue me, to face him at all after such time? Did I so truthfully require answers? I had felt such emotions about him throughout the years, anger for what he had done to father, disgust at his irresponsibility, sadness of rejection... but fear? Not since the day I had first fled from him had I felt the notion of fear toward his personage, and yet that was the result of his sight, a blinding terror which had gripped me from within and led me to flee once more.

I wandered the icy summits of mountaintops and glacier where no man treads, and for two months after, stayed myself from the sight of mans works. Living within caves of ice and stone. I sought lonely refuge within my thoughts, and in my turmoils, I raved. I was angry at the fear that I had felt, angry at myself, the world, and at the creator who had inspired such dread excitement within me that I, like the coward, hid from life's activities. Yet what alternative had I to this? Was I not destined for such solitude? Friendless and without hope to behold or touch in that desolate yet beautiful land?

By this times end I had settled somewhere amid a sea of ice, and thinking my isolation safe, I calmed to surrender myself in more hopeful thought. For merely a few days this calm comfort surrounded me, but upon one afternoon, I heard the shouts of a man echoing across the ice, and was stirred to discover their source. Only to the frightful sight of my eyes upon seeing the cause of such commotion did I observe then the sight of my creator once more.

I knew not how he had found me, or by what devices he had accessed this wilderness, but somehow he had arrived amidst the vastness of those endless chasms, at the very same placement as I had meant to hide from his form. However in place of fear, my mind found within it the fires of rage. My blood felt as if it boiled beneath my skin and I staunched my body to confront the man at last.

In this state I departed my shielding hideaway and lumbered across the icy ridges toward his person in furied haste. At first revelation of my approach he wasted no breath before accosting me with curse and blighted names. He called me a devil. He shouted accusations which I did not understand and dismissively threatened my life as if by some bolstering degree, he thought himself stronger even than my stature which he himself had crafted. I grew angrier still at this...

In Mary's lustrous words she recounted this scene with such creative flourish that she made me to sound eloquent by comparison to truth... but in honestly I was not so well spoken at the time. My passions and rage inflamed as they were, along with his own, I found myself shouting at him in indignation while he in turn continued to threaten and curse me with the vilest of concern until at last, I stood by his presence, now towering above him. He moved as if to strike me but I continued to walk ahead with such speed until he was forced to stumble backward onto the frozen ground. A flintlock clattered across the ice beyond my legs and He moved for a knife, but this I grabbed with one hand and discarded with a sure and powered swing to send it sightless over the waves of frozen precipice and ravine.

He looked up at me then with due consideration even as I aired my grievances full with forceful lung. Shielding himself with his hands, he displayed humbleness at last as he listened to my torrential exposure of wounds both deep and old. For minutes I raved this way in pacing before his trembling form and yet never did he rise or move to arm himself again, even as my anger turned to tears and hate to fear, expressed openly and raw for the first time to the man who had brought such woe upon me as to create this wretched form.

I beseeched him in sobbing fury. "You accuse me of some unknown murder, and yet you would, with a satisfied conscience, destroy your own creature. Oh, praise the eternal justice of man! Yet I ask you not to spare me; listen to me, and then, if you can, and if you will, destroy the work of your hands." I shouted.

I told him of my first memories and his evil upon me, then of the perils I faced pursued by villagers with injury and confusion, I told him of my time with Conrad, my questions to my being, my loneliness and desperation at the life I was maligned to live, and yet not with escalating sympathy did he calm, but with humorous restoration to his cheek, I saw him nearly glowing until at his first chuckling laughter I stopped fast in my tracks and peered with vile toward his placement before me... and while my own words may fail my memory, his do not.

"Oh you wicked wretch." He laughed, pulling his body beneath him to stand as he dusted debris from his coat and legs, now standing fearless and composed as if I had relieved him rather than expound to his reasoning, my causes to hate. "How you have struggled with this weight that you should ponder and fret over the meaning of yourself."

His laughter increased with arrogance. " What ridiculousness I might not have imagined. I should tell you truthfully then that these were not any intention that I might have felt to concern your mind! I am *not* Conrad. Nor do I aspire to his aims, and am glad to hear of his death! He has contaminated you poor creature. I am aghast that you would wonder so much at this! I had no goals as you imagine to resurrect or perform any miracle at the creation of some new life or race upon the earth...

You fancy yourself a man then? Frightful foolishness, my aims as they were in earliest pride were simple, so utterly simple in their perfection. I wished to prologue the virility of youth and stay of my beauty! You who have neither, nor have ever tasted their sweetness could not understand, and in ignorance have placed your existence in such tumultuous inquiries as never needed occur had you not fled like a cowardly beast!

Look at me now! Look at me! You who have seen age I am certain. Do you see before you a man of his fifties as I ought be? Or am I not still a countenance toward the earlier prime of life, to scale these heights, to locate you in your hiding? *This* is my doing with you! This extension of grace is what *your* body has provided!

You were not the ends poor creature, but merely the regrettable means by which to draw from, a spring head for the fountain of youth and eternal life that pulses within you! I made you as an incubator! Don't you see? You need not worry about such troubles of spirit or humanity. You are a cow to milked, crafted for the nectar which propagates freely within your veins.

I crafted you not to act or think. Ha! Surely yes I made you to be beautiful as one also might craft any fountain, but you were never meant to set foot beyond the darkened room in which you fled from me or to see the world which has contaminated your mind...

These things, this "Life" you say you have lived. They are corruptions to your purpose. You have eaten from the forbidden fruits of knowledge and like the folly of man have found despair at their touch!" He continued boastfully.

But then a calm took his voice. Almost in sympathy he changed in continuance. "Take ease in this. Now calm yourself and return with me to my home so that you might fulfill your purpose, and in return I will diminish these thoughts from you so that you may never be troubled again. I will dull your mind by removal of its higher function and you will be happier for it, for your timing is fortuitous! " He smiled.

"It was merely a fortnight passed from this day that I used up the last draft I had taken from you in our short time together before you came upon me at the funeral of my nephew, and I dismayed that I might grow older still without further actions or will to retake such work as you once required to create. I did not know in truth that you had not murdered the child. Forgive my prior accusations dear Creature, for I thought you more stern than you are, but it seems you have not the taste for vengeance so much as the piteous sympathies of pain and weakness that my former mentor has poisoned you with...

I sought you so that I may kill you and take what is mine, but alas if you may be tamed...

You see, I am to be married once more, and with your gifts, my young bride will soon find me on our wedding night returned to my former glory of youth and vigor with no need more for the temperance I have taken to extend the scarcity of what was left from our last encounter! For now you have returned, my prodigal son, and you will have the greatest of joys to behold, to live as you were intended, to extend my longevity and now make more youthful and beautiful my bride that I might live forever beyond the ravages of time and decay for the world to never lack of my charms."

He laughed heartily once more and I stood shocked at the audacity of his proposal. No remorse, no pity, no sense of responsibility toward my story seemed to touch his heart, and as boastful as a man could be, he stood before me now asking that I willingly sacrifice myself to the nature of his requests so that he might what? Live everlasting while I sustain him as a beast of burden wherein he has removed my very identity; My higher mind, my ability to function and reason as a man, and he calls this my path to happiness?

What sort of devilry was this man before me, my creator? When I spoke in return to his words, my own had lost all emotion. My voice low, and spirit broken, I fell within my heart to the depths of resignation and loss.

"So you make me not your Adam, nor honor me as your equal

but mean that I should supplicate myself before you as my creator that you may have all the graces of life which you would deprive me? And in this you will end my suffering by making my mind feeble and unable to comprehend such sufferings?" I questioned without emotion to show his eye.

I looked to those eyes then with outburst sudden and great. "Accursed creator! Why did you form a monster so hideous that even you turned from me in disgust? God, in pity, made man beautiful and alluring, after his own image; but my form is a filthy type of yours, more horrid even from the very resemblance! Satan had his companions, fellow devils, to admire and encourage him, but I am solitary and abhorred. Why my crafter, create me in your image at all? Why not stitch a lower beast as you could and take then from it which never knew itself? You have made me the size of a bull, but would a bull not have served you well rather than to give to me this mind?!

Do you not hear me speak and recognize the language? I speak many now. I write, and hunt, and I sing. Hand me a flute and I will play it. I know not whether these are things learned or remembered but I have done both of these, and you whether meaningful or not in this result, have been the reason I exist... and yet as you say, would I not be happier without this knowledge?"

I considered this momentarily. Perhaps he was right. He after all was what he was, and in ignorance might I not know peace at last? But at what cost? I had meant to do as Father had asked once and amend myself to coexistence with my creator... was this the means alone?

I could not... Curse myself as I might, I could not do as he asked, but this did not prohibit all alternative. For though he may never consider me an equal of worth, but I did possess that which he desired, and in turn might he not provide for me a different sort of peace?

He answered then one of these questions as he could. " Why make you in mans image you ask? Why would I not? If one has the abilities to craft such an achievement amongst the history of earth, then why should I settle for the creation of a lesser form? By making you as I did you are compatible to suit the needs by which you were designed. That which is man within you, makes you able to supplement that which is man within me and could not have by my mind been created otherwise.A woman I suppose might have been optioned in your stead, but upon view of the resulting form I fear I might have turned my passions to dust had I done so."

He continued to smile in spite of my change in countenance. Truth had not worked to sway his heart, nor sympathy, but this was a man of arrogant nature... A trait which I knew with understanding through many a text for such wicked prides and vanities as I might play on those to my own advantage. I stopped as if an idea had only then touched my thought.

"Now that is a thought. I confess, dear Creator that I cannot do as you ask in trade for the favour you propose. You must understand that I have come too far and hold too high an esteem within myself to act as less than I feel. Perhaps I may never equal yourself, however meager as this mind I possess, it is my own and I cannot acquit its existence any more than I should ask you to volunteer your own sources of happiness, for you are indeed the semblance of virile youth as you claim, and I wish not to take this from you...

The desert mountains and dreary glaciers are my refuge. I have wandered here many days; the caves of ice, which I only do not fear, are a dwelling to me, and the only one which man does not grudge. These bleak skies I hail, for they are kinder to me than your fellow beings.

Yet you are right. I am not as stern as you, and have no taste for vengeance. Yet it lives within me now even as we speak. I was benevolent; my soul glowed with love and humanity; but am I not alone, miserably alone? If the multitude of mankind knew of my existence they would do as you do, and arm themselves for my destruction?"

Thunder resounded and I feared avalanche if we remained.

"Yet it is in your power to recompense me. A new species would bless you as its creator and source; Many happy and excellent natures would owe their being to you. No father could claim gratitude of his child so completely as you should deserve theirs. Come with me shortly and I shall propose an surrogate to your own concepts."

At this, with the start of rains coldness above, I applied such forgiving allowance that I permitted Edmund Breda to collect his firearm from the ground and walk at my back as I led him to the cave which I had so recently claimed as my shelter. I helped him over the ice, and after entry, started a fire that we might sit round its warmth. He had called me his prodigal son, but here I was to consider not the tale of biblical return so much as the words themselves. Prodigal; to be extravagent, wasteful, prideful or rash... he was each of these, and I was the result, his own. So returned the prodigal son to his creator I thought, but not as intended, and not to the liking of either.

I would entertain him for the duration of the rains harsh wear, and in this I would build if I could a new form of bond, a mutual agreement if he would concede to compromise that might prove amicable for us both.

Thus as the fire burned I began once more.

AND LEAST TO SUFFER

It is amusing to think at times just how entranced I have long been by fire. Upon my first sight of it I was burned, and never again reached to touch it's embers so much as ignorance might drive children or the simpler minded, but I find its movement hypnotic. With irony I also fear the heat of flame much more greatly than might be so if not for my first memories. Its power to consume and destroy aside, it has also connected in me some form of mortal dread which none else holds save the figure who sat across from me then.

Some time later by his very actions I would learn further reason for these concerns as it should be noted in truth that my very blood burns in the manner of oil when set to great heat and air exposed. And so along my greatest fears and mysteries I and this and we, sat athwart from each, both flame and creator, begging not control but complimentary service from one as I had been taught to coax the other.

"You have endowed me with perceptions and passions and then cast me abroad an object for the scorn and horror of mankind. But on you only have I any claim for pity and redress, and from you I am determined to seek that justice which I vainly attempted to gain from any other being that wore the human form. I am alone and miserable; man will not associate with me; but one as deformed and horrible as myself would not deny herself to me. My companion must be of the same species and have the same defects. This being you must create."

I finished speaking at this and fixed my look upon Breda in

expectation of a reply but he did not. By this, the confusion upon his face spurred further implorement.

“You must create a female for me with whom I can live in the interchange of those sympathies necessary for my being. This you alone can do, and I demand it of you as a right which you must not refuse to concede... and in trade for such kindness, I will offer to you that which substitutes for my blood and you shall have of me what you wish, along with what others may come from us as who might hail you our creator as benevolent and beloved in name. For as long as we shall live, you shall live as well, and in gratitude we will exalt you from afar, being of no bother to any other, having acquited the company of man to seek our own placement far away, from whence we promise to return only as needed that we might supply to you our life's blood in return for our very continuance and joy."

Breda smiled at this and spoke once more. "Such an offer is enticing my creature, however I do refuse it. No torture shall ever extort a consent from me. You may render me the most miserable of men, but you shall never make me base in my own eyes. Shall I create another like yourself, whose joint wickedness might desolate the world. Begone! I have answered you; you may torture me, but I will never consent.”

"You would urge me begone from within my own dwelling?" I asked calmly. "“You are in the wrong,” I replied “and instead of threatening, I am content to reason with you. I am near malicious because I am miserable. Am I not shunned and hated by all mankind? You, my creator, would tear me to pieces and triumph; remember that, and tell me why I should pity man more than he pities me? Especially that of your form. You would not call it murder if you could precipitate me into one of those ice-rifts and destroy my frame, the work of your own hands. Shall I respect a man when he condemns me? Let him live with me in the interchange of kindness, and instead of injury I would bestow every benefit upon him with tears of gratitude at his acceptance. But that cannot be; the human senses are insurmountable barriers to our union as much is as your pride and arrogance. Yet mine shall not be the submission of abject slavery. I will revenge my injuries; if I cannot inspire love, I will cause fear, and chiefly towards you my arch-enemy, because my creator, do I swear inextinguishable hatred if you refuse. Have a care; I will work at your destruction, nor finish until I desolate your heart, so that you shall curse the hour of your birth.

I intended to reason. This passion is detrimental to me, for you do not reflect that you are the cause of its excess. If any being felt emotions of benevolence towards me, I should return them a hundred and a hundredfold; for that one creature's sake I would make peace with the whole kind! But I now indulge in dreams of bliss that cannot be realised. What I ask of you is reasonable and moderate; I demand a creature of another sex, but as hideous as myself; the gratification is small, but it is all that I can receive, and it shall content me. It is true, we shall be monsters, cut off from all the world; but on that account we shall be more attached to one another. Our lives will not be happy, but they will be harmless and free from the misery I now feel. Oh! My creator, make me happy; let me feel gratitude towards you for one benefit! Let me see that I excite the sympathy of some existing thing; do not deny me my request"

"You propose," he replied, "to fly from the habitations of man, to dwell in those wilds where the beasts of the field will be your only companions. How can you, who long for the love and sympathy of man, persevere in this exile? You will return and again seek their kindness, and you will meet with their detestation; your evil passions will be renewed, and you will then have a companion to aid you in the task of destruction. This may not be; cease to argue the point, for I cannot consent."

"How inconstant are your feelings?" I pleaded. "But a moment ago you were moved by my representations that we might worship you, and why do you again harden yourself to my complaints? I swear to you, by the earth which I inhabit, and by you that made me, that with the companion you bestow, I will quit the neighbourhood of man and dwell, as it may chance, in the most savage of places. My evil passions will have fled, for I shall meet with sympathy! My life will flow quietly away, and in my dying moments I shall not curse my maker. Yet every day from now until then I shall live to produce the object of your desire and by your will you will have this at your whim!"

Edmund pondered only briefly before response "I consent to your demand, on your solemn oath to quit Europe for ever, and every other place in the neighbourhood of man, as soon as I shall deliver into your hands a female who will accompany you in your exile."

"I swear," I cried, "by the sun, and by the blue sky of heaven, and by the fire of love that burns my heart, that if you grant my prayer, while they exist you shall never behold me again without the granting of gift and oils for your continuance. Depart to your home and commence your labours; I shall watch their progress with unutterable anxiety; and fear not but that when you are ready I shall appear." I breathed in ecstatic joy.

"Oh that shall not do." He responded. "I have taken leave intended as guise for other pleasures at this time. The pursuit of you was an unsure game in this and I have a wedding for which I must prepare, yet I am not expected to return so soon, nor would I pursue such grisly endeavors within my own home, town or country herein... No, you must come with me to another place where we both as union may pursue this work. I will send word of my postponement to the young beloved for which I am intended, and she will await patiently my return."

By this time the rains had passed and the sky calmed as soft yellow lights reflected from the clouds above in the dim setting of sun. Breda thusly agreed to stay with me for the evening within the cave and we should depart upon the light of a new day, but I confess in my mistrust I found no rest myself, even as he slumbered peaceably on the hard surface of the caverns floor.

In the morning we rose, and without offer to myself, Breda heated and consumed a small meal by the fire. I said not a word against him, but doused the flames afterward and made ready for our departure.

I could not by his side, traverse the canyons and heights of those majestic environs as I had on my own, but instead walked and moved at his pacing along the easier paths and climbs until we reached sight of a town nestled within the softest of valleys below.

We both knew that I could not follow uncovered for risk of sight by these peoples so unsuspecting, but trust was not easy in the absence required. Edmund gave to me a map, and marked upon it a place with wax pen that I should meet him in three days time. From there he swore to me that he would procure transport for the both of us across the oceans passage to the land of the Scotts, where upon those shores, he would fulfill his promise.

I thought to offer a gesture of good faith on my part by giving to him the blood from my veins, however having no vessel by which to carry it, or need of its use at the moment, I felt that such payment in advance may deter his conviction to uphold our bargain.

So as gently as could be conceived between us, with great trepidation on my part, and disingenuous nature to his own, we departed ways; He descending toward the town below, even as I studied the map to determine my own way forth.

DM: Ya know, you tell us that you barely remember what you said and that Mary wrote it out better, but I recognize half of what just came out of your mouth almost directly from the book.

CR: Steven, I thought you agreed to play nice.

I chided the doctor once more.

AG: Fairly there is a remote possibility that having been involved in both the event and the later retelling in Mary's words, that I have either inspired more of them than I recall, or have recalled her version of them more favorably than my own, and simply substituted for the preferable phrasing Doctor, however I doubt that much if any of my creators words had made their way into that fictionalized account.

DM: Well yeah, you've got me there, but despite all of that, it still rings suspicious to me when its almost verbatum... Entrancing and tragic yes, but suspicious. Just ya know, while we *are* talking about suspicion and all that.

CR: There is just no satisfying a fan is there? It is getting to be incredibly late though, do you guys want to continue or pick this up later?

DM: Honestly I've cleared my schedule and don't have to be back at the lab until I decide to. I want to hear more. He still hasn't answered the questions I wanna hear about most yet. How are you feeling?

CR: I've got nowhere else to be.

DM: And you big man?

AG: I have no objection to continuing, as far as that is what you wish and can remain upright in your consciousness, then I would choose yes be, to continue.

CR: Maybe a brief pause though, for bathroom breaks and such? I can hit pause on the recording.

An agreement was set and I stopped all recording while we each did what we needed. Before returning to our proceedings, I grabbed several pillows and brought them to the floor so that we could sit more comfortably. After finding our new seating adequate, I dimmed the light of the room and Adam began once more.

AG: When I had arrived at the port nestled within the home of the Dutch, I made way toward the place for which Breda had fixed our meeting with much anticipation. Would he leave me here without arrival of himself, or perhaps lay a trap by which to capture or destroy me toward his own ends? I simply did not know. With such dread fantasies amok within my minds eye, I made decision to climb atop a nearby roof and wait with watchful eye from above for the arrival of his form and shadow.

I stayed here for one night and a half day in wait before I witnessed the due and planned arrival of Edmund himself. I watched as he conversed with men along the docks nearby before some exchange of payment was made, after which three strong looking lads were summoned to move his belongings from carriage toward a ship at moore nearby.

Seeing this, and verifying that Edmund as promised to me upon our agreements was quite alone, I climbed down from my perch and made way to meet at the predesignated point within an alley shared between two businesses of ancient and persisting commerce. It was not long as such before he appeared at the entrance of the narrow passage and came to meet me most hurriedly.

He looked not surprised to see me, nor begrudged at my presence, but hastily explained in low tones the placement and nature of our soon to be passage. By dark of night, I would steal aboard and stow myself within the cargo hold of the vessel, which was laden with spinners and looms bound for Edinburgh, a cargo requiring no maintenance nor interference throughout the voyage onward, and would assure my absolute seclusion were I to remain below with them throughout the journey.

Following these parameters, I did as I was asked and stopped not to investigate the accommodations or placements Breda had booked for himself. I stole myself onboard the ship by nights embrace, carefully timing the comings and goings of the crew from some distance; As to not cross paths with another soul, and by the most discreet means possible, I adjusted myself below decks to make a home amongst the stacks and crates along the furthest most wall of the hold. Being below the waterline then, I found no porthole nor source of light to pass the hours, but instead took comfort in the gentle sway of the ship as I fell to sleep some time after.

When I woke, it was not by light of morn, nor passage of time, but instead the sounds of men who moved above. I heard the entrance to the hold opened, and observed through the cracks of several large crates, two sailors who moved by lantern's light, inspecting and accounting the number of their cargo in preparation for departure.

Their discussions, though brief and course in nature, informed me that these things surrounding my safe disguise, would be unloaded upon arrival, and the hold filled again with a curious commodity which I found thankful in the moment was not to be carried while I remained aboard, as the stench of it would have likely been untenable without release by airs movement. This cargo was of course to be a weighted measure of fish and of oils counted by barrel and in disguise of a smaller number containing drink to be exported hence afterward to France.

By fortune and design, I remained unseen by these men even as they climbed upward once more to seal me below without knowledge. As mentioned, from my humble confines, I was unable entirely to discern the light of day and passage of time by traditional means, however by what must have been the second days passing hours, I had discovered with keen ear, that I could account for these through the movements above me, by passing recognition of footfall and actions paced.

Only twice more through our move across the sea did any men enter the place of my concealment; Once to procure a barrel that was taken above, once more to retrieve a trunk which I recognized as one which belonged to and had been loaded for the personage of my creator.

I knew not the pangs of hunger, nor the need to relieve myself of waste, as these things fall far between for my body and occur infrequently within me, but neither did I slumber in excess, choosing instead to pass the time consumed by thought in the darkness which I inhabited until at long last, I heard and felt the slowing of motion that signalled our arrival and mooring at Edinburgh.

If by chance we had arrived at any other hour than we had, perhaps the crew would have discovered me as they unsealed their hold and removed the contents which hid my person, but alas it proved of little concern when I discovered after some hours, that the ship had grown largely devoid of the sounds to which I had become over that time accustomed. The crew it seemed, had prioritized leave, and few remained aboard as we had arrived by the closing of day unto nights folding dark.

Nearly an hour passed in this stillness, but again at last and with anxious reveal, the sound of the holds opening, drew my attention. It was Edmund.

"If you live still, now is the time for departure. Do not respond in word to me, but wait a measure before you unshield yourself. I will go above, and tap three times my foot when the way is clear. Depart eastward from here, and await me by morning beneath the furthest pier south. I will come for you assured and true. knock now upon the nearest plank if you understand monster."

And so despite his cruelty, I knocked, and so he departed thus, issuing as he had claimed to follow exactly these actions, and by suit I followed course as requested. My exit from the ship in due course was a sight for me to behold, as the bustling life of this port proved miraculous in its vitality. I heard the distant sounds of musical instruments and raucous activity not only within the buildings nearby but along the streets themselves, and though I yeared to inspect their sources in man and womankind unlike my home and memories held, I made way instead beneath the piers, moving by great strides to grab along the pylon and post which held them above, until I had arrived at my destination.

So far in this undertaking, Breda had kept to his word, and again by late morning he had continued thusly, arriving in single mast sloop, alongside my blind. He waited for me to board before setting course along the coastline in the direction of north. I determined in sight to my confused recognition that his spirits seemed high, and his countenance unbothered by my company. So unlike what I had known of him to these times, I hesitantly accepted when he shared with me a loaf of fresh dark bread and large side of smoked fish as he directed our movement along the sea.

I looked toward the beauty of that countries cost and while It was not inquired of me how my days had been passed or what state our journey had left me, Edmund talked at great length of his pleasant encounters and interactions with the crew, until it seemed he had all but lost the breath to speak. At this time, he took the opportunity at last to ask of me the few simple questions which concerned him, chiefly as to whether or not I had the ability and knowledge to sail the ship on my own so that he might take rest without obligation further.

Responding in the negative, I was surprised when my creator took the time from his own pleasantries and dutifully sought to school me profusely in the workings of not only the vessel we sailed, but indeed the theory and practices of several others which he had taken the chance to captain over his years. He showed me with great excitement this knowledge as if the pleasure of teaching itself invigorated him equal to the activity he so clearly passioned, and for the first time I had beheld within him, he seemed to me a decent and well standing man which I had not known before.

After many hours complete with trial, failures and eventual success, he celebrated unabashedly in my progress with joy before he willingly relinquished full control of the vessel to my hands under instruction of where I was to guide us during his slumber. Yet I was surprised when he chose to sleep not below, but on deck by the pulpit as it was referred, open and free to view the stars which appeared now above us.

By early morning the following day, a favorable wind had carried us toward and beyond other ports, the last of which Edmund recognized as Aberdeen, the final in which we must pass before arrival upon our destination he told me. Sharing once more a meal of bread, fish and some strong drink which I did not care for, he continued with kind guidance to direct me toward land until we were able then to anchor ourselves along an outcropping of rough stone which wound its way toward a cobbled cottage overlooking the cliffs.

"Be most cautious with the supplies and I will start a fire upon the hearth as the air grows chill in these climes and damp sets in early along the coasts." Breda instructed casually as he stepped from the vessel to shore.

I must confess that the carrying of these was no great weight to myself, yet stepping at first to land from the swaying vessel, nearly put me off my footing as I shouldered their bulk. I trudged the contents of this luggage upward along the sloping stone unto the cottage in short time and as I stepped inside I was met with the the earthy scent of age and decay.
The array of furnishment and lighting told me at once that this abode had been utilized previously in similar efforts and I wondered naturally if part of my own construction had been assembled in that place. Breda himself seemed to take note of this, as he answered my curiousity without request.

"Many a night I spent in this wretched hovel during my experimentations to consider creating another of your ilk. Ultimately, a pursuit I chose to abandon before it's start could begin in earnest. I am glad now to have you with me, as the peoples of this shore know my face too well; For in days since, I have visited often and found pleasant the distractions afforded. Yet as we work I should not myself be seen for this reason, lest damage be done to those reputations by the work required."

He bade me to set the luggage along certain areas of the main room even as he showed me to the humble quarters within. The cottage consisted largely of a central area as described, but with spaces adjoining it comprised itself in thirds by measure of one bedroom, sparsely furnished, and another that seemed to have been an office of sorts, housing nary a trace of presence bar that of a long desk beside its window, and low cot along the bordering wall to the door. This would be my stay as we began, and further onward to planned completion.

I found the cot suitable astonishingly, not only to my length but also the weight of my frame, and upon closer inspection was able to determine that this was no cot alone, but an operating table of sorts that had been fitted for the work of immobilization to a body of my size, as straps wrapped beneath it and around, so that the buckles of their fixation hung low to the cobbled floor.

That first night we conversed and sat amongst the tools of my makers trade within the central room, and like friendly neighbors we spoke of trivial things, uneased yet comfortable enough to abide the endeavors to come...

Little could I imagine the events to follow, and if I had, might have staved the mans skull right there and in that moment for the fury and horror they would inspire.

BETRAYED

That night I slept soundly, and whether by trust or neccesity, we found one another to be decent in composure the next morning. Breda shared with me freely the duties of his work at the beginning. Much of his requirement was spread along the tables within the room and it seemed as if he had thought to bring the bulk of supply that might be utilized within, yet I knew not what many of these tools and vials were purposed for, save the cutting and stitching implements which proved obvious by nature.

Some of these contraptions were pieced together in construction to my sheer bafflement, as large tanks took form alongside low boilers and cabling which I did not understand. By noon of the third day, we moved toward the beaches of that rocky environ along the waters edge nearby and spending our day for nearly the remaining light, we toiled in the gathering of eels which seized my muscles to touch as electricity emanated from them into my hands.

These it was explained, were to fill the large copper tank I had assisted to assemble with such curiosity prior. Still further however proved odd in my assignments as I was sent day by day to the fetching of strange work such as the collection of eggs belonging to sea foul, or the procurement of certain grasses along the cliffs nearby.

One day upon entering the cottage I found Breda at work extracting the fluids from a creature I did not recognize. I call it a creature, though at the time it could have been described to be a gelatinous flower and I would not have known otherwise. I asked about this as he proceeded and excitedly he described to me the pains by which he had taken to procure the specimen, as it was a rare form of aquatic life found only in particular regions far from this side of the world. Its toxins he said, could kill a man within moments, yet within it, he remarked, dwelt life undying.

I might have thought more about this toxin had I some sense of foreknowledge, but since I had not, I gazed simply at the delicacy of his work while he proceeded, and then I did afterward asssist to replace the tendrilled creature back to the jar from whence it came without allowance of its touch to my skin.

We had resided this way in busied work for some weeks, and at times I had peered into the copious notes and journals Breda spread across the rooms, but I did not yet fathom the extent of how he aimed to craft a body, having not yet neared the remotest considerations of grave robbing or otherwise, until at long last I was told one evening to prepare myself the next day that we should sail once more to Edinburgh.

The journey was short and my questions long, but upon arrival I was sent by dark of night along with a missive to meet with two gentlemen residing within the city itself. There I was to pass to them a sealed letter by way of a mail slot at their apartment's door and to return in wait by the sloop once more. I did this with great curiosity, lingering to peer through many a window before my return, but upon arrival I found myself anxious to venture further while we waited for so longa time, that it seemed I felt, that I might have explored half the countryside in such interim. For two days after, we floated in solitude, moored off the shores of that town, and not once more did I step foot to land before upon the third night, these men approached at last.

They pulled behind their horses, a cart laden with human remains, some fresher than others in their decay, and Edmund as if the essential of business mannerism, asked that I choose from these not the body nor countenance of most liking, but instead, the largest of female frames by which we might create my companion. I admit without guilt that this tasked sickened me a great deal. However it struck no cord of pity or wretchedness to my maker, and at long last we had sorted through the stacked corpses of our delivery until one such selection had been made.

Payment was given, and the men departed even as Edmund and I loaded this poor body onto the deck of our craft and set sail once more. The stench was abominable even wrapped within tarps as she was, and I twisted within with every fiberous notion of reality to what we pursued, until arriving early by morning's light, Edmund asked for me to pick up the burden of this form and bring her henceforth to the room prepared by my own, as he could not carry such weight nor traverse the rocky pathways himself if he were to assist me.

Again I followed his instruction without contestation, and soon laid this poor girl upon the table before us. I could not watch as Edmund proceeded to disect her body and remove the bones within. I could scarcely stand to be within the same walls, but in lieu of my participation, I was asked instead to carry the buckets of flesh and organs removed, downward to the sea where I was to cast them amongst the waves without ceremony or consideration of the life they once held.

Four days more he proceeded to work by these conditions as I saw bones sawed apart, placed within tanks of glass and hooked to wires that reached to and from the tank of eels nearby. I saw as Edmund crafted and molded the increments of each uppermost vertebrae to recreate or imbue them with molten copper, and he told me as much had been tasked the same in my own creation. I witnessed the arrangements in preparation for so many horrors that I cannot name them all, and I sank within myself to know the depths at which my request had demanded upon us both.

At long last, when these things were done, and it seemed the final requirements could not be fulfilled without flesh by which to dress the skeleton, now modified, enlarged and constructed in whole, Edmund made of me one final request. He asked it of myself while we sat for breakfast in the cold damp drizzle of that country, a tradition which had long since moved outside of the cottage itself so that we might dine by open air, uninterrupted by scents and scenes disturbed within.

"Now my child" He spoke sweetly. "There is the last of it to be tended. We have need of that which will create for you a bride by your request, but as such I have chosen specifically a form most pleasing to myself as you have never known, for it is by your need that my own should be met.

Some months ago, I tell now, after the first agreement to my nuptials were agreed and proclaimed, I came to this wretched place once again, as I had many times before, seeking such pleasant distractions as man requires in such times to relieve his bodies need, and by unfortunate chance I was less cautious than I ought to have been.

I received a letter some time later informing me of this calamity as I was named father to a coming child by the whore I had lain with in my time spent within this land, and I confess to you now that I have found the solution to each of our woes in a single path.

She, that whore child who would crush my future by her corrupted and growing appetites, lives only a days walk from here you see, and quite alone within a country home aside from a mother and younger sibling, whom I have favorably also enjoyed from time to time. If you would but walk that length and fetch her for me, I will do with her what must be done and after which utilize her form to craft your bride."

He smiled wickedly and I was astonished.
"You mean to kill her?" I asked.

"Of course my calf, how else do you propose I obtain the remaining materials for the oil which animates your unsightly form? By fortune we are in luck indeed that she is with child to such degree as to provide exact our requirements. It is no more but in fact less, than was required for your creation, and by this we shall both have as we desire. If you are to be learned from, then it is no bother to concern her memory for she will not know the origins of her flesh by more than you yourself know your own. She will neither remember me as lover, nor the child to be lost, and as this new form is so much smaller than your frame, merely the one should suffice I should think." He snickered carelessly.

I staggered upright and away from the man, seen clearly now for the evil within, but I found my limbs heavy and disobedient.

"I will not!" I shouted, realizing only then the numbness to my lips.

"Ahh, yes I feared as much... Worry not, I am less than disappointed. How did you find your seat this morning? A bit itchy I should think. It never ceases to amaze how hearty you are to pains my dear boy. I dressed nearly the length of an entire thistle with toxin and yet you set directly upon it without care... Now you may care I take it, but it is too late. It should not kill you at least, but should merely make you more manageable.

Come now within and lie on your bed. I shall tend to the rest."

I do not recall entering the cottage, nor how I came to be upon the bed within, but by next recollection I found myself waking, strapped fast and tight along the operating table which I had utilized for slumber the past months. Edmund stood over me with smug delight, and moved toward my eye then, holding within his grasp a great needle, which I saw attached subsequently by hollow tubing to a large pump and glass jar nearby. I struggled but could not move freely.

"Ahh he wakes at last. Good. I could not draw such from you while the poison affected you so. I might one begs to believe, foolishly poison myself if I had. Now, by estimates which I have figured most easily, I convey that the blood within you, nourished these past months by hearty food and drink, should number in volume enough to last my bride and I some two, perhaps even four hundred years before requirement comes once more. Of course then I shall have to craft a new being by which to drain such life once more; but such is the cost.

You have proven far too troublesome in the end, stronger of mind and sympathies than needed, yet weaker of heart... A true failure only in mind. As for the waif, unfortunate I suppose. I shall simply have to stay clear of this spent and impoverished township until such a time has passed that she perishes on her own accord. I might have been more careful. Really I should, but who so could resist the temptation of one so feeble in mind while rich in lusts?"

He turned only for a moment, so self pleased and amused at his own words that I seized the opportunity to rip with all of my strength the bonds which held down my right side. I was not at full motion, but was able to do this alone before

Breda spun to face me with much fear in his eyes. I rolled and thrashed, table still bound to part of my body, and I fell to the floor even as I perceived the cascade of light which the door allowed entry as it was slung open in the fiend's hurry to depart.

By the time that I stood, all was found in vain as my wicked companion had thrown over the contents of his table and with them the still lit lantern of oil which set alight the contents of so many jars now shattered around me. My struggle toward freedom persisted even as the fires grew. The blaze rose quickly and before I could escape my last, these had consumed the room in flame which burned my flesh, even more at the peircing of my wounds where set to open air, the fire caught alight the oils of my blood as if the liquid itself were fuel.

I scrambled outward, crashing the door to splinters and with it the remaining entanglement of my bedding. Yet my person was burned and aflame in many a placement as my blood continued to feed the heated fury surrounding my wounds. By at last I had burst free to pursue, I saw only in my anguish that the sloop had set quick sail without me and Edmund with it, had escaped. Rushing none the less, I sprinted toward the cliffs and leapt to swim after him, but all was in vain as the toxin and injuries left me too weak to pursue at speed that vessel and he had sailed beyond my sight already.

I tried to shout, to swear my vengeance upon his evils, but my mouth filled with water and I struggled to make it back to shore, thrown by waves upon the rocks and beaten against their roughness.

When I had again set my foot to that hillside view, I saw the fire out of control upon the cottage, taking with it the notes, the tools and the gathered supplies... But this I did not mourn. No other should die so that I might escape my loneliness... But by this and for the sake of justice I did swear death upon one.

I had loosed a man upon the world both evil and foul, given him life beyond his years and allowed his escape. Without more of my blood or cooperation I knew it would be only a matter of time before he tried yet again to form another, only this time not in my image and mind. He would make as he had intended me to be, a helpless creature whose innocence would be his prey.

For this offense I swore vengeance in my rage. I would murder he, his bride and all that he loved. I would raze his leavings upon the country of his home and I would scorch his name from the earth! As I knew no rest I would leave no rest for him and his! Justice would be done! By this I bound myself in intention and cried mighty into the skies and sea.

"I will find you maker! I will find you and you shall tremble at the whirlwind of my wrath! Your wedding night shall not pass without my presence and a grave shall be your bride!" I called out in agonized oath of intent!

THE FIRST PURSUIT

Knowing not if my escape had been observed, I made my efforts to catch my maker with haste, but without vessel by which to sail or move across the seas I was forced to turn south towards the port of Aberdeen by land. If he thought me living, then Surely the scoundrel would return to his homeland to protect his estates. However if he presumed me dead, then I knew the arrogance of him would stray no other course but to move that same direction with aims toward the marriage and bride he had so often spoke.

I walked across that land in anguish and fury, healing from the physical wounds of my body, yet tortured within. At first I stayed true to habit and hid myself from all sight. Even upon the reach of Aberdeen, as I skulked throughout the streets in disguised exile, I seethed in anger as I searched for passage. I could not await the time it might require to overhear some degree of circumstance to lead my path toward a ship bound forthwit toward the destination I required, and so by night I snuck myself within the offices of the local authority, and scoured the logs for record which would inform me. Yet through this too I remained unseen.

This was just as well I learned, as the strange accent of the peoples were not only difficult to decipher to my ears for inexperience with them, but also the intersection within their dialogue of a language unheard elsewhere, created within their speech much greater the difficulties of understanding. The written word however was clear enough, and by this I selected a vessel on which to stow myself as I had once before to the shores of mainland Europe.

It was not easy at times to remain so concealed, yet carefully I proceeded until the timing permitted that I successfully made my way into the hold of a large vessel bound for the coast of France, which was as close as could me managed without delay. However it's contents brought with them not my ease or rest, but only further acrimony toward the whole of mankind, as I found below decks the filth and ruin of what emptied cargo it had most recently transported, in the form of fellow man woman and child, shackled and kidnapped into enslavement where left to anguish in squalor and degradation, they had lived for times unknown below the deck of the vessel.

For this reason and more, I burned internal with increasing and ceaseless hatred and disgust. By dawn's light when the crew had boarded in full and the ship made to set ready, I had already hidden below within that hold amongst the shackles and stockades for such a time that I stewed with sickness at the thought of those above. I had since found the bloody scratchings along the planked confines where the poor and wretched had gouged the wood itself in attempts to free their bonds. I had sat within the remaining stench of human refuse and blood left behind uncleaned and forgotten, and all the while I festered in enmity towards any who would engage in such trade.

These practices, I knew of by studies and word alone prior to this. I had never seen a slave nor any man in true bondage, and yet as stomach churning and vile as they may have seemed then, to face the tools of that wicked business while already in such depths of frenzied vengeance which played within my mind... It tore at what part of me I most fervently held as virtuous and caring until it seemed that all love and hope for man had vanished from my heart.

I found comfort only in belief at such things as greater than man, and to my shame I used the words of my fledgling faith to justify myself in what would come. For in Psalms did it not say the righteous shall rejoice when he seeth holy vengeance: and he shall wash his feet in the blood of the wicked? This then was not so evil within me to seek, and I arrogantly awaited my chance to act as the right hand of wrath upon those whose wickedness wreaked such disgrace. Yet I stayed as Conrad had insisted in his life, hidden from view for the good of the world, and saftey of my self.

I know now the folly of these thoughts and excuse as they were in personal indulgence to my baser being, and yet they stayed my patience only enough to await my most sought after of opportunities to bear such action down upon my creator, else I may have slaughtered the crew itself for their own crimes and profession.

Still I did not hold to the binding of my secrecy for long. I held below decks it is true for the short days of voyage over sea, yet at the very moment I heard the call of land toward the entry of new portage, I burst from my hiding below with such ferocity and volume that all above did witness me in terror.

Playing into the knowledge of my inhuman appearance I roared at their sight a listing of their sins and payment due for such heinous work they had engaged, as if I were truly a demon brought to life by the draw of suffferings which they had committed. I carried on at those men with frenzied admonition and accusatory judgement until at some length I had actually pitched myself atop the mainmast, where I proceeded to call down the might of heaven that it was to take them in misery, before launching my body from that height in extravagent view and quickly sinking below the waves. I vanished from their sight before senses could motivate them to defend themselves and in this I count myself shamefully fortunate.

In truth, I would swim to shore unseen while leaving them in dread and dismay at what had just transpired, but the motives within me celebrated in joy to know their fear. I had not only unshielded myself from hiding, but called out men for their wickedness and made myself righteous in mind for doing so as their superior, unafraid to display for once my physical form and strength in broad day and view. I flaunted these by action and used them to my own purpose to strike terror in their hearts with hopes that they might repent from their lives and this too was shame to my person, for while right or wrong might they have been in any action, I had taken a perverse pleasure in the thought of their deaths a hundred fold, and imagined the devices for many days by which I might commit murderous intent upon the whole of them. The sheer hypocrisy and pride by which I commited this should have brought me low with remorse, but I instead took relish in freedom by words of holy origin that I had fashioned into a shield upon my heart.

I justified these thoughts by twisted repetition of doctrine which spoke reverently of judgement and violence for those purposes deemed holy by God, and so I found my peace in imagining myself a tool of his will and permissive to act accordingly. This temptation of pride I continued as I moved to shore, and this I utilized to deny myself responsibilities toward good or forgiveness even as I motioned my body forward with unconstrained purpose.

I did not hide you see. Rising from the sea and rushing forth across the land for days forward; my form frightened and plagued the countrysides of that region gleefully while I moved within the exposed light without care to disguise a single moment from any who might see my visage. I walked by roads as if I they were my own properties until they proved indirect, by which time I traversed the woods and towns without pause or caution. Such was my singleminded fury and selfish need for satisfaction that I meant to reach by any means the place where Edmund Breda returned and would let no qualms of discretion nor fear of reprisal stop my advance.

Some fled before me in terror when I was seen, as many cowered and shielded themselves. Others armed their person and did fire weapons toward me in the days to follow, but I would not stop. I bellowed at these times in quotation of both scripture and epic, borrowing words from the like of Milton and Dante with equal flourish to the testaments of old which I also quoted until I myself felt as if a demon had sprung forth from my own inner depths which deceived itself into fashion as an avenging angel.

In earnest I know that it was fortunate that none followed or laid siege to me in advance, but who in truth could have stopped the might of my conviction as it was? Who could challenge such heated emotions and logic as I held to, while coupled with my capability and fortitudes? I did not eat. I did not sleep. I did not stay my foot or stray from course to march the whole of distance between me and my quarry. Past numerous injury and attacks I charged undeterred so that by the time that I at last reached the city wall of Breda's home town, the word had reached before me of a coming storm; a monsterous demon, an angel of death intent on murder and wrath. Yet to this lasting day I swear I harmed not a soul, nor injured another living thing despite my bitter passion and goals.

None but the foolish would have believed this of course. The idea that the violent and raving monstrosity they had witnessed, would traverse such great distance inspired by murderous fury and yet seek no other relief for their foul lusts of vengeance either within wilderness, wilds, or even township, where frightened men and women dared to strike its form? And yet it is true... and for this too in small providence, I am grateful beyond words.

For by the time I did reach the home of my abhorred creator, I found within it a woman prepared for my arrival that she might greet the apparition of such gossips and rumored report. The doors in fact were opened, and though nary a servant witnessed my entry, blame cannot rest on any who might, for believing whatever superstitions would have told them such, that I was a devil hell bent on destruction; For my arrival was followed by cloud and thunder almost as if orchestrated supernaturally to coincide.

I marched my way up stair and hall until finding the quarters of that estates master, I stood at its threshold to an unexpected sight. I had thought to behold Breda himself before his bride, but in such lamentable timing, Edmund was not home. Instead what greeted my eyes were two forms, both female, both standing in wait; One a young woman of stature and sharp beauty, dressed in finery and coiffed to excess with an air of confident power as undoubtedly Edmund must have loved, for it reflected in her the same striking quality he held of himself. The other, was a plainer girl, dressed in servants garb and with beauty befit, yet at conflict of her current state. The servant girl, it was clear firstly, was very far along with child, however this would hold little comparison to the condition that captured attention most readily. No, the first observation to be held and recounted was much more dire and apparent all at once, for the Lady Breda, in true shadowing of her recently wed husband, was in fact standing behind the poor girl, gripping her body in most forcible restraint, with a knife held tight against the servants throat. This upon entry I saw, and with shock I stopped solid within my tracks.

"By devil he spoke truth to your appearance" She laughed wickedly. "I had scarcely believed until now that I see your person that my husband could be truthful in such descriptions, yet here you are. Oh yes, dull form he has told me of you! Good fortune that you are slowed by such cumbersome nature that he arrived such time before the word of your appearance amongst the peasantry had to confirm your continued existence! However he has kept no secret since from me and I have embraced his greater qualities for good and ill long ago." She continued. "Do not look so surprised upon me! Did you think my husband so foolish as not to warn me of your coming?"

I looked on in horror as the woman held the helpless servant within her grasp. "Is this what you have come for then? That which my husband refused you? The life in trade for a life that you might embrace another of your ilk?" I winced and shrank at her words.

"No? That is right isn't it? It was you who refused the duty of your creator to commit toward that neccesity! But fear not unsightly corpse, for I am less squeamish it seems than even you, and but for the release of our bother by your burdensome presence I will give her to you, the abortion of my husbands hands! Here you arrive so pitifully filled with indignation, and yet for love of a companion you would cease your advances and claim upon us? Has death not enough company that you crave more? Oh that only the living could tolerate you." She spat mockingly.

The girl in her arms shivered and cried. I could see the terror in her eyes but it spoke nothing of her entrapment or threat from the lady whom held her. No, her eyes, pools of tears and despair as they were, looked fixed instead upon my own form in fright that such I knew I filled her more with horror even than death itself.

Was this what I had inspired amongst those innocents whom

I had terrorized in my pursuit to this address? Was this truly how I was perceived? And yet in that moment, having sworn my vengeance, I could not in good conscience endanger this poor mother to be, any more than I would have slaughtered the mistress of Edmund herself.

Thinking at once of that poor victims saftey I moved to stay the hand of her captor from those threats by my own surrender, and instead was met with furious decree.

"Then I shall make her dead and be done with you!" Lady Breda shouted!

I do not know by what instrumentations at this point I moved, but before the blade could but nick the flesh of the pregnant girls throat, my body had sprang forth without thought so that I found myself in single bound across the rooms breadth to seize upon the bride of my creator.

The soft and tender flush of her... I recall with sickness, it twitched in my hand and the sound touched my ears of a muffled snap even as the last heartbeat of her life pulsed beneath my fingers grasp... I watched the life vanish from her eyes.

All at once my pride and vengeance faltered. They fled from me in that moment as the falsehoods they represented and shame filled my countenance. There was a scream and the girl whom I had saved, condemned my fate. A terrified squall of pain came forth from her lungs as she herself collapsed upon the floor of the chambers hold and with it, all was fixed henceforth.

With such outrage I had entered this place meaning death to my maker and his kind, fully intending the destruction of this house and the wife that I had now killed in truth, but now that

such a thing had transpired I found that I had not in myself imagined the reality of the price it carried. In a flash of pity I moved to save the life of an innocent, and perhaps too of her unborn, however too late I realized that I had damned myself in their stead by fulfillment of the promise I had swore upon Edmunds betrayal. I had taken from him that which he held dear, and with that killed a part of myself.
Hearing the hurried footsteps along the hall, I looked to the rooms entrance to see my maker as his eyes met mine arriving too late by less than seconds. My hand still holding the body of his woman, now lifted from the ground, released at once, even as the shock played across him. I watched the birth then of something familliar and I feared in knowledge of its weight that obsession would take him as it had me.

The body dropped lifelessly. He moved to catch her but failing in this by the distance, her ruined form crumpled before me with a gross and resounding thump. Knowing no other action to take, I sped with haste toward the window nearby.

As I had fled from him once before at first and second sights, I now did so with new cause. Breda bellowed as I had with vengeance, but I no longer wished him harm in my heart. I looked back from the windows edge with pity and remorse that I could not measure, but knew without doubt or question that he would offer neither.

So I lept. I ran. I fled from him as a coward and in the aftermath, hell would pursue me as such, rightful and fair that it should. None could blame my maker for this. I had brought upon myself that which I had partly sought and justly he owed upon me, the accusation as so many had seen me upon my journey here that none would doubt him, had he but asked for their assistance in pursuit of the killer I was.

However this was not his way... Out of spite toward my

sympathies, or perhaps to cover his own sins, I could not be certain, but this I do know; It was by his testimony that the blame for my crime, fell upon the servant girl herself, and within the week, as I ran from that place, she was convicted and hanged in my stead... further damning me for my vice and sin.

UNTO THE DEATH

Adam stopped. He swallowed hard and tried to shake his head like he somehow meant to clear the fog of memories that clearly filled him with guilt, but neither the Doctor or myself could think any less of him. We both tried to express that to Adam in our own way by questions that we each felt might distract from or lessen these emotions, but he was stubborn then as he had been before. I spoke first. I was nervous and I waited a while before I could work up the courage to speak but I approached the topic delicately.

CR: May I ask something?

AG: If you will still stay the room with a murderer then yes, by kindness how could I not reply?

CR: Why do you insist on calling your killing of Breda's wife a murder if you were trying to defend someone else?

Adam looked pensive, shifting to one side and back again before he answered with a heavy sigh.

AG: I call the act what it was, because I know to this day within the deepest parts of myself, that despite all immediate causes by circumstance, I had purposely and with premeditated consideration, set my intentions toward death and destruction for such a time as it clouded all other thought. I travelled to the home of my creator with murderous resolve, entered into that dwelling with purpose to kill beyond this, and so in my action that once completed, brought with it the death of they who I had meant to destroy, as well as the death of even those I meant to save. How in good faith could

I thereby claim innocence? Had I not meant mere moments before my actions killed that woman, precisely to commit murder? And in the finality of result, had I not slain her?

A moments pause and diversion from this, changes not the actions result, nor does it remove the long festered motivations which lay below. Without these might I have simply restrained or disarmed that same victim? It should be known that such a thing would have been possible, and yet in a fugued state, I carried forth the extremity of my previous purpose... Though these which may be excused by others do hold sway to relieve their own misgivings about my actions, I cannot reconcile within myself the deed as anything else. So this I speak honestly.

The woman was surely as foul as Breda himself, with coldness and cruelty of heart that I do not deny... However still she was a human being whom posed to me no harm, and though harm she held toward an innocent, by admission of self knowledge, I know my actions to have been wrongfully committed, for the need to destroy her was not absolute.

DM: Fuck...

Steven was clearly upset by Adam's words, but not angry. He struggled to find his own reply but after several deep breaths seemed no less bothered.

DM: I never meant to call you *that* word man... I am so sorry. I accused you without knowing what I was talking about, and I get what youre saying right now, but surely after all this time... you've gotta realize that there's a difference between what you did and what that word carries with it. To say it like that... to...

AG: Please, there is no need to apologize. I say what I say to be honest. I do understand your response, but you must also understand my own. I admit to this guilt of conscience out of desire not to be blamed or judged for crimes, but merely to hold myself accountable none the less in earnestness for recognition of my own state of mind, as well as a fuller understanding of circumstance which surrounds the events which took place.

What's done is done. There is no reversal of it. And for all that followed and all which I owe to this world, I must possess and claim these actions as my own. That is all. Did she deserve death? Perhaps... but that is not my right to judge nor carry out as I did.

This was the first time which I had ever taken a human life, and the only time in which I afforded myself these rages of passion toward such ends on that I would call human. I was changed by the event, and by memory of it, I continually strive to hold myself to never repeat its unfortunate result or to excuse within myself that which I know to be wicked by the words or beliefs of any faith professed.

I know my senses as my compass knows north, and by them I perceive both right and wrong, to deceive myself in such ways by doctrines or technicalities not in line with my inner directive, or worse yet to excuse my actions entirely, would serve only to unburden myself in spirit, to give rise in habitual action that I might continue to perpetrate such things as my heart knows to be unjust.

There was a long silence while these words sank in for each of us, but afterward I sought clarity to an issue which seemed to me entirely relevant in its inquiry.

CR: So... since you've brought it up a few times now... Specifically Christianity, I'm a little confused. Are you still religious Adam?

AG: The answer to that question Ms. Reynolds, should prove irrelevant. What faiths I do or do not posses have no true bearing on the considerations of ethical morality, save for those who by lack of rightful judgement hold within them, the most basic capabilities of human understanding. No man should require doctrine to give to him empathy and knowledge of good versus evils within this world, less he be broken enough within to lack the functions of compassion, care and consideration for those existing outside of himself. Just as true no man should utilize faith to excuse the actions known within to be evil by nature.
Religion as it pertains to morality as guidance in my mind, is simply a motivating principle for the weak of resolve, confused of mind or woefully ignorant of self awareness, that they might seek reward or fear punishment for the works they should by logic and emotion know as right or wrong within the living of their lives without these things. In truth if one knows these not without advocacy or admonition, then that is not the fault of some religious ignorance nor application, but a fault within their inner workings, either born broken or made such by others.

I have lived for over three hundred years Ms. Reynolds. Yes in my beginnings I read and took the words of Christian faith, for those were the words which permeated my settings and the peoples which lived there, but time and placement moved beneath me and I moved with them beyond fear of outside knowledge, so that my learnings and beliefs did not stop at these professions.

I have by grace of time studied every world religion and faith which I could find amongst the living, and though I have beliefs within, and would profess a nameless faith, I consider these a deeply personal matter as was their discovery; A personal journey along the winding paths of spirit. So you ask if I am religious and I tell you without question within myself that this inquiry is irrelevant to any but myself, for my present faiths, unlike those of my past, hold no bearing on, nor excuse any action which I commit according to the principles which I accord morality.

Does this answer you?

Looking back at the recording of this portion, it is clear to me to see that my eyes were wide in surprise, but I was so entirely stunned by the answer which Adam had given, that I did not give an audible reply. Instead I nodded in silent confirmation, and allowed Steven to speak in turn.

DM: Ok, but at the time, you were definitely more leaning in the Christian traditions? Bible quotes, Dantes Divine Comedy, Paradise Lost and so on.

AG: Such were the exposure of my mind, but yes, I wavered within even these much like father had. They held no direct answers to a being as myself, save the further questions of my nature. And as I had long gesticulated for many years in debate with him, I feared perhaps by their claim that I might be either some demonic form yet ignorant to my essence, or simply a damned machination without soul imbued by my creation. Other days I did as Breda first accused, fashion myself to be a man, and by such belief adherent to all the laws and teachings of one that I might one day earn placement in heaven above.

I knew them intensely through extensive studies by that time as I had long searched their words like many others in search of understanding, and like those surrounding me to all directions I had yet travelled, I held to those lines for my only guidance on such matters beyond philospGhy and the words of scholars past. Of course having found no answers which seemed at completion to apply to myself within these, I pitched back and forth in daily confliction as to whether or not to take them as truth.

DM: That seems entirely fair.

AG: Unfair as well perhaps, for I often wonder at the course of the world in many places had mankind merely searched more profoundly within themselves rather than the preachings of their trusted masters.

Of course this experimentation of thought yields none but further conjecture, and that of itself proves reason enough to continue, however by the time which I found alternate possibilities by which to consider, my own courses set as they were, would move naught in much the same.

After the murder of Breda's wife for instance, had I the ability to reverse times course, I would have done so without question, and possibly saved myself the events to follow, but with all things come and gone, regret accomplishes little but to inform our future choice.

My choice however at such time, as wicked as could be in its cowardice, was to flee the vengeance sworn upon me by my maker. It remains unclear how by such persistence he followed my path for I was careful and deliberate in my concealment from even the most solitary of shepard amongst the field or traveler along roads, I dared not follow. Yet with considerable accuracy and speed, my accuser pursued me.
DM: So back to the story then?

AG: If you have no further questions at this time.

DM: None that can't wait til later.

AG: Good. Then I should relay that at first I thought to flee southward. Such was my compulsion that by months of continuous motions scarcely broken by need of food nor rest, I went so far as the great seas of the Meditarranean, but alas by measure of mere weeks within my solitude upon one lonely isle of that warm and pleasant land, I caught sight once more of my maker as he steered toward my shores to land upon them.

Making for my own vessel, I aquitted the encampment I had created and with haste eluded his presence once more, unseen by his eye, yet hunted by each hour, endlessly chased with seemingly no retreat. I thought for once that I had lost him along the edges of the Black Sea, but to no avail soon realized he had followed.

Still further north I moved thru the icy terrains of Russia by whence time over a year had passed since that fateful night. Generally I subsisted on the meager offerings of nature in that place where rainfall might quench my thirst or animal cross my path until by determination that even the remains of any hunt would betray my course, I determined as often as possible to consume only the roots and berries of earth, less fishing upon some shore I felt safe enough to cast any leftover remains adrift in the waters.
It was as if my pursuer could read upon the earth my presence etched in stone, and try as I might, the stalking of my trail continued. I pushed my body to limit and continued northward, but there the snows thickened and the cold increased in a degree almost too severe to support any variant of relief. When the rivers were covered with ice, and no fish could be procured; I found myself cut off from my chief article of maintenance without further sign of my presence, and so in desperate acceptance of fate, I gave up the hope of escape or comfort in favor of remaining ever vigilant, a life lived thusly by remaining only ahead of my predator.

"If you will not take these pains from me then form in my spirit a masochism of equal measure so that with gratitude of heart I might endure!" I cried to the heavens. Though to what end I cannot measure whether answered or not, any being living or otherwise heard my prayer to return response. I was miserably alone, plagued by guilt and burdened by endless sufferings, as the flight of fearful ruin chased my form. Every shadow to my eyes carried with it evil and fright that perhaps in silence my maker had discovered me, and yet never did I consider his presence as happy that such dread company relieve my solitude.

I wove my path in tapestry from land to land with changing course for years, finding not rest in either the peaks of Himalaya, nor steppes of Asia. Even to the jungles of lower China I fled before adjustments west, onward to India I continued, but it seemed the more present any form of life or pleasantries existence, the greater speed by which I was rooted out and uncovered. Several times I would hear the sound of Breda's voice or glimpse his person over distance, only managing myself to freedom by physical feats which he could not repeat.

Skirting once more to the mediterranean after some six years of this, I thought by sea I might at long last vanish from his supernatural prosecution, but even that did naught but slow his return toward my paths, until in desperation and despair I dedicated my routes further northward and over the Atlantic waters until landing upon solid ice, I trekked further by craft and foot than the edge of Eurpoean mans discovery.

No place on earth held such desolation as those deserted plains of frost and ice I felt. Here where no foliage grew and no other seemed to live, I meant to preserve my life only by death in the hunt of what fearsome beast and odd prey I might seek upon the slabs of those frozen waters. This way, I surrendered myself to conquer and consume the white bears or blubbering tusked creatures which defended themselves against me.

No hiding nor burial of snows could disguise the bloody red of their demise, and I knew with certainty that my whereabouts would be evident, but I was not of Edmund's human frailty, and meant in such hardship to outlast him by life, even if such result only compounded my anguish and pains. Noted I should reveal that over this time I had survived such inclimate changes and injuries repeated, as to feel myself nearly proven in imperviousness to death, despite my wishes for it's peace upon me.

Then, one night, after nearly the entirety of a decade running, I found myself helplessly surprised to be be caught at last unawares. However in fickle humor, fate brought forth those who surrounded my camp that were not as I feared, the cold wrath upon me of Edmund Breda or any whom knew him, but instead a most curious discovery of that land's native peoples. Toward my sleeping form they had crept in silence within the endless night of that land, and only upon my waking did allow themselves to be seen.

They stood at a distance with intention, disarmed and open, as if to show themselves to me silhouetted against the whiteness of expanse beyond, with fire blazing before them that I might better sight their presence, and there for many hours they remained. When at last I moved toward them, they did not turn, and within myself I felt hope for the first time in ages that somehow, in some measured way beyond reason, I might here encounter the kindness of one who did not fear or hate my very existence. I approached with caution.

A gathering of four men I found, but to greater pleasures a number of dogs which had been fastened by harness to their type of sledge which carried as it did swiftly from place to place. These animals did not fear me I realized, unlike so many others which had fled from me upon sight or sensation, I was met with glad greeting and lapping at by their number, even as the native men who met me, stood silent without motion.

I knelt to stroke the fur of those dogs as tears rolled from these eyes in gratitude, allowing them to squirm and climb toward me as if I were the greatest sight they could fathom. I wept to experience such affection for truly the first time. Their masters, seeing this I feel, must have looked at me with pity. Knowing not the language they spoke, I startled when one of these men began to voice his words in my direction. I stopped at once from the caress of the canines and stepped backward in fear, only to see a hand extended which bid me to stay as the man stepped forward unarmed.

His string of words to follow could not be translated in my mind, but I was astonished to understand his actions as I witness him to untie a bundle from the sledges face, and gently strike it several times with his hand before stepping further forward to lay this on the ground before me. After these, he stepped backward once more and gestured widely toward the sledge itself. He spoke again only briefly, but I could detect no fear nor anger within the deep tones of his voice, and though much of his face was covered by the hooded furs of his adornment, I could see within his eyes a kindness that beseeched me to trust in the intentions of his party.

By the lasting movements of slow and careful determinings, I found myself some hours later, seated upon the ice amongst those men, warmed by fire and eyed with sweet compassion, I developed a communication between us of french, which at marvelous fortunes they understood. These were indeed the native peoples of the north, but not at home within the region we inhabited at present. They in fact belonged far to the west, and had travelled within season to hunt the creatures which lived here only for a time. Yet in their hunt they had discovered my deeds in the killing of the white bear and tusked walrus, which I had committed without tool or weapon.

They had followed my trail under the belief that I was a spirit, and seeing me then had determined with reverence that I was indeed no man, but none the less alone and helpless. They had sought to bring me only gifts that I might in some way bless their hunts, or at very least agree to peace between us. The bundle which had been set before me contained both furs and tools.

Strapped also to the sledge from whence it had came, were spear, animals fats and oils, meats, and skins. These it was told to me, were along with that single sledge and a team of dogs,what I was to be gifted with no requirement upon myself other than agreement to act as neighborly to their givers, should I see their like in the future.

I thanked these men tearfully and prostrated my body before them in humbleness, but they did not hold that I should do so, and bid me respectful goodbyes with unexpected embrace and encouragement before they turned to depart at last. The speaker for these men, knelt to whisper in the ear of the lead dog which I had been given, and with gentle pat to its head stood once more before turning with final eyes toward myself, to mount his sledge and move away with stoic expression.

I might have been tempted to follow if not for the dangers it would bring them. It is possible in such friendliness that I could have lived amongst those peoples, for they did not see me as others had, and felt such different beliefs and superstition that I know in my heart that they would have taken me gladly as part of their tribes, but Edmund's pursuit would surely follow, and no quarry would he grant to any by my side.

In actuality, I had not seen him then for some time, the longest yet in many years in fact, and part of me wondered if he had lost my trail, or even perished upon the ice. This in strangeness did not bring me joy or relief however, for if I could not live with others for fear of Breda, then Breda for me was the whole of companionship with other men. Should he perish or stop within his obsessions, then somehow, I felt even more I would be alone upon the earth... Yet if this were true, there were also others now that might take me, and at present at least, I had been given the gift of company in great pleasures, not to other men, but a team of dogs which could not and would not judge from me any sighted difference from their former masters or other men.

Peace however never seems to last for long. I had taken to some degree of enjoyment in life once more, even in that sparse and frigid region. I found the beauty of night skies and stars so perfect in their crystaline reflections that I almost forgave my past and believed again in the glory of life... I looked outward at the oceans and adrift upon them the frozen burgs with solemn awe.

Regrettably this habit was also the source of my first sight toward others, when at last their arrival proved immanent. Sailing upon a large ship, I witnessed their approach from afar and retreated some distance even as they continued forward, directly into the icy confines of ocean edge to the freeze itself. I did not know if that ship would contain my creator, and thusly inspired by slight courage the hopes of friendship most recently offered by the natives, I kept them within closer distance than I might have fled otherwise, so that I could by occasion spy on and observe their progress. Until upon one such inspection I realized that the ship itself had become lodged and frozen in place.

Men struggled to free the sides of their vessel, climbing overboard and to the surface of the frozen waters, they toiled and struggled to loose themselves, and I considered the options of my decision that I might even lend my strength to the task if it were possible to do so unseen.

No sight of Edmund appeared from that ship, but in my focuses upon it, I nearly missed a terrible truth as he enclosed upon me. I heard the ice break to my rear and the yip of dogs not my own, but had not predicted the actions of my maker, that he might so quickly descend on my locations by waking hour. It was surely he I discovered, following once more, and now within distance so near that I could identify his person undoubted. I lept to my own sledge and called the dogs to race.

Across the ice I fled, drawing too low and near the ship to escape sight, but all the while devilry chased my soul from happy release until by stranger circumstance I looked behind my trail to see the pursuit abandoned by force, when Edmunds sledge turned aside and wrecked upon the plains of slickened shelf. Stopping short, I called the dogs to slow and turned to aide my fallen maker, but saw on approach the rushing men of the entrapped ship who had witnessed all from their station.

There was a cracking sound as I recognized the firing of riflery in my direction, even as I approached to lend aid, and for this reason alone I turned once more in escape. I continued onward unto nightfall, circling back in distant sweeps to keep watchful eye upon the ships mast over hill, until I found within reason an outcropping by which to conceal my presence.

For three days I stayed in that place, daring not venture nearer, and for three days I waited. Part of me so bound to my makers wellbeing that I looked not in fear towards his eventual arrival, but in distant hope I realized at last the yearning within my heart to make right the wrongs which we had inflicted upon one another and amend my sufferings through peaceful surrender. It was then and only then, that leaving the belongings of my supply, I released the team of canines which had loyally served me and warmed my heart, where after, I turned by foot to meet my fate.

My dogs had run free, my sledge left to it's own, now far away, and my trek had moved me to the ship of men who had rescued Edmund. During my trepidatious approach I braced myself in body and mind to be seized or fired upon, but no sounds nor motion escaped from the ship or its surrounding measures.

The vessel lay quiet, and by courage summoned to my utmost reaches, I found myself scaling its sides to reach the deck of the ghostly sight. I saw with fright the source of such stillness as my eyes beheld upon that deck the scattered bodies of the crew, frozen in death and time, where the colds had taken them. There were several huddled round a burnt circle where it was clear a fire had blazed days before, but now covered in frost and snow, it had failed to save them from the bitter ravages of the north.

With terrorized imaginings I slowly made my way below to find many sights similarly composed, as frozen men embraced one another for heat, or lay solitary upon the floor. Inspecting several cabins I discovered further many that lay in their beds and bunks half clothed, surrounded by frozen bowls and vessels filled with bile and refuse. It was then I knew that a sickness had taken these men, some fever that would drive them to disrobe and wretch to fill their surroundings with that which they could not dispose themselves. In one of these places, ghastly and ruined, I discovered him, my maker, my second father as wretched as he had been, laid out before me a frozen corpse.

The visage of his face echoed to me memories of Conrad, and in a moment I found myself overcome with inconsolable grief. All the death which had surrounded me, so that I might outlive not only my beloved but even my most hated enemy, and left alone upon the face of this globe with no heart within my breast to ever hope again.

Screaming and groaning in desperate cry I became as one entirely lost, and heaved myself over the form of Edmund Breda in sorrow and agony until my energies were spent and my body began to fail. With such tiredness I could scarcely stumble to move myself toward a nearby desk and realized the quarters in which my maker had perished, where not alone lay his body unaccompanied in death, but tended by none other than the captain of that ship, whom had died upright within his chair.

Languidly I pushed his body aside and replaced him. I did not move again that night, nor the next, and for days in stupor as whatever sickness had taken the crew overtook me in turn, I sat vigil over the ruin of that once thriving abode, until at some time I passed from consciousness myself and hoped for death.

Adam concluded his story at this point, but looking back at the recording it was clear, I had fallen asleep somewhere before. It was already mid afternoon and we had stayed awake the entire night without wishing to stop the interview. The recording had continued all this time, and Steven, barely awake himself, signalled Adam toward my computer. The footage shows after this that Adam rose from his seat and approached the device, after which the filming concludes.

SESSION THREE

Interviewer Name:

Cassandra Reynolds: Journalist for "Washington Post"

newspaper and special columnist for Al-Jazeera International.

Second Interviewer and Consultant:

Dr. Steven Malcom of the Boston College Institute for Scientific Research and Advancement: Specialization in structural biochemistry. Published author and Nobel laureate

Interview Subject : Adam

The time is 5:46 pm. March the 30th, 2024

Location: Personal offices of Cassandra Reynolds, Washington D.C.

CR = Cassandra Reynolds
DM= Dr. Steven Malcom
AG = Subject - Adam

Personal notes Italicized

THE OLD MAN AND THE SEA

After a period of rest from the proceedings of session 2, we woke in early evening and found Adam transformed. While we slept it seemed, he upon himself, had formed an idea to inject the dyes which he had told us of previously, and afterward applied makeup. The difference was nothing short of amazing, and even though I knew with full awareness how he had appeared to us just hours before, I couldn't help but to almost felt like I was meeting an entirely different person. In fact aside from his size, I could have met him on the street and never known anything about him was different about him from any normal person I might have passed on the sidewalk a million times before...

Steven was equally impressed and surprised to see this, but Adam explained to us the purpose, even while we tried to ask questions about the transformation itself. He asked specifically if he could wait until later to answer these, because he wanted to take us somewhere before then. Since we have no recording of this, I will describe it as best as I can.

After we had agreed to these things, Adam informed us that we would have to walk to our destination. When questioned for reason, he told us very bluntly, that he was simply too big to fit comfortably into Stevens car and it seemed an awful waste of energy to drive such a short distance either way. This too we agreed to without reservation. It's odd to me that the place he took us was not all that far actually, just a few blocks over from my office. While we walked however, I noted Adam's behavior along the way. Not only did he appear more confident and at ease than when we had first met, but even friendly to passers by who looked up at him as we passed along the sidewalk without pause or break in our conversations, which meandered greatly in topic.

We talked about the park, the river, the weather, and such small things as he seemed to enjoy, but also too of the history within the area. More than once we would pass a building where Adam would launch into a lesson concerning it's history or methods of construction from a time before neither I nor the good doctor had been born. These detours in topic included lists of former tenants, and advancements in architectural trends, as well as what uses these buildings had been used for over their histories, which Adam also seemed to enjoy without reserve.

As for the destination, it turned out to be a small asian restaraunt which I had seen and passed several times before in fact. From the outside, the place looked like it had been built in the nineteen seventies and left to age without renovation since. Inside this was punctuated with dim lighting and seats along the floor like you would find in a japanese tea house.

The most surprising thing to myself was that the old man who ran the place seemed like he'd expected us, and even though the sign out front said closed, he greeted us outside and asked us to come in as if we were somehow honored guests. After that he greeted Adam with a deep bow that was gracefully returned in kind and it was confirmed very directly that they actually knew one another in some capacity which had been previously omitted in mention.

We were seated on the floor, much like we had sat recently along the floor of my office, and the old man brought us bowls of rice, as well as noodles before sitting down next to us. At this point, the man began the process of explaining that he had quite literally known Adam since he himself was only a small child. It was then revealed to us in turn, that Adam had also been closely acquainted with his parents and grandparents before him. The man, who I would easily determine to be in his early eighties, explained how he had grown up with visits over the years from Adam, who had in earnest friendship, stayed in touch without fail through each turn of life through passing years and decades to present, never changing, never aging, never faltering in his dedication to their friendship.

However, this very friendship it seemed, was not merely some light acquaintance or passing familiarity, but enough in meaning for Adam we were told, that not only did he pay for the families' original move from Japan before the man speaking to us was born, but apparently had also purchased and gifted the building where we sat to the mans' parents, in essence, funding the opening of the restaurant over 40 years before.

While we relaxed, and began to eat, the two of them swapped updates on each others' lives and Adam looked at pictures on the old man's phone of children and grandchildren which he knew by name and recognized in sight. All the while Steven and I curiously looked around the room. That's when I noticed something intriguing hanging on a nearby wall. It was an old black and white photo, framed and set simply without much of note to any casual observer. It showed a large family standing in front of a very traditional home somewhere in what I would deductively surmise to be Japan near the turn of the last century. It was certainly aged enough to be some image of the old man's grandparents, if not possibly one more generation removed from even that.

Yet that wasn't why I noticed it, or why I feel the need to tell of it's detail here. In the photo, as mentioned, was a group of farmers, gathered with their families, robed in the fashion of that time. Some were holding tools, others children, or even nothing at all. There were bundles of plants, buckets, even a dog... but what I saw first, was a large silhouetted figure of a man behind them who's head was out of frame. I knew it was Adam. Even without seeing his face, I could recognize his posture, his hands, and oddly enough, I could swear he wore the same exact coat which he'd had on the first night we met. Perhaps the photo could have been a fabrication. The entirety of the evening could be intended simply to convince us further of the story, with the old man playing his part based on some pre-established agreement between the two... But neither men present ever directed our attention toward the photo. In fact no mention came of it directly. It was merely there... And I was left to draw my own conclusions.

The food was amazing, and the evening continued. The stories that were told shed light into other portions of Adam's personal history beyond anything we'd heard so far. I felt that they were of greater interest perhaps only if due to the telling of them by another party, that stood as secondary source confirmation to the idea that Adam was perhaps, in fact, precisely the man that I believed him to be. We were told that the old mans' family had first met Adam when he had saved one of them from what he called a kyuuketsuki a long time ago. After that the family and nearby villagers had given their strange savior a place to stay nearby, and he had lived for several years helping them on their lands while also protecting them from white bandits who had recently troubled the area.

As the tale continued, it was easy to see that much had been passed on almost in the fashion of a family legend. There were bits missing, deemed irrelevant or purposely excluded, but the story continued all the same to result in Adam's seeming discomfort as he attempted to downplay his role from this time with them, repeatedly expressing gratitude and debt owed that he could not repay surrounding some unspoken tragedy that neither would discuss.

What I gained in understanding, was that Adam had formed closer bonds with the family than I would have ever guessed he had in the world. I also discovered to my surprise that not only was another person now able to corroborate several of his claims, but with photographic evidence to support them that neither thought to point out. They talked like old friends for the duration of our meal until when it was time to leave, they parted solemnly with embraces and tears as if to apologize somehow for things I cannot assume. Part of me felt that perhaps it was due to the mans's age. Any goodbye could be the last in a case like that and truthfully I wish that was all I believed. The trouble is that I feel far too confident in also suspecting that there was more to the story than we knew.

As we returned to my offices the conversation again moved more toward small talk than questions of what we had just seen or heard. It's true that both Steven and I wanted to ask, but Adam skillfully diverted at every turn. We talked of the food, the restaurant, the mans' children and grandchildren, even their professions and moves over the years. By the time we reached the door to my humble abode, I can say with some certainty that I knew more about "Bay-lee, moving to California" or "Jonathans' engagement" than about the mysterious photo or any clarity on exactly what a kyuuketsuki might have been.

It hardly mattered either way. The interview continued shortly after in its official capacities, and I began recording once more while our earlier questions were discussed for the record.

March 30th 8:07 pm

DM: Ok you promised to answer us about your appearance. You told me about the dyes before and It's obvious that you've learned to apply a very natural looking makeup, but I honestly can't believe the difference. Why if you can live like that and walk around without people losing their shit, do you still hide yourself away? I mean dude, if I passed you in the grocery ailse I would just think you were a really big guy, maybe the biggest I'd ever met, but still just a dude.

Adam sighed.

AG: Steven, I must tell you that so long I had yearned for

such simple possibilities, that the ability to do just that, overwhelmed me in ways I can scarcely describe to you now. From the time I was first aware of my reflection, I had lived my life rejected by such of the world; Faced with so many cruel expectations, that at times I found myself bitter on the taste of mere sweetness, only to be treated otherwise when it became feasible to me that it tore and shredded my mind in grief even to touch the edges glow of that light i thought impossible for so long.

Unquestionably, for the majority of my years, as I have told, I had hated my own image, finding in the reflection of my form, a loathing no less than equal to the expectations which others had placed upon me by its sight. There is such beauty in this world, and even flawed as all things begin or end, I was humbled from the start by the sheer magnitude of what I could see and wished to be a part of. Yet stretched before this endless line of unmeasurable awe, I had been treated to be such a thing of disgust, bearing lower worth to others than even those abhorred creatures who live and dwell in decay and rot. This was my lot, despite all inner feelings as another entirely, that to see the shape of my own body struck me as it did them, liken to behold precisely that lumbering beast that those who knew me not, had projected me to be.

For too many lifetimes Doctor, I lived and toiled in revulsion at my cursed misbirth, so that I dreamed unrelenting of some glorious day where I could walk amongst others without their impulse to flee or demolish my being, and yet when the time came which I found myself at last able... I had discovered after short experimentations that I no longer wished it so.

It is paradoxical I know. So long I spent in self loathing... Yet by those first years of success in the transformation you now witness, I had come to know and subsequently to lose, a family of my own making, even in finding yet another.

Though the story has yet to be told to you of this, I swear it on my breath and the beating of what heart pounds within, that there was indeed a time in which I had in the wholeness of my being, been accepted within what can only be called by that name; A family of unyielding acceptance and love.

You have now met one of these remaining few, whose embraces so transformed more within me than any outward augment may ever achieve. The man who we dined with this evening, though not his children or others who know me only in name without truth or revelation, is the last of these in my life. For though my appearance to him is known in the manner as it was to you just last night, that unchanged form as I truly am, those who came before him, not only found it in themselves to welcome me not for what I appeared, but to love and know me for who I was beneath those illusory entrapments.

Even still, before those of his line, I knew others. I was loved by and gave my all, to a count of more than merely this... and while that family did choose to take me as their own, and I in turn to protect and to love them duly so; None can truly compare to the love which touched all that is me in every possible way, those who were lost and I shall not see again in my time as the family who sheltered me through those earlier days and loved me intimately as this heart yearns to this day for their breath upon my skin and hold upon my breast.

Tears were moving from Adam's eyes again and without saying her name, I knew he was speaking of Mary.

My experiences with this, have changed me from what was, in ways I have learned only in hindsight when I realized in finality that I would rather accord myself in solitude and genuineness, than to waste another day of effort and breath to disguise myself or make ready the whole of my being to adhere to the outside acceptances of those who judged without knowledge or compassion. Because I have known so profoundly the love of those which accepted me as I am, I confess to you it has destroyed utterly in me, those longstanding needs to bow my disposition in submission for the sake of an idea which I now hold intolerant to abide.

Because I have been loved, and learned myself worthy of love without change, I have grown to love myself beyond the hateful wants of those very changes merely for the sake of acceptance by any stranger who fickle in nature and judgement would reject me based upon knowledge not of me as a man, but merely a figure unsightly to their liking. Those sir, can go straight to the depths of whatever hell exists beyond life or within it, and straightforth I would hope they kiss the expansive breadth of mine own patched and constructed ass for eternity, as well as that of all those they slighted, rejected, ridiculed or persecuted based on such shallow and material measure in their cruel lives.

No. Only in neccesity to move as occasional need requires do I continue with what I feel as a charade and dishonesty with others. Times like today where I venture into a city, able to walk along the streets uncovered, or pass amongst others are rare, yet daunting. As even within them, there shall always remain the fear of one to a million that may glimpse what is below this mask and lead again a crusade against my freedoms.

Yet noted in myself I remain aware in my enjoyment of interaction unshielded from others, and though I relish to be a part of humanity in that way, to walk along the street unaccosted, to wave and smile at children, to open doors for others to happy thanks and smiles, I know also the disappointment and disdain I would hold to see the majority response to my unaltered state so modified... This I tell you, is why that bittersweet pill sticks as it does in my throat.

That was the only answer we were likely to receive and I could tell that the subject held great emotion for Adam. He wasn't only defensive in posture, but nearly irate by that point, railing at the injustices of past pains felt, though no one in the room was truly the source of his anger so much as any and every person alive, less proven otherwise. Steven's eyes were wide in silence and I could relate. I don't think either of us wanted to risk responding with the wrong words simply for fear of being scolded, but something had to be said in order to move forward to hear more of what tragic adventures would follow, and being the professional at hand where it came to de-escalating others, I tried my utmost best.

CR: That seems very difficult Adam. I am so sorry to hear how much pain you've been through but I'm glad you've found peace with yourself. Do you want to continue from where we left off?

Adam took a deep breath and closed his eyes. I watched him calm himself this way as if he realized the change in air and tension that his emotions had stirred within the room. One breath was all it took though, and when he opened his eyes again to look at us, it was like everything had returned entirely to normal. Speaking from experience with similar situations, I will note that this impressed me quite a bit more than perhaps should be the case, but to see a man essentially pack up 300 plus years of baggage and shove it to the back of a closet so quickly as to recover in a single breath... I'm going to say right now without hesitation that it stands out to me as a rare quality to witness so clearly.

AG: That would be welcomed Cassandra. Where were we before?

DM: Um, right well... You had just fallen asleep on a ship in the ice, and were maybe sick possibly? Do you get sick? Sorry, that's probably a question for later, but I still want to know actually.

AW: Ah yes... That's right. I would nearly answer that question later Doctor, but for sake of simplicity, I should likely say yes before we begin. I do contract illness for brief periods on occasion, though never for long and always with recovery. It has happened since this particular instance, though I clarify in truth that this was the first time in my life to which I am aware of experiencing any notable effects of such.

As for what came after; When I woke again from the depths of that particular slumber, it seemed to me as to the sounds of thunder, which admittedly I observed with some addled confusion in my state. I noted also while waking, that ice was in fact caked upon me in half thawed chunks which fell to the floor, creating a mess of slush upon the weathered planks of the cabin. I felt not at all myself as I moved to stand, still shaking the remaining frost from my body. It was in that sickness still perhaps, but I felt weakness the likes of which I had not known since the first days following my initial animation to this world. As I steadied myself against the captains' desk however it became quickly apparent that the ship was in motion, heaved by great waves outside. To this point I was forced to steady my feet while it lurched and turned upon the water.

The still preserved body of the captain in fact, rolled across the floor at my feet from the commotion. Also I became aware that he too was beginning to thaw and concern bothered my thoughts. I looked about, surveying my surroundings. Truly the ship had been not only confined by ice, but anchored Just hours before. Yet I saw through the window that in place of the still plain of icy expanse, a great storm outside did churn the sea then surrounding the vessel, and though darkened, I observed the light of day only to the faint and obscured degree that one might expect within such a storm.

I found trouble in holding my body upright as I nearly collapsed with buckling knee and unsteady security. My breathing was irregular, labored and heavy. My head swum with nausea and dizziness similarly unknown. In this condition, scarcely I managed to open the doors to the upper decks before falling upon them. The rain struck me immediately as surprisingly warm, and I wondered at the means by which the ship had been released from the ice. Had the anchor line broken? Had we ever truly been anchored at all? I never in my condition had bothered to check. How far now had this vessel drifted to bring upon it such warm rains? These questions unanswered would continue for several confused moments , but soon lost priority in the knowledge that nomatter the causes, the situation at hand must be dealt with accordingly at present regardless of their knowledge.

The bodies of the crew had thawed in their entirety. They rolled and turned freely about the decks as the storm continued on. Some corpses slid upon the slick of the doused and worn wood without obstructing friction to slow them from grotesque movement. I tried again to rise only for my limbs to fail me in their strength once more. Desperately, I fixed my gaze upon the throws and violence of the sea and my mind blazed with further questions, but none so present than the matter of how and indeed where I now found myself cast upon such predicament. I lay prostrate where I had fallen as the maelstrom tore and the lightning cracked with fury, until at last with the passing of several hours, the seas calmed and the full light of the sun came to dry my wretched body.

As I dried I felt such heat that I had never imagined outside of the confines of a fire itself. Slowly I crawled over the disheveled and ruined bodies of the crews remain, until righting myself along the mainmast, I stood that I may survey any visible markers of the distance which we had retreated. Yet as I peered to the horizon in all directions, I saw no sign of land; Met only instead in sight, by the blue grey dark of a vast ocean unknown to me in recognition. For some time I recall that I leaned in that position, unable to again move until night fell, taking with it the clouded steel of the angered sky, to be replaced by clear and starlit peace above. Taking stock of my condition in this time, I report that my skin was cracked, and my throat parched... However, still having not the strength by which to remedy these plights, I fell again to slumber, helplessly surrendered to whatever fate might take me.

Upon my seeming resurrection with time, I observed that many days had since passed; Seen evident within the now decaying remains of the ships' men, which lay about my failing frame. It was with slight disgust, not abject horror that I woke to the empty and blank stares of hollowed socket and open maw coupled only with the stench of decay. Their skin, yellow as my own now baked in the glaring sun, driving me to wretch. I moved then, but could not determine why or with what purpose. Delirium began to take me as the days passed. I could count neither hour, nor day as I pitifully dragged my tired body from one point to another in search of food or water.

At times I would fall into seeming bouts of madness, seeing before me the countenance of Breda himself alive and maligned by deaths peace as he would berate my existence, tempting me with visions of sustenance and bounty. However it was thirst which tortured me above all else. What illness had stricken my form which should leave myself the very image of death unable to recover? Never before had I fallen to sickness nor fever. Never before had I felt such weariness nor weight of my muscles.

I do not know how long this condition did persist, only that by days, perhaps weeks, the corpses turned from spoiled and rotten flesh into the slick of putridity. The sinew and fat fell from their bones in great clumps, releasing both bile and blood, blackened with age. I crawled again below the decks themselves and sought some form of relief there, only to find none; Until slowly I lost all frame of mind to distinguish waking moments from tormented nightmare. All became unseated in my mind.

This persisted over course without any personal ability to correct until one day, I awoke to find my bodily conditions somehow improved. My frame was still weak with disease, yet I saw in confused recognition new surroundings. Absent were the woodplank walls and floor, the roll of waves, or sight of death; Replaced instead by stone , moss, and an ever present drip of scented fresh water. I lay on a bed of straw, chained I found to the floor beneath me. Only the light from a small window above allowed me vision enough to observe a door to one side in realization that I had been somehow removed from the ship itself without my awareness.

By the loss of light, I recognized the passing now of two days as my body seemed to recover and my mind became again my own. I listened with horror to the voices of men as they passed into my dungeon from the outside world. English they spoke to be certain; Yet with a strange accent which I had never known and words half recalled in the language of Gaelic. It was not entirely unlike that of the Scots, which I *had* heard before, however also still not the same in equal measure. In eavesdropping, over time I heard the tale through repeated piece and contextual assembly, of a ship wrecked upon the shores bearing no survivors... That is, save one; A man so hideous with sickness that he appeared scarcely human, mad with delerium, yet great in strength. This is partly how I had come to be contained within the local prison.

I also heard the name repeated many times of the doomed vessel which I had been previously aboard. Albatross it was called. The Albatross; The "Mystery of the Albatross", they would say. The local legend grew with each telling, expanded at last to that of a ghost ship, lost well over ten years prior, recently washed ashore and carrying within a lone survivor unmentioned on the registry, with yet another additional body to the belonging names of it's original crew, both found within the captains' quarters.

As I pieced together bits of conversation and argument I discovered also the length at which I had been presently detained. Originally thought a man stricken with madness, I had been first placed into a cell in view of others to monitor my condition, but as I showed signs of life improving over the course of months, I had recently been labeled a devil; A demon disguised in barely human form that must have brought plague aboard the curse of the crew. I learned more still, that the ship was burned in the harbor; That men and women of the town had begun to fall sick as well. My fate was argued to my horror; Hanging, burning, even mention of the removal of my heart to be crossed with nails of iron. As these new snippets of conversation repeated themselves from person to person, my recovery only hastened, brought on by means of terrored excitement I am almost certain.

Not seeing fit to await so gruesome a fate, and no longer want to surrender myself to death after what I had miraculously survived, I had heard quite enough. By waiting until the still of night and all voices absent, I broke my chains and threw myself against the stone of the wall only to find myself presently within another cell equal in composition to the former as the crash around me littered my body with dust and debris. It was perhaps foolish I realized, aiming for the stone rather than wood, Thusly, I adjusted my efforts at instead the door of the adjacent cell.

No matter what fear I held at the prospect of being seized upon by the hands of my jailers, I *must* attempt escape I felt. The door I confess, gave way with surprising ease as I slammed my body against it toward freedoms untold. And though I felt wounds of splintered wood ripping into my flesh, I was only to feel them healing nearly as soon, in essence to confirm my bodies' recovery. At last through the door so ruined in my escape, I had burst forth into a room of some measurable size, which I found empty to my relief. It is there where I discovered keys with which to simply unlock the remaining outer door and did so, however puzzled by their presence within a locked and emptied room, even as I climbed the short stair upward to level of the cobbled street.

It was night, and the passages of stone and dirt, were barely occupied if at all, for I saw none in sight to pause or tarry. How the crashing of my escape had not brought forth any authority or curiosity I could not say. Perhaps the superstitious nature of my jailors had deterred approach, or merely the placement of my cell was muffled enough to sound little in volume from beyond those walls now known to reside partly below ground.

I fled from this town with great speed only to encounter a green countryside beyond its border, composed of rolling hills and steep cliffs, across which I came eventually upon a forest, making way through on to another wide plain of grass. I ran to my knowledge of no less than twenty kilometers during the night, that by evenings' end, before taking rest along the banks of a small stream, I looked with wonder at the sights of living splendor once more.

It was a matter of days before I found a place where my safety felt assured as I located a farm arranged close to the edges of a high and steep stone cliff far to the north of the town. A small shack, backed within thirty meters of this sheer drop seemed to me entirely undisturbed for some time and I determined that if further escape should become necessity to avoid discovery, then I felt it simple enough in theory to remove the planks composing the sheds rear, and climb easily down the vertical descent of that very cliff which faced out to sea. So here I settled to take shelter unseen, and unbothered by nature of the sheds' neglect would remain likely secluded.

As had become mere habit for me by this point in life, I observed the family that lived in the farmers' cottage of this land and found it inhabited by a woman seeming of young adulthood, a man equal in age, and also a small child. All members of the household possessed similar physical traits, pale skin adorned with a speckling of freckle, deep dark eyes, and a shock of thick wavy hair, black as pitch. Their strange accent continued to confuse me as the members of the town which I had recently fled.

Surely these devils' must be equally disposed as all men I had thus far encountered, barring the friendly natives of the northern ice. To think that I once believed that race above myself sickened my heart. Only Conrad and the aforementioned ice men had shown true kindness to me thus far. Only they had held any detectable form of virtue to these eyes and I felt now sure, after the years of my sufferings, that the tales which Father had once shared, were nothing more than fantasies and virtue of an age long past.

I knew not what to do with myself at this juncture of existence and stayed undetected for many months living as I did within my humble shack unseen. It was in my time however spent here in observance to these creatures that I found the virtues of which my father had regaled me with in youth. I saw gentleness in their actions with each other and I recalled the similar actions of those towns I passed on way to Breda's homeland. I saw determination in the working of their fields and care of their livestock. And I observed an earnestness of nature firsthand that left me shamed to have ever supposed them as devilish... Yet still I knew they would fear me.

While seasons changed, and between my nightly excusions to forage and fish, I was able to hear from them much that enlightened my previous state of confusion. I had been cast upon the shores of Ireland... The calendar year and month were now June of 1759. The world I knew had been embroiled in a near continual state of war for the past five years; A time which I had apparently slept within the ice encapsulated ship which bore me to these coasts. Upon the landfall of the Albatross, the citizens of the town where I had been detained; Now known to me as Newcastle, had at once thought themselves to be under attack by the French. However post discovery of myself on board, the tale of the ghost ship and its mad survivor had spread to a point which even in my present location just north of Downpatrick had become a source for conjecture among the residents.

I learned the family name of my neighbors to be that of Miles. Consisting of the young man Alexander, his wife, Ann, and their young son Bryan, they seemed to suffer from similar woes as I had come to recognize during my time with my father. Those woes being the accruement of debt to another, specifically in this case the lease payment of their land. Having seen their plight as well as their virtue, I set my mind to assisting them in any way which I could.

At regular intervals as they slept I would make my way down the cliff side to the sea in order to catch the fish on which I subsisted. Having no way to cook them however, I had taken to drying them upon a wooden rack within my shed, never questioned in scent or sign, the strength of such odors produced within my abode itself, as the smell of the sea drifted easily about to mask any cause for curiosity otherwise. Yet I now took to doubling these efforts in order to procure enough meat to supplement the family of which I had grown endeared; A supplement I began to regularly leave upon the sill of their forward window, preceding my retreat for the duration of daylights time again to my humble quarters. I watched each morning from my residence as they seemed to delightedly accept these offerings.

Even then I became dissatisfied with my degree of aid, and I began on the nights which I did not occupy by fishing, to tend and toil quietly within the fields that they might have in turn a bettered harvest to see their improvement. This included the small work of such things as weeding and nurturing the soil. I often did so by interring the remains of leftover fish entrails and heads within the ground around the seasons growth, until it seemed in short time that this effort brought forth visible result as the leafiness and health of their crop grew by bountiful amount. I happily basked in my accomplishments as the young parents would tell Bryan of the good nature that the Fairies had bestowed upon them.

It had never been my intention to unwittingly cause the trouble that soon came. I indeed might have stopped otherwise to know that in attempt to help any harm might arise. However, upon harvest time that year, the family was indeed in fine order and condition, at want for nearly nothing which I could provide... It is unfortunate then, that this outward appearance of prosperity angered their landowner and in the decline of the autumn seasons, he came to the cottage with men and seized Alexander in cause to escort him to a debtors' prison further north in the place called Carrickfergus.

I awoke unexpectedly one morning to the heavy lamentation and pleas of young Anne and Bryan as the families' patriarch was thrown into the back of a carriage and driven off without sympathy. Whence herein I thought at once to help the family however I might; To cast off the confines of my hidden abode and rush to their aid. My physical fear of man having greatly diminished, I looked at the three remaining brutes who had trespassed to carry out these actions and calculated my next course. It was in this brief pause nonetheless, that Ann rushed one of the men and was shot to the ground. Grief and rage both immediately seized my heart and I indeed then in a moment of fury, threw the roof from my apartment charging the men with intent only to strike fear into their minds. But

I was soonafter the recipient in turn of even more gunfire. The injury to my person as several of their shots collided with my body and tore through me, only enraged my disposition further.

I grasped the gun from the nearest man and broke it cross my knee where then I stepped back so that they might see me more clearly in the light of day. I roared like an animal enraged. It was to my shock that as they fled, one of these scoundrels scooped the young child into his arms and leaped upon his horse. Stooping to retrieve a stone with litte thought, I hurled it towards him, striking him from his mount. As he fell I quickly dove for Bryan and scooped him into my own arms while the remaining horses, spooked and confused, had run towards the safety of the nearby wood. I watched while their riders followed suit but still I held Bryan to my chest as I took him to kneel by his dying mother. With trepidation I released the boy and his mother looked up into my eyes.

She could not move, yet also did not call out. I saw only thankfulness in her gaze as she turned her head towards her son. Had it occurred to me at the time, I know now that my blood may have yet saved the poor woman. However ignorant to this fact, I allowed her to spend her dying breaths with the beautiful child.

“Find your Da Bryan. The fomorian will help ye."

She took the young boys hand and held it close to her lips, kissing it as tears rolled down her cheeks.

“Trust the fomoire."

And with that I saw the life fade from her eyes. Instinctively I reached my hand forward to close them, and the young child embraced my chest in tears. An Honorable Undertaking

DM: What was that she called you?

AW: Fomoire... This is an old Irish myth, a type of fae. Misshapen sea gods, fairies of large stature...

Adam sighed heavily.

AW: She believed me to be one of them. Bryan would later explain to me to the best of his ability just what that meant, for I did not know.

Such a rich culture has that land...

Adam paused for a moment. I note here that in these recent tellings, he had taken a bit of an Irish accent himself, but we did not mention it to him. He sat up straight, closed his eyes only briefly and then continued

As young Bryan watched on, I collected and proceeded to bury his mother. The tools were of ease to find and utilize, yet I found myself lost in painful thought as my present situation set in amongst the torrent of my mind. Here I had been entrusted with the fate of a child, furthermore complicated by an expectation to not only find, but in charge, to free that childs' father from a prison within an unknown township; An assignment more foreign to me than the concept may have been to travel amongst the stars themselves.

Knowing not the first stroke of where I should begin, I calmly collected all the necessary provision which I could imagine into the conveyable package of a burlap sack. I entered the home, for the first and only time, in search of a map by which I may accord myself to my expectant journey. And to my wonder, the innocent child, shaken and mournful as he was, seemed to follow within my footsteps at every turn, silent yet without fear of my appearance nor size. Surely I thought as all human adults must seem strange giants before him, perhaps he had not the thought of scope to my otherness. As luck would find, a map indeed did lay within a modest desk which sat amongst the contents of the families' cottage. Having now the required tools to begin my journey, I turned to face the young boy kneeling as lowest I could towards his height, as I took to one knee before him.

“Bryan isn't it?" I asked.

A gentle nod came as affirmation to the childs' attentions. He sniffled and wiped his balled fist over one eye.

“Bryan... My name is...”

For the first time in my long life the idea occurred to me that I had no true name since Conrad's first observation of the same. Father had spoken to me using no short manner of descriptors over our time, yet no constant name stuck truly in my mind; And upon this new occasion, I was indeed in need of something by which to make myself familiar to this child. In haste I began to recall the names with which my former readings had acquainted me during my turn at Wittgenstein and beyond, until I struck upon the title which had so often passed others' lips by which I *ought* to have been called. Adam had been the first of his kind, truly a creation of solitude in the beginning. Was I not the first and only of my kind? Created not from the hands of God, yet still molded into the image of my creator. Pressed now for an answer, I gave the only one that seemed to me appropriate.

“You may call me Adam." I told the boy. With what seemed to me a momentous marker within my life, Bryans young mind seemed merely satisfied that there was a name to which address his next question.

“Are you friends with my Da Adam?” He asked me.

Stunned again by the simplicity and genuineness of this young human being I replied with what first occurred to consider in truthful hope.

“I wish to be Bryan. I hope to be." I spoke.

After this, I took Bryan by the hand and led him once more to the grave of his mother. His grasp of the situation fails me in words. He spoke the echoes of the lords' prayer without falter, and looked upward towards my direction in search of approval. Tears nearly overtook me, yet I withheld their allowance upon my cheek as instinct bore me to save the child from added distress.

We departed then and by the setting of the sun, we had traveled only out of the cottages' sight, yet the child could walk no more. Knowing that we could not rest within the open fields so close still and present on the land of the man who had earlier that very day taken to end young Alexanders' freedom, I then took up the child within my arms and continued to walk as he slept against me throughout the night.

Travel with Bryan proved to be a slow endeavor. His short weak limbs unable to carry him at any length, and as a child required nourishment multiple times per day, it was rare for us to make what I considered to be even a normalcy of speed. Also it became impressed upon me his frequent need to relieve his body of both fluid and excrement. Such a hideous burden I imagined that to be, and became thankful that I had not been created with such frequent requirement.

I aimed to seek forest whenever possible, but more often found it requisite to walk along the shoreline, separated from the open land by means of tall cliff and rock. We took care to circumvent society at each new turn, yet we stopped at minimum twice per day in order for me to prepare sustenance that I may ensure the health of my charge. At night I found he was incapable of resting on the ground as myself, and thus I allowed him to lay his body across my chest to slumber.

Often times we would talk, as I found it important to entertain his limitless curiosity and I chose it best to allow his dominance of our conversation in order to avoid any reveal of myself, that I might strike fear into his heart. We crossed several bodies of moving water during those days where it emptied itself to sea, and by these, fresh water was procured.

I would listen with contentment and humor as young Bryan crafted tales of great imaginings within his own world. Other times he spoke of his mother and father, and their peaceful life on the rolling plains and hills far above us. I found that his company brought new life into my soul as the ceaseless wonder of his worldly perceptions captivated a spirit of pure innocence and joy. Understanding at last, brought me to the facts that humans were not indeed created wretched and ill willed, yet brought into this dominion in much the same way as Bryan himself, children of wonder and tenderness, who through the actions of the world and its troubles, became turned toward afflictive nature over time.

As colder weather encroached upon us I found myself carrying Bryan more frequently than not, until at last it became unfeasible to continue further within his waking hours. Over journeys' passage, it was in the deepest night of December when I at last beheld the lights of Carrickfergus in the distance.

As I could not leave the boy alone, exposed openly to the winds and cold of the sea, I spent my first days now in sight of that place, creating for him a humble abode of shelter and rest, that he may feel secure during my nightly excursions. Before embarking upon the first of these however, I procured the wool of a lamb to lie over his form and I observed through several nights to be sure that his slumber came uninterrupted. Only the infrequent call for his mother on occasion would escape from his lips, yet he never woke. With this time assuring of both his security and unencumbered rest, within the darkest hours of the night I began now to strike into Carrickfergus on a regular order.

Over the following weeks I made attempt to survey the area in search of Bryans' father that I might free him and reunite at least in part the remainder of this humble family. Returning in the wee hours of morning I would take short rest before Bryan himself woke, only afterward to occupy my days within the entertainment and care of the young boy who I felt had become a friend to me.

Oft times we would fish, or take meal in silence, yet more so than not, he would create games and story in which taking up small sticks he sought to match me at battle with sword. It gave me great joy to appease him thus at first gently making imitation of his motions appearing in earnest to battle as he, yet near always by ultimately feigning my own death and groaning prostrate upon the sand I would come to rise quickly and seize his body, hoisting it high into the air as we spun till near collapse. No shortage of strength did it give me to hear the giggles and joyous squeals of that child, and I hoped dearly that upon his freedom, Alexander would allow me to remain by their sides.

Finding the prison took no longer than five days, yet I discovered it at all times to be of heavy guard and more sufficient fortification than I had anticipated. It had now entered into mid February as I spent my waking hours in attempt to imagine ways in which to accomplish my goal. I took at night to learning the various paths and occupancies of the local street and town surroundings. And I established in my mind that the first priority of all men of arms should lay within protection of the close by castle.

Having no accomplice and little means by which to create circumstance in order to distract this nightly guard, I made it my course to then, utilizing the cover of the morning fog, climb upon the castle wall undetected and light off one of the several cannons which sat perched along its fortification. Surely this sound would alert the men and drive them from their respective posts.

Anticipation and anxiety towards being able at last to reach this goal filled me, while I considered the return of son to father, and father to son as my own honorable pursuit; A nearly divine assignment with which I had been tasked by the highest authority, that being not only the love of a mother, but a dying womans' last wish. I made design to lay forth this plan within the following days. However as the sun rose near the time of nine on the morning of the twenty first, Bryan and I together spotted ships advancing toward the township quickly from the east. Soonafter, the three of these landed near Kilroot nearby, and we observed a score of men marching upon the town.

Lifting Bryan in my arms I ran to the camouflaged safety of our shelter and for two days the battle seemed to erupt and subside as if by tidal influence; Until on the third last, a calm seemed to fall within the battlements. Only the screams of the injured could be heard from our retreat. By night of this third day, I took Bryan against my breast once more and traveled to the prison with haste. I found it unguarded and quickly began with my free hand to bring down the doors and gates in order to gain entry.

I discovered to my disgust the occupants of that place to be without food nor water, lying forgotten within their cells where during such time of battle, these men and women had been left to perish without further attendance. I set Bryan behind a pillar and began to free each and every one of them, at last coming to the cell of Bryans' father whereafter I led the boy to the door of the cell and stood him beside me as I unhinged it from the walls surrounding. Upon first freeing from his imprisoned state, Alexander took the boy in his arms and embraced him, lifting him to his own height in order to look into his eyes with joy. Only *after* this did he turn to look upon *my* countenance.

Instead of appreciation, I watched helplessly as anger flashed over his face. Ushering Bryan behind his own body he separated the two of us.

“Monster! Why have ye freed me?! Where is meh wife?” He shouted. Hearing this, young Bryan began to cry in protest.

“Da! Da! His name is Adam! He's brought meh to ya!" He pleaded.

Alexander seeming to ignore the exclamations of his son, continued to shout. “What have you done with my Anna beast?!”

Bryan pulled at his fathers' ragged clothing.

“He is ma friend Da! Mother asked him to bring meh!" He exclaimed.

“You ave bewitched meh son!? Where is meh wife? What measure of trickster are ya to release me from ma bonds only to steal the heart of meh child?! Do ya believe you can bargain me freedom to make a changeling of meh boy? You shall not have him!” Alexander continued in anger.

Never in this slew of insult did I have occasion to either answer nor defend myself. Instead the father reached for an iron bar that I had wrenched from his cage and held it at length to distance me from them until his back was to the open door. As he took Bryan into his arms and rushed forth from the Prisons' walls I heard again the fire of cannon and shouted for him to wait.

“There has been an attack. The streets are not safe!" I warned. I pursued him out the door instantly to find that the battle had resumed indeed. Fires burned in the street providing only flickering light amongst a thickening cloud of powder smoke, and Alexander in his haste had fled towards the walls of the Castle. I pursued, calling out repeatedly of the dangers ahead, but within the smoke, I briefly lost sight of both father and child.

Suddenly a sound pierced my ears with such devastation that it brought me to my knees. Ears ringing, I leaned forward to place my hand upon the ground, only to make a discovery that tore my soul from my very breast. There on the dirt before me lay the pair. Bodies broken and twisted by the impact of cannon fire. I saw the father still holding his dear child, my unspoiled companion of such beauty and innocence... both dead.

As morning eventually came, I found myself wandering in stupor through the streets. I had lost care for whether or not I would be seen. I had lost the will to continue on my journey. Was life to be an ever continuous string of tragedy? What cruel hands of fate conspired against me? Despicable wretchedness of this world, I wished only to be done and through. I had seen the potential of man, and yet now even it was snuffed unrecognizable by the machinations of their war and vile. I wished to be struck by cannon myself, yet the battle had ended. The soldiers within the castle had claimed their great victory, and I was left to persist amongst my agony.

I lumbered along with careless step until something caught my eye. I observed the image now of a hangman's' noose lifted above the levels of the street. Perhaps if nothing else could take my life by injury nor sickness, then I may still find my escape through the extended adjournment of my very breath. I do not know why the thought of drowning never entered my mind, yet I made my way towards the grim vision of my own demise. Calmly and nearly without thought I placed the thick rope round my neck and walked forward unto the drop.

A HAND OF GLORY

AG: How does any man move beyond the loss of hope? By what means can any one soul continue his former path after such a change has blackened his world? To rise from defeat and press on is an admirable quality, yet never does one question how to rise again once they themselves have chosen the end of their days... That is until the time with which that terrible reality has come to lay before them.

I woke to my utter dismay upon a heap of the dead. Discarded without care nor thought as only merely another amongst the number destroyed by the bleakness of man. My eyes peeled back in revelation of the dim sky above. No wonder, nor thankful thought filled my heart. I lived, yet I knew not why. Were I so damned that my soul would not even come accepted unto hell, or was that indeed this place between heaven and abyss which my life presently existed. I did not know. Yet here I lived.

Breath continued to fill my lungs. Birds of the sea continued their squalls... and around me, men walked as if nothing were more wrong in this world than the necessary labors entailed in reconstruction of the material pieces of their own existence. Nothing motivated my motions nor relieved my heart, yet as day turned towards night I took to raise my body from the mangled flesh that was my bed. I instinctively steadied my first movements in order to support my frame, yet with strange sensation felt a curious affliction upon my left hand. As I looked towards the place of this curiosity I discovered not my left hand in accuracy, but instead the blunted stump of an empty forearm made all the more hideous by a single protrusion of broken bone.

Somehow the newfound awareness of being without my lesser

extremity affected me with little shock. Why should I care now for a single part of my bodily self when I no more desired the life which it forced upon me. Should it come as any surprise to my mind that the very creatures capable of snuffing from this world the purity and innocence of a child, might turn to remove a single hand from a hanged man? For what purpose should one require such a strange affectation I worried myself little at first occurrence. Yet as I fell again upon the pile of these unfortunate wretches, my mind turned towards the processes by which I had been created, and the sins of Edmund Breda.

What new hell may be brought upon this earth were another to have taken up his own pursuits now? Rather more dreadful, that they may hold intention more than the arrogant selfishness of my creator, yet truly seek more violent aspirations? Another such as myself created as a tool for war, instructed within the dissolution of baser individuals than the likes of my maker...

I rose at last with new purpose. Should I not be able to join in the joys of man, was it not still my least responsibility to protect the innocent from that which may be corrupted of myself? For this I realized that I had lived and must persist. In order to prevent the dark from within my being set loose upon an unsuspecting world, I must now make it my direction to act beyond personal pain. By the light of torch and lantern, I stood again within the dark of night and set my heart to the pursuit of an unknown thief.

Upon short accord I learned that the battles of Carrickfergus had ended. The occupying force having been composed by the French and led by a privateer known as Thurot, had left in much the way they had arrived, by both their own volition and shipment. Yet now they departed with a small band of hostages in the form of local dignitaries. The castle was returned to the rule of Ireland as if no purpose had driven the invaders actions but to plunder the necessities needed in continuation of life. Thus it was confirmed, that in utterly pointless violence I had lost the boy Bryan that another man may take bread and clothing from the mouths and backs of a people not his kin.

Though my heart longed that my pursuit may allow me to avenge this fact, I knew not as truth whom had fired the cannon which took from me the child and father. Nor did I know who had absconded with my appendage, where I felt my own responsibility must lie. It was then with great fortune I came to learn of the strange hanged man found in the square. Talk reached my ears of the suspicions which many within Carrickfergus had decided were the makeup of my fate. There was discussed by several to be a prisoner and mutineer, brought by the ships themselves, apparently hanged for the murder of several crew prior to landing.

Lauded as a hero to the townspeople my hanging body had been taken as one of their own, yet not before desecration by one of the retreating French. No less than six had witnessed Thurot himself in the act of removing my hand on his final progress from town. These I heard, as often I am capable, from whispers and tellings at a distance while none paid me mind, wandering those ruined streets.

Knowing the inaccuracy of these assumptions, I still could not deny the events recounted by half a dozen individuals. I would have my justification. I would pursue. Yet knowing full and entirely the twelve and some excess hour of prior departure of my quarry, I could waste no time among the dwelling of self pity nor allow myself the luxury of one moment more spent in sorrowful mourning. Indeed I had a ship to catch, and if they themselves wrought and toiled under the guide of a privateer, then I myself must become a pirate!

The acquisition of a vessel now being my immediate priority, I raised the collar of my slicker, ducked my head and made haste toward the docks. Though not tied, yet anchored offshore by a short distance, I spotted a small cutter. Being of the ideal nature to my requirements I dove headlong into the water and made way quickly onto deck as I surveyed the small vessel for sign of owner or sailor. Finding neither, I hastily raised anchor and made ready for pursuit.

Other small vessels nearby also busied themselves amongst tasks similar to my own. As I would later learn, I was not unique in my effort to retrieve something taken from the town, for as I mentioned, the captain of the departing forces had kidnapped several local dignitaries upon his exit.

Through night, while sailing forth from that harbor, my vision remained clear as I spotted sails in the distance, and directed my course towards their position on the horizon. Glancing back into the town of Carrickfergus I could see fires still alight whilst men and women moving about their business aimed to extinguish them. No mind was paid to the single ship sailing away into the night amongst the half a dozen others, nor were my actions of any perceived interest to the nearby sailors who were to join in their own pursuit.

By morning I could more easily ascertain my progress upon the chase given. I had gained during the night easily closing on the three tall ships. Fair winds persisting, I knew that within two to three short days I would be side by side with my quarry. Peering to stern, I observed nearly half of the accompanying pursuers out of sight, turned back in boats and dinghies ill equipped or ill prepared to cover the distances and turmoils of the more open sea. However being of sturdier countenance and requiring less of provision, I continued onward as the wind filled my sail and advanced my former speed.

Few days into my pursuit, as the sun rose shallow against the horizon, I heard the low thunder of cannon fire over the waves. Looking out, I saw what I presume now was the Isle of Man to one side. Three British naval craft were closing with the lead ship to the other. I utilized the strong wind coming off shore in an effort to maneuver myself round the far side of the battle taking place before me. Even in my near fugue state, the matter of self preservation led my actions accordingly. Had anyone looked out upon my direction I would have clearly become a target within my lone cutter, less than a kilometer off, closing towards the now *six* ships of tall sail. Yet fortune for it's fickle bit, played in my favor. All eyes were surely pinned to more pressing actions and I assured myself silently that this was the case.

Having no way in which to conceal my vessels' presence any longer, I swept in from starboard stern within a quarter kilometer. I neared no further to the “Maréchal de Belle-Isle” as I later knew it by name, before leaping into the cold of the Irish Sea. Now, allow me to say at this point, that while I care not for the opinion of anyone else on the matter, you may wish to note the following. If you are ever led to believe that climbing aboard a frigate from the waves is simple under any condition, then you have been lied to. If you are made to believe that it is easily accomplished by stern and without rope, nor ladder, then please assume it to be a fiction altogether.

Without the advantage of my accustomed bi-dexterity, a difficulty only further compounded by the pitch and heave of a full on battle and the icy wetness of slick algae growth upon the hull, I myself found the task nearly out of my capabilities despite myself of the clear physical advantage I otherwise present. Yet I managed, a point that to this day I still take some degree of pride in.

As I peered over the decks for the first time, the light of current conditions presented me with a near impossible choice. This was to either be a search for vengeance, or to consist solely of the search for my absent extremity... but not of both. I knew that in the light of day, in the heat of battle, there would be no concealing my sudden countenance aboard were I to climb onto the upper level. However with all cannons facing port, I quickly chose a simpler, and might I say safer option. From my position, I clung between two of the six pound cannons, yet scarcely below my feet was the empty gun port of a twelve pound monstrosity, and though it may have been out of use to the crew, it was not to myself.

Squeezing through this entry, I found the gun deck polluted and diminished as powder smoke vented out the grate above me. Yet to my satisfaction this portion was nearly devoid of crewman nearest my end, with no eyes cast my direction. Coming in near to the captains' quarters as I did, I wasted not a second pushing through to search for my severed appendage as I closed the door behind me. I am unsure why to this day but some part of myself expected that I should for some reason find the hand of my body nailed above the entryway to this room but it was not.

As if possessed, I tore through the contents of the cabin paying no heed to order nor concern for the wears of what I assured myself was soon to be a lifeless villain of a man. The sounds of battle continued above deck and mostly toward the bow, an increase in footfall led me to the conclusion that we had been boarded. This only increased my sense of urgency all the more. Still I found nothing. The gunfire lessened and slowly the commotion of pained screams and hasty steps became orderly marches and silence broken only by orders.

Then at last I heard no more sounds of powder and ball, no sound of metal against metal. It was all too clear a sign that battle over, the ship had been overtaken. Looking quickly to the window I thought only for a moment of jumping overboard, yet conviction held me still. I looked down to the place where my lost hand belonged... No longer was there an open wound nor protrusion of bone, but a smooth and freshly developed layer of pliable flesh.

In my pursuit, I had taken little time to notice the healing of the area. More often, I had felt no pain, yet simply the impression that things were as they had always been, as if my hand were still in fact present. It was only when I required use of it that its absence seemed a reality more than a driving thought. However that thought now upon this realization became more imperative. I knew not what dark sciences allowed me to heal thus. What is to say that those machinations from within this body would not affect the independent hand in similar fashion? Even if it lay undiscovered, was it a possibility that it might grow another form as easily as my forearm seemed content to begin regrowth of a new replacement for its absence?

When the door to the cabin in which I stood was kicked open, I did the only thing which I could. Palm open, I slowly turned with my arms raised above me, yet it was not the eyes of a soldier that met with mine. Instead, I looked upon a woman. Her gown and hands stained with blood, clearly shaken, and with cheeks streaked by tears and soot, she looked not terrified to see me, but steeled with resolve. She thrust her hand forward towards me and in it, I saw my own.

“Here!" She cried as I noted her English to be without French accent; Her voice that of a woman between anger and sorrow.

“I told him. I told him not to take it... Unholy. And for what?” She spoke more as if to hear the words herself than to inform me. “Luck? Fortune in battle?! I told him!Even before the wound healed itself...” Her voice lowered to a mutter as she looked away from me at the ransacked cabin.

“Stupid man...Damn you Francois.” With her voice raised again she looked back towards me, and I lowered my arms with hesitation to move further. “Damn him... Take it! Damn you, take it and know that he is dead!"

Tears now flowed freely down her cheeks as she began to lose composure. Her extended hand shook, yet she stood firm. As I reached for my own severed palm she closed her eyes tightly and turned away. I do not know who she was. I do not know why she was aboard. I took my hand from her and quickly, yet with as little sound as possible, climbed out of the window, looking back only in time to see English soldiers rushing through the door behind her.

TO BELIEVE IN THINGS YOU CANNOT

DM: Ok, holy shit stop...Stop. Stop. Stop. I can't hold it in. Sorry. I just can't.

AG: Yes Doctor?

DM: You sure?

AG: You certainly seem to be.

Adam's lips spread thin as one eyebrow raised slightly with a small nod.

DM: Right... Ok, So I have to address the obvious here. You are saying that you can be frozen for years and then revived? Which, hey cool trick and all, but seriously, that alone is worth every bit of study that might ever be conducted regarding your capabilities, even despite anything else on its own merit. Then you tell us that what? Yu can not *only* regrow a limb given enough time, but that a limb once removed from you, possesses at least to some degree, an ability to heal itself independently?

AG: That's correct.

DM: No... That's insane! But continuing on anyway; Your'e also implying that *you* are in fact, partly the inspiration for "The Rhime of the Ancient Mariner" *and* that you were physically present at the Battles of Carrickfergus during the hundred years war?

AG: Possible to likely concerning the first... Definite however to the second.

Steven sat back.

DM: Ok then... Just checking.

CR: Are you saying you... believe him Steven?

DM: Oh, honestly I have no counter to it at this point. Merely clarifying to make sure I'm hearing everything right. I'm just rolling with it. I'm good now. Tell us more please, unless Cass has any other questions.

Adam chuckled.

AG: Well then, I appreciate the leniency to your skepticism Doctor. Ms. Reynolds?

CR: I might have a few... I'm less versed in the history or the science obviously, but if I'm following, you did say the year was 1760 right?

AG: Yes, by that point it was.

CR: And you were stranded again in the middle of the ocean I take it?

AG: In actuality no, by some miracle my vessel drifted yes, but not beyond range of my capabilities to reach it once more.

CR: So you swam back to it?

AG: I swam back to it and reattached my hand. Yes

DM: Reattached! There it is. He said Reattached. Your'e

recording right?

I ignored the Doctor's question as rhetorical, signalling for Adam to proceed.

AG: Yes. Understandably, I was forced to rip the skin which had grown over each seperated piecement with my teeth, but yes, I was able to fasten the wayward form back to myself utilizing rope and canvas until it had healed together once more.

DM: Time frame?

AG: It functioned again by the following days sunrise.

DM: Unbelievable...

CR: So where did you go next?

AG: I had nowhere to be and I was heartsickened such by recent events that I sailed onward to France and lived in seclusion for several years near the outskirts of Paris.

CR: The catacombs?

AG: Did not yet exist.

CR: Oh, ok then... Other people?

AG: Not for some time. I'd built for myself a humble home far away from others' eyes and I believe it was in fact near five years before I found cause to move myself from the area. Though by that time I had procured for myself many pleasantries including new texts which I enjoyed reading, and had taken to learn for myself how to adequately cook and prepare complex cuisine. I even by happenstance had come to own livestock.

DM: After all of that, you just went off and lived alone?

AG: It was easier at the time. All that others had offered in this world was not what I considered by then, meant for me to be a part of. I was separate from humanity, and thus I separated myself from them. This did not mean that I had to forsake those crafts which man had created, merely that in not being a man, I did not belong with others.

Unclaimed or untended lands could be homesteaded perfectly well in secret, provided one had the motivation and means to do so. Hiding was merely a matter of not drawing attention to myself... So in solitude, at last some measure of peace... Isolation, and peace...

CR: Interesting. So why did you move? Were you discovered?

AG: Actually no. I heard rumors of several murders that had taken place in another provence and felt compelled to investigate.

CR: What provence.

AG: Gevaudan.

Suddenly Steven burst into laughter.

DM: Nope, not doing it. I can only take so much

CR: What?

I sneered at the Doctor over the prospect of another interruption.

DM: I'm drawing a line now. I'm willing to go only so far, but he's about to blow his credibility if this goes where I think he's headed.

AG: I assume then you are famillиar with the rumors surrounding Gevaudan Doctor?

DM: Jesus christ man! Seriously?

CR: I'm not. What's Gevaudan?

DM: It's a place, not a what... but it's famous for a string of deaths *during* the time he's talking about, where people claim a *beast* was responsible. And unlike our friend here, this one I outright refuse to believe in!

CR: What kind of beast? What's so crazy beyond what the man has said so far that you're not even willing to hear it?

AG: He speaks of A werewolf Ms. Reynolds.

DM: See? See what Im talking about?! I knew it! Lycanthropy is a purely psychological condition! There is zero basis of evidence for the physical transformation of a person into, into a frickin werewolf!

Adam laughed quietly and shook his head. I was bothered by Steven. He seemingly, was not.

AG: As I too believed at the time Doctor. Believe me. In contrasts to both the peasantry and constabulary of the region; I held no superstition toward the existence of what I would encounter. I did not anticipate any beast as had been described. Though the nature of the incidents did cause questions in my mind as to whether by experimentation, such as with myself, another might have been born into being by greater mysteries still.

The tale was simply too much to resist in the end. I found myself curious, and so longing for belief that some alternate, yet intelligent form of being might company me upon the earth aside from man... I gave chance that I might see for myself. By that I did quit my residence to seek further answer only.

DM: So you were bored, and lonely, and you like a good mystery. I can respect that, but I mean... Well, did you find something?

AG: While the statement of such may prove to your consternation... Yes... I must relate most staunchly that I did.

Steven sighed, rubbing his forehead while smiling with bewildered resignation.

AG: Consider, I travelled to that region at great risk to myself, during the heights of a local hysteria wherein hunters and common folk alike, roamed the woods with weapons in hand. I took upon myself the hazard of either exposure, or entrapment, purely to investigate with no honest pretense of what might cross my path more than a murderer or some otherwise human fiend. Yet, I could not in good conscience ignore the possibility of something else if there were even the remotest chance that the perpetrator had indeed been inhuman.

DM: You made friends with a werewolf then?

AG: Oh if only that were the case sir. No, unfortunately I cannot make such claims. I nearly lost an arm and potentially much more to that creature...

By the time that I first laid eyes upon it, I had been at the work for nearly six months along a singularly brutal trail of destruction and sign which others had ignored before me. Though I tell you truly that it was not as you might suspect in form of some hulking giant nor true animal.

Still I must emphasize the inhuman quality to be clear. It was ultimately one night upon the full moon while I rested near the fire that it came; Unprovoked and sudden as a crash of lightning from a blue sky. It attacked me within my own camp as if I had held personal offense against it, but even I was shocked at the sight.

To describe it, I must begin with it's size. The creature was as I said, not some hulking beast, but instead that height of a child rather than a man... And it's form... Though covered in the thickest of gray fur, it stood and moved as human, yet with muzzle and tooth of more canine features. As well too its hands and feet were punctuated by fierce claws upon their ends, which tore at me with a great and mighty strength unmerited by its proportion.

I fought for my life indeed! So strong was it's hold, even after I had overcome the surprise of it's initial attack, that I felt true mortal threat at it's hands. Gratefully the fire proved illuminary; Else, I would have nearly lost the first and only opportunity that I would have to inspect it otherwise. By this however, I quickly came to realize that not only was the horribly tortured being mad, but alternately frightened by even it's own movements and form. This I noted even before I could realize the obvious traits of it's body, which unexpectedly marked it with certainty as being in truth, a female adolescent not so dissimilar to a human in many ways. With a blend of pity and terror, I saw within it's most golden of eyes, the darting frenzy of unbridled lunacy and confusion. Yet I could not stay my own defense at length enough to attempt reason.

Such realizations though brief as they were, held possible only between repeated advances and struggle throughout the night; Until by dawn's rise, and exposure through the trees of that forest, it seemed as if the creature were pleading not for my lethal destruction... but for its own.

They were fleeting, these moments I describe, but I swear that in them, of its most apparent clarity before being once again taken by mania, that this woeful being wished me to release it from life and had determined refusal to cease our battlements until I had done so.

It tore me in shredded ribbon many a time. Even at one point, by lifting me first above its shoulders, the creature had thrown me against the trunk of a nearby tree with such force that several branches cracked to fall from above us. Yet, I swear that I defended myself only by neccesity the entire while, until at last in exhaustion, it began to faulter. I saw the receding length of its claws and fur, expose behind that beastial form, the true and pitiful sight of a very young woman, who in final collapse did at last perish by such multitude the wounds inflicted upon it which did not heal as my own.

I had not meant to kill I attest. In time, I would have taken the poor wretch to bury in remorse and sympathies, had terror at the incident not still pounded my heart when the sounds of others advancing upon our position forced me to hide. I climbed promptly then upon a nearby face of stone which overlooked the grisly scene but concealed myself thoroughly as I had grown accustom. I never did find opportunity again to see the body or discern any further answer than what I have spoken. A party of those same hunters who sought the beast, did find instead the remains of that naked girl, and in assumption, deemed her to be only another victim of their quarry before taking her away I assume, or rather have hoped in years since, to a proper burial.

Soon after however, by all means the killings ceased. Local legends sprang up surrounding the incidents, including the tale of death by silver bullet that now permeates the typical retellings of horror and mythos. I, for my own part, departed the area with haste after these proceedings and returned to Paris in order to gather my belongings with intent thereafter to exit the country entirely. I heard in passing of the many wolves which had been slain during that period, and even one twisted through taxidermy, which was taken to be displayed at court as the great triumph of some renowned hunter, pomped and prided to have ended the nightmarish plague of death himself. Still throughout that time and to present, I hold no explanations for that afflicted being whom fought me to such degrees that I'd scarcely imagined throughout the night of that trial.

I, of my strength and qualities known, even during those years of pursuit from Breda, having faced creatures from the tigers of Asia, to the white bears of the Arctic circle with little concern for death, had never faced such brawn or ferocity as that child who struggled to contain both within herself. And I know good doctor that you have no cause to believe these words, as I offer nothing but the tale itself, but somehow I swear to you once more, within this world there may remain further mystery than we can answer through what knowledge we have acquired thus far. Even in centuries since, I have found no scientific basis for what I witnessed, including the monstrosities of formation brought to light by any other I have set myself either with or against.

Steven sighed and raised an eyebrow toward Adam.

DM: Fine, you seem genuine in your story, and I can believe that through a night of long fatigue and some attacker which you didn't recognize, that you believe what you say. Maybe you ate something poisonous earlier without knowing it, but I promise you there is no such thing as a werewolf.

Since in light of the story told herein, neither Steven nor Adam were aware at the time, or have become aware in any year since the true identity of the Breen child described; They insist on no redaction or alteration to these accounts. Though condolences are extended toward the Breen consulate for this unfortunate incident in sincerity and remorse at our collective, now former, ignorance to all Breenkind.

CR: Ok guys, agreeing to disagree is fine. If there is no more of this, then I would ask instead, where you travelled after leaving paris. Adam?

AG: That is agreeable to me if it is to Doctor Malcom. As said formerly, I did return once more to my home and collected what belongings I could not bear to part with, before taking leave of France entirely. I made my way by vessel toward the lands of England, toward the city of London, where I took residence within the abandoned structures of a former millhouse.

CR: You stowed away?

AG: Not at all. I had years before, constructed a small sailing vessel for my own amusements by which no man could lay claim but myself. I utilized this to cross the channel, having set adrift the cutter which I had taken from Ireland upon my first landing on the shores of France.

The world was changing around me. I had endured enough of my solitudes. Realizing it was in truth a great sense of isolation within which had motivated me to seek answer in pursuit of the creature, I felt drive to be nearer to city life then; Not for comfort or beauty as afforded by the countrysides which I had come to love elsewhere, but instead the greater dialogues of man. For the age seemed to me as if some more fateful awakening had turned within humanity, and I wished in earnest to witness these shifts from within.

However, if it should present to you no argument, I would like to close our session for the evening before the hour grows too late. I have promised to visit my friend if I could, and do not wish to keep him waiting.

CR: The man from the restaurant?

AG: Yes.

DM: I think that would be fine. When do you want to meet again? I can stay here if Cassandra agrees.

CR: Of course, yes. By all means. Is tomorrow too soon for you?

AG: Tomorrow sounds delightful. I shall return earlier in the day unless there is objection.

There was none. Since Steven was ok staying at my place and I was happy to be his host, we both wished Adam a good visit and stopped recording to say our goodbyes. Adam even allowed me to hug him. Steven shook his hand before he left with lighthearted jokes about still not believing in werewolves. Which Adam shrugged off with laughter and good cheer, even while we stood to watch him leave. He waved from the elevator and I closed up the office until the following afternoon.

SESSION FOUR

<u>Interviewer Name:</u>

Cassandra Reynolds: Journalist for "Washington Post" newspaper and special columnist for Al-Jazeera International.

Second Interviewer and Consultant:

Dr. Steven Malcom of the Boston College Institute for Scientific Research and Advancement: Specialization in structural biochemistry. Published author and Nobel laureate

Interview Subject : Adam

The time is 3:25 pm. March the 31st, 2024

Location: Personal offices of Cassandra Reynolds, Washington D.C.

CR = Cassandra Reynolds
DM= Dr. Steven Malcom
AG = Subject - Adam

Personal notes Italicized

◆ ◆ ◆

A TALE OF TWO CITIES

March 31st 3:25 pm

CR: how was your visit with your friend?

AG: Bittersweet... His wife passed during the pandemic and I've not made way to see him since. He was saddened to hear of my plans, but hopeful that your discoveries by them might prove fruitful in the prevention of such troubles in the future.

DM: So you told him what we're doing here?

AG: I did, and he supports it with your assistance. We are both old men after all. He understands my motives. He wished for me to bid you visit him often if you would, to remember me when I am gone. Also, he insists that you will be treated as family hereafter should you do so.

DM: Still plotting your death I see.

AG: Still and always with hope toward what contributions it may ease in the overall sufferings of others.

Adam said this politely, almost jokingly, but his steadfastness was clear.

AG: Shall we begin?

CR: London.

AG: Yes indeed... I cannot tell you how marvelous to behold

the city was at that time. Even in it's filth and the division of class, one could sense the spark of progress within the whole of mankind, which at any moment might light a figurative powder keg of change to throw the world either inexorably forward, or in totality, destroy its foundations.

I wished to be a part of this, and though it may be easily assumed that my form would greatly inhibit any movement within the city around me; I found it quite simple to disguise myself with little more than smears of coal dust and darkened clothing, so that by night and early morning, I would often gather discarded papers and materials which told me of the world further than the limits of my ears.

CR: Speaking of which, that's come up a few times now. Can you tell me just how good your hearing actually is?

AG: I cannot. I can only say, that for the extent of my senses, I can hear more clearly than any man I have yet to meet, and my vision in darkness is equalled in this measure.

DM: We can test those later. You were saying?

AG: Yes, the coal dust... It is remarkable how this minimal disguise allowed me free passage without conflict, but in such lack of true discretion, my size and shadowed figure when seen, remained a constant subject of whispered tales and speculation within the local areas.

My odd ally in this was in fact the most tasteless of divisions among the peoples of that time. For try as any might to convince themselves otherwise, it was in fact so entirely common for those of wealth or stature to avoid eye contact with the impoverished of that city, that none but the odd beggar or similarly destitue would gaze my way beyond the briefest of note to observe any further detail than the silhouette of my person. And yet in those desperate and poor, I found myself largely ignored as well, due to fear of interferance with one unknown to them. Save the errant rumor or legend of the shrouded monstrosity who lurked beyond the abandoned storehouses of the west end, I seemed to hold little interest or impact upon my surroundings in such a way that even within one of the most populous urban cities of its time, I was all but invisible and unnoticed to my neighbors.

Strangely, the decayed buildings of the immediate area surrounding Lambeth provided my settlement quite easily as well. Despite the population of workhouses nearby, I found along a winding but less frequented passage near one of the underutilized ports, a series of large factories and warehouses nearly forgotten in disrepair. One of these especially held interest on my initial entry due not only to its size, but also the great emptiness wherein, that I witnessed such grass had sprung up along the broken floors, that it seemed almost as if occupied by a small field or meadow which had forced its way into existence within the buildings shelter. The walls were covered in ivies and nearly so overgrown with it as to appear forested from within. A portion of cieling too had collapsed inward, allowing for rain and sun to fall equally upon those grounds until even trees had grown to some modest height along the borders. I found it beautiful.

One wall of this vacant structure of course was shared nearby with the furthest reaches of a factory workhouse engaged in the making of pottery. However, none who worked therein seemed ever to wonder at, nor venture towards the great building behind them, so overgrown and decayed it was by outward sight as to remain almost unseen, even as they passed it daily to and from their more important goings on.

This was where I settled, and even by the sounds of my

daily toil and acquired livestock, I remained unmolested or intruded upon. I was able within this homestead to turn the earth below, and thru allowance of that great hole within it's ceilings, produce in placement of the meadow, a small garden by which I might sustain my needs. Of course the Thames lay just beyond, within ease of a moments walk, but so filthy were the waters within it, that I feared to consume the fish which lived there.

Similar to my previous abode in France, I constructed for myself a modest cottage, even beneath the forgotten lofts of that singularly abundant room. And thru many efforts, I eventually procured for my uses, several foul in addition to a single goat, which I peaceably kept unseen or bothered within for quite some time. In time however, the local peoples who might have happened upon my solitude, had by such suspicions come to fear the placement of my residence through tale of those same legends and rumor concerning what brief encounters had led the most forgotten of them to glimpse and describe of my person to others.

I never strived to build upon such things of course, and on rare occasion that some person would cross my path at any distance, I maintained politeness and silence within what shadows I could afford concealment until they had departed. Still to these people, I was more specter than life, and unbelieved by reports to any greater authority that might have investigated my presence, I was through superstition and suspect origins, left to my own devices, both close enough in proximity to observe city life, yet far enough removed as to not suffer threat of encroachment for many years.

By day I stayed within the unassuming walls of that great forested building and I could hear beyond the far border toward the potters house, the chatter and discourse of workers within. This gave me ease to listen to them intently, almost as if I myself were included amongst them. Fortunes smiled brightly that on occasion which I could aquire such things as new books or entertainment to satisfy further my curiosities, I found them in abundance. For in those days the written word did spread across all classes and tiers of London society as if wildfire moved its passage.

The talk especially of those colonists across the sea within the new world, struck chord within me of great interest, as did the news of France, which often occupied conversation and concern for many. Even unto the declaration of secession made by those same colonists, I had apprised myself in marvel at the continual stream of progressive ideals which struggled against the established rules of Europe, and wished so fervently that I could share in the discourse of those days, that at times I would creep along rooftops to overhang eave with listening ears at the gossip of peoples from every walk of life. Or even by pressing my ear directly to the farmost wall of my building, I would hear every word spoken by so many within, until I found myself replying as if in genuine conversation to those who never once heard word from my lips.

By that time I had lived in my placement secretly for long enough to watch from my distance, the growth of children recognized in frequency of the local surroundings, and I marveled too at the grace of those less fortuned than their brethren, even as my disillusionment solidified toward the gentler aristocracy which fed upon their works.

Worldwide, new lands were discovered at such great pace that it seemed as if all the globe were convulsing in expansion even to rip from it's moorings the philosophy and upheaval of nearly every nation's accord, until in rebirth, it breathed a deep and heavy rain upon the refuse and abandoned thoughts of the old ways toward the crying splendor of a new dawn. Alongside these occurrences London itself was seen changed throughout, as paved roads and irrigation sprawled outward to every corner, and projects of development sprang up nearly overnight. The peoples within these veins moved and toiled as passionately as ever, and yet educations rose, idle thoughts transformed themselves into great works of writing, and inventions brought with them mysteries anew by the thousands.

Still I wandered in my solitudinous existence as a fixed point upon the earth, stopped within time and unmoving by age, isolated, I observed without participation and though entranced by so much change, remained half broken by my heart's desires mixed as they were with loathing of memories long past. Further tragedy evaded me during this time it is true, but the depths of my woes carried with me the weight of my own historie's missteps and regret like anchored chains. So when by mysterious event a frightened and mad soldier did enter within my walls by one fateful morning, I chanced myself to reveal to him my presence in aid to his worried state.

"Fear not soldier. None but I dare enter these walls for dread of its mystery. Whatever pursues you will undoubtedly cease, if only for that superstitious credit you seem to have overcome. Are you well sir?" I called out to him from the concealed and shadowed placement of the reading chair I had positioned within the loft some years before. Admittedly I had taken in my early hours many a time to sit perched as thus, so that I may view the outline of the growing city through the missing section of my bulding's ceiling and roof, but it was purely by luck I had assumed such placement prior to the strange mans entry.

"Whose voice is here?! Are you the shadowed creature whom gossip attributes this shelter? Have you some disfigured affliction?! Show yourself to me! I swear no matter your form I will be friend to you, if only you conceal me from those whose mean my capture!" He shouted wildly, without knowledge of my directions.

There was promise in his words and chance that I might reply, I did so. "Shall I agree, I must know firstly the truth. Have you cause for such pursuit in earnest, or have you simply offended in principle these men who chase you so?" I asked calmly, stepping without sight toward and down the stairwell to the floors below.

"I have fled from indenturement within the king's army, and have no desire to fight that battle which wages overseas to preserve any land there which I have never stepped foot, or fight those men to mortal death who by their own words ask only for freedom from tyranny! Will you show yourself?!" He asked again, turning then to my sight as I stepped finally onto the same level as he beyond my gardens plot. He looked toward my silhouette in anticipation as I revealed myself from those shadows and into the light.

His eyes squinted as his voice lowered. "What type of man stands before me? Your vastness portrays much... I had not believed the tales, but as they say, you indeed look the complexion of a revived corpse from some giant of antiquity sir. I would hope not to offend one of such bearing, but by reflections of age I am certain you are already ware of your own sight. Is their any name you know to your ailment that I should fear to approach?" He spoke in sincerity.

"I hold no contagion upon me if that is your fear. Simply cursed by birth I appear as such, and with further reasonable explanation, I can offer none to be understood. I ask only that *if* you should flee this place, you bring not more to my humble doorways. Afford me continued peace within these expansive grounds I beg of you kindly." I informed with gentle speech.

The man gazed curiously, but he did not turn to run, nor did he attack. "Allow me to eat from your gardens. Hide my person within them, and I shall bring no others to this place I assure you. Have you name my gracious host?" He asked, slowly closing the distance between us so that we may face eye to eye.

"I am called Adam by any who would speak to this disfigured form, and you sir?" I asked him gladly.

"I am Ruthven." He responded. "And I shall speak with you kindly sir Adam, if you would accept it."

Thus were the beginnings of my first dealings with the man whom called himself Ruthven; Not of stature or grand introduction, but simplicity and quiet, as two men unknowing to one another, gave considerable accord to the peaceful company of another lost soul within the quiet and forgotten shell of that building's chamber along old Londontown's neglected borders. So curious to this day how I had not immediately worried myself toward his motivations, or suspected the lying nature of his tongue, but all cannot be known when it most certainly would save us. For those troubles which follow, are somehow it seems all but inescapable at times, and fate's weaving hands, complex in tapestry.

I allowed the man entry then and pulled from behind the cottage construction by which I lived within, a half divided barrel, so that he might sit and take rest. This he did, and at some length while he ate raw the hearty fruits of my garden with ravenous appetite, we began to speak without barrier between us. I learned that he was not new to soldiering, but after enduring the hardship and danger of battles countless in many regions, had seen upon his last station, such inconsiderate treatment of the common peoples, that he had forsworn the legal payment for his freedoms, and set out without allowance to desert his post and flee from service.

Coming as he had from such destitution and debts that motivated his original enlistment, he revealed that his mind could not abide further the distaste he felt toward the privilege and entitlement of many above his station, until at last he swore finally to leave their employ in search of some better quality that he might find elsewhere in the world. Further still, when his ranks had been called back to London, the place of his birth, he had set out swiftly in departure. But soon missed by his superiors, he had been pursued and labelled rightly a deserter, though not from what they swore as "duty" he said, for he owed no *duty* to any beyond himself, he expressed, and could be called by his heart to owe not a single person alive any more than to his own drive and course.

These proclamations were of great interest to me, and so starved I had been for discourse for so long the years, that I asked several times his thoughts on the state of the British empire, as well as the embattlements it had engaged with other powers and philosophies abroad. What he asked of my histories I withheld in all but the simplest of telling; That I had been originally from Geneva, but born without wealth, name, or titles, with such an affliction that I appeared unnatural and fearsome to others, and so in retreat from the world which would not accord me any measure of employment or tolerance, I had chosen to live in secret by the work of my own hands, or by what meager luxuries could be procured freely from the refuse of the city. This he accepted without further inquiry, and in trust neither suspected the others company of so dark the secrets we kept.

Those secrets by which we did share however, would hold to such agreements that for a time after that first meeting, Ruthven and I resided in that place together as neighbors, if not friends. Kept in secret this arrangement, Ruthven was able to venture forth as required and return by his own choosing, which afforded various benefits to myself as well, to bring to me that which I could not attain for myself. Truly he was a criminal in the eyes of the law and resorted at many times to activities less than savory to my personal virtue, though in the knowledge that no one was physically harmed by his crimes, I turned blind my eyes to these truths in trade for companionship.

However after several weeks passage I came to note a most unfortunate malady of the young soldier. It seemed that upon certain intervals of time, a fervent mania appeared within Ruthven's countenance. Agitations would seize him in barely restrained agression, and his temperment became uneased even to withstand without nervousness, that I could be faced with him. He would rave and pace in frenzy, snapping in shouts and profanities at even mild activities which infuriated his emotions. Though not permanent in their stays, these times occurred almost by cycles according to a predictable measure of weeks, during which his sustained absence could last for days on end before eventual returns found him drunken and stinking of flesh.

This continued as only the slightest of interruptions to our neighborly demeanor of course, for he always apologized afterward and insisted no offense for his prior transgressions against me or any other. We would resume shortly to normalcy as it were and resurrect such friendly interactions at all times between us without malice or resentment to be had, until one night while within his manic state of violence, I found the man to have slaughtered my dear goat, and was seen drinking from it's neck, the still warm blood of it's body.

When I approached him, I saw at once the returned mania and fury which had become regular place each month, but I had never feared the man, not even then. Thus to my genuine surprise, I was aghast when he lept at me and bit into the side of my arm so forcibly that it tore a large chunk of my body with it. Even when I struck him to the ground, I could scarcely believe what had transpired, and saw the flesh still lodged between his teeth where he fell unconscious before my feet. I knew not what had possessed him, but still I had known the cycular lunacies which compelled his countenance so often, and never suspected or seen such savagery as overtook him that evening.

Part of me should have feared the interactions of my blood with his own, but the idea that through a bite, my body might somehow change him, would never have occurred to me aside from the prospect of possibly healing any wounds or brightening his health. Yet, when he woke the following day, I found him changed indeed. He seemed at once cheerful and bright, but also somehow sinister. His words were spoken differently, and his nature seemed suspect at even the slow rise to stand which darkened the room of moods and happiness.

I feared even in his calm then, that again he might lunge at or attack me with violence, though I cannot say why. He had simply changed. His body looked no younger nor older, no healthier nor less. His skin appeared the same as it always had. Even his posture seemed no different to me. However still, this evident transformation had occurred on some level unseen, which stood stark and bold in contrast to who he had been at other times. It was as if the manias and fury that on so many occasion had filled his person, had then merged beneath the surface of him and persisted now even within his calm. To clothe a wolf in sheepskin and see it from afar, would have been like this day, to see Ruthven's true face for the first time.

"Ruthven dear friend what has become of you?" I asked.

"Adam, my neighbor what do you imply? Am I not the same Ruthven who has awakened from such troubles before many a time? And yet you observe I am better now for it?" He replied with arrogant disdain.

"No my friend, what change has the drinking of blood wrought to you?" I questioned, for it was clear some occurence thus transpired, had altered his person.

"No no, do not lie there neighbor. No change has occurred by the blood of some mere goat! You my golden champion of a man! This is your doing! So unlike any other, I have stayed from question to the truth of you, and now I know the godhood of sweetness that you conceal from this world within. What wonders are you for the flesh to bestow upon me such gifts I now feel? I am freed from the shackles of my body and mind for once, and recognize the might of strength within. No blood of whore or animal has ever resulted in such the delight of my relief. For you alone have cured what ails me in every way and I stand renewed in thanks!" He shouted triumphantly.

The horror at this realization was unspeakable to me, but I beheld my friend confess to it firsthand, having professed to drink the blood of whores and livestock by comparison to my own; Meaning that such horrid action was held common to him. Fearing that I had unknowingly housed a murderer those past months, I recoiled at the thought of my blood bestowing upon him any advantages or changes which would aide in those deeds and attempted at first to lie.

"I am nothing of the sort." I insisted. "Merely a malady wich you have mistaken, and in delerium attached some unknown quality. You are not well friend." I continued calmly.

"Lies!" He hissed. "You have given to me life unkown and

you deny this! More I demand! More and I know I shall be cured forever from my urges and cravings of the flesh! If you shall not give it freely than I will take from you every drop!" He shouted, leaping toward me with inhuman speed. His strength as he struck me was unbelievable. I had never seen the man able physically a single bit more so than any other man of similar height or build, though now he possessed it seemed, those abilities equal to my own.

I stumbled backwards in surprise and rubbed my jaw where he had struck. I tasted blood within my own mouth and feared another blow of such force. Driving by my own charge, I pushed him backward into the garden itself until sun beat down upon us from above and all at once felt his opposition give way, as a shriek filled my ears. Ruthven recoiled from the light and retreated to those shadows beyond as I stood to watch. Observing his own shock as he reached one arm outward into the sun's rays, I witnessed the ill effect it had on him. He shrank before the heat as if seemingly drained of bodily energies, and upon this realization, filled with fear, he turned from me to flee.

I heard the boards of our home's entry move, and listened to the clatter of his footfalls upon cobbled stone, but could not match his speed as I chased after him. I soon lost sight of his person between two nearby buildings. Knowing not the intentions he held, but afraid that he would betray our secrecy to others and return with further demands for my blood joined by them, I chose that day to pack my belongings once more and depart from yet another abode in sadddened disappointment, not only to have lost that friend who looked upon me kindly, but also a settlement which had truly been most favorable to us both.

Collecting my things in some haste I began to see for the first time, quite by chance reading of headlines to the papers which I meant to discard, some trend of connection between Ruthven's extended absences of past and the following reports within those days of missing persons and murders committed within the same areas which we had inhabited. How could I have missed such things I wondered? Had I truly been so blind to him by need of friendship that I had chosen to ignore those signs? Had he been, this entire time, so stricken by madness that these were his doing or merely coincidence? I could not know, and did little to investigate.

The year was 1779 by then, and leaving London altogether, I could not find my original vessel. I stole a half rotted barge along the Thames toward greater port, where upon arrival, I secreted passage once more as I had become accustomed. I returned myself through these winding paths and passages across Europe until I came once more to Geneva in my shame.

HOME AND AWAY

I had not seen the countryside of my birth for over fifty odd years, and yet still it appeared magnificent in beauty to my eyes. I had departed London, leaving behind a fiend of my own indiscretions, with no concept of the scope to what havoc might come of him, and yet feeling firstly the responsibility to prevent his further empowerment, I fled his presence and returned to Switzerland once more, carrying with me two trunks of possession which weighed upon my back even strapped as they were, the most comfortably that I could arrange them.

With no place other to live, I thought at first to return to the frigid regions of the sea of ice, and make myself home within the caves I had once fled. However upon much deliberation given during my journeys to arrive at the famillar placements I had once roamed, I decided in place of this choice, that I would settle myself more accordingly near the castle of my birth. Knowing as I did the forrest and surrounding countryside, I felt it quite possible and indeed likely to avoid detection travelling onward into Germany. However given my experiences in London, I determined it also to some benefit after arrival that I might encourage a level of superstition surrounding my yet to be established campus.

So I travelled onward toward and past Castle Frankenstein, to set about the work of securing a retreat from the world once more in the woods of Odin. Of course having grown quite adept at homesteading by then, these tasks were performed with little difficulty to myself. Until once again within the seasons changes, I had grown in that place some meager crops beneath the shaded forrest canopy, and obtained several egg laying foul within range of my properties.

In time I produced not only a cottage for myself, but also a woodshed and coopery for my foul, along with a smokehouse and small pond, which I irrigated to support my gardens and ducks. Hunting became a more than common pursuit during this time, and while I preserved meat for myself, for some considerable measures I abstained from the acquisition of another goat for milk and cheese.

Ruthven was but a distant thought I admit, and though I missed the gritty news and bustles of London, I settled quite nicely within the tranquil forests of my homeland. Marking my territiorie's edge with carvings of mythical figurements and eerie constructions intended to deter motion further. I felt myself secured by their effect. Also indeed, I did promote a level of haunting gossips concerning my lands where opportunity was presented, but these were made all the easiest due in part to the reputations of those who bore responsibility for my origins in beginning. Some good it seemed, had settled from the rumor and myth of my father I thought, as the tales of his disgrace and the later destruction of the House of Breda, had blanketed the whole of the castles presence within a shroud of suspicion and fear, even to those who possessed ownership of it.

Still, this proved only half measured in requirement as the woods of Odin held legend to their own possession of dragons and dangers from more ancient tales. And my carvings reflected such power over the minds of others that they feared not only haunting, but witchcraft had left its mark upon the shaded labrynth of that area.

I did find it more difficult to obtain news during that time, and doubly so the endeavor to procure for my pleasures new books which might fill my time. However there was much occasion in which I travelled for such things and found them more available to me nearer the cities. Almost two years had come and gone before I would happen across the indecipherable consequences of my earlier association with Ruthven, and still it baffles me the turn of events which transpired.

By means unknown to me at the time, Ruthven the deserter, the lowly and destitute, the hater of wealth and entitlement, had manipulated his way into title and lands which established him as a now lord of some properties around the countries of Europe. One of these properties being close to the location of Inglestodt, had come to his attentions as in need of inspection before he took full possession, and quite by chance I saw tell of this impending visit within the discards of a local journal to that area.

Preparations were made for his arrival as if he were a travelling dignitary. Word spoke of the affluent Lord to visit with curious excitements by the peoples of the area. Scarcely could I believe even upon further detail that this was the same Ruthven whom I had known. However with curiosity, I lingered within the locale of the city for several days in order to view his appearance, until this very thing was confirmed to my eyes.

The "Lord Ruthven" of whom the news had spoke was indeed one and the same the man whom I had shared my time with in London. Not only had he obtained both land and title in the interim, but also reputations for respectful and stationed accord which seemed at complete odds to the personal history I knew of him.

Suspect as I did, that he was in all probabilities a murderer and deceiver, I also felt owed to him the allegiances of friendship and pity for our shared time together and his predominantly fair treatment of me in spite of my appearance. So in this state of mind, knowing my old neighbor whom had never feared my presence might at the very least entertain a conversation to explain himself, I awaited his arrival and subsequently followed his carriage to the estate which he had set his visit. Some time after nightfall, I made my secret entrance to see him.

The mansion was large and gaudy with fashioned adornments, placed low in perch by the side of a clear and beautiful lake in such a way that reminded me of my makers own. However by first sight of Ruthven, who rejected it would seem all servants stay or tending within the home, abided alone that night within the vast halls of such palatial surrounds, I could see apparent the outward demeanor of a man almost bored by the expectedness of my arrival.

"And now returned, the blessing of my old neighbor and friend... How fair was the passage to me in this place?" He asked me low from some distance.

The surprise on my face may have been apparent, but impossible for him to have seen, as he faced away from me at the time by the burning light of a parlors fireplace. Still he continued. "Do not worry yourself my dear Adam, I have told no one, as none have told me. I merely felt your approach and direction by that which is shared between us." At this remark My wayward friend turned, and I could see upon him the strangest of gazes which looked toward my person not as one who sees, but more so one who is blinded, as they might gaze longly toward the mid distance without true sight of clouded eye. The calm that surrounded him was like death itself. And again I felt the ineffable grip of some darkness which moved at his presence.

"Have you nothing to say to your old companion chum? Some remark of question perhaps? The entitlement? The lands? The freedom from prosecution for my abandonment of the kings army? Or, are you bound more to the question of those vices you had long been unaware during our time together? Perhaps the inquiry of murders you might have surmised to be my doing? How unpleasant...

You are perhaps still the least vile of all men I have known my friend. No vice, or lusts to have deemed to touch your soul and solitude, nor greed to pursue the power which by rights you could easily take with but a grasp of your hand. They are the rest of such disappointing lots I confess, that none other have capable within them to meet that level to which you have spoiled me with." He continued.

"Ruthven..." I muttered pleadingly.

"Oh, do not force me to chastise you for lies my guest. You stand in *my* home now, and I shall be honest with you without fail if you will but return the favoritism I grant. Shall I first begin as proof to this in explanation of what questions you *fail* to ask?

I feel that the tale would be of great interest to you... For it is made possible only by your gracious bestowments. For instance, did you know that your blood possessed such powers? I have never seen them used by yourself in the ways which I have discovered, but surely you were aware before me of some extent to their miracles... Or should each their magics bestow a seperate set of gifts per personage, and I the luckier have simply been most fortunate?" With these words I witnessed Ruthven vanish from his stand before the hearth, only to reappear near instantly along the opposite side of the rooms breadth.

"Oh? How interesting. A gasp and racing of heart tell me this you did not anticipate. So first of my questions you have answered, and I shall answer yours." He looked upon me intensely with gaze both gray and vacant. "Come, sit." He gestured with his arm toward a chair by the fire, but I did not move.

"Well then, that suspicion is confirmed then. I hold no sway over you, nor would I have expected such. Oh Adam, you delight my heart to no ends. All others I have met since the day we last parted, have held no such constitutions or defense against my wills. This station you see, I had but to ask of it and was gifted all that my imaginings could desire, granted first clemency, and then lordship. I have ever since walked within the worlds of those I most despised and found little entertainment but by their ruin and disgrace, until I have become so intolerably disinterested by their vices that even the draining of them or their children has offered no warmth or fire to these veins.

Oh do not swallow such at this, those urges you have witnessed before; They were born of unbridled neccesity at the cravings I have held my entire life, those which drove me to hysterics of violent release. You knew the madness within me and yet never questioned the smell of flesh upon my returns that I know now you *must* have recognized. I only killed then for scarcity of available choices otherwise. By the need alone I felt to consume their blood and flesh, I would have been persecuted and labeled perverse if they were spoken of. Even the base whores which I did pay for their bodies would refuse such simple request that would stave my maniam and yet they would freely give to me without contestation the carnal lusts of their sex instead. Those who witnessed my needs and died on account were a forced burden upon me who now has no need for such indiscretion. As now I may simply *will* those in my service to forget I ever did touch them at all. Is this not better in your mind that I might relieve those craven cravings in calm and secreted ease?

Why not should I, who was their indentured, be capable now of calling them to my service in their vain and dispicable lives, those which preyed on others so cruelly yet now in peace and ignorance provide for my own?" He continued coldly.

"Yet I am alone as ever and you are the only who might conceivably provide me with companionship my friend. Forgive me my melodramatics at our last sight, and stay with me now. I will make others accepting of you and provide so much for this if only you will give to me what I desire."

I was aware then by glimpse of a barely discernable grimace upon his lip which spoke of some sadistic pleasures within him, but standing still and without sign of my anxiousness, I asked the neccesary question of what it was that he desired. To which he answered while circling my body slowly.

"It is *you* Adam. It was always you I now know. By your blood I was cured of my delerium and gifted these attributes, but not devoid of those cravings which continue to drive my neccesity to drink from others. I know that if you simply allow me to drink once more, then I may be cured entirely, and in addition to this assume a greater level of control by which the two of us could reshape the dastardly habits of mankind away from greed and war, class and prejudiced against the less fortunate. I know for certain your mistreatments by them would cease. We could cure them all of these, I am assured in this. If only you will give to me that gift once more in greater volume... dear friend" Ruthven had stopped behind me in these words and awaiting my response I felt as if I were held at knife's edge.

Like the proposition which I had once made to my own maker, I now faced a creature of my own responsibility, whom I feared more powerful than myself. What he asked of me unnatural as it was, seemed at first tempting to consider for its benefits to all, but what right had he or any other to usurp the wills of man and seek control over them even for some imagined good to come of it? Yet by what escape might I flee his presence with such speed he possessed and the means to call upon others in my pursuit?

Helpless, I stood there for long moments before a memory compelled my actions. I was disgusted by the thoughts of Ruthven's confessions, but more so by his seeming apathy towards the implications of these proposals. However, if my own suspicions proved true from recollection, then by time alone my escape from him would require no aide or involvement of another.

I spoke to stall for time. "And if I entertain this, you feel that you would cease your consumption of their blood and flesh for less need of it, but what if the opposite proves true old companion? Even I do not understand how this has come of you or what malady has originally compelled your thirsts. My blood, has grown within you powers, which I have never seen and without knowledge of what the greater introduction of this might produce, I do not know that I could aquiesce in good faith, but merely an ignorant hope instead. I will sit as you asked, and if you will do the same, we shall discuss these questions further before any accord." I replied.

"I agree to this and have missed our long chats friend. Let us explore what options lay before us and I swear to you a peace as gentlemen, that we might rekindle our acquaintance." He responded smoothly, his frigid presence slinking away like the chill of a serpent who crawls over the skin, until seated at last, I followed to face him from the opposing chair...

Steven at this point had moved as if to question Adam's story several times, but every time he leaned forward, Adam would raise a single finger to ask his patience a bit longer. I wasn't sure how much more this could go on by that point, but again I saw Steven concede to the request knowing that soon the floor would be opened to him for all that he wished to ask.

AG: We talked for hours, and in fact through the night, as I questioned deeply the intentions of my former neighbor, growing no less concerned but in fact realizing with true horror, the depths of his delusionary concept for the future he wished to create. Only by the first light of morning which I knew to come soon, preceded by birdsong, did I dare to express my dissatisfaction with his answers or openly declare my unwillingness to participate.

As I had feared however, these responses evoked within Ruthven the first true emotions I had seen since my arrival, and with fury he turned against me in vile "You will agree or I shall take it from you!" He shouted, but I did not wait the coming attack. Knowing his speed now as I had witnessed directly, I anticipated his action and allowed his charge to lead him directly into the burning embers of the dying fire, whilst I fled toward the nearest of doors onto a balcony facing east into sunrise. At which point there affixed, I leapt over it's edge and ran across the lawns of the estate past many guard and servant, all of whom stood watch outside as if unmoving statues bound in place by invisible chain.

Turning to look back, I saw thankfully the gambit's benefit to me as Ruthven withdrew hastily from dawn's light as if unable to force his body beyond the barrier of it's rays. I did not know at what distance his strange sense of my presence would dissipate, but hoped at the least, that with distance between us I might lose him better than I had my maker years before. With these thoughts I returned to my home at great speed with some hope that he would be stayed until nightfall at the least.

However I knew then the truth of a question which long plagued me prior. How had Breda consistently pursued me so many times over the years of our chase? How had Ruthven gained foreknowledge of my arrival to his home? It seemed apparent then that as he had said, those who had taken from my blood, could feel its pull like the pull of north moves the needle on a compass. This nearer to any other thought, troubled me much.

QUESTIONS OF LIVING DEATH

DM: Now?

Adam nodded calmly.

AG: Now.

DM: Ok. Alright, good.... Umm... So I kind of thought somehow the werewolf might be the end of this, but I'm struggling here again. Ruthven was essentially a vampire *is* what your'e saying right?

AG: While I am not partial to that word purely due to it's supernatural implications, yes, that would be the most fitting terminology which comes to mind... Albeit, not for what he was originally. Though I feel his disturbed compulsions may indeed be the same sort or type which originated the myth of such things in others throughout history, but primarily for what he became afterward, I would certainly attribute those qualities.

CR: Right... So to be clear, your'e not saying that supernatural vampires exist.

AG: No.

DM: Just that in this case, a guy with some sort of mental disorder, gained abilities because of exposure to *your* blood specifically.

AG: Well, I can't entirely say that I believe it to be mental disturbance alone unfortunately. In years since, I have seen evidence of certain physical deficiencies and ailments which may have greatly contributed to Ruthven's compulsions as they were.

DM: Really? Such as?

AG: Actually Doctor, these are a matter which I'd very much like for you to test in a labratory setting as they may relate to my blood's interaction with others. Merely as a threat to my peace of mind, I would adamantly insist. You see, there is this very pressing concern in me which borders on near paranoia around such matters.

I know from trial and later successes that this is not the result experienced by most where my blood is concerned, however the threat is quite real and present that I should possibly pose risk to all mankind if improper exposure should contaminate the wrong individual. It troubles me greatly.

DM: You're totally serious then?

AG: Gravely. I have witnessed firsthand the result of how my blood interacts with different individuals if introduced through a variety of methods, and for saftey sake I feel that extensive experimentation and documentation are neccesary for reasons you will soon understand.

Adam wavered nervously before reaching into his pocket to remove a small scrap of paper which he handed to Doctor Malcom.

Being as your employ, affords and involves directly, your access to genetic samples pertaining to such a wide variety of afflictions and conditions... Doctor, I have compiled a list of those which I feel most likely to have been suffered by Ruthven himself.

If at all possible, then I feel it would be prudent, if not the singular responsible course of action, to test the interaction of such samples against exposure to my blood within a controlled setting prior to any experimentation with others.

Steven took this note and looked over it while muttering to himself as he read. After this he looked back toward Adam.

DM: This is interesting... You realize of course that more than half of these are benign nutritional processing disorders though? Do you really feel these are more pressing than the possibility of psychosis?

AG: I have given much thought and time into this consideration over the years Doctor. Admittedly I have gone to such lengths that I researched both you *and* Ms. Reynolds at long ends even before setting out to arrange these meetings at all. I had to be certain that neither of you personally held any of these conditions yourselves. You truly have no concept at this moment of the threat that is posed if I should be correct and another incident occur. I assure you, by my tales end, you will be equally inclined to cover any and all possibilities, however remote, in order to prevent such misfortunes.

DM: Wait, what kind of research? There's stuff on this list that a lot of people can have with no idea that they have it at all. These require specific testing. Either of us could have half a dozen of these and it wouldn't show up on our medical records or anywhere else unless we asked to be tested specifically. Are you saying you got access to our blood or tissue samples somehow?

AG: Oh, not at all. I apologize. No. I simply observed each of you for several years and took record of your daily habits including diet, excercise, general health, interactions with others, mood, and so on. It was nothing more invasive than a typical marketing algorithm. Actually, the bulk of information was collected by a third party organization which was paid to share it with me from your social media and personal device data. All I had to do was use an old company name to receive the results and apply what criteria that I was seeking, in order to verify that neither of you posed such a risk.

CR: Don't worry Steven. I already followed up on it when he told me. Actually I interviewed the head of the company that sold our information for an article last month.

Doctor Malcom looked stunned. hIs mouth was slightly agape and he looked toward me almost without motion, save his eyes.

DM: And? Is there an expose that's gonna shut them down or something?

Adam and I both laughed.

CR: Of course not. They're a normal company. They collect the same data that everyone else does. Adam just lied about who he was in order to gain access to it. Public scrutiny won't shut them down unless they overstep the law. It just makes sure that they double check who they're selling to and stay upright. Besides, Adam's company is legitimately real and could legally use all of it regardless. He just doesn't do anything with it. I looked into him too. The company has been around for like a hundred years, filing taxes and basically just sitting there without producing anything.

DM: But... my device information...

AG: Is already viewed hundreds of times each day by companies wishing to sell you things Doctor. I consider my use of this data more pressing and of ethical merit. All records which I kept have been utterly destroyed since. I assure you, I have no care for your browser histories. I merely wished to be sure that you showed no concerning malady which might endanger these proceedings. You do not. Perhaps there is a touch of high blood pressure and an above average penchant for antique medical journals and werewolf movies, but nothing of worry to me.

Doctor Malcom blushed and shrank in his seat, swallowing hard.

DM: So, the list then? You really think these things matter *that* much?

AG: I do, yes. Partly this list comes from a mere theory of course. It must, but much of that theory is informed by further dealings with, and observations of Ruthven himself. While I do believe some form of psychosis existed in comorbidity with his base affliction, I strongly suspect the origins of his initial cravings to have been genuinely marked by a bodily deficiency which was merely amplified in function due to the specific outcomes of his exposure.

Furthermore I have seen the limited extent of mutative properties capable within my blood's nature beyond Ruthven, and can thus conclude that his gained ability and functions were driven not by any neurological proclivity, so much as some specific difference to his physiology which predated exposure, allowing my blood to act as a catalyst to natures already present within him long before we had ever crossed paths.

Whatever psychological repercussions there were to this originally, I feel chiefly to have been a result of his actions rather than the drive to commit them. As these were calmed rather than exaggerated by the healing capabilities of his bite to me, and even persistent in bodily compulsions at his weakest states, never returned with the same detriment as what had been prior. It is undoubtable to my personal opinion, that the cyclical nature of his mania itself was not only predictably caused by a physical defalcation, but in fact temporarily sated by the actions which he took as a result. So long as those particular needs were satisfied, Ruthven's health remained stable both of mind and body.

DM: So, you obviously suspect something akin to a metabolic myopathy. I see particularly you have L- Carinitine deficiency underlined next to pellagra and Lactate dehydrogenase deficiency, but erythropoietic porphyria is further down the list. Why that order?

Doctor Malcom seemed to recover quickly from his embarassment the more he spoke of the topic at hand.

AG: Ah, over the many years following the previously described account, I studied Ruthven's dietary habits as well as the time periods in which he seemed most peaceable and subdued. If porphyria had been the chief culprit, then his bodily reactions to garlic would have amplified his thirsts rather than suppress them, also his aversions to sunlight and the localisation of rashes observed, lended to these hypothesis along with several other factors.

DM: Interesting... interesting... Then what can you tell me about those dietary habits and cycles?

AG: His cycles, by my best observations, involved predictably intense agitations and short temperedness as described previously, coupled with difficulties of communication including slurred speech and poor execution of actions, weakness, fatigue, vomiting, confusion, behaviors as if he were inebriated when he was not, complaints of pain to his neck, lower back and hips et cetera. There was also the greater photosensitivty to his eyes and body.

During these times he would drink great quantities of milk and eat of raw garlic, both of which seemed to afford him some measure of temporary relief to those mental deficiencies. He also seemed unable to resist strong peppers and vinegars, which eased his bodily pains. However chief amongst all of these was the consumption of red meats, often raw, and the drinking of blood both animal and human, after which he would return to seemingly perfect health and mind.

DM: And the photosensitivity, you described him behaving as if the light drained him of energy, but not actually causing burns or lesions correct?

AG: Yes. Outwardly the sun seemed to cause no harm to his skin in the early days. Yet his direct exposure to it seemed both painful and debilitating all the same, particularly affecting his eyesight at times. I learned that this, over time increasing, left him nearly blinded in whole by days light.

DM: I will definitely be looking into this. I have a few other thoughts, but I can start with the analysis as soon as I get back to the lab if that's what you really want. Were there any signs akin to dehydration that accompanied his symptoms? The appearance of hair growth or visible receding of his gums, or maybe elongation of his fingernails?

AG: Both. Also his injuries would bleed less the longer it had been since he'd fed.

DM: Do you have a time frame? Or should I hold off until after these interviews are all finished?

AG: Afterward would be fine. It should be easier to do while I am present for any further samples needed.

DM: I agree... I can't believe you have me even considering this... A medical explanation for the vampire myth is insane, but you may be onto something.

AG: Insanity perhaps, or as I feel, simply the extension of logic and science applied to historical misconceptions.

I watched the two men talk with a complete lack of input to contribute on the topic, but other questions swirled and circled in my head all the same. When it seemed like they had reached a pause to their conversation I eagerly asked the first of these.

CR: On another note, Adam you seem very adamant to refuse Ruthven's proposal even though it could have meant freedom and companionship for yourself. Why?

AG: Why did I not entertain the thought of subjugating others under the guise of mankinds betterment? Miss Reynolds I am surprised you would ask such a thing.

CR: I am a journalist. Of course I'm going to ask.

AG: Fair as that is, I would think you know enough of me to determine the answer for yourself.

CR: Maybe, but it would be irresponsible of me to put words into your mouth. I'd like to hear it from you. Do you not hate people or feel like they should be better? Do you not feel like you could have helped to persuade them to act less selfishly or to reduce the motivations of greed and wealth? Ruthven's idea might have ended war and poverty like he said. How do you reconcile with those emotions?

Adam paused to think.

AG: How might I express this most succinctly? First of note perhaps should be that I do not consider it morally or ethically prudent to force upon others, those behaviors or actions that they had not decided upon within themselves. Freedom above all, to follow one's heart and mind toward genuine action and the pursuit of personal authenticity, is a value I hold more dear than even their goodness and consideration of others. If one's private will is to be usurped, even under pretense for the greater good, then with it goes any illusion of this.

It is my wholehearted belief that mankind cannot be forced to behave admirably in my mind, or all admirable result would fail in import. Their actions would become a mere echo of their masters... and growth removed, stagnation of true progress would result. One should not anticipate a betterment of internal condition by diminishment of choice, nomatter the external change it forces. Personal choice is the requisite of personal responsibility and vice versa in turn.

Ruthven may have been capable of forcing others to behave better toward one another for a time, but by what measure in this world should humanity be reduced to automaton in their actions? Would it truly remain humanity for all mankind to hold bound by the constraint of anothers will, behaving as kind slave to choices beyond their control? No. I reject this now as I did then. No matter what ill or even dispicable behaviors any man engages, or lessening of his burden to follow blindly, they are his to commit and in his beliefs to justify as it is in his responsibility to face their consequence.

People as a whole might appear monolithic as sheep to be herded for lack of seeming thought and individuality, but that itself is a lie. I would not make the world to cattle simply for satisfaction of my own ideals without forsaking those ideals at their very core. And who then would it be determined could lie worthy of such control? Even a blameless and selfless god, should not unspool the quality of mans free will, and Ruthven was none of these.

He like all others, including myself, was a mercurial and flawed individual even disregarding his self entitled feign to righteousness. He was a murderer and predator, a parasite even; Who labeled himself as deserving for no reason aside from his disdain and intolerance of what he perceived personally as wrongdoings. Even in agreement with some values he did profess, intolerance itself is the marker of corruption and vanity.

Mankind is flawed and I would beg of Doctor Malcom's input to this further, as I feel he and I share certain perspectives in this regard which may better illuminate within your transcriptions the nature of my words for your reader.

Even in my judgement of others Miss Reynolds, I consider it my own failing to accept at times those traits which I find distasteful, as I am not better nor is anyone better than their neighbors, even when we feel it just to assume.

Doctor, Speak true, have you not hated others for their small mindedness at times? Punished yourself for feeling judgemental ire toward them only to turn from that within your heart and work tirelessly to benefit them as a whole? And should someone pose to you that ability to change that nature of man, to make them think as yourself, would you then agree?

Is it not owed to them the choice?

Steven looked stunned to be put on the spot, and rubbed his chin before answering. He sighed.

DM: Yeah... umm... Wow, that's a heavy fucking question. *He chuckled.* I get it. I mean I've noticed a few things where I agree that you and I might be very alike, and I've had those questions too. I know I'm gonna paint myself into a corner here but he's right Cass. You're right Dude. I don't want to be a judgmental dick, but I sometimes hate people as much as I care about them.... It feels like I'm just watching a bunch of sheep who cant think for themselves... and I blame them for it. I judge them for not taking the time to *think.*

Maybe it would be better if everyone were on the same page and nobody had to consider the consequences of their actions. But ultimately questions of what we *can* do and what we *should* do require a deep dive into our own beliefs and choices, not some new law or king telling us what to think. It's hard work. It's a lot of hard work.

People like you or me, or Adam here, may not always realize that sometimes, and it's hard for us to accept, for *me* to accept, drives me a bit nuts to be honest, but that's because I don't think I have the ability to turn it off or put it away like that, and so I never stop. Not everyone is geared the same.

It's not because they're stupid or intellectually incapable, at least not all of them I hope, and I've thought about why a lot. Do I believe people are so selfish or lazy or greedy as a whole? No, not like some people might I guess. I think that people go along with whats presented to them because they just don't have the options, energy, endurance or personal drive to tackle all of life's bigger issues on top of the day to day worries that fill up the rest of their lives ya know?

The effort to avoid discomfort is natural, and yeah maybe I see that as a failing, maybe I see it as a weakness, but you know as well as anyone, that to choose the alternate path is to choose struggle over and over again. It hurts; that questioning, the confusion, the disappointment, and ultimately the choices, because it means taking on responsibility for all of yourself... but removing that? No I mean come on... Even if they wanted it, Even if people by the millions people stood up and said "Make my choices for me", that's a terrible way for anyone to learn. It would stop progress, not drive it.

Yeah a lot of people take the easier way. They satisfy themselves with the comfort of someone else telling them what is right or good, how they should behave, what actions they should take, whether that be a religious doctrine, a political view, a leader, or maybe a social trend where they can put their faith. They take their cues and follow what gives them comfort, try to feel better by choosing one or two things they can handle thinking about or taking action on to do the minimal amount of good that lets them sleep at night. Then they escape with distractions to keep themselves from facing the never ending pain of bigger and harder questions or truths. It's just how they make it through the day... But does that mean they should be deprived of the choice? How could I think less of them for that, or wish anyone to be forced?

Look I don't remember the actual distances, but the general idea is the same regardless. Pavlov tried this thing right. If you put a steak in a dog bowl twenty feet away, but then put plain dry dog food in a bowl five feet away, the dog will eat all of the dry food first almost every time. He wasn't looking to uncover some secret truth about dogs alone, he was studying base behavioral trends that might apply to people too... and I think that they do. Is that disappointing?

Maybe... but the average person is just average because they feel average. They don't want the weight of the world or feel like they could carry it if it were on their shoulders. They have enough. They turn away from the extra responsibility in favor of the feel good, easy, answer because its the closer bowl.

Everything is basically path of least resistance. Which bowl is closer? Which option takes the least effort with the quickest gratification? Is there a price attached to one over the other? How can I avoid the shock, no matter how minor it might be? Ruthven even is doing the same thing there. He's looking for the easy fix to a problem which is tantamount to human growth.

Some of us will do the opposite thing. That's always held true. We'll walk the extra distance for something more, something better, push thru the shock even if it becomes paralyzing, do the work, carry the weight, and then wonder why the people around us are hanging back... but what kind of person would I be if I couldn't get over my petty little resentments of them for it or I thought it was within my purview to change them against or without their will?

The choice is what matters. Right? Dude you gotta tell me if I'm even on the same subject here. Sorry, that was a tangent.

AG: No, that was very in line with the topic I feel. Would you agree Miss Reynolds?

I stared blankly with my mouth hanging open searching for appropriate words before I could answer them.

CR: I think that's probably more than enough for an answer to my question. Are you sure, you two arent the ones related?

Both men chuckled nervously and looked toward the floor at the same time.

CR: Ok then, ignoring that. I'm assuming from what you said of your chance to study his behaviors that you and Ruthven crossed paths again.

A PROLONGED COURTSHIP

AG: Yes. After I had fled from him and returned to my home, it is true that I did not see Ruthven for some time, but that did not mean that I forgot or ignored the severity of his shadow. In fact I took great pains to follow any news of his person wherever I could, especially upon his returns to Britain.

Years in fact passed, and while I noted for that time the isolation of my own activities, I uncovered regularly the documentation of Lord Ruthven's social reputations as reported by gossips and listings within the papers and gazettes which circulated those english written periodicals which found themselves within the borders of Germany. In truth, so many well to do travellers from abroad frequented by this time the scenic venues and summer homes within our countryside, that upon their departures, it proved quite simple to rummage the discarded belongings left behind and procure by consequence great volumes of information such as this.

Still I too wished to travel once more. Discovering one such trove of literary treasures along with several letters of correspondence, I had been stricken to read the words of a woman that came by my possession, and found within them such prolific challenges to thought that they evoked within me the provocations of delightful considerations which I compared easily to Voltaire or Paine themselves, both of which had passed by that year. It was with great dismay I learned also of her passing, but by chance in these correspondence that I obtained knowledge of her family, who seemed at greatest pleasures the epitome of forward thought and grace.

However within those same correspondence and some further revelations, I deciphered with concerned heart the involvement of their household with that of Lord Ruthven himself. As within my mind it became clear that he had held some hand in several tragedies surrounding them, I made intentions then to visit and observe that family remaining of the writer whom I so admired in Somerstown. There I decided at the least I might shield those souls further from his intrusions, as surely they seemed the like precisely of what prey Ruthven fashioned preferable to himself.

I did not acquit my new abode easily mind you, nor with light heart approach the task of such. As I understood all too well what risk of exposure it would bring should my old acquaintance detect my presence. However moved deeply by feelings of connection with those peoples, I could not idly sit in saftey while one of my own responsibility continued to plague and feed from their livelihoods. So I shut up my doors, loosed my animals upon the land and prepared departure carrying only what neccesities I felt required for the journey. So that came to pass and in the year of 1804, I travelled once more to Britain.

Habit had taken me by then to secure these travels easily and without suspicion by others to a point that I enjoyed the endeavors of sailing and trekking over distance, but upon arrival to the shores I had known before, I was taken aback at the sight of change which brought with it a greater level of challenge to the continual circumstances of secrecy I required. Lights now filled areas once shadowed in night. People moved at all times along the streets. Even in earliest of morning, the task of veiling myself became near impossible to achieve, and more than once upon my endeavor I was met again with terrible encounter and violence which directed fearful stranger against me.

Had I lived so long in solitude and peace that now the most basic of mankinds vitriol left me shocked? Or had the whole of Britain somehow become more calllousedd toward their fellow beings? I did not know. Simply put, the cities themselves had become rank with the scenery of despair, and despite all written proclamations that inspired hope from afar, I was twisted in twine by the disturbing presence of disregard for even the common decencies once afforded between neighboring strangers. I was pelted with trash and refuse from windows above, chased by lantern and gunfire, even at one point stabbed by the knife of a child as I retreated through an open alley past the burning fires of the poor.

Such was the condition, that by my arrival in Somerstown, I found myself shaken and filth covered, leaning to wash my body and face near a lake... There then, was when a young girl approached my sight, running with tears that stained her face, not *from* my presence but toward me instead. She darted behind my crouched body and utilizing it as a blind, leaned fearfully her face to search for any pursuer. I saw none who followed, and in fright I stayed dreadfully still for fear of her reaction to my person when she might be bothered to observe further *this* visage,

Adam moved his hand over his face, seemingly forgetting in the moment that the dyes within his body remained, leaving him not his usual self, but instead the more normative in complexion and appearance to a person of average sight.

but soon I realized in that state, her rigid and frightened form felt to relax, even as she slowly emerged from hiding to stand at height directly before me.

"Thank you sir giant." She said meekly, wiping the tears from her face. "I did not mean to intrude."

I felt a catch in my throat by stunned emotion as I almost teared to be treated thus after that which I most recently endured.

"Are you not frightened child?" I asked.

"Not of you sir." She sniffled. "I am running from home. My brother and sister have been cruel to me and I cannot bear them more."

The girl was near seven or eight. Her flowing brown hair and deep dark eyes stood starkly against her pale skin, and she was dressed most plainly in a long but pristine set of skirts and coat. Quietly she looked at me with bemusement, even smiling, she brushed my hair from my face and wiped away a tear which I had unknowingly shed down the side of my cheek. She called me odd, but not insultingly, and soon after began to regale me of the story which led her to run from her siblings.

They were named Charles and Claire, but were not her true siblings she swore. They were the children of her stepmother, and blamed her for what they had done to a woman named Louisa, who seemed by her story to be a housekeeper which they had pranked most innocently before placing the account on the young girls shoulders. Her name she told me... was Mary, and in short time I discerned truthfully that this child was one of the very family whom I had come to shield from my former acquaintance.

Adam's voice cracked and choking back tears he continued almost reverently to describe these events.

Her mother had been the writer Mary Wollstonecraft whom I had so admired, but the child herself was surnamed Godwin, and by length of her professing tongue, she blamed herself for her mother's death as well as her father's financial woes, claiming that if not for her he would never have been forced to marry again and bind her so woefully to those siblings who now troubled her.

I questioned these assertions of guilt and attempted reason as she described to me such things as clearly no fault or control might have owed to her their responsibilities. However as children oft will, she persisted in assumption of her centrality to them until at last I conceded merely to comfort her with repeated gesture rather than to convince her otherwise.

Through all of this, young Mary was so incredibly gracious to me as to not once react with fear or apprehension at my presence. She cried and professed her heart's deepest of troubles while I attempted to ease her mind. Until by release of these thoughts, she teased at my hair and pawed at my face with innocent delight, even urging me to make faces at her while she returned in kind the laughter and play of her age. Now lighted from worry, this playful encounter continued until at long length by the setting of the sun and scarcely broken conversations, until she had fallen asleep upon my lap, gripping so tightly to my coat that she nearly wrapped it round herself in slumber.

Still, sitting quietly there, I heard at some distance the movement of several others as her name was repeatedly called in search. She did not wake as I stood, and walking gently through the edge of shadows where I could, I approached the borders of a garden where I placed the sleeping child upon a bench to be found by those who cared for her.

Years later Mary would reveal to me that she thought I had been a dream or imagining. So often she had spoken of me to others that they did not believe her, and so in time also she had assumed our day together to be a child's figment of fancy during emotional moments, but no such questions existed within myself. Not in the many years to follow did she understand until much later, after our genuine knowledge of one another, the threat which hovered over that scene... For turning to walk from where I had placed her, Ruthven indeed stepped out from shadow to reveal himself present.

"Pretty pity friend. You must have known I would feel you here." He said. "Why do you intercede in the affairs of this family?"

I stopped. "I should ask the same of you with warning before you reply. Any harm you bring to these people shall result in your destruction should you continue." I told him.

"Walk with me." He asked flatly.

There he moved and I followed within the shaded moonlight of Somerstown gardens. "You know my quarry as I have told days before Adam. These people are of little vice and no concern to me. The father has paid his debts and I confess I hold no further interest to them now that the mother has gone. Her words alone intrigued me such. yet now without her, should you wish to guard them so, I will nary intrude with exception to my interests in you. So again I ask what brings you here so far from your Frankenstein abode. I should ask however how castle life finds you these days, for I know that area which you haunt in ironic concealment." He spoke.

In truth I learned by this the limits of Ruthven's detection of my presence. Surely he had sought after me following our last encounter, and in vain been incapable of isolating my whereabouts beyond the castles location. Just as the compass spins upon certain surroundings to that place, he too had lost trail of me, and now baiting for information looked to entrap further knowledge from my own lips.

"Well enough that I keep to my own." I replied. "Though *your* company it seems so well documented *Lord* Ruthven. Have care you might toward such publicity, should someone in time notice your ageless truth." I returned.

He raised an eyebrow at me, and I felt at once for it to be the most telling expression of change which he had expressed thus far. "Fearing that thru me you might be discovered old friend? Have no concern toward this. All control aside, none look to note such things in the frivolous circles of aristocracy. Would that I could remain eons undetected and all to their discernment would be praise of my fortunate health and blessings. I am patient by measures untold, and without you have none that suspect the illustrious name and title of my person toward any more than mine mysterious bachelorhood which baffles their senses." He dismissed.

"And shall I, who know you alone, have cause to fear another attack should I refuse your previous offers?" I inquired.

"Patience does have its limits old friend. I give you time to see my way as righteous, but should you prove bothersome, this too will pass from me and know in truth I shall have what I desire by any means. For now however, I bid you stay. Protect this family as you will and in knowing one another's nearness we may both keep watchful eye until that day comes. Would you join me for dinner if asked?"

I knew in his sentiments some ulterior motives must be their cause, yet I could not detect them by such short interactions, and so I agreed to his invitation and followed Ruthven toward a carriage which then escorted us away until we had reached his lands. Even entering and seated to dine, with every word within his presence I searched for clues of what intentions he held, and still could not determine them. Yet with each response of my own, I remained careful to navigate as one sails over treacherous waters.

It was horrid to bear the sight and service of those who waited upon us that night, as even the setting of the table itself was performed by others seemingly mindless to our presence while they carried out each task. All within those walls and even to the greater properties whom Ruthven employed, were not by silence alone marked, but indeed driven forward without waking consciousness of action, the vision of animated matter whose souls had lost ownership upon the flesh. I saw among many the signs of teeth and bites partly healed where he had eaten and drank from their persons, but pain or acknowledgement showed neither to them as thoughtlessly, wordlessly, they stood nearby with vacant gazes.

I spoke to him without question of this, and observed without contestation, though sickened within, I witnessed as the subtleties by which he revelled in that sense of control. My questions pried closer to what weaknesses and strengths he possessed and in due course managed to appeal to that pride which would see them each demonstrated to me without fear.

As observed before, I was shown again the speeds of his movement when chosen, but also witnessed the faltering energies that followed. I saw his commandment over his servants, which extended even to his mercy the threat of their own life without question or knowledge, but took count of what limits he could extend this by inquiry of his staff's number and duties in line with how he came about their replacement when needed.

Where once he could control only two or three at a time, now he boasted of forty, but by slip of tongue revealed the nature of their enthrallment required that he feed to them his own blood, and that their release while he travelled brought with it such "disappointment" to him. For without continual replacement, the longevity of these effects waned temporary to merely a fortnight or less before replenishment proved neccesary.

I asked what methods he employed to disguise the lost time of their days when this occurence transpired, and to further dread learned that such expiration came mortal upon them for if continued beyond that length of time. Their bodies began to decay as if dead, and upon release even within this span, those of his employ would often suffer madness afterward with no cure. These "unfortunate" circumstances he utilized as reason not to cease his actions of course, but to beg my assistance in extension so that such "neccesities" could be avoided altogether.

Purposely again I stayed until daybreak so that I might guage his responses to sunlight once more, and as such when time approached, I was entreated to observe that by his own volition, Ruthven did step outside of his doors to escort me to the waiting carriage whose coachmen sat stiff and had remained stationary throughout the night. His steps forced as they were and with visible effort, proved to me two qualities of import. Firstly that it was not impossible for him to bear the brightness of day in totality, but secondly the tolls which it took upon him in equal time, as I saw his composure weaken and energies decrease, even by that short walk in dawns early glow.

Departing politely, I felt unequalled the relief to leave that man's presence and thereafter shuddered at the thought of what he had done to so many poor men and women already. No matter the cost to myself, I knew certain the absoluteness of my resolve that I would never concede to his wants of me, and in truth deduced likelihood that the only end to his horrors and deeds would come by death alone.

This troubled me of course, not only by the thought of killing the man himself, but by equal measure my lack of knowledge in how to carry forth such a task while his healing, strength and speed might match or exceed my own. This of course is not to speak of what innocents he might employ at his disposal to stave any attack or even the protection afforded by his notoriety. I knew not how to stop him in truth, but he was correct in one regard.

Should I remain the protector of the family whom I had come to see originally, our presences to one another would in fact remain known and with watchful eyes we could avoid that surprise which ignorance makes capable, should the other move without knowledge against us. However this I feared still a trap somehow, and despite my temptations toward such action, I chose instead to return once more to my wooded cottage near the castle of my birth, where I would remain uninterrupted for twelve more years. All the while knowing Ruthven's transgressions and growing power, allowing them to persist and doing naught to stop him, I retreated from the world and planned for the day I might face him once more.

THE SUMMER WITHOUT A SUMMER

CR: Twelve years is a long time to watch from a distance.

DM: Fuck that, twelve years is a long time to wait while you know what's happening.

AG: Yes, but twelve years is also enough time to orchestrate a noblemen's downfall with purposed movement. It is no small marvel to me the impacts of the written word alone, and in anonymity that which may be accomplished through the selective spread of rumor and misinformation.

So many letters I wrote during those years to cast suspicion upon Ruthven from afar, utilizing the languages of business and gossip. Bit by bit his estates were dismantled, his power usurped and even at last, the word of his untimely death was spread across Europe until all vestiges of his former luxury were ruin upon the earth, until at last I feared he would come for me, seeking shelter from what remained.

Yet also in this time so much else had transpired unbeknownst to my person, that I could not anticipate the changes of life to follow. For part I knew of the wars which had ravaged much of Europe as well as the Americas and beyond. I knew of the changes in politic and thought. I followed the news of advancements in industry and technological progress, but not the private lives of the young girl whom I had met by the lake that day in Somerstown, or her family. She had grown. Her stations amongst the society of her birth changed and with them much scandal accompanied. The affair with the married poet Percy Shelley cost her much, including the closeness between her father and herself, but to this I was unaware.

There is a great deal to be said and written regarding those events, however to my knowledge at the time, I would not encounter these themself so much as to become entangled in the consequences of them after the fact. No, when I first saw her once more, she had already eloped with Percy and travelling along with others, had taken tour of the Rhine which led her nearest to my own doorstep. This time and her accompaniment filled with rumor the countryside gossips and tabloid, even before her arrival, and at those I finally took note once more of the recognized name and heritage of that strangely beautiful creature.

I saw her at a distance on such fateful day as if by destiny. I had been walking nearby the castle's garden in search of herbs you see. That was when she came with others to view the sight of my conception unknowingly. Instantly I was entranced, but further still as curiosity spurred me to follow their party from that place forward, I traced their paths, leaving behind my own worries of home while they travelled also to the lands and cottage I had shared with my father, along with many other placements which I had seen and known before. I was transfixed by her sight and that of her lovers, as I observed quite clearly the interactions between the party to note active relations between several of them as such to be just that.

Days of distant examination told to me that Percy shared his bed with Mary herself, Claire her sister, and to my surprised impressment, his most recent entanglement Claire's lover Byron as well. Mary in turn also shared bed with Claire in addition to Percy, and though seemingly participant in many dalliances outside of this, seemed content with the presence of those two alone. Whose child she carried by then or whose son aside from her own clung to her hip was unclear to me for certain, but credit given to Percy as the father seemed due and sensible given the circumstance.

After the first of their tours which I observed following carriage, foot, and floating vessels along rivers edge, the group was joined still by others and settled themselves near Geneva in division of two villas of shared estate along the shores of a scenic lake outside the village of Cologny. Despite this and excessive time more spent upon the water in small boats, also interspersed by walks near the shore, the rains of that season often meant that the group remained cloistered as it were within the walls of these buildings, and would have been lost to my sight had I not dared to approach closer to peer through their very windows.

Understand that I know the transgression of this and though privacy concerned me not by that age, I am aware of the improprieties of such actions by any other standard. However then, I saw no harm in observing these moments of other's lives as I had never myself known the true inclusion of social interactions with so many at once. Over a month passed this way, and I witnessed much. My animals left to fend for themselves and cottage abandoned such time prior, I felt no shame or doubt that I should return in due course to correct all left untended, but for that time, I was drawn to stay and to follow these beautiful young friends without full understanding of why.

Claire, the sister of Mary, lover of Byron and of Percy, was beginning to show signs that she was with child. Byron, who I found to be both beautiful yet arrogant, took this news indignantly as the would be father, and behaved ill toward her afterward less passions or inebriation moved him otherwise. The physician Polidori who accompanied them, seemed primarily entranced by the fellowship of Percy and Byron themselves rather than Mary or Claire, and the women while not tending the children or engaged otherwise with the men, shared deep and passioned love for one another.

For his part Byron was a boastful and conceited man of brilliant tongue and fierce argument, but his treatment of young Polidori who adored him so, proved crueller to me than even that of Claire who loved him firstly. The party of them enthralled my curiosity the like of which I had never seen, to reject with such ire the conventions of society and within their own form anew, indulge those strange and wonderful bonds in defiance of the world around them.

Scarcely could I fathom the change from that little girl I had once met, to see firsthand and feel arise within myself the urges of such passion. Yet it occurred to me the freeness of love given was not contradictory to how fondly I had once been treated without judgement by her. Having watched voyeuristically many a night by then as Mary's sleep had been disturbed often in nightmare and unspoken terror, I took it upon myself on the most fateful of occasion to enter her room with simple intention to comfort her thrashing woes without waking her from slumber. Had this been the child so kind to me? Kneeling beside her bed, I did nothing more than stroke her hair and speak gently in that darkness, but felt her reach for my hand in peaceful thanks. For several nights this repeated itself after all others had turned from that space, and for several nights Mary continued to sleep unknowing of my company.

Adam sighed heavily.

It is perverse for me to consider now the lengths of intrusion I dared take. I was no less than a stalker to so many over my years, yet without relationships to bind me to those proprieties of human interaction, I was more a creature still than man in spite of my minds keen awareness.

But then of course, there came the contest. Fuelled by the smoke of opium and dryness of drink which they often engaged, each among these young libertines it seemed were all writers in their own light; and storytellers as they will, do love the sharing of such things between themselves almost as freely as the love for affectionate lusts and bodily pleasures I might note.

Of course by instigative quality Byron I believe was the one to propose the challenge that came. In hindsight the simple events of that night have become legend by Mary's own account, but it remained a small thing then, that after so many ghostly tales of horror spent by firelight to entertain one another, an idea was posed that each there present, should create and write an original work of that genre which might thrill and provoke the others.

Since that time, many have speculated and written of this contest of talents so humbly began in what has been labelled the year without a summer, there by that lakeshore in Geneva. And through it all I have been not participant, nor known as more than the subject of fictitious story woven as result. Even in my strangest moments I too have wondered at times if Mary did somehow conjure me to being, complete with memory and life before this, for to myself, all which preceded, all I had ever known, might be equal to nothingness if not for the awakening she crafted within this heart.

From that challenge of friends however, I truly began you see. I found courage to reveal myself at last to the girl who had once welcomed my presence without fear. For in listening to the tales that each spun, and even those read from "Fantasmagoriana", I observed that Mary in particular remained near fearless at even the most disturbing concepts of each. In fact for every single horror presented in all of that time, she discussed afterward with curiosity and calmness the explorations of theme and detail which might reveal some deeper truth to human nature or mans philosophies.

The girl, now a woman who I learned with sorrow had lost a child not long before, spurned by her beloved father for affair with one of his very followers, lover of a sister, and mother of an infant son, daughter of one of the greatest philosophers I had yet to read in all of my own pursuits, was truly fearless to any earthly concept save that of societies chains themselves, and I thought in foolishness perhaps, but hope none the less, that here was a heart who unlike any other, might care to know without shock or horror that very story of my own existence. Not in part, but full, should I only but risk revelation of myself to her glorious mind.

So again after all others had departed and Mary readied herself for sleep, I crept quietly through her open window, even as the rains began once more outside. Standing within the movement of curtains my body trembled nervously. I was so afraid. Then a flash of lightning turned her attention, and with a brush still in hand at motion within her long and beautiful hair, I watched in frozen dread to move, as she faced my hideous sight at long last.
In this moment of truth and monumental change to myself and all that would follow however, she did not recoil as any other might have to face such intrusion by my horrid appearance, but instead that angel, that glorious wonder of wonders... She smiled so sweetly with excited recognition of my face and form, that to this day I melt at the memory, a grateful shadow of gratitudes impossible to speak in word.

"You?" She whispered in pleasant awe. "Should dreams come so easily that I do not know when I have passed to slumber then?"

I stepped forward cautiously, though my legs as lead, felt weighted to that floor, the flame of lantern flickering from nearby, I dared to speak. "No dream my lady. You remember me?" I asked quietly with shaking voice.

"Of course Ishould remember you. My dear giant; you who have been the dreams of my nightly protection these last weeks, the savior of childhood troubles and imaginary companion upon shores of youth. Dreams are thus and beautiful that you should join me now as if by waking hour." She smiled once more, reaching toward my hand and beckoning me to take her own, even as our first touch surprised her so.

"But I feel you sir..." She whispered. "How can this be? What drink of this evening produces so real the fantasies of my mind that I should brush such touch my very dreams?"

Kneeling before her I confess without shame the tears that welled and fell from my eyes wordlessly, as even then Mary, my sweet and lasting beloved, cupped my face within her hands in pity and to my astonishment placed her lips over mine in the first kiss I had ever known. My heart and soul nearly breaking into splinters, I all but collapsed entirely from overwhelming sensations such as I had never known before.

The touch and affectionate softness of her gift to me lingered in magical bliss and equalled painfully a shameful unworthiness within my heart as our lips parted, and she looked into my eyes. I saw her face by that glow as the single framing of image that will always and forever remain my first thought of her to this very day, and such abiding love did fill me then, that I swam deep the warm darkness of those eyes, plunged as if drowning with no care to fight the depths overwhelming, even as they beheld me at closeness with carefilled grace.

I wept. So profusely I wept that Mary herself, now removed

from her seat did kneel to match me and embraced my body firmly as if I were her own child, until at long last my sobs subsided, having soaked her night clothing and chest. When this had passed she sat back and lifted my chin by the delicacy of her fingers to look toward me once more in my eye before speaking, and thus began our acquaintance.

I noticed while Adam said this, an unexpected sight from the corner of my own eye.

CR: Steven are you crying?

He was. Even on the recording it's very clear to see the tears that ran down his cheeks while he listened.

DM: Shut up. Adam don't stop. Please.

AG: Yes well, that night Mary sat with me without question or further word until by the sound of stirring outside of her room the following morning, I moved to take my leave... but in this motion incomplete, she reached for me and stopped my hand.

"Do not depart once more sir Giant, return to me that I may know your secrets and rest by such comfort that shall keep them." She pleaded gently.

"The others... I cannot." I began. "Seeing me, they will not entreat my presence as you. By night I shall return and ask as your will requests if only unchanged it be... then I shall tell you." I replied with quivering voice before continuing my leave. Her fingers trailed from my hand and I left that room to wonder the rise of the sun while rains still fell.

None that day did leave the walls of that place to seek enjoyment, and very close I stayed to its shadows, sitting long the hours of day beneath shelter of a nearby pavillion of sorts, I paced and worried, sat and considered such combinations of joy and fright that I felt nearly converted into two seperate persons, the happy at heart as one, matched and at war within the suspicious and terrified other.

Which side of myself did win would be impossible to say. Yet by evening I returned, half prepared in will to reveal my past, unknowing of the response I might receive, still filled with thoughts from each internal voice. Mary stood wait for this and upon entry I was embraced once more by her arms.

"Nameless sir, how I have longed this day to see you once more by each telling of the hour! I could not explain the distance I felt from the vitalities of my company and yet Claire, my sister knows well enough the look of my distractions if not their source." Mary gushed. I observed then the basinet nearby and frightened at the prospect of disturbing the infant, I stood startled in quiet.

Before even the telling of my life that night, we sat upon the floor of that room and Mary gifted me once more with that which brought tears to my eyes and joy to my being as with careful instruction and softness, she allowed me not only to look upon the child, but beseeched me to hold him in my arms.

Having in my hundred plus years of life never touched the fingers nor toes of one so young nor frail, I could not refuse such kindness or refute the impact of its miracle when he grasped at my hair with such tiny hands force, that I giggled at him adoringly. He in turn looked upon my face with laughter his own, and I was most joyously baffled.

"His name is William" Mary told me. "after my father and brother. A sister Clara passed before his birth, but he is my joy in that sorrow... Dear sir, your tears do not fall on blindness to what pains you might have seen, for I too understand loss and shame and though I know not your stories, I recognize those traits within you unhealed. Have you a name that I might introduce you by?"

I stammered. "Adam... Some have called me Adam before." I told her quietly.

"Adam." She repeated with softness. "William, meet Adam." She smiled, while leaning to kiss the babe within my arms before taking him gently from me once again to rise and place him back within his beddings comfort. "Now then sir Adam." She whispered, taking seat before me once more with a straightening of her night clothes over folded leg. "You promised to tell me of yourself. Who my dreamed protector, is the man Adam which ageless from the day last seen, comes so secretly to comfort my woes by night?"

I hardly knew where to start, but in time that very evening, without aside of philosophies or sciences which we have discussed, I found able myself to reveal those histories by which you have also now been apprised. Mary listened to my words with enthralled curiosity, but also such expressions of sorrow and sympathy at times that many an instance passed while tears filled her own eyes, where she took my hand in comfort. At other times when I had begun to cry myself, she reached for my person gently to bring my head onto her that I might weep openly as she stroked my hair and encouraged that my words continue. For by her professions that she was there and all would be alright, I felt safe.

By the light of morning my tale had finished and I meant to away once more if not for Mary's insistences and profession of neccesity to her very happiness that begged me to stay.

A TALE TWICE TOLD

We could hear the stirring sounds of others beyond the door and fearful I remained as Mary then attempted to persuade me that I should reveal myself to them, not only in sight, but to repeat the details which she had been told, that they too may know the wonders and wretchedness of my past. When I asked her why I would do such thing she replied that "Percy and Claire I swear would embrace you for these with such compassion toward those woes that love compelled. They will take you as our own as you have stirred my heart Adam. Please trust this. Even the physician of Polidori with such keenness of knowledge may bring understanding to what and how you are before me and him too I trust!" She insisted.

"And Byron?" I asked. " He who rejected your sister so coldly and mocks that man who trails his steps in admiration; Would you ask too that I entrust my safety to he, despite the afflictions of my person, to give freely an openness to assault from such a crude and volatile specter?" I asked her.

"Trust not in Byron perhaps then, for he is as you say. But trust in me in his stead. For I trust he should hold to that which he values above all else, the professions of his own greatness and indifference to worldly convention, which you to him shall represent in whole of being the proof of his assertions against. He will be astonished by thee and in self ennoblement unable to concede otherwise the truth of his baseness, keep the secret of you for vain pride alone of that knowledge no others possess beyond us." She asserted with consideration.

"Why?" Again I asked. "Why should I expose my person to

those who might harm me or sever by their choices the peace I find in your company?"

"Because dear Giant, of the peace I find in yours Adam. I wish you to stay... and to do so unseparated from my family and loves. Hearing of you is to know such wonder in this world a person of so great a strength to have suffered your life, yet with tenderness and beauty remain in goodness, a virtue unseen yet rejected by others mistreatment carry a soul worthy of my love. I wish their acceptance of you that you might remain with me, not secreted by night, but shielded in our private communities of more than these small hours, so that I can be with you longer and they shall share in my grown affections for your presence... I know what risk I ask of you, I do by understanding know. One who having been spurned and outcast by so many for your entire existence, that trust in such bonds seems impossible. Yet by faith in who I know them to be, I swear if you should face these risks then rewards you cannot yet conceive will meet you for that bravery."

I was unable to refuse her, not for the desire or hope matched in what faith she held of her consorts, but for want of pleasing her alone I conceded to remain. While she prepared justly for these revelations in advance, to gather the others and forewarn them of my presence as well as appearance before coming to retrieve me from that room, I agreed to stay and follow thru with her plans.

Further for assurances in case her beliefs in the company she kept proved unfounded, she insisted for my own protection against any unpredictable shocks that might follow, I must enter she directed, clearly holding young William within my arms. For none might shout or act in violence while I sheltered the form of a babe near my person, and this would prove me both gentle and loving by nature she argued.

With those motives Mary departed and I stayed, awaiting her return that she might bring me forth to that waiting audience. The thought to flee that place back through the open window occurred many times during this and though I did not, fear gripped most fiercely at my heart in disbelief of man's goodness so present beyond one person of beautious exception. Even as the door was opened, I heard the voice of Byron from the further room in wicked jest.

"Tasked with the creation of horror, she crafts instead some pantomime and staged play" He laughed. "Only a womans imaginings would indulge such. Who then shall play this disfigured creature you speak? Your beloved sister who stands by in wait while we..." Byron's voice trailed upon my exit of Mary's chamber into full view upon the upper landing. "My word! No game has she lied" He whispered in awe from below.

Polidori gasped, even as Mary, by crook of my arm, took me in the direction of the stairwell that would bring me further. With the child william within my hold and his mother by my side, I proceeded down thusly to enter the room where each stood wait.

Percy and Claire appeared wide eyed with wonder and excitement to gather toward me hastily, but with caution. Even as Byron stood unable to move, he looked with skeptical glance toward the smoking pipe within his hand, as if my presence were possibly some delusion brought forth by its contents. Polidori however, nearly white with shock, trembled to approach inspectively as he circled my body to gaze upon it.

"Dear friends, this is Adam." Mary told them, still holding my arm within hers.

Claire was the first to say her thoughts aloud to her sister. "Mary" She whispered. "This is your giant by the lake..." She said in surprised gasp before looking more to me. I felt Mary's body shake in small giggles.

"Then now you believe me sister, if only Charles and father had ever the sense to do so." Mary replied.

"Charles and your father are fools indeed." Joked Percy through scoffing breathlessness before regaining composure entirely. "I for one shall not be. I am most pleased to meet you Adam. For much it seems I have been told in truth of your existence, that now from Mary's dreams you appear so far from home in glad company, a traveller from an antique land." He offered, extending a hand in greeting.

"It's alright Sir Adam. I shall take the babe." Claire said softly, reaching gently for her nephew so that I might shake with Percy. Nervous as I remained, I handed him to her and reached forward where Percy gripped modestly my hand and placing his opposite over top of it in addition, smiled at me most genuinely.

"Come then, do not let your legs be stone gentle man. We shall sit and listen as my love has told us a tale awaits from your presence." Percy continued, breaking the shake to take my opposite arm in crook that he might lead me forward by open side along with Mary as co-escort into the adjoining parlor. After this, all were seated with exception to myself and the young Doctor who continuing to circle and gawk at my presence could not be moved to speech until such time Byron asked in annoyance that he be seated and cease his "childish" actions.

I was irritated by that when in obediance Polidori took seat upon a chair as if he were nothing more than a scolded adolescent. I spoke not against it however and looking around the room, I observed the patient faces of unjudging peoples which sat ready that I should begin for them some recitation of histories past as if I were nothing more nor less in their minds than a fellow poet or writer joined in their company. At first I fumbled to begin, even as Mary smilingly encouraged and spoke preceding in greater introduction.

"Adam, be not afraid. Should it help if I stand with you?" She asked kindly. I nodded in reply and Mary rose once more to join me, taking my hand in hers to face the others. I realized that since my arrival amongst them I had said not a word. At first effort to remedy this, my voice cracked and I felt flush upon my face the embarassed blush of shyness.

"I... I am Adam." I managed at last. "And I know not where to begin but in apologies... I come amongst you I fear with no plans or true understanding of why, aside from chance of circumstance that I in truth have followed you and spied on your friendships with envy and wonder these last weeks and months since your passage through my lands and tour of where I once came to be.

As seemingly you have heard the tale before, I once met Mary in her youth, and having recognized her sight, compelled myself... No... That isn't truth... Feeling compelled by unknowable yearning to be near to her kindness, I have wronged you in secretive my pursuit of your party that I might in proximities and voyeurism, relieve the sorrows of my deep presiding solitudes which I had long deceived myself to be untroublesome. For in truth I am alone within this world and have been such for longer than any of you have lived, so rejected and... " I began to cry once more in shame.

Mary then stepped before me and placing her back toward the others took my face once more into her hands to speak quietly.

"Do not be saddened now love. If I ask too much, then I shall remove any request I have burdened upon you and we may sit without neccesity where you will be welcomed without further demands of such difficulty to explain yourself, simply to join the company of our evening."

Momentarily I looked away and sniffled, unable to meet her gaze, as such grace she offered felt nearly unbearable to my person. Yet overwhelmed as I might have been, I summoned within myself a determination to press onward, thanking her for such concern, but insisting continuance for my own need to express at that point, the truth of my being to others. I asked only if I might sit upon the floor rather than stand to tell it.

Then in full view of all present, Mary leaned my face toward hers to place a kiss upon my brow before moving to sit upon the floor herself and urging me to join. Seeing this, the others too without question or complaint, raised from their seats, and placing pillows upon the carpet surrounding, joined us closer then, that I might feel at comforted ease. Even Byron did this, bringing with him both glass and pipe that he should remain without cause to retrieve them later, which might interrupt what would follow.

With this I found voice to begin in earnest. Telling to them the same which I had relayed to Mary. Of course this took considerably more length than before as I was stopped many times with question and upon revealment of the events which occurred upon the ship called Albatross, much Jest occcured concerning the author Coleridge whom had based it seemed his most famous poem upon my sufferings. However also among these interjections, including the brief task of laying young William to bed, much gravity and curious mind came from both Polidori and Byron concerning themselves with details of Ruthven, whom it seemed they had known once thru introduction and name.

"The villain remains then? Alive and with reason to hate, you tell us now that he may seek you wherever you are even to these shores, a vampyre of man which has bested you twice? God damn the risk that you carry among us now." Said Byron indignantly.

"Let the man be Byron. After what he has told I should stand in his defense unto death if need arise! Could you not see within sympathies and sense that he has been through enough that you would spurn this miraculous being once more even amongst us?" Scolded Percy to my amazement.

"Then what are we to do then by your bleeding heart Shelley? Endure the wrath of one who might drink the blood from our very veins? Let you go first as always into such romantic ideals." He debated.

Unexpectedly and with quiet apprehension another voice spoke. "We might depower his abilities thru revelation." offered the doctor Polidori.

"How is that?" Claire inquired genuinely.

"Oh" He stammered "The contest I mean... Here we have tales presented that speak such horror as we previously endeavored to create, and yet purposed they might become. What if we should write in them truth, and by such in name forewarn others and protect ourselves against this Ruthven under guise of fiction?"

"More than that..." Mary interjected. "Adam's tale itself might be told in this way, should it draw forth or warn against any other such as that Breda he spoke! For surely he seems more the villain to me than this Ruthven..."

Claire nearly rolled her eyes to hear these words."Sister, you say that merely for the harm that Breda brought him surely, for I see as clearly as others your affections lie with this protector of which you have so longingly dreamed."

"Truely?" Scoffed Byron from now standing placement across the room while pouring himself another glass.

"Mary's mind is her own Byron. If love she has for this man then beauty that holds, and I should embrace him for what happiness her heart beats." Percy defended.

Never had I dreamed such a thing in my days that so quickly these lovers would accept my person amongst them, much less with professions of seeming love and loyalty to guard my continued presence rather than turn from my sight... Yet there they stood, not one but now three at my side and another willing to engage toward this end while only Byron agreed with even the slightest signs of reluctance.

With a sigh Byron surrendered his argument both exasperated and cold before at last approaching my place upon the floor with extended hand and greeting. "Concessions demand then as financier of this party, I welcome you creature to share our holidays within these grounds. And I suppose as the others seemed fixed upon this new direction to our endeavors, we shall pen our own version of these accounts creatively. Though I insist this be in amendment to the current competitions aims rather than in replacement of them."

"Most graciously... most graciously to all of you, I too surrender to these invitations." I breathed heavily in response. It was odd to say this, as if a fog surrounded my mind, and I realized the probable cause that came from the drifting smoke of Byron's pipe, though without knowledge of its contents to this day I cannot assert what levels this might have influenced the others.

Percy himself was overjoyed to hear this and proclaimed loudly afterward. "Right then, it shall be! Let us celebrate and make merry this evening in preparation for this new accord! That by the morrow we craft our tales inspired from the histories of this mighty man amongst us and indoctrinate him to this family of fiends we are!" The others cheered and toasts were made.

By that time, evening had settled over the villa and none could mark what hour by night it was, for clouds covered the moon and with thunder cracking outside, they carried on with drink, dance and intoxicant smokes many hours further. Even to my own degrees I attempted to join within that revelry finding the taste of wine bitter, but the sensation of smokes most pleasing within, until taken by Mary's arm, I was swept away from the company of the others in direction toward the stairs which led upward into the hallways and bedchambers above.

Upon the way I recall that I stopped to look curiously at a painting which seemed to depict some devil who sat atop the supine form of a beautiful woman. Mary noting this, told me of the artist and informed further that he had once loved her mother but betrayed her for another woman. Afterward in her heartbreak she told me, that her mother drank such quantities of laudanum that she almost perished before the chance to ever meet her father. I admit that surprise at this story found me curious. Having read the works of Mary's mother personally, I never might have guessed such thoughts would pain her so. For it seemed to me by her writings, much like had presently observed with Mary herself, there stood a deeper conviction professed within her that acclaimed the practices of free love to many partners in following of the heart, rather than those conventional doctrines and practices which demanded monogamy as the only rightful and approved form of love's expressions.

Mary herself without prodding, also felt the need to explain this to me. "Never did that action move such by jealousy I gather from the story that father tells, but the rejection that came with it was no less harsh... For who in love and goodness does not feel the stings of heartbreak to be spurned by those they would love while offered no love in return?" Mary trailed. "Oh Adam, you who have not known of loves sweetness, let us not linger here by such dreary depictions, but come with me to bed and find not the haunting of demons or pains past." She continued while urging me onward with pulling arm.

Following that insistent guidance upstairs, I was surprised to find lantern lit and bed made where Percy stood wait within Mary's chamber. I had not seen the others pass us, nor suspected such greeting, but he held a flower within his hand, and while I anticipated its gift to Mary, I was confused at first why he should instead bow to offer it toward myself. "Claire will be with us soon." Mary told him quietly with a giggle, before taking the flower from me.

She placed its petals upon my lips, and closing my eyes I leaned to her pull for those petals, which soon replaced by her lips, she substituted with a kiss that affected me deeply enough that I nearly stumbled forward. I could feel her hands as they pulled at my coat and began in earnest to disrobe my body, but could not resist in such humble fashion to stop these motions. Unbuttoning my shirt and peeling away the fabric even while the kiss continued, Mary embraced me with softness and touch. Then, in realization of another feeling which caused my eyes to open, I observed that Percy now knelt below as his hands also joined in effort the removal of what remained. He stripped away the belt of my pants and tugged at their sides to lower them, but stepping back in surprise and break of Mary's kiss, I looked at them both.

Seeing my trepidations, Percy ceased his action and stood gently with smiling reassurance. "My beloved Mary has found you worthy Adam, and by my eyes I find you marvelous that she may love another as I had once hoped such happiness may find her. For by her joys my own are multiplied with each, to feel the growth of love.

These freedoms and encouragement moved her little toward Thomas, nor Byron as I might have dreamt; Yet you a dream unknown to me have somehow held her heart since before we me,t and through all her life she has loved you, all the while you have known not the love of any.

Therfore by virtue of love I wish to welcome you my friend to the race of humanity in fullness of heart and body, that you... Adam, most beautiful and unfathomed man who has suffered so greatly the touch and rejections of violent aggressors, may know within this night both man and woman here, who shall henceforth love you as family amongst us, for as long as you will stay our company." These words rang within my mind even as others met my ears from another unexpected.
"And I as sister now to lovers of both, shall bear witness in this welcome to hold you further, as brother to me thereafter should you accept. I will embrace thee the same" Claire's voice sang softly from behind me where she had entered the room unseen.

I could say nothing. Even as Percy stepped closer once more and pulling me forward, kissed my lips himself, tears flowed freely in wondrous awe the turn of fortunes that had transpired. Panic momentarily filled my mind and breaking our kiss, I wondered in fright. "But the sin..." I whispered desperately.

"Sin from thy lips? O trespass sweetly urged! Give me my sin again." Mary quoted, as her hands pulled my face towards her own and kissed me further while Percy's lips seized at her neck in passionate suckle. The door was closed then and Claire, drifting her hand over each of us in passing, moved to recline by the rooms opposite walls.

So profound in me is the memory of that night. Stripped of my clothing by their hands I stood before them while caress graced the most despised parts of my self, and yet even with their beauty exposed in full I was embraced for everything equal to their own hearts beating in time with mine as passions moved them in loving embrace. To witness the form of another man so flawlessly created and woman so artfully composed in softness and grace, I was humbled to be wrapped by these in the throes of love where I touched the moist entrances of their flesh and taken in by such trust, exploded with passions unbridled urgings until planting my soul within Mary's womb under watchful eye of her lovers, I took also with apprehensive form the seed of Percy's lustful gentleness even as my own flowed from myself to her whom had first accepted me in body and being.

The details matter not as much to speak of that one might note afterward when Claire drank from these fluids, or that after that still, shared kiss with Mary. But to reveal that this persisted until spent and indulgent in happiness we collapsed to the glow which came with such activity. She also came then to join us in bed before realization could prove that due to my own size, we could not lay together in slumber therein.

However, refusing of course any alternative, Mary and herself, spread upon the floor all of that bedding perched with pillows and pallete that we may all lay together without separations between us during our following rest. In truth it was near light of dawn before we slept. Yet with each in turn draped over and between one another, we seemed an endless tangle of bodies entwined and at peace with such mysterious movements of time which brought us individually to that placement within the cosmos, that we might become as one for those brief moments of ecstatic expression.

Adam sighed bittersweetly and a silence hung in the room while Steven and I caught our breath. Unfortunately that ended when I coughed and could think of nothing more to say aside from what follows.

CR: Adam... that's beautiful...

DM: Um, yeah but well... Can you really publish that Cass?

I sighed and scrunched my face in thought.

CR: Ya know... If anyone says anything against it, I think I'll just take it somewhere else...

AG: We should likely stop for the evening.

DM: What?! But the next day you started writing the novel!

AG: And tomorrow I shall tell you about it, but the clocks hour draws late and the two of you require... rest...

CR: He's right Steven. We should go to bed. Adam, do you want to sleep here in the office or do you have somewhere else to go?

AG: Respectful to your invitations I should leave you for the time. Will you stop tape?

I walked to my desk and stopped the recording, but afterward noted the sadness on Adam's face. Even during our goodbyes it never seemed to shake, and I knew the pain of loss that he felt to remember his story to us. It had drained him. After he left, Steven returned with me to my apartment and we waited for the following day.

SESSION FIVE

Interviewer Name:

Cassandra Reynolds: Journalist for “Washington Post”

newspaper and special columnist for Al-Jazeera International.

Second Interviewer and Consultant:

Dr. Steven Malcom of the Boston College Institute for Scientific Research and Advancement: Specialization in structural biochemistry. Published author and Nobel laureate

Interview Subject : Adam

The time is 6:34 pm. Aprill the 1st, 2024

Location: Personal offices of Cassandra Reynolds, Washington D.C.

CR = Cassandra Reynolds
DM= Dr. Steven Malcom
AG = Subject - Adam

Personal notes Italicized

April 1st, 6:34 pm, Recording begins

CR: Stop it Steven.

AG: I hope not on my account? I am pleased to see the two of you happy.

DM: Oh no. I think she just hit record.

Walking into frame Steven and I joined Adam to sit on the floor again, having not moved the pillows back to the sofa from our previous session.

CR: Welcome back.

AG: So we are ignoring that then?

CR: Just for the camera.

AG: That is fair. Shall I resume or is there question first?

DM: I have one. Claire... did you and her ever?.. ya know.

Adam laughed before sighing.

AG: We did, but not for some time and not out of the same affections for one another as we each held for Percy or Mary who truly delighted in love for both of us equally.

CR: So what? You became an item, all four of you?

AG: A family... yes.

DM: Not to act surprised, but I didn't realize just how progressive they all were. God, especially for the time, I mean here it is 2024 and people still can't wrap their heads around polyamory as an idea, and all of you are living it out openly during the 19th century.

CR: Don't you go getting any ideas Steven.

AG: Truthfully for my loves, such a thing was not with thoughts of any progressive agenda, but merely an act of freedom toward their own hearts which spawned belief professed and fought for. Without the will to bend toward those constraints of society I honestly feel they afforded themselves little other choice but to stand in defense of their way. Percy had already published such controversal works that even the church despised him and Mary's own mother before her demonstrated within the words of her writing, the fires and passions of such same liberty, long before the current affair between that grouping housed at our first meeting. It served further only to solidify such an image within the eyes of others.

I certainly had no ambitions to *seek* such a lifestyle. I had never once dared even imagine the love of one person in such manner, much less the embracing of myself for all that I was by three, who devoted to me the same affections they held one another. Like them, I could resist not the love I felt in return, nor deny that I felt it. And with no need to restrict my feelings with exception to the rules of a society which would not afford even my existence, nor answer to what nature I might be whether human or other, I fell deeply in such wondered blissful appreciations and care for those three persons all, that I could imagine afterward no reason to follow forth with any arbitrary societal rule which might look down upon the beauty of our relations.

Who could judge and defame the awe of pure affections and concerns that any person might find in companionship? Of what matter was it to them if it harmed none while elevating the joys of life to those involved? Sin? Yes I had read the works and words of the church and society as you know, and long attempted belief such that I held to those so fiercely for fear of damnation. However why? I wondered once more should I place faith in those proclamations of virtue, when I knew not with assurance that even my mere existence might lead to damnation itself, nor that such fates might be avoided by adherence to their laws? For I existed not of any making they described. How then by incompleteness of knowing could I even be said to reject those principles any more than embrace them while being not a part of their design?

Yet by choices, I had indeed become a part of that family which then taking me in loving care made me to feel worthy and beautiful as I had truly never felt before them. All this in spite of all forgiving graces claimed by such faiths who's followers had spurned me from the world. And again I also asked, how these who harmed no person in loving one another, had sinned more greatly than those who would in harsh judgement or self righteousness, look upon the impoverished with cruelty, murder thy fellow man or condemn them to fates worse than death by deeming it right to rule over them, enslave and sell away their freedoms, then stripped of their liberty or had forced upon them such systems that required by very nature the classist structure of their life where few above draw power from the toil and works of those below by stepping upon their backs to climb ever higher?

What hypocrisy seemed clear had wrought in favorance to the actions which I saw as sinful in others, had looked to these bold and intelligent youths as deviant or perverse? So owing my allegiance to mankind's potentials in empathy and grace, I could not right within my heart any such verdict of guilt that I should side against those I loved for fear of so called damnation. For I would be damned truly if I persisted against the honest leanings of my heart which felt rightness here, where unquestioned wrong before had excused itself by gilded words at odds with the teachings of prophet and saviors whom Europe's most prestiged of faith claimed to follow.

Adam sighed. Clearly the topic was one he felt passionate about and in my mind I could see him fit easily among the group he described, not only for defending them, but also for the convictions displayed. Wanting to get back to the topic at hand however I tried to remind him then where we had left off.

CR: So after you guys woke up, how'd the writing start?

AG: Ah yes, thank you Ms Reynolds. Diversion roots so easily at times.

DM: Wait, I have one thing. I looked into this after what you described to us and have questions. Ok, so you said you followed Mary, Claire, Percy, Byron *and* Polidori from Germany back to Switzerland *before* they took up their stay for the summer or the writing challenge was issued, but history documents that they didn't meet up with Byron until arriving in Geneva and had come by way of Italy and Paris, only touring the areas you described weeks after that.

Adam smiled widely.

AG: You are in no way mistaken Doctor. For these were among the first alterations that were made by each of us to assure the secrecy of our acquaintance. Each writer present had both written letter and kept journals during these times and with thoughts that their truth may reveal to one such as Ruthven my whereabouts or retreat, it was decided by all involved that these were each to be written over in revision so that it appeared only possible that I resided not in Germany as Ruthven deducted, but rather Switzerland, where we meant to depart by summers end. Thus these fictions protecting shielded, if it should ever be needed, my residence within the wood of Odin.

DM: So you're saying that the first thing any of you did was rewrite your own histories?

AG: Only so far as the month of May, after departure from Paris. Nothing prior to this was neccesary, and even these were mild in adjustment. For instance where in truth Claire, Percy and Mary *had* met Byron along *with* Polidori at a hotel in Geneva during May, which we knew could not be altered in record by our hands; All documentation surrounding this time was imperative to us only describe intentions to and recording of their stay within the Maison Chapui, as well as the Villa Diodati respectively, there also in Geneva where we resided currently, without mention of the travels taken further at that time.

By this simple twisting of events, we reasoned with all purposely omitted and destroyed written record of their travels onward to Germany and beyond, before return to these places, that doing so established a trail of clues which would lead Ruthven upon their forthcoming publications to assume I had met them here alone, rather than following as I had from closeness to my home. And by this, he might seek me nearer those estates than elsewhere, even while I travelled with them further still.

Also decided after this, I would in fact lead our group again along such places as they had recently seen, to show them firsthand the truths of my story and how to locate my home without use of compass or map if secrecy should demand its occupation at a later time. This was to be a journey purposely recorded with corroboration of others while agreement struck with the landlord of the rented estates there in Geneva, for an account to be made of one matching my description, seen upon the lake itself long after our departures. Whereafter he would keep watch for any suspicious company who came after, such as Ruthven himself, who might seek my whereabouts in Geneva.

DM: But you said Ruthven already knew you lived near the castle.

AG: Twelve years prior yes, but never having found my abode and given the odd magnetism of the surroundings, we concluded that it's secrecy must remain for sanctuary's sake if our plans turned sour in fruit and brought his wrath upon us.

DM: So you backdated letters and journals just to throw him off a trail he might never even find?

AG: Indeed, and better for it, we had for later these actions proved worth their efforts in weighted gold as you shall see.

CR: Ok, so you changed a bunch of letters, but how seriously was everyone worried about this Ruthven guy that they were willing to do that?

AG: Greater still my dear than you suspect. For before Mary set pen to paper in any attempts at her work, the arguments surrounding creation of that which bore the warnings against Ruthven himself filled the house for several long days. None wished credit upon their names to risk this endeavor, and still more concerning to each remained how to insinuate his evils most aptly that might hold to memory, so others knew of his wickedness without overtly being capable to tell the tale as I had relayed it thus far.

In eventuality Byron himself did take to craft a story which he felt both accurate enough in depictions and filled more so with superstition and recognizable traits of folk legend and lore, yet short enough to be easily read by a wide audience. That the work to be titled "The Vampyre" was assured to limit any free capabilities or resources Ruthven had to wage further evil deed. However he did this with refusal to accept authorship upon eventual publication and demanded that the words be written by another's hand while he dictated them. Even despite this, credit would find him still to a level that eventually forced his repudiation of that work for his own protections and would drive young Polidori to ruinous fate in his stead some years later, having been the claimed author by that time.

I tell you their fear of Ruthven was such as especially stricken for Byron, his very poem "The Darkness" which would stand later as his entry within the competition, was directly described, such literal nightmares he feared that in the end, how by Ruthven's destructions that only he and I would survive all others before death took each of us in one another's presence.

"The crowd was famish'd by degrees; but two
Of an enormous city did survive,
And they were enemies: they met beside
The dying embers of an altar-place
Where had been heap'd a mass of holy things
For an unholy usage; they rak'd up,
And shivering scrap'd with their cold skeleton hands
The feeble ashes, and their feeble breath
Blew for a little life, and made a flame
Which was a mockery; then they lifted up
Their eyes as it grew lighter, and beheld

Each other's aspects saw, and shriek'd, and died
Even of their mutual hideousness they died"

Excerpt from "The Darkness" by George Gordon (Lord Byron)

Breda was gone you see, and I being embraced as harmless to mankind, was of less dire need to warn against another's pursuing course to recreate a being liken to myself. However Ruthven's evils not only persisted, but so close to each of us had they come, that the only one who had yet to either make his acquaintance directly or be known to have held interest to him in the past, was Percy alone.

DM: How long did he wait to write that poem?

AG: The Darkness? With ironic ire, I must admit that Byron drafted a version of that poem during dinner one evening simply to prove his assertion of the dangers he felt my presence brought with them. He revised and edited at length for quite some time after of course, and complained in hindsight at some imaginative difficulties he had writing any story at all, but perhaps most telling was that of how lasting it's impact would prove, given its original recital. As it was was meant chiefly in purposes a simple jab against what he saw as the foolishness of sheltering my company.

CR: But he allowed you to stay?

AG: He did. I believe he feared further my departure and with it what protection it provided at that time than the presence of my personage or what it might bring. For Byron feared the future nearly as much as his own sobriety. Though his recent divorce afforded some degree of pity for the man, Mary more than once remarked at concern for the judgement of our lovers, that each at some point had taken to lay with him, and truly believed Polidori's love of him to be masochistic in nature.

DM: What a dick...

AG: Regardless... Our stay, as well as our forthcoming travels, were for the time only possible by his leisured consent, and still he assisted us each day. Just as his contest itself had brought forth within me the courage to make myself known to Mary and led to those events, none that happened then could possibly have transpired without him.

CR: On another note, is there a reason you refer to him and the doctor only by last name or title?

AG: In the case of Bryon, yes. He insisted upon it. None called him by his given name at that time. John on the other hand simply answered most often to Doctor or Polidori, so that no other name seemed more appropriate, even as I say it now.

The troubles were, that the endeavors so changed within that competition of writing, and with such curiosities and want to indulge ourselves in the splendor of company, that even within that household of illustrious credit to their pens, little but Polidori himself did much actual writing beside further journals and letters of notation for a time; Until by chance that was, that Percy and Byron began their planning of a boating tour around lake Geneva by which freedoms Mary, Claire and myself were able at last to begin in earnest, a new work, while the doctor performed edits on Byron's transcribed words which he had taken down days before.

As for that new work, with which you are well acquainted, I have told you much of this already, but in summary I shall say further that the base structured outline of story within story which came to define Mary's words, were brought about at the suggestions of Claire, while I gave input primarily to detail and perspectives which Mary then endeavored to include amongst her own personal motives and concept.

Yet with Percy and Byron being gone from us for several days as we began the creation of our text, I remained only as persistent in the defamation of my own form as in my insistance on my creators fickle and careless nature, which revealed to me as previously stated, Mary's deep and lasting hatred for Breda's harm to me that she attempted to temper by inclusion of Percy's more admirable traits and her own upbringings.

I wished to make neither of us sympathetic in truth, but only to prepare a story which would entice the mind of a man such as Breda his self or Conrad before him, in order that any pursuant to such ends might come into the public eye or seek out the author of that work with question concerning its similarity to their pursuit... And therefore at last should one come forward this way, I could press my ever growing inquisition into the nature of my being.

DM: So the book in a way, was a dog whistle then?

AG: By modern terminologies yes, precisely.

Continuing further, Mary was often insistent that within this, our endeavor must be adequately disguised as a story of the purest fictions, prefacing the entirety of her work with a clear and adamant disclaimer for what she swore as our own protection. The words of this she would revise more than once, and wholly shift in credit, much like the novel itself which changed over time with each subsequent edition. Yet through every subsequent publication, this she continually insisted none the less.

Though as time went onward and even after the first

drafting of Mary's tale, my time with her as well with both Percy and Claire, began to change my self views. Being ever surrounded by my lovers and indeed true conditionless affection, I began to see the potential for a life less horrific. Through togetherness of family I faced the ups and downs of a shared set of journeys and tragic griefs so that I came to understand the true weight of loss with which my creator had inadvertently come so close to end by my creation... Had Mary and I met at another time perhaps, I might have saved others and spared her much pain herself. And it was in this time that I began to forgive Edmund Breda, not for his actions, but for their possibilities.

Mary, having already understood this, breathed life into our fiction with a growing sense of something larger at work, and though I would not allow her to describe me as her claims would have held otherwise... I did relent to her ever growing depiction of my mind in relation to the actions of the creature with which I identified. Be that as it may, I also retained my insistent demand over the depiction of his brutality. If my sympathies had grown five times from knowing this brief measure of domestic life, then it was by no less than ten, which it had expanded my guilt. I expressed this to my mind within the horrors perpetrated by my doppelganger. Though as always, Mary balanced these too with reason and understanding, leaving our tale to take on a life of it's own.

My time with Conrad became the time of the blind man, and that of my time in Ireland to form the basis for the creatures observances of the cottagers as he called them within the novel. Each separation lasting, would become our creatures rejection in mirror to each involved, those pains they had felt to be spurned by another, even including Claire's heartbreak by Byron wherein she still wavered by passing day between sadness and fury. By this I did allow for our narrative to take on more sympathetic tones, eventually framing the context of my creator's mind equally into that of my father's and eventually Mary's own as described, until we had imagined a great purpose and even dignity to his character.

The day came I realized, that I could recognize very little of Breda within the life of Victor Frankenstein. With Claire's growing influence upon our minds, we had eventually created for him a love story beriddled with tragedies that proved both reflectant and ultimately foreshadowing of our own lives. Certain moments of Victor's life would be that of ours as we poured our collective griefs into the accounts, with his loss of mother, and sibling being only two of these stark instances.

By the third draft, we had not only begun dropping adumbration to my true history within this strange tale, but outright reference to matters that as seen by our use of quotation, might have in fact given away more than intended. I believe that it was finally in this mistake prior to publication, that we inadvertently allowed the knowledge which Ruthven would eventually use as window to our thoughts that he might torture us most successfully in later years.

When Percy and Byron had returned, the lot of us meant to travel again through the tours which they had previously taken, and for purposes of later use, view my homes location where I would collect my things before we made way to Chamounix. Byron and Polodori by this time wished not to be included in any written words of this however and though they travelled with us and observed with many questions of their own, It would seem to posterity as if they had remained within the Villa while Mary, Percy and Claire conducted research for the novel in development.

Utilizing this deception, Byron drafted defensively many partial works which might have lended credit to his assumed stay in Geneva and even by implication of them, my lingering presence. However finding himself either unable by inspiration, or perhaps design, to complete these tales, he shut them away afterward for several years without use or publication.

We had collected my belongings by then as planned and with all present then aware of our potential sanctuary's location, we took aim towards differing paths, even as we remained disheartened that Byron, unmoved by sympathies, would reject his unborn in Claire and leave her to our care alone. Still we parted ways as friends sometime nearest September if I recall. Polidori wished us well, and Byron jested that he hoped never to set eyes on any of our persons again. But leaving for England, we bid our farewells and afterward arrived at Portsmouth.

TOO SUSPECT TO BE COINCIDENCE

I must say unsurprisingly, that travel proved much easier with Percy's assistance in particular, but the suggestions of Byron elevated this to a degree that I might call invaluable. As he had learned long before, ways in which to disguise the presence of his varied company in secret and discretion during times abroad. By such expertise and certain arrangements, I was able thereafter with the gracious help of my companions in fact, to come and go aboard ships *and* carriage without sight by others, even within broad daylight of a busied port. Staying not below in hold or darkness alone, but passing my days within upward cabins alongside my newfound loves, was such joy to me and only more in reason multiplied such owed gratitudes toward their assistance.

From Portsmouth however we were taken to the strangest of settings considering, as lodging for Claire and Mary, along with young William, had been secured of all places within an abby in Bath, while Percy and I travelled onward to London. Parting was difficult admittedly, but with Claire pregnant, financial security as well as safety was of paramount importance. By day while Percy worked to secure fortunes which might better provide for the five, but soon to be six of us, I scoured the darkened and foul places of London for news of Ruthven, secure in the knowledge that our lovers remained protected even within the walls of that faith which Percy railed against and was despised by in turn.

However nary a month had passed before news of tragedy came to us in surprise, when Percy receiving such alarming letter from Mary's sister Fanny, took immediately for Bristol to see her saftey kept, only to discover that she had died before his arrival could find her. As she had taken that night to an inn, and was discovered by note of suicide and bottle of laudanum, to have ended her own life.

When first we heard of this and grief took my companions, there were no doubts to the explanations of laudanum overdose or cause brought on by some hidden love professed then for Percy unrequited and unbeknownst. However these revelations like the blow of a hammer, struck down on poor Shelley, who then entered into the depths of a depression in shame, writing at one time with guilty heart "Friend had I known thy secret grief, Should we had parted so", in expression of regret and self loathing.

Mary too blamed her own hands in that tragedy, feeling that Fanny had long suffered within her shadow and that she had done not enough to include her within their lives. Only Claire in her grieving could refrain from self blame and though she tried to assure Mary of guiltlessness for their sisters passing, I sadly report that during that time, cut off from Percy and myself, Mary attempted more than once to take her own life. So tortured she felt by the unfortunate confluence of condition which separating our family, was compounded now with accompaniment of that news so wretched that she could scarcely breathe by day, and writing to Percy begged visitation to relieve her lost heart where mysterious change in humors had exaggerated all feelings within her.

Agreeing to this only briefly so that we might move myself secreted within his travel, afterward he would return to neccesary endeavors at hand. Percy begged me to stay with Mary and Claire during that time so that joy may find them once again and not all of our family should be divided. Having found no news of Ruthven, I agreed to this easily, and joining together once more in shared grief, only I held any suspicion that Fannys passing was orchestrated by another, or that Ruthven himself had discovered my renewed interest in and acquaintance with the family.

Perhaps he intended to draw me out I wondered, but not until later that same year in the month of November did I voice these worries when we learned that Percy's estranged wife Harriet had then gone missing. In my heart by this news, I knew these events so closely bound could be no mere coincidence of misfortune, but the hand instead of that fiend who had the power to compel others against their will even to death, and saying thus at last to Claire and Percy's ears I feared for our families saftey.

"Truly you believe this creature has discovered us and killed our sister?" Claire asked once.

"That I cannot say, but with this latest of news I confess those suspicions seem supported." I answered.

"Then speak not of this to Mary until proof further, for in her current state I fear she would pursue that man to murder in vengeance." Claire replied.

A month after this, the body of Harriet Shelley was found in the Serpentine river and in the apparent suicide letter, she requested by word that Percy take custody of their son Charles, but to leave their daughter in her sister Eliza's care. Unconvinced and partly unaware as my lovers remained that Ruthven was responsible for these deeds, actions were taken to follow those requests by Shelleys late wife.

Though even this was not easily accomplished. For despite by then securing financial means and indeed marrying Mary against his own professed feelings for that institution, within St. Mildreds church before the start of a new year. This all the while coincided also with a long wished reconciliation with Mary's father, so that they might live beneath the same roof in what would be considered sanctified matrimony. Percy fretted and worried much over the prolongued custody battle with the court of Chancery as one does, but ultimately our fate was left to hands of others as each of us in turn, bowed and bent to play our parts within the chains of life so bound.

Much is to be said of the intricacies of domestic tragedy and tedium herein. It is unfortunate to report such things, but such is the measure of life that while in my solitudes years may pass with little to report aside from days of reading or loneliness; That to occupy space within this world and connected to the lives of others, it is a complexity that so many events should transpire of horrid note, that speech of them requires more the approach of times relayed between, than to speak of the truth in day to day love or living.

As for the wedding itself, I watched from the shadowed confines of a balcony while ceremony and recitation of vows legally bound my lovers into what society considered its only form of legitimacy, much to our own ire. Even despite this, that event's happiness did bring final a mend to the rift between Father and daughter at last, and Percy was accepted there foreward with open arm,s even while Claire had remained absent for such event as she being kept secret in her pregnancy, was still such stayed within the Abbey at Bath.

Later after those exchanges of vow however, our unit of lovers once again joined in secret that same night, while Percy and Mary both scoffing with mockery and ridicule railed against such changes in perception as this procedure afforded them by society, and with much celebratory action we four did engage most rebelliously, naked amongst the cold night beneath the gaze of stars, where we did bind our love in *private* ceremony, each to one another by word and consecrations of our own

design and truths. Whereafter this, we consummated our union further in every sort of so called deviancy that we could devise that evening.
This we aimed to worship eachother in full, that the day itself would hold for us the same gravity and importance it meant to others, almost as if to create a sneering joke which none other privy to, might sustain our animosity whenever came the mention of marriage or concession to their wills. For if God should exist, then surely love must be his nature, and by love divine no lighter celebrations could be more reverent than this.

Of course after that night, having moved once more temporarily and in great relief reconciled with her father, Mary lived again along with Percy, on the grounds occupied by the Godwin and Hunt families for a time, before following further to live with Peacock in Marlow while Claire still remained sequestered and alone, unknown in condition to her father and mother. I, during this time of course, unable to reveal myself to those peoples for fear of greater risk, took residence elsewhere, and to the suspicions of none, I was visited easily within a mausoleum nearby, which with my loves assistance had been outfitted most luxuriously, to become my haunt and our retreat for that winters duration. Having of course the greater freedoms by this point than the others, I visited Claire most often to see to her wellbeing.

I cannot count the hours and joy by which with wonder I watched the growth of child within Claire, caring not for who their earthly father might be. For I meant along with Percy, to act as gracious patron, protector and teacher to that soon to be birthed infant, just as I had grown to love and care for William, who by that time took to my arms as gleefully as to his own mother and aunt.

Shadows still remained over our company however, as

thoughts of Ruthven not forgotten, hung heavy a cloud over our happiness. But within a fortnight following the marriage itself, Claire gave birth, and brought into this world an infant girl whom she named Alba. Yet by Byron's letters of insistence would be renamed Allegra in time, which I to this day have difficulty recalling, as for in my mind she will remain always, little Alba.

By March, in success of achievement Mary and Percy moved once more, this time into a place called Albion house and shortly thereafter Clair with young Alba and myself, did move to be with them, rejoining our family as one for the first time in several months. It should have been most joyous indeed. However even by this in truth, the courts conclusions of custodial duties came down in unfortunate conclusions, forbidding of Percy that custody of his other two children by previous marriage which should have been his! They found placement of both into fosterhood instead, citing as reason, the issues of abandonment and atheism which proclaimed him unworthy in their eyes to care for his offspring.

Angered and saddened by this, we clung only tighter to that happiness available to us as we endeavored to assist Mary in completion of her writing. All the while, the time was spent evading requests for financial assistance from her father, and arguing in stress over debts brought on by Percy's endless generosities toward others. For my part, I had never utilized money or accrued debt of any sort, and while I survived comfortably in secret so long my years, I could not forgive the notion of just how influentially vital the concerns of wealth seemed to be to every person in my life. I should have loved to away with them all back to my humble cottage, and never another thought given to debt or finance. I argued this often.

These things are not necessities to our living. I would say. We do not have to struggle in this way. We have each other. We need not pay another for the rights to live upon the land or purchase from any those same necessities which we might produce ourselves. Have we not within us the necessary means to perform all vital function outside of these places? Free from all but ourselves, we would not be alone! Why do we abide this as if no alternative exists? Has humanity not existed long before these confounded systems, and should it not continue if all of this artifice fails in futile fall to nature? Can we not care for our children, grow from the earth that which we need, and live our days free?

I advocated these things of course, during a time where such was still possible; When great lands remained untrodden by, or documented to the governments that proclaimed ownership of them. Much has changed since then. And while legality still comes to question, it was not unfathomable to carry out in such way at that time.

Though, as is life, partners do not always agree. We all felt this in some way. It was expressed repeatedly in philosophical argument. The option however, seemed at such great odds with those other ambitions and causes to stay, that I could not sway them to the application of these ideals beyond word. They often expressed such things as how they *wished* that it could be different, but this was simply the way of a world which must be changed.

Their common belief in fact, was that we could and should do so through word and writing; That seeing these problems as we did, our charge in responsibility was not to retreat from society, but to alter it instead by means of radical thought and concepts put forth to others. I would have led then by example I argued, but in earnest, I feel that fear of such changes or loss of luxuries to which they had always been accustomed, truly influenced my partner's motives more than any of their minds would admit to themselves. Only one at a time did any of them ever seem fully amicable to the ideas of escape or retreat as it was seen, though this too wavered and changed to and fro in opposition to the other opinions, seemingly at times by the day. And always, I remained outvoted.

However realizing as I speak of this now, that these topics are still quite relevant and debated, and that this will be published in due course, I will honor and respect my love"s deepest expressions to those ends. I know full well that there are those who even to this day might say to me, that I should simply give what is owed because that is the way of the world; Regardless to having no true sense of which societal laws I do or do not adhere to at present. I pay my taxes and owe no debt mind you.

Still so in aside from my tale, I would return heartily toward those individuals, that my soul remains in opposition to the base argument and assumptions presented by those words. In fact I say today for the record, in radical expression of thought and belief; Fuck every conceivable notion of that. I have not changed these opinions. No person should ask payment from another, for that which every man, woman and child living on this earth, naturally inherits by right; These being the free use of the earth and it's resources in any way seen fit to them, so long as it harms or intrudes upon no other living person.

Consider, those who ask payment for these things. They did not make the land, nor water, air, plant, nor animal. If any should seek recompense for these, any of these, which they are not in *useful* possession of, or having transformed through their own work made their own; Then I would argue vehemently, that these things simply are not theirs. They are not any person's to claim for work they had no part in crafting! Nature is their owner! And payment due, lies only toward nature by carefully respecting, preserving, and tending to that which gave us life, being the earth and all upon it!

Adam sighed and calmed himself.

But I digress. It was only our connections to others that chained those imaginary concepts to our allegiances of toil and torment. For without need to hold within society, and by way of sustaining ourselves alone, we might have been happier, safer, and more in tune with each of our natures... Instead we dreamed of ways to profit and sustain through money that which was disallowed by society, in the simple living of life on this earth. This still saddens me.

Partly to this, and also our original intentions, in May of that year, Mary's work on our novel was completed, and with it came accompanied in celebration the showing signs of her own pregnancy, while Percy took part in the political and literary distractions surrounding their mutal friend Leigh Hunt, with whom for a time they had also lived previously, yet I remained unacquainted out of neccesity.

Though my repeated questions of society and why we must live as we did, frustrated all the more every member of our household who had long felt the same; I alone had lived apart from those constraints at any point. Each they grew in their immovable angers toward that system regardless. Percy in particular, sided with me most often that we should in fact move the entirety of our family to Odin's wood to be done with the artifice of civil life, and I believe if not for Mary's family, or the import of their works to publish, that we might have won over the others to do just that.

It was during this span in fact, which he drafted almost venomously the work of "Laon and Cyntha" in which he poured his outrage and romanticisms of many sort. He cared so much for that work, and so deeply personal it affected him when it was rejected and decried by those surrounding us to such a degree, that it only increased his disillusionment with the cultures of Britain and beyond. So it was that by September of that year, having cause to celebrate not only the birth of our new child, also called Clara, as well as our anniversary to arrive in Britain together, but the weights of social pressure and judgement, had nearly overwhelmed our lives in that stead.

And I swear I began to abhor not man, but the society in which mankind abided, by such unnatural dispositions and opinions, that I took thereafter the perception within, that all of my troubles and woes of life, had originated not by man's cruel nature, but by the regrettable invention of intractable social influences which corrupted more than they could correct, until not even man knows himself any more than the average would follow and echo what they had been taught to believe in place of reason or compassion.

DM: Dude, those are definitely some are lofty and idealistic opinions that I'm pretty sure you could discuss all night if given the chance, but I see the dillema... It sounds like a very busy year for anyone to go through though. Just putting all the philosophical stuff to the side, two newborns and one infant in a house of four adults who kept you secret through all of it? I can't even imagine how you found time to be anything aside from a full service babysitter.

CR: Yes, we should try to stay on track. I won't edit any of this out, but I would also like to know more about the children.
AG: Of course. I apologize. Honestly I have to tell you both however, that if not for that task and the love of those children, I too might have suffered more the weight of our troubles and pressure from the outside world. I confess to you the upkeep and affection of such innocent life, it is what gave to me the very strength and joys unequalled by my spouses so that I remained steadfast in my ideals beyond such practicalities which they saw first. For I shouldered no other burdens but this aside from the vigilant watch kept for

Ruthven himself, and though busy it was, we abided in love throughout all petty and limited squabbles that came between any of us.

It was with wondrous eyes I watched the marvels of human development when William had begun to walk. And at the verge of speech, I should say that he looked to me as second father. Even unable to speak my name properly, he called me Aiden instead, a habit which would follow afterward to become my name to him in earnest, as all else in the house accepted his calls for me without correction. This was all of course before our enemy made himself clearly known to us soonafter.

CR: And how did that come about?

AG: Ahh, the sting of it. To my dismay it came to pass that Percy and Mary both did publish the documentation of their tours through Europe quite innocently, and yet somehow this had shown our hand... Even doing so anonymously and with such cares as we had taken; These I fear, were what confirmed for Ruthven from his hidden watch abroad, that which he had already suspected. In them he surmised that I had indeed met Percy and Mary along their travels, and as he had felt my presence, not only within Britain some time before, but now likely it occured to his mind that I lived alongside my loves. He assumed as much and afterward extended forth efforts at proof of this, for he could detect my presence at no place else.

DM: But you said that your deceptions and rewritten accounts worked before and that you'd explain how.

AG: As they had in truth, for it would be learned later that within the time Ruthven had first grown in suspicions of my presence and baited me to emerge by the deaths of Fanny Godwin and afterward Harriett Shelley, he had falsely deduced by subsequent inaction that I could not have been occupied as he surmised, and so in this time and for the following months, he had departed the shores of Britain to search for me elsewhere.

Furthermore, delayed as the letter might have been, it reached our hands nonetheless revealed to us by Byron's spies, that Ruthven had indeed proceeded with focus toward the countryside of Geneva surrounding the Villa Diodoti, where word of his sighting had reached back to Byron himself that he should relay to us this information. If not for such diversions brought on by our careful revisionism, Ruthven surely would have descended upon us sooner, and in doing so caught our family further unprepared and vulnerable during our own dramas and turmoils which he had partly instigated.

DM: But the publication of Byron's work "The Vampyre"... Why hadn't that helped?

AG: Because dear Doctor, much like Mary's own work in this regard, the actual date of publication came long after the need for it arose in full. Where we had rushed to publish Mary's novel as soon as any possibility allowed after Ruthven's reveal, it would be another year before Byron and Polidori carried forth to release their own work, even still by then, arguing about the risks to their selves in doing so. Polidori in the end published under Byron's name out of sheer preservation to himself if not spite for our former friend.

Mary of course had named our novel with the title of "The Modern Prometheus" insisting that one day the resolution of my quest for understanding would bring fire again to mankind. For she believed that that the "wonders of my existence" would usher in a new age of health and benefit to all humanity, a term in which she lovingly included myself, despite our inherent difference...

We published anonymously at first, but as the tale had truly become Mary's own in storied art and word, we rallied behind her with unanimous insistence that the only name given credit be hers and no other. And since Ruthven knew unquestioningly the truth of my habitation with her and our family, it would afford no additional safety to do otherwise. Eventually by its second publication some five years after the first when it had already been adapted to stage, she accepted becoming known as the author of what by that time would be popularly referred to merely as "Frankenstein". Though fate's interventions saw that I would not be present to witness it by then. However in the beginnings, it was most important simply to have that work released. For if any should come forward with knowledge of how I was crafted, then by this information we hoped to also find weakness for what element within myself had given power to Ruthven as well.

CR: Ok, but *how* did Ruthven reveal himself? I get the relevancy, but it's hard to keep track when you skip ahead then back again.

AG: Apologies, and thank you for your continued patience. As has been noted, these were very busy years indeed. I shall clarify. He, that is Ruthven, had still been about mainland Europe in search of myself when Mary and Percy's travelling accounts were published and read. Afterward he left the surrounds of Geneva and sought out Byron in our stead, who was in Italy by then. Though by his own hand, our friend had already written to warn us of our pursuers last seen presence near Diodoti as mentioned. Ruthven did not know this, and arriving so soon following whence this message had been sent, he worked by threat and coercement to force Byron into compliance of his will without that knowledge.

If Byron did what was asked without enthrallment, then

Ruthven thereafter promised that he would leave alone his person and estates in peace and saftey. So by our understanding of the threat to his life and little choice that Ruthven had given, we blamed Byron not for what came after, but thanked him instead, that he had forewarned us even before then, though at unknown peril to himself. Of course what that villain had asked from him came to us as an altogether different communication to arrive shortly succeeding the former.

In this Ruthven, whether to pain us or tempt our minds to rash actions, tauntingly claimed open responsibility for the deaths of our loved ones, as I had suspected all along. I shall not quote the text, for it was filled with despicable boasts and longwinded threat, but it's contents further expressed his intention to destroy all which I held dear if I should not willingly meet him to give that which he sought from me. If I did not do this, then he swore upon all the earth that peace would know neither me, nor my companions, nor their acquaintances, and that such pain should be wreaked upon us, that it would remain until as he hoped truly, that I would beg for death by such time that he mercifully took what he wished in it's end.

DM: Wow, and that's just paraphrasing? Jeez... So he didn't come for you directly then?

AG: Not as of then, only by such grace that our misdirections had placed a sea of ocean between us for the time. Yet he was coming for me the same, and in foolishness to warn us, unknowingly Ruthven gave scarce yet adequate time for preparations that we might evade him.

CR: Ok, I think I got it. Let me try to go back through this real quick. So you left mainland Europe and came home with everyone to Britain, but when you got there Ruthven felt your arrival, or thought he had. So that's when he killed Fanny and... Ok what was her name again?

AG: Harriett.

CR: Right. So he kills each of them, several months apart, by enthralling them to commit suicide, complete with letters, hoping that it would draw you out, because you were with people close to them. But when you didn't show yourself, rather than look for you with Mary or Percy, he assumed that he'd been wrong about feeling your presence, or that you'd gone back to Geneva?

AG: Partly correct. I must assume that he did observe both Mary and Claire, as well at times as Percy, but by so many a time I was not living with them, and he saw no evidence of my presence. When Mary attempted suicide herself, he would have assumed my absence and followed Percy, but I had returned then to Mary in light of those events. We all moved so often in such short months, and apart from one another in addition, that it would have seemed merely favorable in our instance, that a shell game was afoot where none had been planned as such.

CR: So because he can't find you there, he follows a trail back to where you'd recently been, thinking you must have stayed, but while he's looking, he accidentally tips off Byron's people, who alert Byron to Ruthven snooping around?

AG: Yes.

DM: Until he gets hold of the published travel logs, and then because their bread trail ran cold, he sought out Byron himself, who had already sent word to you in Britain about Ruthven showing up at the villa right?

AG: Yes, however when he found Byron in Italy, after those letters had been sent, he had no way to know that we had been warned.

DM: So Byron ratted you out as being in Britain, but only because he'd already warned you first that Ruthven was after you?

AG: That is right.

DM: But Byron still ratted you out?

AG: As I said, he was under threat of life if he did not, and was promised to be left alone if he complied. We did not blame him for that. Ruthven could have easily enthralled him to compliance and extracted more information if he had not offered what he did. Byron openly confessed as much by letters which we received alongside Ruthven's own draft of threat toward us. He must have written this almost immediately after being first clear of him. For those to arrive before Ruthven could pursue, they had to have required several favors called in to expedite their delivery in such a way. We... I, could not begrudge Byron in this instance.

You must remember the speeds at which travel was limited during those years. Receipt by Mail was constrained to those same. For those letters to reach us in time at all, was nothing short of... miraculous.

A STALKERS SHADOW

CR: I just want to make sure I have everything straight. He had your address though, confirmed that you lived with Mary, Percy, Claire *and* the children, confessed that he had already killed two of your extended family, and then found Byron, just so he could let you know all of that before coming for you... Why tell you so much instead of just surprising you? Did he honestly think you would go to him?

DM: No, no... It's control... Right? From what you've said this guy thrived on control. He wanted you to be afraid. I've seen it before. It's a stalking mentality... He wanted you to know that he didn't feel threatened by any of you and he wanted you to feel trapped... didn't he?

AG: That is precisely what I deduced Doctor. Which is why the first actions we took after this revelation were not my surrender, as none would concede to this, but to prepare in our own way to take that very power from him. People like Ruthven, if fortune should choose he be called a person, desire power by their mind as compensation from the world at large, in trade for times in which they felt powerless... And this in understanding brought forth our plans, for not only did I know Ruthven the lord and fiend, but also Ruthven the soldier, who fearing for his freedom had struck bargain with myself so many years before.

Drafting letter once more to Byron, we immediately made provisions to sell our estates and upon news of Ruthven's upcoming departure from Europe, to travel after the publication of Mary's work to meet in Italy, so that Alba, or I should say Allegra, could be secured in saftey by Byron himself, whom Ruthven had granted amnesty. However to our heartbreak the consequences of this required Claire's severance of contact with both Byron and our child thereafter by Byron's own decree. A clever ruse I must confess.

If not for his further specifications, then such a thing might have been missed, but while Byron may have been selfish to a fault, he was no monster, else we would not have entertained such drastic measures. We might not have done so even then, if not out of seeming necessity and desire so strong to protect our child. However within his letters, he as the girls father did afford one allowance should Claire wish to see their daughter further, and this stipulation was the following request; That at any such time as the mother, being Claire, wished to visit *Allegra*, then Mary and Percy Shelley must *also* be present.

This of course by extensions unspoken, served also as request unspoken, in demand for my own presence in his knowing of us. For he understood well enough our feelings and love for her in equal to Claire's, and would not abide the presence of one without our others.

The suspicious side of me wondered somewhat if this might also have been some intelligent demand to give protection of his wellbeing, that if I should be the risk, then I should also be the guardian if we should break his agreed peace with Ruthven. For even in assisting us, Byron could not help but be who he was, and as I understood him then, in selfishness first he placed at all times, most highly his own concerns for wellbeing and safety.

By these plans, and unwilling to abandon one another, we swore ourselves afterward until providence might show to us another path, to live a life most restless in nature by travelling as I once had, one step ahead of our pursuer without allowance of his nearness to catch us unaware. I still would have preferred the woods of Odin defended and isolated, but as said, these alternate options were not favored by all.

We planned at this while using the guise of Mary's text so that we might search without suspicion for any who should lend us aide to defeat the shadow at our backs by unravelling of the mysteries which spawned my being. Yet first in preparations we meant to depart from Albion house in favor of a staging ground elsewhere in London, so that we might take more eased rest in our securities for the time between.

DM: Ok, but you're already giving up almost every comfort and convenience. Why didn't you just go to your cottage near the castle in Germany?

AG: It was the isolation. My spouses still held so much faith and hope in the worth of Mary's words to possibly assist in other ways that which we would forfeit had we fled entirely to solitude. This was held for that time in reserve as a last action when neccesary, given what others had failed by then. We would not risk its exposure before.

Thus intent along these lines, we carried forth with those other plans, disguising their motivation easily beneath the cause of escaping the tyranny of civil and religious judgement as well as pressing debts which Percy was *known* to suffer from. Leaving London for Dover to undertake our journey and arrive in Calais the next day, we travelled then through France, staying in Lyons during several days in March, where from afterward we made way to Italy and stayed further in Milan for three weeks of April.

The travels as one might estimate were not eased upon us while carrying not two but then three children along our endeavors. William for luck and grace had grown old enough to entertain his own mind as often he played sprawling on the carriage's floor with marbles and blocks. While at other times filled with questions, he would crawl between our seats and chatter away at the views of the countryside surrounding.

After Milan however Percy left Mary, William and baby Clara under my protections for a time in what is now called Tuscany, while he, travelling with Claire and Allegra to Venice, went to see Byron simply so that they may make arrangements. However in arriving there and finding Byron absent, they discovered that the arrogant man, fearing for his own safety lest the meeting being discovered had been some trap by Ruthven, had sent forth only a messenger to retrieve his daughter alone, leaving our loves to say farewell unwitnessed by his shamed eyes and without our opportunities afforded to do the same.

Infuriated to hear of this at first, I was surprised further to hear after their return to us, that he had in fact invited all of our company afterward to *stay* at one of his residences so that we might say our farewells more properly to the daughter whom we loved.

So mercurial and mysterious has been my judgement of that man even to this day... Regardless, we meant to do just this, hoping to see Allegra at least once more. However, after our arrival and subsequent arguments with Byron, as he had thought Mary and myself would have travelled along with Percy and Claire originally and might have been followed, we made ourselves comforted within those walls under the false senses of security that Ruthven remained in Britain still.

It is hateful to admit that unlike his abilities to detect my own presence, I never held such capacity to know of Ruthven's nearness to myself and have paid dearly on that account many a time. But none were to be so shocking as his first arrival there. We had settled for some weeks and grown comforted in what we believed the safety of Byron's estate. Perhaps trust was our mistake, or arrogance. Even I have thought at times that he in fact was punishment incarnate for our perceived sins, however none of this changes the course of time while present becomes past and future to present.

Entering the bedchambers one evening quite late so that I might sing to young Clara while changing her bedcloths, as often I took this task happily so that all others might rest; I spotted his form. He stood to my shock, leaned sinister over the rocking crib in that room without even the most remote of previous suspicions which might have warned me. For none of my senses, despite their acuity, had detected his presence.

Rushing forth at haste, I meant with no shame in my heart to kill Ruthven even before discovering his evils. Yet upon seeing our child... still and lifeless within...

Adam's breath shook.

I was brought to my knees in such overwhelming sorrow.

His breath caught repeatedly as he struggled to complete his sentences.

He fled through a nearby window at speeds that left him vanished beneath the clouded skies... even while his mocking laughter rang out long from places unseen... It sickened my heart further, but I could not move.

I did not know then my abilities to revive another, nor had I, might have been able to carry forth those tasks neccesary with shaking urgency to do so upon an infant who henceforth by my beliefs even now, then would be never aging and vulnerable to all the woes of growing mind without body to match... And so she died...

Adam was sobbing.

AG: She died, without having truly lived... and I, in depressed impotence, I could do nothing.

There was a long pause as we allowed Adam to shed the tears needed. Steven unfortunately spoke too soon regardless.

DM: Wait... what makes you think she wouldn't have aged? Also what do you mean by abilities to revive?

AG: Is *now* truly where you would ask this? After I have described these events? There are *no* words in any language I have learned which appropriately describe the wrenching pains that come with the loss of a child and yet you would stop my telling now to ask *these* questions?

Adam sneered at Steven, exhaling through his nose in the first display at frustration I would nearly call anger, which I had seen him openly express toward either of us during our interviews, but I could not blame him for it. Seeing this, Steven shook his head quickly, and backtracked his words

DM: No. No. My apologies. I'm very sorry. Go on.

AG: As I was saying, (*He began sternly*) each of us struggled so to carry on with even the slightest of joy for so long after that event. We searched for reason or blame amongst ourselves to such volume even to strain the devotions we held for one another.

Percy blamed himself as Mary claimed personal responsibility one day and cursed each of us the next, but through it all we mourned equally in fury at Ruthven, who had taken our beautiful girl from this world and stolen our joys through malicious evils unspeakable to any who might call themselves a man.

Even Byron, having been present still with us there, railed at the deception that Ruthven would break his words of amnesty and descend upon us within his own properties, swearing cruel and vicious response in kind if any harm should befall Allegra herself, whom I still believe he feigned devotion to more out of pride than true affection, even if it is ill natured of me to think such things...

I, for my part, cursed my own existence and begged each of them to allow me to depart from their company lest further tragedy befall on account of my presence, but even this they refused, including Byron, feeling that no loss prevented could be made its worth by giving up that which they also loved, or in his lordhsip's case, might signify our defeated dispositions.

"I will not trade the affections of my heart and passions of life for some unassured security and protections which would strip even more joys from my days!" Mary insisted angrily at these suggestions.

"Nor should any, for if we abandon one another and allow you face his evils alone, then Ruthven has won his aim to destroy us." Percy added.

Claire was silent, her eyes cried to exhaustion so that tears no longer fell from them, until with no more ability to speak she shivered at these thoughts.

"The fiend is enemy to freedom of all and must be defeated. If you should face him alone and he defeat your person, then all is doomed and the world forsaken! You shall stay by others and they by you, else armageddon befall us all, you Goliath of inanity!" Byron raved.

"And you too would stand by our crooked family for these things to come?" I asked him sharply. "What of Alba?!" I shouted, forgetting of her changed name.

"Allegra? A convent! Surely even as Ruthven's gaul might extend, he would touch none within the saftey of a convent!" Byron shouted, revealing for the first time those plans which further after would indeed result in Allegra's extended securities.

This of course spurned even greater argument in our grief and such shouting persisted that it became indistinguished at times from our wailing tears over the course of the following month while we stayed ourselves at Byron's home repeating these arguments in cycle over and again. The halls and rooms echoed such with noise and painfully heated debate that I feared its impacts upon young William who innocently knew nothing of what cause brought forth the conditions so changed within us.

Only Claire and I seemed able to retreat from this to care for the children, for the passions of all else raged with firey heat. And while Allegra understood nothing aside from the differences between calm and fury, William would run to me for security and hide beneath blanketed forts in confusion at what storm had taken that house within.

"Aiden, why does mother cry so?" He would ask me. "Why is Papa angry? Where is sisssy Clara? " and I could give him no answer to satisfy that innocent understanding of it which he alone possessed, until like a child myself, I too began to ask such simple questions within. Why must death exist I wondered? Why must all that is beautiful fall to ruin while I remain untouched? Most of all, how could such monstrous form and evils come of the man I once knew and housed as neighbor to me in trusted companionship? Has life's cruelty no end?

Departing by Novembers early days little had been resolved in truth, and Ruthven who had not returned, seemed all but impossible to guard against, even within Byron's homes. This was of course lest we ourselves take leave of them while Byron held custody of Allegra still for her own safety. To pursue any other course would mean that all should be suspect and endangered equally. Which we would not allow. As for this, Byron did mean to send young Alba to convent at first availability, as he swore he would join us afterward. However even that would be some time later and I for one, did not believe him. The rest of us must leave, we established; That now being Mary, Percy, Claire, William and myself, as we still mourned at the loss of not one, but two children in so short a time. And inconsolable in grief, we travelled from there. We moved heartbroken through Ferrara, Bologna, and Rome to arrive within Naples a month after.

Admittedly such attentions were poured into William then as we clung to him in all the love that could be poured from the whole of our hearts. For I confess we needed him, that remaining child, as if his love in return were the only thing that redeemed us in any part. We doted and indulged him so, that for a brief moment in that dark season, a glimmer of light shined upon us and we found only barely such strength to go on.

DM: Is now a better time?

Adam sighed deeply in resigned submission and answered Steven's previous question, in my mind simply to lay it to rest so that he could go on.

AG: I only assumed that by my own lack of aging and Breda's also, followed by Ruthven as well, that my blood would result in the stagnation of bodily growths such as maturation, healing one only as they were, rather than allowing for change.

DM: Fuck... I was afraid that's what you'd say. I don't know if this will help or hurt here but... Adam, aging isn't the same in bodily function before someone reaches maturity as afterward.

Not getting old, doesn't mean not growing up, it just means not falling apart. The failures of the human body in breakdown mostly occur due to age by an inability for someones genetic duplication to properly replicate cell instructions... It's got more to do with the degradation of mitochondrial function and shortening of the telomeres than...

Steven could see the frustration on Adam's face.

Look, I'm just saying that in theory, and I don't know if it would hold true in practice or not, but anything that could repair that type of damage, it wouldn't stop natural maturation as a process. It would only sustain them at the peak of health once they'd reached that point.

AG: Yes Doctor... I understand this *now* as science has progressed, but histories so long passed cannot be rewritten or pains removed, else I might have in hindsight returned Father to life, or even Breda. Further still i would have returned that father and child who perished by cannonfire during the battle of Carrickfergus. I could not know this then, just as it helps not the past to know it now, but only the future that it may be put to use.

DM: Damnit. Why do you keep having to say things like that? I can't just say nothing. At risk of pissing you off possibly more, I have to ask the follow up now. Are you honestly implying that in times since all this, that you have... like literally revived the dead?

I could see that Adam was tired and frustrated, but wished to press on for whatever reason to what came next. I'd seen the brief flash of annoyance that washed over him, but calming his temper quickly, he continued.

AG: I am not angry with *you* Doctor, simply ill of heart at this that is difficult to speak of and wish to achieve the telling of what follows. Those answers shall come later. For where we are within my history at this time, I would think you might find the following account of equal interest should you stay your questions until I have finished.

DM: Sorry... Sorry. Go on.

AG: Where was I? Naples, yes? That was it. Having arrived in Naples... and seeking respite after so much pain and distance, Mary and I for the first time at some length, found in one anothers forms those comforting affections of intimacy as we had come to take solace in as part of our relations.

We lay together for the first time in many months one night, without Percy or Claire in company. For neither of them it seemed, held the humors to seek this same release between us. I feel that this was due not only to the general sense of depression for the recent losses we had faced, but more specifically that those had filled them each with dread and fear toward the possible conception of another who might also be lost in turn.

In support at this I would note that Percy himself did still for reasons all his own, feel compelled to engage in several drunken dalliances during this time, but remained absent from our bed alone. Perhaps it was a need for distance and the lack of intimacy present with those strangers should conception result, however such closeness was essential to Mary and myself and together we held no such fears to divide us. Of course we did this without knowledge that my body would hold within it even the capability to conceive, and for this too we would suffer greatly the following consequence to that ignorance.

By dawn the trailing day therefore, came our complete astonishment to see clearly without question that Mary, now swelled in form and vomitous of stomach, had grown pregnant with child overnight... This fact revealed by such rapid growth and change within her womb over a single night, that she appeared then as if some 6 months with child by the sun's rise and waking hour, even as she rushed from bed to expel most violently that which had been eaten the night before. There was confusion from all, and at first notice, anger that she had somehow hidden her condition, as if secrecy were even possible. Yet William's response itself calmed this by so fundamental a question that it stayed those flared tempers directly.

"Aiden, made a magicked baby inside mum?" He giggled childishly, and with these words the truth revealed to us wholeheartedly so that all stood still in truth even as his laughter continued. All was not well however. Within days further, Mary became contorted in pain by each passing mark of the clocks chime, her body's rapid transformations left her riddled with affliction as the procedures of gestation quickened such as they were, had placed strain upon her so fervently and with implacable demands that they very nearly killed her.

We witnessed helplessly these changes by each day as in fear for our beloved's life we could place no blame on Ruthven nor any other but ourselves, and remained in careful care to hide from the world the unexplainable haste of her secret pregnancy while panic took us in turn to care for our dear wife. However within the span of a single month, the most horrific and strained growth continued at expeditious pacing until labor arriving, brought forth the full tortures of Mary's agony to punctuated extremes, wherein her screams and pain could be hidden from none.

Yet then, within mere hours after the event had begun, like William at the month's start had naively implied, as if by "magic", an infant girl was born. She came to us in blood and spectacle, which unmatched by any natural occurrence, had nearly torn dear Mary's body asunder during her delivery to be certain. And still we worried over Mary's health that she may not survive. Yet thankfully and by untold miracles they lived, mother and child both, they lived.

Truthfully it was not only in her survival that we did find relief, but in first inspection of the newborn girl as well. For by chance during the throes of childbirth, Mary, while cursing my name and all fates at play, had gripped my hand so tightly, burrowing her fingernails into my very skin, that the yellow fluids of my blood trickled from there into the water of the bath in which she lay, and promptly they healed her from those deformations and wounds which the babe's term and delivery had carried with it as issue and payment. Seeing these things altogether in succession, untold joys at that blessing, though terrible in its effect by then relieved, saw Mary restored in health, having brought within this world a babe of my own fathering, unanticipated in every way.

This grace and providencial greatness was such in enormity, that even Percy, so devout in atheism, nearly thanked God for such a gift bestowed as wonder overcame each of us to behold not a disfigured or alien child to match her father's countenance, but instead the most healthy and average looking infant as there had ever been upon the earth. For days afterward our joys abounded. Mary had recovered in full and even in secret amongst us, as none else knew or could be told of how this babe had come to be, we celebrated her arrival and William was overjoyed to welcome his new sister.

Yet in this too we found new depths of despair to dawn upon us that truth which must *never* be told... For born of my blood, here innocent and beautiful to behold, Ruthven's aims might now be accomplished not by prey upon myself, but in discovery of this defenseless infant the possibility of his ascensions to desired power. If this should come to pass then he would surely descend upon her in my place to fulfill his evil aims, and with no ability to detect his whereabouts, any life she lived would be bound to us at all times without freedoms or joy her own. Panic took us at these thoughts and in long discussions we considered every option.

The only saving grace we felt was that Ruthven for now knew nothing of our child, and in knowing not, could never prey upon her. In the end, the only way to protect her as we determined, would be to keep that secret of her origin and not ourselves be near enough that suspicions arising, could be connected of us to her birth or life ever after, lest Ruthven even unknowingly in attempt to pain us further, seek to destroy her as he had Clara before, might inadvertently discover her parentage and sup himself that innocent's blood to rise even greater in strength.

This could not be allowed. We knew so achingly in our hearts the singular course of her salvation, that my only child, who bearing no resemblance to me, must not be taken from that place or raised by us, but given to another for the sake of her continuing safety and chance at life's living to come... Destruction so wrought, wrung dry the tears from our eyes, for even in loss there might be hope not for our sake, but for her own.

We named her Elena Adelaide, the second name of which had been inspired by William's own moniker for her Papa... and for one month we cherished her, being certain of her natural growth and health, that she would display no further miraculous traits as to draw the attentions of others. We listed Percy as her father, registered her custody to a woman whom we met mostly by chance named Marina Padurin, and allowed her to depart us, never to see our child again.

After this I thought to depart as well, but in furious tears Claire cried out first against her usual nature in protest."You will not Adam! You will not! And we shall not see it done! You are *my* husband! Just as Percy is my husband and Mary my sistered wife! We shall not sacrifice or surrender willingly one more member of this family ever again! Leave now and you will see my death! For I will not allow your absence to provide my safeties!" She shouted between heavy sobs.

So broken she appeared, so wholly disassembled in heart that I could not turn from her then, nor could the others. For they assured her even as we wrapped our arms together round that fallen form in comfort, that her words were true and none shall allow me banishment without equally destroying our family's wholeness. This we did and by this I was sworn yet again, even before the carriage which carried my infant daughter, could pass from our sight.

Adam closed his eyes and breathed deep. When he opened them, I saw that he was looking at me directly.

This child of which I speak Ms. Reynolds... My child first named

Elena... She was... Within a year and some months you see, fearing Ruthven's potential discovery of her as gossips had spread that perhaps she were the child of Claire and Percy...

Her name was changed and documents forged proclaiming her death, even as she was secreted away further from our own eyes into the lost mysteries thereafter. It took so long to discover in truth that so beautifully she had been adopted and raised within the Reynaldi family as I would later find, and to have lived a long and natural life complete with children and grandchildren of her own...

She was *your* ancestor Cassandra.... This I know you both have questioned, and this is how such came to pass.

And you, being the last of that line, having changed upon imigration in name from Reynaldi to Reynolds, are my last living descendant on this earth. So , you are as such the last vestige of my beloved Mary who I may cling to... and I have found you to tell you this and more before I die... for I wish you to know from whom your line comes. I desire this so, that another... That another, may continue to love her... To love my Mary, after I am gone...

Adam had streamed into quieted tears while revealing this. I was speechless. Out of respect and a need to gather ourselves, I stopped recording.

A FAMILY ABIDES

As one might imagine, much was discussed during our short break. Things were pretty difficult, but ultimately the evidence which Steven had previously analyzed was already enough to all but confirm Adam's claim before the explanation that had finally come of it. So there was a sense of relief and confirmation to have it out in the open at last. However being so personally involved in the nature of those discussions, it can be a little hard to sort out what type of description to give here. There was continued crying on all sides combined with as I said, relief and happiness from both Adam and myself. Most of what we discussed are things I would like to remain off record for now since they pertain a little more to my side than to his.

We did take advantage of the break to eat a bit and excuse ourselves for other pressing neccesities as needed, but soon after we were ready to get started again.

Recording resumes, April the 1st, 9:23 pm

CR: Are you sure your'e ready?

AG: Yes.

CR: Ok... Then my first question has to be about Marina. You said you met her by chance. How long had you known her? How did that happen? And were there many others you'd met during your time in Italy?

AG: We met her acquaintance on our first night in Naples actually. She had come seeking Percy, having heard of our arrivals thru local gossip and published columns in advance. Such was the nature of notoriety endured by writers at the time, almost to the levels to which modern celebrity attracts papparazzo, yet without the cameras or extremities of privacy interrupted by those proverbial lurkers in the hedge.

It just so happened by these things that being a follower of Percy's works, Marina wished only to meet him, and after doing so made such an impression that she had grown somewhat close under a brief period of time to all but myself. This admittedly was not entirely uncommon.

Though my telling of it may appear at first as if we restrained all contact with others, in truth we met many, and Mary, in promotion of her novel, even conducted business during this time despite our woeful troubles.

There was one incident which I recall while still prior to our deep sadness and mourning. Percy himself had demanded this quite indignantly on her behalf that she refute the conjecture of a british magazine writer who had sworn that he, that being Percy, not the magazine writer, was the rightful author of *her* work.

Even after this and all that followed, none but myself could avoid the notoriety which trailed their persons, and many kinships were formed throughout our travels. Claire met a man called Trelawny who was quite taken with her, despite her rebuffing his advance more than once. That individual however, being a naval man, had found in Percy instead, quite an interested party in discussing all things nautical to an extent that Percy for a time, attempted to convince us each the benefits of life upon the sea.

Also during this time, Mary worked at the already published novel with edits abounding in preparation for later editions to come that might include outlet for our many heartbreaks and changes in circumstance since penning the original drafts.

CR: Can you tell me anything else about Marina? Did you ever get to meet her personally?

AG: Only the once... and at some distance, still obscured within shadow enough to stay the potential of hysteric reaction. Despite this, I was told at length of her keen mind and belief in love, as well as how comforting she had been to Mary and Claire for their losses. Also that she had lost a child of her own most tragically the year before, which is partly why our decision had been to place your ancestor in her care, not knowing in foreknowledge the need that would arise to falsify her death and move her once more in times to follow.

CR: Her "belief in love"... Did her and Percy sleep together?

AG: Not so likely as I could discern. Percy as previously mentioned was given more to the comfort of strangers or men during that time, and she was closer to him than that.

CR: Did that ever make Mary or Claire jealous? Or you for that matter?

AG: Understanding why people ask such things, it has always seemed none the less humorous to me in the gulf of misunderstanding that our world instills regarding that. I do not think it intentional that the majority do leap to those assumptions, and yes at times jealousy did occur, even to the point of argued resentment. For unfair divisions of time or lavish affections regarding poor choiced lovers that were warned against, still affected our family.

Yet so rare it seems to cross the minds of the average person just how great the joy can be in feeling bliss or happiness expanded within their partner's enjoyments, that jealousy ceases to be a primary motivation, and instead becomes the basis for understanding and security. By sharing the source of those feelings and seeking rightful correction or compromise together to relieve them you see, we found only strength and trust which was gained, not lost.

CR: But what about between Claire and Mary?

AG: Sister will be sisters, even whilst married to one another. Albeit Mary often exaggerated this within her writing to others that she may disguise their true affections together. For many had suspected Allegra at first to have been fathered by Percy, including their own father in Britain. So it was that in keeping up appearances, Mary did in fact feign so far as resentment for her sister to cast off many suspicions over prolonged periods. However truthfully she wished only for her happiness and protection, and would never upon pain of death have seen to cast her aside. Claire was Mary's Elizabeth, and as I have said, what truth she held of thought for her may be found within those expressions of Victor Frankenstein's love for that character created in her image.

DM: Did Mary ever sleep with other people?

AG: Not so often, and with less enthusiasm or outward needs as Percy... We found satisfaction together, Mary, Claire and I... and while shared equally in our love for one another as in our love for Percy, chose not to pursue further entanglements at readied chance, aside from those who sparked within them some special quality that might merit further exploration. This did happen on occasion, but sadly none held fast and true enough in form and thought to bind the risk of addition to our household.

Percy himself was... complex... and though it might drive

us mad to indulge his many varied pursuits, we saw the need within him, and understood that such drives were not of purely sexual nature, but motivated most often by an unquenchable thirst to quell unseen pains or satisfy within another that which he could not bury within his own heart. For in the giving of pleasure to another, just as in the overly abundant financial assistance he seemed incapable of refusing the less fortuned, he found what I might call the divinity of service and peace which he lacked by way of religion or faith.

CR: Wait... So are you saying that sex replaced religion for him?

AG: Indirectly yes , suppose that was part of it. To be more succinct, I might say that any spreading of love and joy replaced for him that which was called religion at the time. It filled his heart and gave purpose to his life to be of service to another which he saw as worthy, and though the impulse comes to many that they might call such things selfish, I simply cannot assign to him that which I might easily say of Byron.

Was there some level of inherent selfishness to seek comfort in that which sustained and eased the pains his heart and brought meaning to his days? To play at dalliances with others in his time of grief that he might feel relieved to bring them happiness without exposing the depths of his own despair or sharing with them that intimacy reserved for us? Possibly so... But why would that bring jealousy to any of us who knew with absolute security the depths of his love and affections? The only action which could have possibly driven him from us or us from his heart would have been to deny this of him, and as he saw the prospect of that, chain his being to limitation.

DM: Compersion... I've heard the word before. Had to look it up. Its the opposite of jealousy, like extreme positive empathy where one person feels another person's happiness vicariously.

AG: Yes Doctor, though the term may be used newly, the meaning is essentially that and the same.

CR: Ok… so, how did William handle losing another sibling?

AG: With saddened acceptance regrettably. By such time he had become unfavorably accustomed to loss and departures, and while he took joys in having a sister again even for so temporary her stay, his attachment to others aside from the four of us, seemed almost remote. We had first noted this with odd inspection of his seeming relief to hear that Allegra was to be taken by her father, even before dear Claras death. As some animosity toward her had seemingly grown within him, possibly due to our negative feelings expressed regarding Byron himself or partly in misplaced blame for Clara's absence afterward.

Mary wrote once even how this very oddity to us, caused question in her regarding nature versus nurture as it applies to the goodwill and graces of innocence. Not that *I* could blame this on any but ourselves, having moved so often and suffered so much within his short life, what else could be done but to adapt or seek answers within our own dispositions?

In so many times since then I have oft wondered what type of man he might have become, that child so curious and playful… If only Ruthven had not found us again.

CR: Oh my god no! Adam… William?

AG: Sadly…

DM: Fucking hell… Seriously dude, I am so fucking sorry… If I could travel back in time, I'd kill this Ruthven asshole myself. I swear man.

AG: Calm yourselves please, I can bear it for the moment if you can stand to hear more. Temperance and forgiveness are virtues learned in the fullness of time and though I regret nothing of my eventual actions to end Ruthven's reign of terrrors, I know myself not faultless in the victimhood of circumstance that drove his motives despite the depths of evil which possessed his heart.

DM: Just skip ahead. Get it over with.

AG: As you wish. After my child had been secured away in secret, we travelled from Naples to Rome, moving into the Palazzo Verospi by that March, now in 1819. For the while we lived therein even in knowing Ruthven's presence seen nearby. Mary you see, was again pregnant, by Percy this time, and was strained to travel further if could be prevented.

When word of Ruthven reached us that an English beggar clothed in shambles had been suspected of several deaths within the area, we meant to make our stand rather than than flee. For it seemed to us that these conditions implied his desperation if not weakness.

Other motivations and angers perhaps clouded our judgements in this decision as well. Having lost Clara to his hand, and then given up our Elena to mystery, we clung to hopes concerning Alba and deeply wished her return. Also we wished saftey for the child yet to be, and should we continue as we had, what chance would there truly come toward that end?

Truthfully, letters had come from Byron in code that told us much of dear Allegra by that time, such as her learning Italian in place of English, and her growing similarities to himself, which in vanity gave him much joy to behold. Yet in fear that Ruthven had haunted his presence in anticipation of our return, and also the difficulties arising from raising one so like himself in temperment, Byron had sent her to stay for long periods with his friend Richard Hoppner, whom was at least he told us, a wealthy and upstanding british consul, bordered by defenses both secure and great. Hoppner's wife however did not care for Allegra and sent her to stay with three other families in as many months.

Percy responded most angrily at such injustices and revealed through secret phrases, Ruthven's presence nearer to us. This was done in hopes that Byron might reclaim the child and assume his fatherly duties in earnest. But as I say, it is my belief that these emotions prompted directly those decisions for us to stay, in hopes that by doing so, Ruthven's threat may be brought to an end so that we could reclaim Alba in removal from Byron's dismissive and irresponsible fatherhood. By that time Byron had publicly labelled *us* the offenders in lacking care or upkeep of *our* children whom we had lost, as he would tell others, that they had died from sicknesses brought on by neglect, even while knowing the full truth. What denial could we offer? Helplessly we endured this slander without retort, and in those days grew only to resent Byron himself in addition.

We, during that stay I mention, defended ourselves with all that could be done to keep watch at every hour, even procuring the assistance of some nearby residents who sought to catch the local murderer. We convinced these men that we of all surrounding peoples should be exceptional in cause to fear this fiend due to our families shared nationality with him, and those notorieties which might prompt his aims toward us. Being in reason enough to be believed, this they took at face value that they should keep vigil over our home, and in doing so likely catch that murderer at which time he made advance against us.

Yet this too was for naught, as unbeknownst to us, Ruthven did enthrall these men to allow his nightly entry unsuspected, even while we thought ourselves safe. The tragic result of this was that in doing so freely for so prolonged a period, Ruthven had laid plans most foul and had repeatedly drank from dear William while he slept, not at once, but over a span of weeks, leading us to believe at first that he had contracted illness rather than what evils he suffered at Ruthven's hand.

In this time that William suffered, we remained ignorant. Though doctors came to treat him and every effort made to extend his life deemed his sickness to be malaria, without cause to suspect our lasting foe. When the time passed that he too had died, William was buried within a protestant cemetary by ceremonies which I could not attend. Afterward the others, joined by friends in mourning, stayed late into the night at the home of another, where provisions were laid out and fellowships continued.

I had not been forgotten, merely a victim of further circumstance. Left in my grief, I stayed alone within the halls of our home all the same. So it was that with all others away then, Ruthven came for me that night, leading those same men who we had thought our protectors. He marched before me within the courtyard with laughter and gloat at his cruel deviancy to reveal to me of his own claims, what actions he himself had committed and how. This was all at once the first suspicion and confirmation of the truth to dear William's death and with no other near to protect at that time, I charged at that devil in unrestrained fury.

None I felt but sheer evil could commit such wanton acts of barbarism, and in barbaric fashion I meant to destroy that man for his crimes! Only in this rush, I came to be surrounded fast by guards so turned against our family that I was held at bay with flaming torch and pitched forks that I could not reach my quarry without first injuring several innocents. Still I would not desist, and throwing off these men with aims not to kill them, I reached Ruthven in person where grappling with our torturer, I fought against his strength and speed even while others beat and stabbed at my body from all encircling sides.

To see him, clad in beggars rags or not, he had not changed a day since our last encounter aside from the look of his skin and eyes, which now pale and ghostly matched not my own, but some other type of being also not quite human.

Ruthven laughed maniacally. "And yet do you wish for death old friend?! Have you had enough of your charade to be one of these chattel and love amongst them who would leave you alone in grief?"

I roared indistinctly and grabbed at his shoulders, meaning to rip the head from his body, but flame had caught the blood spilling from my veins and soon a blaze surrounded us as we continued to struggle. Then, suddenly and without warning, I was rendered unconscious by what would later prove to have been a rifle shot to my head.

I did not wake for several weeks. My body had been found the following morning by my companions and moved along with our belongings. My loves took me by that time in hopes of recovery, to a Villa near Montenero. Though I woke at last after this long stay of their tormented anguish, I for great part had not yet entirely healed. Mary was the first to see this, and followed by Percy and Claire wept in relief that I lived. However I could not share in this. Knowing the truth of what my presence had cost, and at last determined to break the hearts of those I loved, I confessed to them of now knowing of what had happened in honesty to dear William. And despite all argument and protest, I stumbled from that place into the night air with determination to seek out Ruthven once more and put an end to that pursuit, even if my death should result.

Being less than recovered of course as mentioned, I was followed and stopped before I could make it far enough to evade my loves. Though they could not dissuade me, in tearful concession, they reluctantly accepted my resolve to leave them for this task. It was with greater pain even still that each of my beloved spouses bid me farewell that night, under the promise that should I survive, I *must* return to them.

I had not the heart to kiss their lips or embrace their bodies in my shame, and departing in desperate pains, I walked away into the night, not knowing if ever I should meet the sweetness of their company again.

CR: But Mary was still pregnant...

AG: With a son... Whom I would meet but once, in all his years to come.

DM: Where did you go?

AG: Ultimately, I boarded a ship aimed for the Americas. Knowing him as I did, there was no doubt to my heart that Ruthven would pursue me first in priority, forsaking vengeance upon my family to do so. Therefore, I baited his arrivals to this. I extended my wanderings until I knew undoubtedly that he followed, all so that he might see my destination bound before I ever embarked upon my passage chosen. I meant to take him so far from those I loved as my body allowed.

I hid myself from all eyes notice, save his who watched me from shadow nearby. This new trick was one as which I had learned not so long ago then. Obscuring my face from others in mid day behind a barrel carried on each of my shoulders as if I were loading supply; None thought to question or delay any large figure so heavily burdened in labor. Every fiber of me knew that Ruthven would give chase, and in this I breathed easier, some dark but lightened satisfactions. I had chosen my vessel wisely, and my timing more so. Despite his speed, strength or gall, he would not risk exposure here at his weakest.

I had moved downward into the hold, filled as it was with teas and spice. There, it was through a small window below decks that I looked out to observe anxiously his movements. As the hours passed and daylight waned, part of me feared that he may attempt to stow away as I had within the same ship, or to attack in force by night's cloak, but hopes remained that instead, his malicious patience would see him meet me once more on foreign soil. I knew that there was only one other craft which paired with my own, would follow closely the same course to those distant lands, each departing by the next morning light. I knew that it sat near, within the next slip, and I meant for him to take it. However if he did not, then our fight would be there, exposed within that busy port, even under dark of night. Both our secrets would be laid bare in what destruction we could wreak, but one if not both would perish for sure. This possibility I accepted in risk.

Still, morning's light would bid the crew to set sail with the rising sun. So I watched through that night, his pacing, his planning, his ire restrained, growing bolder as he emerged from the alley nearby to question those workers upon the docks and discover the destination of both vessels in wait. Shortly before dawn, I looked to see him vanish in a flash, only to make way unto that partnered carrier by such skilled and practiced use of his speed and silence that no other noticed but I. In this sight too I held some success to my credit so early on. I had been proven correct. He would indeed abandon the lands of Europe in my pursuit, but not to risk public exposure in assurance of his own destruction.

So it came to pass that each of us sailed by the schedule of men who knew nothing of our presence. Separately we travelled together without word spoken between or sight glimpsed for that time. The voyage was long, and desolate was my heart, but watching closely that ship which followed, I could not know before arriving within upstate New York, the ghastly fate which I had inadvertently sentenced toward that other vessel or it's crew. They followed our lead each day. I had seen it. However I learned by our entry within port, to my further guilt and shame, that Ruthven by journeys end, had killed the lot of them at sea and fled the ship before it could be searched.

Yet I had watched the sails raised and lowered only the day before. He could not have manned those tasks alone, even at his speed. Further, these things had been done beneath the full force of a noon sun. Which meant to me only one possible alternative, that such death, even on the scale required to murder them all, must have been carried out only in the last hours if not moments before arrival. The ship had not been anchored, nor had it missed it's mark to dock by any measure more than my own height. How had he done this? Why? Even I, watching thru every open moment which allowed my sight of that ship, did not see these actions committed, nor his escapes. I remained addled in confusion by what he had done or how it had been accomplished until I recalled the power of his thrall. Murder by distance... He could have escaped days before without notice, and upon his departure inspired the crew to carry forth upon their duties only to slay one another at a previously assigned marker once he had safely distanced himself from notice. This was not my doing I knew. Yet the fault was mine the same.

For my part, I fled as well by what methods I could before our own occupants might be detained or questioned.

DM: But how? I assume the barrel trick wouldn't work again in this case. You can't just dive overboard. There werent cannon ports. You said yourself the window was small... It sounds like he trapped you.

AG: That is because he meant to. Fortunately the anchor chain of that ship emerges from the shelter deck thru a rather sizable hole, which with a deal of contortion and dislocations, I was able to climb thru before descending the chain itself to the water. True that I had to sneak my way up another level before I could reach that point of egress, but that is the lovely thing about cargo hatches. They rarely emerge within crew quarters themselves.

CR: You fit through the hole meant for an achor chain?

DM: Oh no Cass. That's actually plausible.

Steven motioned with his hands a distance apart from one another to demonstrate the size in lieu of description.

CR: Oh... Ok. Wow that's some hefty chain.

DM: Mmhmm!

Steven nodded with widened eyes and closed lips.

AG: It truly is Ms. Reynolds. Anchor chains of that scale were still relatively new in use aboard the English merchant vessels, and had replaced hemp cables not so long before. I'd never actually looked at one so closely. Still, the size that men craft works often boggles my mind. Even one of my size is dwarfed to think of the scale to which some things are created and intended for use.

I cannot fathom what thoughts any man has to create things so much bigger than his own means to control them, aside from the drive to utilize powers even greater. I don't sit well with it honestly. It unnerves me. To consider that a singular component of some design is larger in scale than any one man can even lift on his own, would be to me, a sign that it should not be made. Personally I am limited by this.

Yet no limits seem to exist where it comes to mankind's cooperative ambitions. Were the world filled with those of my small mindset, no footsteps would have made it to the moon largely due to this. I would have insisted that every component be of scale for a single person to easily construct, maintain, and manage if needed, without anothers assistance. That I fear is merely another product of forced isolation and self reliance that I have never overcome. Even then, to climb down the links of that chain itself, it baffled me. Yet in years since I have seen things so much expanded and enlarged at never ceasing ends, that now looking back I should miss the quaintness of a simple chain so scaled.

Regardless, I did make my escape with intent to lead Ruthven on such a chase that I might ensnare him alone at placements more suitable in isolation. So by land and secrecy, I left port alone to step out within that alien country. I set such course toward some wilderness far from prying eyes, yet arriving days later within bordering lands of a township nestled within the Hudson valley, I instead fell victim to my own ignorance of what powers Ruthven had attained. This I heard in rumored panic by that which he had enacted in wait, arriving in advance of my journeys.

Such had been the success of my defeat before you see, that he felt secured not to attack me directly, but employ instead a soldierment of others to stay clean his hands from conflict between our enabled bodie's strengths. Still due to his plans at this, I soon learned to my own horror the extent of Ruthven's sway over man not only in mind, but also in form. As tales from this township began to be told in following days, of corpses removed from their graves and sightings about the region, of long dead neighbors who had been seen walking along the roadside nearest a particular covered bridge specifically.

This I confess shocked me to hear and though I could not by previous encounter confirm such abilities, I feared in truth the legitimacy of such words, knowing only in my conviction that Ruthven must be responsible by some means. However, here to hear in their telling, while hiding amongst the roomed stocks of ale housed in darkness by a local tavern, I encountered an unexpected ally. For one man, a stranger to that town, though robust and aged, remained seemingly less skeptical than all others.

He made it voiced his ambition to witness these hauntings and revealed himself the brother of an author of keen mind and insight, whom he felt would find much interest to hear of the town's woes. I, hearing this and without another to entrust with the truth of that danger posed to those peoples, chose then that should he be worthy of trust and strong of heart, that by nightfall that very eve, I might reveal myself and explain the mystery of these happenings in exchange for his aide.

DM: That seems quite bold of you.

AG: I had little to lose by this point, and much more cause to risk such a thing. Authors, it seemed as I had known several by that time, even those not courageous of disposition, have in my experience a boundless curiosity that conquers often the expectation and rules of societal accords. This I theorized might also be proved true as well to one's sibling. Though I could not be certain, and yes there was much risk involved upon this gambit.

Unbeknownst to me at that time the man of whom I speak was also a congressmen within that state, not that I credit much stock in those matters these days. However at the time, in that frontier of early America, I held this in great esteem to discover. What strikes me as humorous today of course, is that even when I had knocked upon his door in night's darkness and he opened said door to greet me, I was met not with a man terrified at my presence, but instead a welcoming if not wary disposition that treated me at first sight as if I were entirely average to look upon. In fact, taking me by the fire of his lodging, even as I noted a loaded rifle nearby, he showed himself intrigued in fascination to hear all I might tell without seeming judgement or annoyance at my intrusion.

Of course also as tends to happen, and not at all by my prompting, Mr. Irving saw fit within very short order, to record what of these tales had inspired him, and by creative pen, to send their accounts to that same brother, the writer in England, whom within mere months of our adventurous pursuits to follow, had published several disjointed parts of those actions within a series of stories he titled "The Sketch book of Geoffrey Crayon".

DM: Washington Irving I assume?

AG: Was the brother of the man I met, yes. Though I must admit that I sought him out quite rashly in retrospect. Part of my trust and decision may have been influenced unfairly by his name, despite the irrational merit of such thoughts; As when I first heard it, I could not help but think of the only other William I had known, and his parting so fresh in my heart. Perhaps I merely wished within some wildness of mind unconscious then, that I might imagine this man to somehow be an older version of that child whom I might come to know in substituions to my aching at his absence.

DM: Adam, if I might ask, has no writer you've encountered ever formed a wholly original idea?

AG: Why Steven, you surprise me. Would you consider Cassandra, a journalist and writer herself to be unoriginal? Ideas, even original ones, grow from inspirations well, and though the shadow of my life has cast long upon this world;

Credits lie with authorship *however* inspiration is found. For words described that untold before might be revealed, require flourish and skill to document even when unchanged in story. Would you pose that I should claim authorship myself or assume those works inspired by my life as belonging to me rather than one who records them? I think not. I have been merely a player upon the stage wherein too many touched by horrors adjacent, have taken pen in hand to create new concept and telling from the ashes of my wake.

DM: Ok sure, but here you are telling us now that not only did you inspire Frankensteins creature, which I believe of course, no objections there. But also Rhime of the Ancient Mariner, several poems by Byron, Percy, Mary et cetera, but also what I assume now will be Sleepy hollow and possibly even Rip Van Winkle by Wasington Irving... And all but one of those because you *also* created the first vampire who your'e chasing through upstate New York, because all the tragedies in Mary Shelleys life were caused by him and not random circumstances, illness, or personal irresponsibility.

It's such a huge claim! And even *if* it's true, all of it, or even most, it almost seems too revisionist to account for. Your stories basically have you Forrest Gumping your way through history and classic literature as if you were the main character of the world for literal centuries. What about the power of *their* words and *their* contributions to the world when you say that *you* were the source? If there is even the *slightest* chance that you're embellishing, or that *any* of your story is a lie, then it discredits so many people... I just have a hard time with it. That's all.

AG: Understandably... Yet no Steven, I do not lie to you, and I would discredit no one. Only the deepest admirations and gratitude exist within me for what so many have taken from my woes and passed onto the world which others have felt, learned from, or been inspired by in times since. And only within me exists the deepest of regrets that my presence brought with it such devastation to those same which I loved. I know your respect and admiration for their names and histories you have been told, and I mean not to diminish it in the least, only to expand upon your knowing of them as I knew them for the people they were, that you may with deeper understanding, view the enormity of those contributions in context.

However let us take this theory and test it against the nature of the vampyre as writers have made him in contrast to what I might have spoken. Firstly vampyres had existed in various forms as we have discussed, often misunderstood maladies and mental illnesses, afflictions and so on, from times all but lost to history. Being embellished by folk legend or perhaps even yes, cursed immortals that I know nothing of. That is where from Byron's words he proved able to source and label Ruthven to begin with.

My blood gave power and control to a man already monstrous, and his form he did became template for what would follow, but I did not create the concept itself, just as I did not instruct Mr. Irving to craft what would come into his tale of a schoolteacher in pursuit of a land owner's daughter.

What I can tell you, is that immortality as most often depicted, comes accompanied by guilt birthed from the loss of humanity. It is the repetition of evil deeds, the taking of life, that sustains the ever living. And in this it is deemed that the nature of man is somehow evil. tHis si a sentiment by which I do not agree. However, what of one not birthed by some change, not chained to that imagined loss of humanity? Born instead of its absence into the glowing lights of hope to achieve it above him, and be spurned instead by people not beautious but hideous in form?

What place within these popularized concepts has the immortal which will *not* feed off of life, but would give it instead to all? Guilted in their own way, in my way, by their very survival, sustained with dark gift and curses so different from the popularized vampyre? Should I take this personal? I would.

Ruthven was not a creation by my choice, but in balance he found existence thru my mistakes and became in truth my burden to bear. For in him shadowed the mirror of myself, that he should become a guiltless killer craving for power and death, while he did not concern himself with losss of humanity, but rather considered himself above it. He had lived as I had not, been afforded that which I had lacked, and yet rather than reach for personhood, had embraced titles and substitution along with that monstrous aspect pursuant to the life I now refuted, much as my own creator had refused me long before.

Once I had begged for companionship so that I may know love and in anger killed the love of another. Yet and despite this, having found at last without my creators evil deeds, loves to call my own; My creation had begged also for that I would not give freely, and in anger he had killed the loves of my heart. Would none write of this cruel poetry in symetrical aspect?

In my creation's tasting of blood and acquired power over life, he craved destruction alone, even though for centuries to follow, that image of him would persist romanticized by authors whom I would *not* meet. Is that the originality you seek? That ever I remained the monster, for in his form the Vampyre became beautiful and in temptation of his beauty even my warning against him, drafted by Byron himself would inspire the first of these endless motifs?

Ruthven, the prototypical of classic figure that would come to redefine the putridity of folk legend and horror into lust and beauty, the low to high born and the nature of evil into tormented lover by the scribblings of our contemporaries... Such is the insidious translation of writers to what ends they may take inspiration and craft originality; That from the cold and damned nariccisssm of the known poet too afraid in ego and self preservation to even pen his name to the tale. I would suffer these indignations for centuries later, only now to face your inquisition to my honesty after all you have been told?

Steven you are more intelligent than these questions and kinder of heart than to attempt harm to another, but your timing and placement of skeptical over curious mindings do marr the acceptance of realities to your ear, so that I fear in bias you seek their rejection, even when it serves you not.

I pity this of you my friend, for it limits your view and alienates those who bring forth innocently what challenge it faces to the setness of your preconceptions. Have a care that the wonder which originally inspired you does not fade to jaded stubbornness so that even the most sought dreams of your youth cease in magic when you have met them in waking life.

Doctor, please, I would like only that you listen to your heart rather than that rigid structure of your learning which urges you to question these events at each turn.

DM: I am trying...

AG: Then continue to do so and I will abide your questions in the nature which they are given. For though you may not see it firstly, I am open and vulnerable to speak such things and it pains me to tell them.

DM: I understand...

Steven hung his head and I could see that he was sorry, but also I have to admit that I understood where he was coming from, and despite my wholehearted belief in Adam, was also finding it hard at times to accept what he was saying.

CR: Adam, would you like to continue?

AG: I shall, though I feel sorry for my defensiveness. Steven, I apologize.

DM: It's ok. I want to hear the rest.

AG: Mr. Irving, as I was saying, had accepted my presence and offered what assistance he could. Though my tale abbreviated as it was, had lasted the night all the same, and we did not sleep. Instead, we struck out within the saftey of that next morn's daylight to investigate the accounts of the townspeople which we had each heard tell. While I kept to the forest surrounds until we had reached the bridge, Mr. Irving, being of some age, walked directly those roads which led us to the scene.

CR: And what did you find?

AG: Horror, dear child... Most ghastly horrors. It was not by the bridge itself, but tracking disturbance of leaves and trailing of bile, that we followed deeper within the surrounding wood until we had reached a clearing near dusk where fogs settled low within the valley. That dimness and shadow, affording Ruthven free passage, had also given to him concealment, and unknowing to us, we had been surrounded slowly by such creatures which he had brought to animation against us.

I might have known if I had ever cause to question, but did

not realize until then the extent of my bloods power to do these things. However to see the desecrations it's corruption yielded, chilled my very being when the lantern lit by my companion revealed the lurching and mindless forms of those corpses which Ruthven now commanded. Even headless, one dressed in foreign soldiers garb, lunged forward with his arm in immediacy, wielding a sword that slashed my coat even while I evaded harm to my body.

Caught by such surprise, Irving shouted at once that I should find the master of these corpses, even while he fought them off. For their strength and speed were minimal, though their visage grisly and aims equal in hazard to the malicious intent of their maker. I peered into the mist of fog around us, and needing no lantern myself, did spy Ruthven at distance, where he stood upon a jutted stone to view and control his puppeted troop of the deceased. Shouting at him I ran, along the way seizing upon a large boulder to raise above my head and throw toward his body. This he dodged, leaving it to pass his person my hairs breadth, it crashed beyond with sound like the peals of thunder echoing throughout the valley.

"No more!" I shouted, even as his speed allowed him to escape impact, but this was enough. As in his distraction, the bodies stopped within their tracks and revealed some limits of his control. If only I could reach him and focus that attention needed to stay his soldiers, then I knew my companion would be not only freed temporarily from harm, but also given such opportunity, might gain ground to fire his weapon accurately enough to outpace even that swiftness which was my opponents advantage over me.

Ruthven however also knowing this weakness, trained eyes upon those moved by his will and directed them then toward myself to slow my advances. However, the mistake was his, for my partnership though new and without reason for such trust, proved invaluable when this too presented Mr. Irving that opportunity for which I had hoped. Firing once, somehow calmness steadied his aim and in an instant, Ruthven was struck midcenter through his chest while all enthralled by his person dropped lifeless along the leaves around me.

The fray was short, and seemingly won, yet unfortunately this proved not an end to my opponent, as somewhere in the fog, he fled, injured but alive to heal and regroup. Irving rushed to my side where I convinced him quickly that we should track the trail of spilled blood before the villain could escape. In fast agreement we followed with haste for nearly an hour until breathless and exhausted as my companion had become, we lost the trail along waters edge, once more finding ourselves in view of that town's covered bridge where all traces vanished.

Those waters proved a barrier to our pursuit, but as defeat had not taken us, my companion celebrated all the same such claims of victory in battle, and urged me with logical reasonings back toward his lodging that we should gather ourselves and discuss what had transpired before chasing without trail the spectre who had brought such ghouls against us. I allowed this, less for want to stay the pursuit, so much as willful desire to keep my present company in abled aide for times more suited to his abilities. For he had taken the shot which damaging Ruthven more than I had ever been capable, brought with that the proof irrevocable to his vulnerability at last.

Though he was as , a stocky fellow, and somewhat congenial for my experiences, I found in Irving a singular courage without question. His brothers writings of heroes and histories as a soldier, were envied so long in him that he professed himself prepared as he said, for all great adventure he could seek, even amid his fifties in years. Reminding him at that time that I was over one hundred years of age, he laughed heartily and slapped a hand upon my back. Age, he stated had also levied in his heart, a sense of responsibility that those who possessed the means to protect another, were bound as he saw to do just that, and this to his mind had led him to that current position within congress from which he had sought such temporary relief and distractions from when he'd discovered that towns trouble.

"How can one turn away from such a story or the burden to solve its mystery?" He laughed. " And here I have met a giant who napped beyond years, fought a headlessman and faced a specters ghouls all in one! And that toss of the stone sir! Over one hundred in age indeed!" He continued proudly with laughter.

For the time of my remaining stay, William Irving allowed me the use of his room and the joy of his friendship, while we scoured that countryside surrounding in search of our injured opponent. Speaking often of his younger brother Washington whom he felt Mary might find friendly in some capacity, he did mention the intent that he should write to him and tell of what adventures we'd had, but also instructed that should I ever require assistance once more, that I should call on him in his stead. For younger in years and more experienced in soldiering, he felt incapable himself to pursue another battle as we had faced together, and wished for me a worthy champion as he saw fit within his sibling.

Though in days to come, my pursuit of Ruthven continued. I left that place having found in William Irving a strange sense of renewal by his friendship and cooperation, and in spite of the fact that I would not see him again, I would be surprised to learn of his death only 2 short years later. However it proved to me a fortune in worth to know him then, and in meeting with him by those strange events, providence would shine at later dates unknown. For I had inadvertently begun a journey quite unexpected then, which entangling my life with that of his brother unseen, would by the end of things prove also those means to defeat my enemy at last.

As for Ruthven, he had managed to escape for the time, but in his injury I found also hope, and swore onward to complete the task of my responsibility to protect the world from him, so that all which had been lost might not be in vain.

ONWARD TO THAT BREACH DEAR FRIENDS

AG: For several months I tracked Ruthven across the lands of America, and during this time seeing the beauty of that landscape, I could not escape the capacitie's of its people reflected therein. Though many of it's native inhabitants bid me with welcome and awe, I remained pariah to those settlers from my own homelands and beyond.

It was of great interest to me that I learned the use of new tools and methods taught by those tribal peoples and for the first time in years, took again to hunting as my previous companions personally ate not of meat. However I could not hold account of how my heart yearned for them, and knowing by that time Mary my love must have given birth, I longed to see them once more at the completion of my most pressing of task.

I did not know the troubles that they faced of blackmail or scandal which arose from the mysteries surrounding my own child, nor how Byron's disposition had turned against them entirely, else temptation might have carried me home by this alone, especially to learn of that child's supposed death which by grace had been concocted in whole to protect her once more. Though in passing at several instances I did hear tell of new publications which my loves had written during our estrangement.

Also within the following years during this absence, I would later learn of the death of dear Doctor Polidori, whom having published at last the story of The Vampyre under his own name, had seemingly taken his life out of prolonged depression and mania. I fear knowing him as I had, surely this came about from that suspicion and terror of Ruthven's vengeance to come. Although I knew then in certainty that Ruthven had not departed the lands where I held pursuit of him; This was impossible to determine by the knowledge possessed within the dear doctor. Alba, by then known only as Allegra had passed of illness within the convent school which Byron had placed her, and I grew more distraught to think I was not present to console my loves even as I mourned this news.

DM: I have to ask. Sorry. What papers reported all of that and how did you find them?

AG: As I have said before, stories of Percy, Mary and Claire, much like Ruthven during his years of lordship, circulated to the interest of others due to the status of celebrity which people of the time followed much the same as those today in fame are spoken of in tabloid and news. There were periodicals even then, which specialized in this, and knowing the like to report on these things, I sought out their remnants in the refuse of travellers and townships.

DM: That's nuts to think about.

Not so strange dear Doctor as the thoughts which would come to haunt my days. I read of these things only with the most scarce of details mind you, but I had thought so to protect those I loved through my own absence; And knowing of the impossibility to Ruthven's involvement, as I not only followed his trail but by that time had faced him more than once in combat since leaving the Hudson valley, my heart was torn to discover that no distance could save my spouses from such tragedy all its own to lose yet another child, another friend, and soon more than that. As further than this, by months to come, I did also hear at great pains... The most terrible of news which struck the heart of me in truth... to hear that our beloved Percy too had perished.

Adam's voice cracked.

I learned of his drowning at sea in the gulf of Spezia where he had sailed with friends... only to wash ashore, his body ruined beyond repair and cremated some time after. How could this be? Such a fine man, and skilled a sailor, that without intervention of another, he had perished in such way. It did not make sense.

I wailed openly at reading of this news and alone within my encampment, made nestled within the mountains of Appalchia, I turned my focus then to what could not be avoided. What worth was it I asked, to have taken leave from those I loved for their protection, only that such grief they faced alone would come even without the evils of he whom I followed so far from their shores? Vainly I had assumed all responsibility for our woes and meant in earnest to ease their suffering... yet now without me, they suffered the same. As I too felt torn apart without them, only to learn of these things months after their occurence.

Percy... My dearest genius of a man who had been so loving and kind to me in defense and ferocity, and our Alba, that sweet and beautiful child, both gone from this world... In addition to one who had aided us so thoughtfully... And I had abandoned those who needed me for what? Had I done these things in futility, only for Mary and Claire, both surely heartbroken beyond consolation, to face this without me in defeated returns to Britain?

I saw these reports over such times repeated and giving in their telling the rise to such speculative gossips in cruelty and ignorance, that I could no longer justify my prolonged distance and abandonment of them... Until by choosing all my own, I made up my mind to cease the search for Ruthven and turning my attentions homeward, made way to seek passage once more to those lands I had quitted years prior.

However stopped in this, I faced instead the wrath of my former neighbor's jealousy, who seeing my turn in directions away from his trail, descended upon a local tribe and slaughtered their entire camp, simply that I would continue our pursuit as if a game he wished not to end. In wretchedness upon seeing this brutality, I knew despite my conviction to rejoin them, that I could not leave as of yet.

In this darkness I thought the most vile of options to attempt that same desecration of the dead which Ruthven by my blood within him had achieved. Should I raise those deceased of innocent form which he had dispatched, only to bring them against my enemy as he had once brought back the dead to his advantage? So bloodied were the corpses of that tribal village, and so unfair their demise, that I slashed my wrists to let loose the blood of my veins and attempted to heal those wounds of their bodies, but none would rise.

After a day at these endeavors I left in shame and anger to know not what means separated my abilities from his own, and walking toward the rising of the sun I continued onward toward the coast, until nearly a week having passed, I was alerted one night by snapping twig, that another watched my presence. Then... from the darkness, a most unexpected form appearing, I saw the likeness of one woman whom I recognized from before.

She belonged I thought to those dead, that tribe which Ruthven had destroyed and I attempted in vain to resurrect. I recognized this. Entering my camp she looked at me with despair.

"Why have you restored my life Nunnehi?" She asked in English.

Shocked as I was, I could not answer, but stood to face her questions.

"I walked within the great valley alongside my people when sun shining bright, I woke to find their bodies where the white spirit had left them. Knowing not what else to do, I followed your trail here." She told me.

I could not tell this woman any answer she might understand, but spoke to her instead of my pity for her people and how I was to blame for their destruction, but she would not accept it. Nor would she allow me to think I had cast evil upon her to return the life which she had lost.

"You are not the white demon who killed us Nunnehi. Not all medicine heals those who have passed beyond. Do not weigh your heart with his actions. Leave me to warn others and I will carry your tales south with me to rejoin the people." She insisted. I spoke with her at length then, afraid that she might like Ruthven, have risen with evils set within. Discovering none and assured that no lasting illness shadowed her revived body, I could not contest when she offered the following.

"I will leave you now, but thanking you for my life, I wish you well that you will catch the spirit who did these things. Take this, the knife of my brother, and when you face your enemy again, end him for those he has taken." She continued, placing a knife on the ground between us before standing to turn away.

I watched her then in stunned sorrow. "Donadagohvi

Nunnehi" She whispered in finality, walking almost silently into the dark. Though I know this word to mean "until we meet again", never more did my eyes know the face of that woman, but in such conflicted emotion I was shamed to see her go.

DM: Wow... Your'e sure she was dead?

AG: As certain as I breathe.

DM: Any idea what set her apart from the others?

AG: In years since... I have considered this question at length to determine only the volume of my blood which I spilled into her wounds bore such difference. Unlike the others, Ruthven had slashed large the wound which took her life, and causing greater loss of her own blood, in my attempt to heal that, I filled more openly the cavity of its measure with that which I gave.

DM: So, just the difference in amount?

AG: Also as I would learn later, the lack of what remained within her to be replaced.

DM: So, it wasn't that you added your blod so much as that you'd replaced hers? And then you left and never saw her again?

AG: Yes, as I have said... and no. For all of my knowing, she may still live to this day, though I would not know where to seek her. Still, following onward towards the sea, I reached several days later the port of Wilmington and in result did reach for writing of the only man I knew of whom I might send in aide or message to Mary and Claire. For Byron having become unreachable in address, had also become so foul to my mind after dear Alba's death that I dare not seek his word. However even this I find impossible to separate from those hateful accounts of action which he had committed against my family's honor such as I would learn later from Mary's own lips.

And so I wrote to that Brother of William Irving, being assured once upon a night that he might knowing some bit of my histories, be willing and honourable by word to perform a task at my behest. I asked him as unmet stranger, that if agreed, he would alert Mary to my predicament and passing condolences. I also asked that he being an honorable man, would see to her safety while I continued my chase of that fiend who plagued so many innocents on my account. Secreting this letter to post by night along the contents of a carrier's satchel, I left the borders of that town unseen and unmolested.

By this time so much had occurred... So much changed... and yet I could not escape the madness of Ruthven's plaguing torments. As now he had committed them en masse against strangers alike, in knowing my compassions for humanity, leaving only one other to tell the tale should it be believed. So having sent letter to Irving without knowledge of his receipt of it, nor any way to communicate further, I waited several weeks alone and unmoving in my encampment's placement, now along the coast of Carolina, all in hopes that Ruthven might meet me once more.

At last this too came to pass. Yet I admit upon his arrival that I restrained myself greatly to greet him unmoving while I allowed his shadowed evil to sit before me. So often in those years I had witnessed that face, smug and unflinching in countenance, able with ease to sway the minds of other's and in his unquestioned beauties, draw forth victims by choosing calculation. Only now to see it once more, then reflected with my own burning hatred at the memory of littered bodies he had massacred for no larger purpose than to seek my continued presence, I seethed. He sat then, exposed by the light of fire between us, and I burned equal in rage to abide it.

"Have you quit the chase so soon then that you will finally concede, or is this to be another ill begotten clash between us?" He asked insolently.

"I have come to bargain." I told him.

"At what old friend? You have but one thing I desire."

"At agreement to conditions that you may have it." I spoke.

With barely a motion of his face, I saw the surprised intrigue of a singular raised eyebrow. "I am listening." He responded

"You wish power, control, the strength of what my blood has given amplified without end, and yet you knowingly possess more strength, speed and attributes unique than myself, in addition to the ability to walk amongst others unchastised for your likeness. What else might I bestow with the gift of more that you do not possess? You have taken from me all that I held dear within this world and yet still you bait me with the blood of innocents and I ask then; What use is my resistence if the cost equals nothing more than humbling myself before you... but I know in truth that which you deny to yourself." I began

"And what is this?" He asked me.

"That these things you have committed come not from desire alone to control all others. You do not wish to be supreme above them and feed upon their flesh in solitude, but as displayed by your unwillingness to see me leave you in peace, a greater desire for companionship which might join your company. It is what you seek from me, you take from me, and I have learned now enough to realize that it is for this yearning most of all you must seek my blood, that you should make another like yourself... In my foolishness I have been blind to think us so different. And so I shall extend to you the bargain which I myself once suggested to another.

Should I give you this, I wish that you do nothing more or less than depart from the company of others. Stay your hand at their destructions and live with whom you choose, but plague this world no longer. Set up township in some distant land if you will and rule over it's peasantry to your satisfaction and pride, but cease in stripping them of will and life. Feed and release them as their honored count or king, but do not kill them friend. For we both know that you do not require it. Agree to this and I will give to you that you seek..." I pleaded.

There was a long pause, and I watched Ruthven's face as he rubbed his chin in thought before reply.

"No... Adam you are a fool, and I regret nothing more to hear that truth than this lack of clarity within you. You are right in one regard. I *have* found such powers to surpass you and though I may not inflict my will upon the whole of the world without your blood, there is little assurance that any change would grow within my purview even with its additions. In honesty friend I grow bored with these fantasies.

It has been more delightful to see your torment than any greater power you might bestow, and I see now where your heart truly lies, that you, so lonely and desperate for their company, pine for what you believe I lack without a single understanding of the difference which marks us. I have no such need for them as you so clearly hold.

Go then, see your *beloved* family and I will allow it for the present, but after I have supped my fill and taken vengeance upon that simpleton George Gordon for his arrogance to write of me in that book you and your collaborators orchestrated, I wish to travel a bit where I have not seen in this world. Perhaps I shall for a time take your advice into account and resume lordship someplace, but I *will* find you once again and we shall end this by *my* choosing, not yours.

Take what time you have my friend, and advise your loves to the same, for these are limited in scope, and to my knowledge your beloved Mary has one son left to take from her, with or without your presence near. Hope only that he tastes so sweet as young William that it might prolongue your chance for goodbyes. You may take me at my word, and depart for now... I have no further use of you."

Hearing these professions my heart exploded at last with fury and I sprang forth without warning to end him there, but was caught by the throat, even while still midair above the fire itself. And Ruthven, gripping tightly without any seeming effort on his part, thrust my body upon its coals, before leaning near to my face even while they burned through my clothing and into the flesh of my back.

"Tsk tsk." He hissed. "You should know better than to attempt this *after* I have fed. It *shall* be my choosing friend... Not yours." he repeated before loosing his grip of me and vanishing from sight within a blinks time.

I coughed, sputtered, rose from the fire and sand upon that shore in pained tears and anger. I sat through the night, helpless in my way to stop him. I knew that I could not do this alone... So long I had tried, and bested by him at every turn he prevailed over me. What good was this to continue? No man alive, not even one possessing my strength or healing could take this devil without assistance. I wept.

At last by morning once more, my renewed decision had been reached, and boarding a merchant vessel soonafter, I faced again in my life the shackles and chains of a slavers hold, but I could not bring myself to the same furies as before. I felt chained as well. Despite the evils of Ruthven, man too seemed less in wholeness than those singular souls I had encountered who showed to me exception in their tenderness rather than demonstrative of humanity's divided natures.

So *if* I concluded, that mankind itself was altogether to be riddled with evils, then the lesser of these I would make amends with to serve greater purpose. Travelling first to Belgium and afterward exchanging that vessel for another bound now toward Greece, I swallowed all pride and distaste to seek out Byron himself. He was easy to find in that place.

Upon arrivals I found the man was drunken, dressed in curious garb and armed as well. Furious to see my return of course, he ushered me within hallway to hide from sight that his mistress would not see us. He spit such insults as I had never heard from his lips even as I attempted to warn him of danger, and through this all he dismissed me, agreeing only to provide Mary's address and to tell her not of my presence. Had the whole of the world turned rotten from within? Slavers, murderers, wars unending which moved from shore to shore under newer and more fanciful names proclaiming guise of principled righteousness, even gentle people of settlement's who friendly otherwise, sat complicit in the genocide of their neighbors native to those beautiful lands which they corrupted afterward by driving them out. Now even Byron the self interested coward, armed himself as if for battle, and growing in vile nature turned on former ally. I was sick at heart. I left Greece unsatisfied by the next day and sailed for Britain with unformed intentions.

There, upon familiar shores, I made passage onward in the

directions of my love's home and staying hidden, I watched from afar to look for any sign of Ruthven's betrayal to his word. He did not come. For weeks and then months he showed no signs of himself and I observed the life which had become of my beloved. Claire it seemed had moved once more to Vienna and begun relations thru letter with an old friend, Trelawny , the same man who had taught Percy the art of sailing and after his demise identified the body.

As for my own correspondence, it seemed in truth that my letters *had* reached the American Irving, and friendship found him indeed amiable with Mary, whom had been told of what I asked. However also after this, his introduction of her toward his acquaintance John Payne had seen her pursued romantically to her chagrin as she rebuffed his advances in favor of continued communication with Washington himself in hopes that I again might write.

Also it seemed to me that Mary had occupied her time with publication, and working as a paid author, put forth the bound collections of Percy's former works in addition to her own continued prose, only to be halted by his father under threat of suspending the allowance he afforded her for the upkeep of their remaining child, his grandchild, named after his father, Percy Florence Shelley.

To see these things was agony. My family scattered and gone, only Mary remaining with her son, a single mother supporting child and faced with such troubles, yet brilliantly consistent in work and talent. The world indeed seemed bitter. During this time word reached my ears later of Byron's death and having seen my last of him in such conditions and treachery, I mourned not. Mary to me was that only light remaining, and even she seemed dimmed by all the world around. However I feared so the risk of my approach that in knowing of my return she might beg of me to stay, and at truth I would be forced to tell her of Ruthven's remaining threat that in my failures and abandonment, he meant murder still upon her only living child... For at that time, I knew nothing more of Elaina's continued survival.

This however proved ill fated to last, as Mary watched each day the shadowed places she knew my habit to keep, and in under a years time, seeing me by keen eye despite my attempts to hide, she met me by evening, and tearfully took my hand in silence, leading me forward with leaded step toward her home.

I could not anticipate what words she might speak, nor had I chanced to guess might I have stricken upon any one of them indeed. For in those years of my absence, even among the hardship and turmoils of life, my beloved had steeled herself in purposes unseen. She searched all those days, against every obstacle, and nearly alone it would seem at times, for ways in which Ruthven might be defeated, so that I might return to her in fullness only when these dangers had been conquered. Still further unbeknownst to me, Mary had laid plans, which waiting only for my returned presence, hinged on this so that the trap would be laid to begin.

For then however we walked silently, and entering her home while Percy Florence slept, even before she would speak these things to me aloud or embrace my presence, she took pen in hand, and drafting letter to Claire, told her that the time had come, before sealing its contents and preparing it for post at first light.

AG: Shall I continue further? I see the hour and you have not rested.

DM: Screw that! I'm not stopping until Ruthven is dead dude. Plus you just hooked back up with Mary!

CR: Same. Now spill.

AG: So be it. The letter which Mary had written contained instruc...

DM: Ok no, first you have gotta tell us about the reunion. Please tell me you guys did the whole tearful confession, holding eachother, crazy passionate sex thing.

CR: Steven!

DM: Come off it. Don't pretend you don't need to know this.

Adam chuckled slightly.

AG: I am sorry to disappoint in reporting only some of that truthful. Tearful confessions and holding of eachother yes, I can verify this much. She told me of all which had happened since my departure and we each cried profusely as I relayed to her my own storied troubles. However it proved more difficult to engage in the rest you might hope to hear of, as we *talked* through the night more about the mournful circumstances and loss of our husband than any topics which might bring comfort.

Polidori had perished. Byron too by that time if you recall, and continued dangers remained not knowing if Ruthven, in keeping that word he swore to me in Carolina, had been the one to take his life, or if the man's own foolish vanities driving heroisms redemption for posterity, had led to death by other means. Adding to this were also those plans Mary revealed to me, and explanation for Claire's absence. We spoke through the night's entirety until Percy Florence, now nearly a young man himself woke seeking his mother.

Of course, having never met my personage or even in truth being told of my nature beyond that of a name mentioned in passing, I could not appear so strangely within that childs home. "He is returned from Boarding school only for the summer before day school begins" She told me, afterward asking that I hide, and directing me henceforth toward an adjacent room which secreted by disguised door, had in fact been prepared for my arrival some time before. Yet to Percy Florence, I was little more in knowledge than that of some stranger acquainted with family from a time before his birth.

Honestly the night marked such new beginning for Mary and I, that if anything, it had taken form not entirely unlike our first fateful meeting spent tearfully seated upon the floor while exchanging tales of woe. Though not strangers to one another of course, how should one account for all which had changed us?

However if you would allow, I might relate instead of these matters, the contents of Mary's letter to Claire, which hold much more import to all things concerning Ruthven should his end be the aims to which we must reach before you shall agree to rest.

You see Claire, through some contrived acquaintance known

to her man Trelawny during his many travels, had found within Russia an individual both studied and capable it seemed of dispatching with Ruthven once and for all. And thru the establishment of contact with him, procured for herself a position to be taken up as governess to a family who alllowed his stay upon their lands in trade for past services wherein he had relieved that family of as was claimed, a vampyre, who once plagued their home region.

Mary's instruction within the written letter was for Claire to secure passage and make ready the journey that I should be travelling with her, after first my arrival in Venice, to follow onward into Russia to meet this man. After this it was meant that with his aide, he and I might hunt Ruthven down, at last capable of his destruction. Further even than this, Mary drafted that next day while I stayed hidden from view, a letter to Washington Irving as well. Having been told of me in trusted word, and also Ruthven's threat by both Mary as well as his brother, Mr. Irving had enlisted himself in service to lend where possible, an additional assistance most welcomed indeed.

For in the days following his first knowledge of Ruthven, and having been informed by Mary of further details, Mister Irving had formed within his network of associates, a list of those who having suffered the losses of their own families to Ruthven in years past, wished to see his end as equally as any by our own wills to pursue him. And by time now alerted as had been planned, Irving told these compatriots just how and where to meet another vessel, which provided by Trelawny and having been stocked with weapons, he had procured through involvement with the disputes in Greece, would go in advance of us to Ruthven's last known whereabouts, also in that country.

DM: So he was in Greece? And Byron was in Greece when he

died, but you aren't sure if he killed him or not. Why would he stay?

AG: War makes easy to disguise the actions of murder which might otherwise seem evident Doctor... After all, is war not man murdering man under banner of other men's cause or ideals? Even when righteous or just, death remains death, and if committed by one upon another not in defense directly, is it not still murder? Not to say there is never to be reason or just cause. Ours for example was just in my belief, and though Ruthven was no man in my eyes, nor myself, I intended to murder him the same for the good of others.

DM: Ok, we've discussed this. Your definitions of murder are a little skewed.

AG: Are they? Or is the normalcy of other terms a twisting of reality so that it eases the minds of self proclaimed peacekeepers to convince them that the righteousness of a state or groups abstract purpose, excuses those same actions otherwise condemned if committed for equal reasons by one man carrying forth to perform them alone? If a man kills another man or woman, it is murder... unless his reasons are lended convenience to others under disguising terms. Is that not accurate? And who sets those terms but the same society which outlaws those deeds without their consented approval otherwise?

DM: Fine, just get back to it.

AG: Very well, so it was not quite possible you see for Mary and I to resume as we had been. For within the time these letters took to arrive, I was set to depart once more on continued quest and urged to finish that task before returning to her. Only on the single night prior to this departure would Mary and I consumate any continuance of loving touch. For thereafter it was unknown the time it would be before we met again.

Truthfully the span of these tasks went on no less than three years following that night. And for those years our only communications came through coded letters moved thru shifting channel of shared friends or family which found us on occasion long after their writing.

DM: Three more years? You didn't kill Ruthven for three more years? Ok maybe we do end for now.

AG: No need. Three years after all is not so long in telling. I can summarize these quickly if you wish.

CR: Are you sure?

AG: Easily.

Steven and I looked at each other for confirmation but both nodded in agreement.

CR: Then by all means...

AG: Well, to begin, meeting Claire as planned, I travelled to Venice whereafter we did continue to Russia, and I was introduced to a stern cossack of a man called Anton Viestberg. After some convincing, he assured to my satisfaction that he did indeed hold proficiencies enough in capability of tracking and containing someone in possession of Ruthven's characteristics, that I agreed to his aide most humbly after demonstration.

DM: He kicked your ass didn't he?

AG: He held his own, which is no small feat I remind you.

Having first been tasked in tracking my person over a two day contest, he located my hidden presence where then we battled with swords until each disarmed, faced one another in hand to hand combat until proven to my own satisfaction I conceded the duel with gladness.

DM: Mmhmm...

CR: Stop it Steven.

AG: Admittedly I do not know how he came to these skills and can offer no confirmation of his claims to have killed one or more which had been vampyres or any other strange being of enhanced or supernatural capabilities, however I can say that the man was both highly skilled and deeply cunning in strategy, which to me mattered most of all.

As for Claire, she took up her position as governess and remained within that household in Russia, an anchor to facilitate our correspondence with Mary while Viestberg and I made way toward Greece to meet with Irving's men. Only I should note to the surprise of Sir Viestberg, that upon arrival, we found not all indeed were men, but also women who equally wronged by Ruthven's crimes sought equal their own vengeance. Truthfully the presence of those women included withing our ranks proved invaluable to those endeavors many times over due to the prevailing prejudices of the time that even Ruthven suspected them so incapable of harm, that he bid them no attentions up unto his very death, despite the clear and ever present ability that many held greater than their male counters over our course.

Coming to the place which Trelawny had told us of in Greece, I met with those sworn and bound in purpose upon the decks of their ship, and for the first time in my years, was welcomed by not one or few in number of Europe's citizens, but all who stood together there and bent their knee to the direction of Viestberg and myself. These introductions stand still in strangeness for me as I was not only allowed to walk openly amongst them, but welcomed and lauded for my dedications and sworn rivalry against Ruthven, despite what part I held in his creation.

Having faced him before and pursued his presence across the Americas, those men and women present, afforded me respect and degrees of admiration which humbled my nature not to lead them, but to serve them each that we may accomplish our mutual goals, setting right what had been committed against those we loved. They called me their captain, and Viestberg their General, titles to which I hold no pride to this day, yet accepted none the less. And in this party of brethren I was taken as friend to converse freely and become familliar with every man or woman who joined us.

Also meeting us then, joined for a time Trelawny himself, who out of friendship with our family, even having never met my person and despite his prolonged involvement within other altercations which divided his attentions, lended all possible assistance he could during our weeks time there.

CR: So they weren't afraid of you?

AG: Upon first sight admittedly, I did witness a mixture of shock and fascination, but not that repulsion or fear which I had become accustomed to in expectations where I had been seen before. The only person who failed at this upon meeting, as if he had already been familliar with such sights, was Viestberg himself when we'd first made introductions in Russia. Yet despite that I found him almost disinterested to questioning during our travel together at first. He truthfully remained throughout, so stoic and quieted, that I questioned for a time if he held to any singular joy in life aside the successful pursuit of our quarry.

Our crew of course, now formed in completion, made sail after this from where they had anchored themselves at distance from Ruthven's hunting ground, nearest an island outcropping under the guise of belonging to those unnumbered foreign mercenaries which had come so far to join in the ongoing disputes and fighting. Viestberg and I consulted first and listened to the details they had gathered, taking Trelawnys advice into account and structuring our attacks to purposely corner Ruthven within a series of caverns nearby, so that his speed might prove less advantage.

Knowing not his exact location however, our party skirted the coast while divided in search. We made landfall in waves, whereafter battlements ended or injuries sustained, return to our ship afforded the members of our party a mobile base of safety to regroup or be treated. In this we held at bay those men whom Ruthven enthralled for nearly five days, advancing so far as several of our own claimed even to have seen the whites of his eyes before having taken such a shot to his shoulder, wounded and without option, that snake forced his way through their ranks, killing no less than ten men, including five of those which he had enthralled to serve him, before fleeing unwitnessed. He departed the area entirely.

I, for I could manage, engaged infrequently then, meaning only to reveal myself once Ruthven had been cornered, that I might face him directly rather than utilize my strength against those helpless souls he had controlled to his will. Instead, I directed such strategy and plans along with Viestberg from the ship itself. That in it's freedom from battle, allowed me the task of treating our wounded using my own blood. I having learned some bit at least by then, did this not by ingestion as seemed to have corrupted Ruthven or sustained Breda, but through direct application upon the wounds sustained, as I had come to witness more appropriately that this method healed them without further changes to the body or mind. As for our perished, I dared not attempt their resurrections but instead mourned their honored passing along with my crew, unknowing still the means by which my singular success at this had been achieved.

After that series of attempts however, it seemed that Ruthven, having attributed his defeats to Trelawny's involvement and tactics rather than knowledge of my own or even Viestberg, had made his way toward Ottoman lands in escape. And though Trelawny remained to fight in Greece, wishing us the best of luck and stocking our ship full once more with supply, the rest of our party in turn followed that trail.

Within those further lands, being forced to anchor our ship, and leaving only two to guard its security, then proceeding on foot, Ruthven evaded us for several more months while we pursued. Yet his innate detection of my whereabouts made this effort most difficult. Among the most successful engagements which followed was one particular to stand out among others where laying a trap, Viestberg along with several of our most capable fighters, filled the back of a wagon led by two of our fiercest women, and covered themselves to lie in wait while journeying through a narrow valley between two remote villages.

With careful planning, one wheel already weakened for such purpose, broke along that road and to any unknowing it was believable to appear little more than the misfortunes found by innocent travellers stuck by night along rivers edge. Moving far enough from myself to alleviate Ruthven's suspicion as neccesary, this ruse met with a degree of success, when lured out of hiding, he came to them feigning gentlemanly assistance with intent instead to feed.

However much to our opponent's surprise I was told, for I was too far to witness firsthand, Viestberg and his patrol managed to catch him unawares long enough to not only fire several shot, but also inflict many assorted wounds to his body by swords edge, before Ruthven unfortunately escaped. He did this by flipping the cart entirely and killing both horses as well as one of our men before sunrise crested the mountaintops nearby.

Another attempt some time later saw our adversary locked fast within a borrowed barn and strung by rope to lift his feet from the ground so that he could not run, however breaking free with ease and crashing a wall to splinter in escape, I arrived only in time to hear the sounds of gunfire and witness the bodies of two men torn asunder within.

I thought perhaps a chance might prove more beneficial at one point to lure Ruthven to me alone and face him directly, rather than hiding myself and allowing our compatriots to secure him before my approach. I entered the mountains, leaving the main party behind to settle within a ravine flanked by overlooking ridge to three sides, where only one man upon each of these would lay in wait that night surrounding my camp, prepared to fire upon signal when my lantern had lit appropriately the face of their target.

However in this he showed again that which defined his nature, by entering the low valley beyond at visible distance and calling out with voice "It pleases me to see you are making friends my brother! However I fear you choose them poorly! Have care they keep better mind upon their shoulders than these have, or else you should have fools for company!" He shouted wickedly before raising his arm with a toss; Whereafter I was met in falling disgrace which landed before me with thudding rolls, those decapitated heads of my volunteers who had surrounded me in wait. I chased as I could, yet Ruthven vanishing from sight just as quickly as he had appeared, evaded even this.

Open battle had not succeeded due to Ruthven's ability to sway others to his side. Trapping him alone had not succeeded due to his strength and speed, and following him proved only a double edged blade as our most reliable means of discerning his whereabouts came not from discernable trail over land or sea, but merely the bodies left in his wake, as if to flaunt his continued freedom every bit as much I knew, as to sustain his unnatural powers. Barring this, his paths were covered over from our detections almost entirely, and for six months we travelled after that failed endeavor, simply seeking his location without fortune or progress to show for it.

In fact this continued all the way into the lower region of Wallachia until superstitious rumor reached our ears of a Vampyre returned to the former castle home of one Vlad Tepes, a place called Poenari citadel. This creature they swore, who taking residence there had enthralled a small army to his service, was to them none other than Vlad himself and had sworn himself Count over the area nearby. Knowing immediately the truth that this was Ruthven, we followed quickly to that place as well and arriving within weeks were met with confirmation.

However this was not as one might assume a fortunate turn at first. We attempted to lay seige to the castle not knowing the number of others he had brought under his control and despite each new strategy none prevailed. I believe to this day that his action was one of intentional mockery toward my pleading request made before, that in assuming counthood and lands he might see fit to end his games and tortures, but instead he used fear and power to garner loyalty while continuing to enthrall others at whim to set against us.

Ruthven had gained from this move, the most frustrating of fortress that we found it nearly impossible for our group to ascend the multitude of steps required to reach it without great loss of life and injury from above. And yet no other course seemed better suited toward achievement.

This siege continued for over a year and a half, while we lost many to its efforts due to steep mountainsides and river below, leaving only the staired entrance a point of egress. However Ruthven too lost even more as his thralled army died by overextensions of his powers limit, and without means to leave his citadel or feed further at the last of his subjects enthrallment, those same powers diminished until even the reanimated dead he engaged against us, became less threat to defeat than mocking sign of his sick and twisted persistence.

That was when Viestberg and I decided our plans to scale the mountain's steepest side alone by mid of night, while leaving our remaining group to light larger their fires and carry on loudly from our established camps that such approach might go unnoticed. However the keenness with which Ruthven could detect my presence proved even this to be partly in vain, and arriving over ledge of castle wall, I was met by his laughter instead.

Viestberg, who was undeterred by this, urged my calmness and landing on his feet atop the castles walk, he began to circle Ruthven with voiced taunts of his own, striking with carried sword to deflect each attack despite their speed.

"Defliled leech! You show face to cossack with laughter as if you believe you are great? Oh Count that once Lord who slithers away time and again from battle. You are parasite!" Viestberg called out with booming voice. "I waste not even spit at you!"

Ruthven Charged him, but again he parried with sneering disdain.

"Little man with shiterot words... I could toy with you until age alone sees you pissing yourself weak as the child inside your mind. Why ally yourself with this fool against me?" Ruthven hissed.

"This friend you call such fool, is more the man you should ever see, yet matters not. I would face you same without him and in result wipe from this world another flea who costumes by the holy form of man!" Viestberg returned.

I joined him there, and together we baited Ruthven's arrogance for such lasting time that he had no escape when the sun rising to the east blinded his eyes.

"Damn you to hells fires!" Viestberg shouted, as he stuck deep with sword Ruthven's now decrepid and withered form. Yet retaining enough strength to do so, Ruthven did throw such force his arm with backhanded strike, that Viestberg unprepared, was sent over the walls edge even as I charged forward.

"*My* choosing!" Ruthven shouted in pained laughter as he threw his head back defiant to the end. Meeting him in full force of fury and with every ounce of strength I plunged my hands deep into that wound around the hilt of Viestberg's sword, until ripping to each side, I tore at Ruthven's body and wrought him entirely divided in two, whereafter each part of him landing so far from eachother, I knew no healing would aide any recovery.

Turning without pause to savor the victory or breathe relief so much as a sigh, I ran to peer over that castle steep where Viestberg had been cast aside, and was relieved to find him still gripping below, the sides of an off countered stone which had caught upon the strap of his pack. I reached to pull him up, but seeing my blood covered form, he recoiled with curled lip and grabbed instead for another stone as he climbed once more over the walls edge and heaped himself upon the ground to rest with laughter.

"No offense my friend. You should wash." He chuckled mightily, pulling a flask from pocket to drink and restore his body before spitting toward the remains nearest his placement, only to rise soon after. "Gather him." He instructed. "In time even this will heal. He must be burned."

So I did as asked, and lifting one side of his body, tossed it over shoulder while Viestberg took the other. Together carrying Ruthven's remains, we descended those stairs toward our camp to see the last of his necromanced minions collapsed round every side, until entering below the company of our remaining party, we were met with cheers and cries of ecstatic proclamation and tears of joy. Our defeated enemies remains were further divided by blades and hands alike upon careful guidance before being doused with holy waters and blessed with prayers. They were carried then onward toward those still blazing fires which had lit the camp through night.

There each portion of Ruthven was cast on such pyre that burned his earthly remains to ash before our anxious eyes; Forever ending the reign of the Vampyre whom had tortured so many and taken so much. In the end for him in desperate time, left alone and diminished, ultimate defeat had taken his power forevermore not by singular my rages or pain, nor by strengths greater or some heart most willing to sacrifice, but the efforts of those wronged, who banding together with loyalty and friendships earned, fought for the sake of love, rather than the forsaking of it.

DM: Holy shit... Dude...

AG: Now shall we retire before another day passes?

The room was silent only briefly, but Steven couldn't resist.

DM: Tomorrow... I have questions about Viestberg and the others, plus what the Native woman called you.

AG: Then they should wait for that morrow Doctor.

CR: Right... Normal time?

AG: Indeed.

I stopped recording.

SESSION SIX

<u>Interviewer Name:</u>

Cassandra Reynolds: Journalist for "Washington Post" newspaper and special columnist for Al-Jazeera International.

Second Interviewer and Consultant:

Dr. Steven Malcom of the Boston College Institute for Scientific Research and Advancement: Specialization in structural biochemistry. Published author and Nobel laureate

Interview Subject : Adam

The time is 7:48 pm. Aprill the 2nd, 2024

Location: Personal offices of Cassandra Reynolds, Washington D.C.

CR = Cassandra Reynolds
DM= Dr. Steven Malcom
AG = Subject - Adam

Personal notes Italicized

◆ ◆ ◆

DETAILS TO BE DISCUSSED

Adam arrived per usual at my office where Steven and I were waiting anxiously. We had already eaten and settled in for what would come, but expecting him somewhat earlier, we had already prepared a list of questions discussed between us.

April the 2nd, 7:48 pm, Recording Begins

CR: Welcome back.

DM: Hey there Big Guy.

AG: Good evening.

CR: Would you mind if we started a little differently tonight? We've made some notes

AG: I should find that appropriate given that so much of our time of late has been consumed informally by my prolongued narrations.

CR: Good. Don't be nervous.

AG: Where would you like to begin?

CR: Well, how about something simple. You describe so much time spent alone, years in fact, and we know that you're and avid reader, which I'd like to cover later, but maybe you could tell us some of how you passed your time. What type of hobbies or activities you might have skipped perhaps?

AG: In earnest?

CR: Yes.

AG: Delightful. I would be pleased to answer.

Hunting as you know I have mentioned; Carpentry and cooking as well, which first born of neccesity, later became sources of great joy to explore further in practice and skill...

Many activities in my years of solitude spent my time, but I would not call as such hobbied, those being primarily fundamental to life, such as gardening or the care for livestock.

Woodcarving of course allowed me many hours of enjoyment, poetry, painting, long hikes, boating, study of language, scientific experimentation, and climbing. For a time I attempted to engage in cave exploration, but being limited by size, encountered obstacles which gave much less enjoyment to that activity as a recreational pursuit...

Though sledding is a certain delight for me when seasons permit, and for the past century or so I have taken great enjoyment in the pursuits of mining. Not that I have direct use for wealth mind you, but it has been by this that I have been able to provide for others in cases such as the Fukiharo's immigration or what is now Hiro's restaurant establishment.

I also greatly enjoy movies and music.

CR: Interesting... So you have a gold mine somewhere stashed away?

AG: I do.

CR: Near your current home I assume.

AG: Yes.

CR: Which is where?

AG: Perhaps some day I shall show you personally, both of you for that matter, as for that information to be included on record, I would prefer not to say.

CR: That seems fair.

DM: I'd love to visit. Ok if I toss some questions out?

AG: Toss as you will Doctor.

DM: Nunnehi?

AG: Immortal spirit people. Native American fairy lore of a type.

DM: Do you ever find that sort of thing interesting? How every culture you've encountered seems to have their own names for what they've called you?

AG: Without fail. I find it quite mysterious to be honest, that the lens or perception by each culture has informed not only what I am called, but how I have been received by those of so many varied beliefs, and how within them each culture has possessed some form of being to share traits they see reflected in my presence.

Such matters have led me many times to question if others not entirely unlike myself might have existed before or exist still somehow, also unknown or hidden away as I have been, only seen by carefully chosen encounter or scarce accident.

DM: Which would be why despite your scientific leanings, you don't discount the possibility of things like werwolves or vampires beyond what you've encountered.

AG: Doctor, would you have believed in me if not for all evidence offered to your very eyes? Even after such, your skepticism has been noted and discussed more than once during our times here.

CR: What about travel? You've been so many places it seems. Is there anywhere you haven't been?

AG: Four entire continents in fact. I have never set foot within Africa, Australia, Antarctica nor South America. I have also remained stranger to most heated deserts on any continent, and I have never made it so far as to explore the Pacific Isles. I should have liked to see more if it were possible, yet over three centuries is quite enough to settle for what wonders I have in fact witnessed, and I shall not regret these oversights to end my life without them.

DM: Avoiding that topic, what if any fantastical tales have you heard or seen evidence of in your lifetime that you might be most inclined to lend credence to in promotion of further study or the lightening of skepticism?

AG: Intriguing question from *your* lips Doctor. This is quite enjoyable honestly.

Let me consider... Firstly I might respond with the study toward some presence of psychic ability amongst certain individuals that extends beyond superstitious or spiritualistic explanations. I have seen too much in far too many instances that I could *not* dismiss this outright, and might wonder if perhaps there were something more to those ideas which unexplained as of yet, does exist outside this reality, perhaps accessible only by individuals set apart somehow through mental capacities uncommon to most, such as a mutation or evolutionary advantage which having presented itself mysteriously in peoples from every placement on this globe, might explain the phenomenon of shamanic or psychic experience, however removed from the context which typically accompanies their telling.

After that... I might say almost in expansion of the same vein, the extension of scientific consideration toward shared concepts toward beliefs in general, that which supersede regional superstition or shared psychological motives; Such as how each culture round the whole of this world has some form of vampire mythos, or fairied lore... Even in example of this how seemingly every area of the globe shares some version of that which has been called a dragon, and while science has dismissed this possibility outright, cheered the discovery of dinosaurs whose very skeletal remains spread globally beneath our feet, would explain precisely that in cause.

And lastly perhaps in furtherance of that same conception, I would think a secondary evaluation of sciences seeming need within the last century and a half, to self inflate it's importance by renaming ancient ideas and perhaps truths with new titles, merely so that it might dismiss former wisdom in favor of labelling such things as new discovery, despite their seemingly obvious ties for any who has lived long enough to witness in full scale this self aggrandizing revisionism to occur.

I have a deep and profound respect and love for the processes of scientific discovery and illumination to bring the world out of darkness into betterment of understanding. I myself am a logical being, but also I am product of experimentation which has yet to be replicated to my knowledge by any other that

I have found in a long search for just that, and yet I remain also existent in course of my three hundred plus fifteen years, a consideration too bold and fantastical for science as it exists within mainstream circles to have deemed worthy of serious consideration that I might exist already without their knowledge; A discovery too large to go unnoticed, and by presumption deemed impossible, lest I do as I have, and literally expose myself to open scrutiny, bearing evidence in advance before I might even be given any benefit of doubt...

Subsequently to be left until my meeting of *you* in fact, that exception to this seeming rule of many, to seek my answers and understanding of self instead in others deemed crackpots, or spiritualists as my father once was, and creator would have been labeled as well had he made himself known to that community which rejected the absolute pursuit of knowledge in favor of convincing others that their minds already full to what limits they could conceive, not only possessed answers beyond them, but also to deem all else unknowable in their arrogance.

DM: Definitley a passionate answer... But do you have other specifics like Ruthven or your werewolf story? Like maybe within your encounters with Viestberg? Didn't your friend Hiro say you saved his family from a what was it called again?

AG: A kyuuketsuki... but back to the former, to be frank I did once read the account of a man claiming to be the reincarnate soul of an angel, which admittedly in fascination planted in me the first inkling of idea for this interview process itself, but that aside, Doctor If you are asking this simply to know more about Viestberg, or later on the kyuuketsuki, I could simply continue my story and those answers will come along its telling; As Viestberg and I travelled together after Ruthven's defeat and I did learn much of him regarding what you might wish to ask without saying...

CR: We *could* save the rest of these questions for later if that's what you guys want...

DM: Are you sure?

CR: They aren't exactly time sensitive babe.

AG: Cassandra... you are still recording.

CR: Oh shit! I'll edit that out. Thank you for reminding me.

Seeing as how in the time since first publication, it has been well documented and generally known that Steven and I are married now and have been since before Titanfall, I decided that redacting this seemed kind of pointless for this edition. So embarassment aside, there's not much reason to hide what is public knowledge. Adam Brought us together... Interviewing him reminded us of what we'd seen in one another the first time when we met and we decided that it was worth a shot beyond the one night in Geneva.

DM: So we're going back to the story now?

AG: At your wills.

CR: I think so.

AG: Right, then I should begin from where we last ended. Ruthven had been destroyed, and letters while drafted to reach Mary and Claire, would take time to see delivered from alternate locations. So travelling back through the countries of Wallachia and the Ottoman regions, we made way once more toward our waiting ship to greet those long departed who stood watch over it.

These two however joyed to see us, had in fact during our

absence continued to live aboard that vessel, leaving only in procurement of neccesary provision and being man and woman formerly less acquainted, met us in rejoicing splendor to carry with them a babe who had been born to their parentage during that time. Viestberg delighted in this after the loss of so many, that newly brought, another soul had joined in life the bright lit hope he saw to lessen the gloom during our weary travel.

He insisted however, that none should depart those shores before the joining in marriage of those two parents, which saw with it a celebration to rival any other I had ever seen before, much less as participant been included. Also the child, upon his urgings, was christened and blessed by none other than, being the captain in name, my own hands. The words and instruction he provided to me of course, and despite my lack of any professed faith by those days, I did these things for him without dispute or grudge.

After this, and sailing onward, many of our crew took leave within differing ports along our journey and bid farewell to each of us in thankful heart, until one night by quiet light of a moonlit sea, Viestberg approached me in conversation.

"I am glad to be with you my friend." He stated quietly.

I was surprised. "Thank you sir." I replied.

"What troubles you then with longing eyes that look to sea a man lost? Ruthven is no more. We travel victorious to see your woman with life to live freed from threat?" He asked me.

I breathed deep. "I feel shamed... To confess that these years have been the first true life I have lived, to share with so many... and even in losing such a number under dire course, I have found friendship and freedoms not known before. I love my

Mary as also I love Claire, but my presence within their life is burden to hide and secreted in shame. I do not know what is to come." I told him.

"Adam... I fear I have failed in friendship to tell you what in kindness you have never asked. You are not the first I have known to carry such burden, and though the other looked not as you, his friendship's had lived such time with that secret solitude, witnessed in passing all that he knew. He asked in fullness that I end him kindly, for his only living progeny, in the likeness of Vampyre, had taken from me the family I once had." Viestberg sighed.

"Another?" I asked with surprise.

"Another... without age or injury, born of man however, unlike you say of yourself. He too carried that gold fluid which I see beneath your skin, and with it healed others. His however was drink, not blood." He continued.

"Why do you tell me this now?" I responded.

"In cause that you are a good man Adam... and I wish not to see more pain take you in longevity that you might suffer alone as he... There is a way."

"To end it?" I questioned.

"To raise another which you have loved and make them without murder, like yourself."

Crestfallen to hear this answer, I looked away. "I fear you are mistaken Viestberg. I may heal, even to raise one previously dead once unchanged, yet the only to *gain* my strengths from this, have been wicked and perverse in result, Vampyre in body or devil in soul."

"Because within them sickness lived before. Germaine too encountered this, and I have hunted those created by his folly longer than you know." Veistberg tapped the flask within his coat pocket. "A gift from an old friend indeed... Should I pour it to sight by your eyes, you would recognize this truth from all reflections you have seen of your own likeness." He sighed. "But I am weary and alone as well, and nearing the last of that elixir, I wish no more to live in hunt when one as you may take that cause immortal upon this earth, and joined by love do so not alone."

"It cannot be surely the same even in similarity friend... Those secrets passed with my maker, and I would not dare press my blood to the lips of one I love, lest in perversions growth I cast curse upon them." I answered.

"Then do not give them thru drink that which is foreign to their body." He whispered with a smiling glint to his eye. "You must drain their blood after death, to be replaced within their veins by yours. Do this in part and they shall rise again with life the same as before, such as the woman you raised within the Americas. Do this in full, and they will rise as you, forever after, the same by blood which flowing within can replenish its sources through lifes own living."

I was skeptical, but awed to hear these claims, and soonafter with the growth of shared conversation between us where Viestberg revealed to me things long kept hidden, I heard the tales of vampires hunted and immortal man preceding me who had walked among the lives of many for centuries, befriending king and pauper alike, sustained by drink alone. Yet nothing permitted my belief of such legend, and in recognition of that name, Count Saint Germaine, I believe in earnest that my friend did lie simply to comfort me. For Mary, Percy, Claire and myself had looked to these legends before, and having found no support of them, deemed them already a fiction. By such time I asked at last to see that liquid contained within his flask, Viestberg swore to have drank only days before, it's final drops.

So you see Doctor... I too have looked as you toward gifted horse to inspect the wear of its teeth, and in doing so lost sight of all possibility beyond.

DM: Wait... I thought you said you'd never seen evidence or known of anyone like yourself.

AG: And still this is true, for Germaine in my mind remains as mysterious and likely to me as an elven king or Nunnehi. I cannot discount their existence in comparision to myself, nor can I credit it fully as truth. They were tales to be told, not believed... And even by that time I might encounter another called Vampyre in a foreign land long from then, I could not know their origins, or compare them in likeness to the abilities of Ruthven, for they were not alike so much as different, and only shared in part that which drew their naming.

DM: The kyuuketsuki?

AG: Indeed.

REUNIONS AND FAREWELLS

AG: Onward we sailed, until at times long lasting, we bid farewell to the last of our companions whereafter Viestberg and I travelled once more to Russia where Claire awaited. He and I parted ways in friendship and peace knowing truthfully the shortness of his remaining days unsustained by his elixir. I remained for a time with Claire, so long absent from my life that we shared at length the confessions of our heart, and stories missed with estrangement.

However my love professed a happiness within her solitude, and bidding that I return to Mary, she confided in me the wish to live apart as friend more than lover, that in the fullness of time when death would take her, I was to attempt no such resurrection upon her body and allow her rest in peace. My heart was broken to hear those words, but happiness for her also thrived within and wishing nothing more than her joys in life, I agreed.

Our works done in full, and departing amicably from her former employment, Claire and I sailed once more for Britain in the year of 1836. Arriving to meet Mary under cover of night, once more forced to shadowed life. We met along the area of Regents park where Claire agreed to stay, in light of the passing of their brother, William Godwin Junior, whom cholera had taken that preceding winter.

Having moved once more, Mary's new home held no secret place for me, and knowing we could not live openly, I was taken instead to those familliar surroundings of graven yard where a housing had been established in wait within a mausoleum as before. It would be the last night shared in bodily love between the three of us together, but not so between Mary and myself, for even while Claire became afterward only that friend she had wished to be, Mary visited me often and our marriage continued in hidden scope.

Their father William Godwin Senior, passed in spring, leaving Mary all rights of publication to his works in support of his surviving widow. She began his memoirs then, though never completed them, and later in October, left for Brighton, to be treated for recurring ailment which none could identify. It was a malady I feared leftover or produced originally by the conditions of body which produced our offspring years past. In this time Claire tended to my visitation for her stead, not wishing solitude upon me.

With Mary's return, restored in health early winter of the following year, talk began of plans once more to live undivided by household, for Percy Florence that following fall, would enter college, and Mary, planning afterward to move once more, wished that I should join her. This too came to pass, and for several years following I was kept in secret among each subsequent move, hidden away from all but herself or Claire, even including Percey Florence.

As always, Mary worked and wrote such vast works, continuing as well to honor our late husband by collections and publication of his own, yet often sickness ailed her internally, and being incapable of healing all but outward wounds, I was helpless to aide in her pains. For never would any drink from my veins I swore, and never again such evil come from those changed by their content.

In 1840, Percy Florence and a hand of his companions showed how like his parents he truly was by touring in Europe so many of those places we had once lived, even at times without the knowledge of such. Mary, hearing of these plans asked me one evening if I might consent for her to lend direction for that group to visit or stay within my old home in Germany. Yet knowing only how to locate its whereabouts on foot, neither of us proved able to adequately provide direction which would allow this. So Mary made plans to travel with them.

She sent letters for those months, and while I missed her so, it filled her with pride to see the man her son had become and tell me all about his likeness to our Percy before. This is how I knew him, only in words and remnants left within our home, viewed through cracks within the wall during visit, and never to speak with him or share our lives, even after their return and his subsequent graduations from Trinity in the year that his grandmother, Claire's mother, Mary's stepmother, passed from this world.

Claire moved to Italy following that, having cared for her in her final years while teaching music as profession. In actuality I believe some affair had begun with her new housemate, an old pupil of Mary's mother, but she would not share this with us. Though Mary and I visited her after she had moved briefly to Paris.

I could tell the rest, but in truth those years passed bittersweetly. Percy Florence Married. Mary visited their brother Charles and his daughter. We endured multiple blackmail attempts, some even having originated from my former crew. Claire converted to Catholicism and later forsaking all rational mind, argued me a demon responsible for each and every of our families woes, effectively convincing Mary and myself that she had fallen to mental illness. Even trying to reach out to her became bitter and turbulent to points unbelievable and saddening to us.

Percy's own father, Percy Florence's grandfather, died, finally "falling from the stalk like an overblown flower", as Mary phrased it.... And Mary's health failed.... Slowly in descent over years I stayed her side and watched as my love withered unto death, so that in the year of 1851 Mary too passed to be buried at Saint Peters church while both of us still remained estranged from Claire.

This to me was tragic, but truthful in such time we had discussed its inevitability, and planned that attempt which Viestberg once told, of how I might raise Mary from death that we should be together forever. We did not know in truth if that would work at first, so testing this on several felines used in experimentation, I established its probabilities with concern, only to see shortly after that they appeared nearly certain, by three out of three becoming in fact not only alive once more, but also impervious to injury.

However going against her wishes, Mary's body had been lain to rest within the wrong placement, and at last revealing myself to Percy Florence to remedy this without desecrating her gravesite, I was met with odd acceptance as if he had always known my presence. "She told me once that the day would come when I would understand." He said tearfully, embracing my form. "You must do as she asked, but further after, you must also remain as dead to the world. I will have request for her body be moved to that place she asked in guise that you should do this, but promise me sir only one thing. Make my mother happy and well, never to look back in regret. Grant me this and I shall be content." It was the only time I knew her son, which felt so oddly might have been mine... and for so short a time as we shared our days til deed be carried out, I spoke to him as if he were, departing afterward to see to that which he could not bear to witness.

A casket filled with exchanged body of one already passed was laid to rest in Mary's place then, while I, taking her lifeless form within my oldest mausoleum where we had shared our first night as husbands and wives, carried forth to replace the blood of Mary's veins with my own, much depleting my energies unto the point that days afterward I slept. When I was wakened by touch, it was to see within that gloom, my bride in life and smiling joy, to hold my face and kiss my lips, where youth restored, she looked now in reflection as the image of my own making.

No affliction touched her further, no pains of body or mysterious illness remained. Cured of all and new in life, leaving the other to its own courses of natural progression as she described, we had only but one destination, my home within the woods of Odin.

It was neccesary at first that I teach Mary the ways of our new life, travelling in secret, how to secure passage on ship or make way in shadows to avoid detections, however being not of equal size to myself, it was very much simpler for her than ever it had been for me, and in not long of time thereafter, we made our way to Germany and settled within my lodging of old.

CR: I thought... But she's not with you now?

AG: Sadly no...

DM: But you brought her back. I mean you made her immortal right? And it worked. You said it worked every time, meaning there are probably three housecats still roaming around Europe since then by the by... But how could she die then?

AG: Same as would take me or that which destroyed the body of Ruthven, that mortal fear I have dreaded the whole of my life, mankinds one discovery which entrances and consumes even myself. Fire...

First however was splendor, for Mary did not pass soon from those days. We lived in that cottage for over ten years, reading the likes of splendid modern authors who delighted our spirits to see extend forth new philosophy and considerations to challenge men's minds. I cannot express the love I found for the work of Victor Hugo, in his portrayals of morality and questions of forgiveness.

Mary delighted in the works of Dickens, and though neither of us cared toward the dryness of the author's words, we did read with much attentions and conversation the work of Mellville's "Moby Dick". Also during this time came the brilliance of Whitman and Thoreau, but no writing struck to our hearts the way in which Darwin's "The Origin of Species" could.

We had searched long and varied for the mind of any who thru sciences advancing might understand or utilize for mankind's betterment, that which we now both were, and long past we had all but given up on this errand, leaving Mary's novel attempt as nothing more to us than a singular work of years gone past; Whereafter such vastness of writing persisted in wonderment that "Frankenstein" remained only in fond memory the establishment of our beginnings. Yet here was a new science, full of possibilities and proof evident to us that the world progressed. Should these studies continue and give greater understanding in combination to others, then in time perhaps... One might advance those sciences to our required levels.

However we wondered also if mankind might deserve immortality. Within the following decade then a war was raged overseas where men fought to preserve their right to own other men and use them enslaved without consent or ending... Yet also this war fought to *end* such things in one of the final vestiges of great political power where the practice remained. The victor of this might determine in truth the course of all our hopes for mankind, and in doing so show again those potentials for change not of the exceptional, but of the societies whole.

This of course was all before sweeping reforms within the catholic church deemed larger our blasphemous beliefs and life than ever before, at which time Claire, having joined in extremist views, informed members of that church in confession to our whereabouts. Being able not to specify the exact directions of our home, but indeed to approximate it's location accurately enough, we were forced to flee in advance of a veritable troop of clergy who descended upon our wood with malicious intent, chanting exorcisms and proclamations of piety even as they meant to take from us the peace and goodness of a life unspoiled.

Fortunately we were able to carry with us most of our cherished belongings, yet the infuriating indignity and saddened loss of our home was only a small disturbance in the end, as we considered for some days the adventurous freedom by which direction to accord ourselves.

CR: You went to Japan.

AG: We did. The catholic church was not welcomed there, and peaceful places remained as images of beauty and tales of splendor had long before enchanted our imaginations. We travelled to Japan, and making our way inland, settled at the base of a mountain to build our new home in secret placement beyond the farms and rice patties nearby. It was beautiful indeed, serene and bountiful to view in each season passing, and in building our home with garden and carpentry equal in beauty to the landscape, we flourished. However secrecy proved both short lived as well as unnecessary, when Mary by walk one night in the mid of winter, expressed a strange feeling to know a presence somehow like our own nearby.

I had no such detection, and only by trust of Mary did follow her forward below the moon's light, until reaching the borders of a small farm, we heard the screams of a man and woman. Looking to see before them that which they later called the kyuuketsuki, and identifying with greater concern for our neighbors than desire to remain hidden, we interceded then. Mary, running faster than I was able, took the farmers in retreat while I, following shortly behind, meant to fight that fiend who menaced clear harm toward them.

He was a pale and thin man, with large eyes and a distended jaw wherein he possessed fangs bared both upper and lower in mouth like the maw of a reptile. I fought him alone at first, but soon was joined by others, who with polearms in hand, similar to a knifed lance in shape, pinned his body against a wall nearby, when an older gentleman approached fearlessly to hand me his sword with stern look. I had never wielded a blade of that make, yet taking it quickly with my best effort toward a customary bow of respect, I pulled this from scabbard and cut the head from that attacker, before dividing it further into parts. After this I exchanged that sword I had been given, in trade for the flames held by a shaking torchbearer, and I lit the body to burn.

That was how our friendships began with the Fukiharo family. Stories of our presence nearby had previously become the stuff of children's night stories, having been glimpsed or speculated by the sounds of our home or smokes of our fires, yet now those tales changed. Mary and I were lauded as heroes among them, welcomed into their lands, taught their language, and even hired with traded payments to work their farms. They became as family to us, each of them nearly as beloved to our sight as children and brethren alike, and at last with open companionship and all pleasantries of life provided, we passed the next twenty years.

However during that time, troubles had found our ears that bandits wearing the garb of British soldiers had begun to pillage the countryside. Of course... what cause did Mary or myself have to fear of bandits? We thought. Each of us possessed strength beyond mortals. Each of us would heal. So knowing this, we began our campaign of defense, and alongside the family, and neighboring farmers, we met those men as they came, only to see them turned away in haste, each time diminishing in number.

No less than twelve times this occurred, and never did a single injury befall Mary, myself, or our friends... Until that is, they came by night while we slept, accompanied by priests.

Waking with a jolt, I was held down by several men, but knew also some drug within my system had been introduced. For the weakness of body and slowness of mind I felt, were too familiar to me the effects of toxin derived from opiate distillate. Mary screamed from another room beyond my sight, even as I heard the striking of hammer which pinned my wrists and ankles to the floor by irons driven through bone and flesh. And when those hammers stopped by mine, I knew in the continuing strikes that Mary suffered the same.

I struggled to free myself, screaming and pleading with begging heart, even while chants were given above me and oil thrown over my body. In desperate tears I struggled, until ripping loose the iron pin of one hand, I seized at those men who held my body and throwing one of them from me, the others soon followed. Scattering, they ran, even as Mary continued to scream, and the house was set ablaze on their exits.

This fire caught and lit the oils covering my body, even while my legs and opposing arm stayed pinned. I fought them, ceasing my screams and focusing in determination to free myself. At last accomplishing this I attempted to run in search of Mary within the adjoining rooms, but could not dowse the blaze upon my body, or move quickly on shattered ankle. I fell forward when one of the beams which held our roof, landed upon my back, trapping me without escape. My energies failing and body broken, I tried. With everything I possessed I tried I swear it....

Tears were pouring from Adam's eyes. He was shaking uncontrollably. I quit recording.

The conversation was no longer suiting for an interview to be read by others. Adam's grief made intelligible speech difficult through convulsing hyperventilations, but I can pass on what was learned.

Mary stopped screaming after that he told us. He was rescued by neighbors who pulled him from the still burning house and extinguished the flames on his body, but none of them could make it to Mary. She died, her body burnt beyond salvaging or recovery. Adam lived... and it was something he blamed himself for.

ALONE IN A ROOM OF MANY

12:02 Am, April the 3rd, Recording resumes

AG: I promise you, should I falter again I will make you aware. I can continue.

It was 1899. I woke within the home of Jin Fukihara, having slumbered within catatonia for for six months while tended to all the while by that family. My home destroyed and Mary... gone... I recovered slowly, in agonizing despair, but grateful thanks to my rescuers.

Having searched the ashes of our home, they assured me no chance of my love's survival, yet I could not accept without seeing myself what remained. They spoke true. The whole of it had been burned to ash, and nowhere within did a body remain discernable from that wreckage.

In 1900, I left Japan. I made my way here to your country and I secluded myself from the world. The great states of the globe erupted into war, and even then I did not engage. I experimented with dyes to pass myself as mortal man and in time as you know, discovered this possibility, only venturing forth on occasions when needed... For the company of others felt hollow without love.
I found gold within the mine near my home and pushing my strength against the mountain above, I labored for this beyond need, simply for the work of body and release it gave to accomplish some task. Writing on occasion to the family and descendents which had rescued me in Japan, I continued correspondance until a second "great war" took the world.

I was horrified to witness the devastations wrought by this and though I would have fought to kill every Nazi of the so called third reich which corrupted my homeland. However, I knew that such evil could *never* know of my existence, lest they unleash upon the world those terrors multiplied one hundred more fold. So I watched from my self imposed exile. I observed the rises of technology, along with the rise of political turmoils which darkened my hopes.

Now able to walk amongst men and women unsuspected, and with wealth at my disposal, after the war, I sent money to bring over those who remained of the Fukihara line, and using a false identity crafted some years before, purchased on their behalf a business and home where they began their journey within this land.

Yet in the cold, humorless grey of the mundane, I became trapped by minor day to day proceedings of life. Was I living my purpose? No. I passed each, my time in toil and struggle to achieve a place where that was possible, knowing that the song of my heart would overtake all other desires, and that I would be lost within it of only I allowed myself the freedom. So rather than pursue those passions or live to my fullest, I filled my waking hours with directed actions, duty and unspoken obligation to serve a function, lifeless dedication to practicality followed that was broken, only by the distraction of entertainment or frivolity which did not feed my spirits.

And day by day, that spirit, smothered carefully to preserve its very ember, became a distant and hidden glow that dared not flicker to more... A flame in waiting, a heart sustained on buried hopes alone, waiting for the day it could once again burn bright, if only I could keep it alive until then.

They say that each time we remember an event that it changes in our minds eye, and I have to wonder if I am honest with myself... Since it first transpired, I have played that night in my head a million times, yet part of me still questions how far I have come from the original events to what I now recall.

If with each retelling of the memory I have changed even one slight or another, then what truth is there left to my recollections of pain or regret that might be more or less than falsehood or emotional trickery upon myself? And yet with each time, it feels true to my heart.

Do I now, as they say, only remember the story as one imagines a fiction? Or is that part of me somehow any different from the minds of other men? If I remember my fear or courage, are these merely tricks of regret, or was I in the moment, that which I feel myself to have been? Heroic? Cowardly? Overwhelmed? Was the weight so much to bear that my entrapment true? Or is that merely an excuse I have told myself after the fact?

There is no way to know. We are merely in the end the stories which we tell ourselves, and acceptance of that as reality may be the only peace possible in place of any objective record otherwise writ in places unknown, beyond the reaches of human life. Therefore I cling to the hope that I have not been false, but know that I do not know.

By the mark three quarter past the century before this, I had consumed myself in purposed research. Man had been to the moon and returned. Perhaps the sciences *had* come so far. I left my home and sought out a Doctor claiming to have discovered Conrad's original formulas, but he was a charlatan. Another within the following decade proved so unethical in experimentation that I was forced to take his life in preservation of others from suffering due his abhorrent practices. Still more after that I met with disappointed eyes, but I hoped still.

After the fall of the Soviet Union, and destruction of the Berlin wall, I returned for a time to my old home, and found no remains of its structure. Instead I found also ash, where it being discovered, I suspect those Priest and clergy who sought us, had burned it also to the ground... And so within that countryside most familliar but changed, I continued elsewhere to rediscover those contents buried so long before which contained my father's personal belongings.

They had built a coffeehouse upon the spot... but turmoils some time before had see it closed for repair, and I was able to break through the floors in retrieval of that chest. This I brought with me on my return by cargo ship. As you might imagine, it is difficult for one my size to procure passage by air. Also I should like to note since it has not been asked, that I do in fact drive and own a vehicle. I have a truck, if that might interest anyone.

For another decade, I remained nearest my home, which is in possession of not only power, but utilities and internets as my identification on record states that I am 89 years old. Of course that is when I watched your speech Doctor. I had already taken to following your career with interest you see, but it was that speech which solidified in me the knowledge, that at last a man existed who might truly be my aide, and in this I meant to seek you.

However discovery of you, my dear...

Adam turned toward me.

Came only by chance when seeing the page of your mothers obituary within the paper of this town, I recognized a piece of jewelry worn within her portrait. Once it had belonged to Claire, but given afterward to Marina, linked somehow your family to that woman whom I had once entrusted my daughter in Naples so long ago.

And so I searched, pouring over genealogies and traveling abroad to seek further confirmation, I discovered the truth of my child, and later her line, leading lastly to you, the final member...

Tears were welling in Adam's eyes again.

I wish for these to be my final words on record.

CR: Are you sure?

AG: My story is concluded dear. The time has come. Any further questions may be asked without these proceedings. I wish to know you both, truly I do, for what duration it takes to prepare these notes to public view and begin the task of my undoing I hope to grow close.

May I speak in closing?

I nodded my head and looked to Steven who agreed silently. Adam began.

AG: I might begin by stating this. Time itself is a double edged sword... Having both the blessing and curse of it's abundance, I have taken my days to fill with both thought and action in equal measure. I have seen sympathy in your eyes for my pains, but I tell you that I would not marr my memories with regret nor trade them for the all the comforts of this world.

I have often heard others in their musings, ponder the thought that ignorance is bliss. Yet I for one have often marveled conversely whether bliss itself may lead to a type of ignorance, taking pity on those whose lives have been filled with little more than joy, for the lessons that they have been deprived by such.

You spoke of this very thing several days ago and I have continued to mull over your words. Is as you posited, thought itself beyond the confines of necessity and preservation of life or livelihood not an indulgence I have wondered? For who has the freedom to question but those who have the blessings of worry lifted from their shoulders? And still I rail at the audacity to think such things, for in worry and despair have I not asked the eternally lingering curiosities of more profundity than during times of joy and ease?

I have truly known many of years so fewer than mine, made wiser than I could ever claim, not by age or maturity as so often defined, not by ease or luxury, but experience and thought alone brought to them by facing the temptations of comfort, and refusing to allow themselves reprieve from that which mattered the most to their internal world beyond the external circumstances of life; Having transcended the bounds of those who walk so lightly through the rain without damp or darkness besmirching their forms. I do not feel myself their equal in this matter, but I strive to reach all the same.

My pains and troubles, though many over the vastness of life, were in earnest, the surest form of strength that could be gifted such a meager mind as my own. These in measure were the weights by which my soul, if that be what I possess within, exercised each task to grow in capability and fortitude.
If not for my pain, could I experience the heights of joy? If not for my struggles, could I have learned the lessons of life which were bestowed only by adversarial emotions regarding the depths of discomfort or the burning fires of anger and passion? Could I have loved so deeply if I had never known the spurns of rejection or cruelties of others?

Even in the grip of hate for those who pursued me with such disdain, how could I have learned to love and appreciate the strength of my convictions without their very challenge? By the knowledge of what I did not believe, did I acquire the knowledge of my own values and character. By their example of evils, did I not learn my definitions of goodness? By forgiveness of their faults, did I not temper the shame over my own regretful misdeeds and mistakes?

Yes, at times I fell to loss of hope, despair and pain... feeling as if life were defined by the cruel idioms of selfishness, that acts of love and morality were merely self satisfying in their expression, and that perhaps there were no greater meaning to the turning of the globe but to protect myself and serve the whims of my own desires above those of some imaginary greater good. However through the valleys of hardship and peaks of ecstasy I grew from these thoughts as a child grows to understand the grace of a parent who chastised them for ill resulting behaviors which endangered their very life.

That sense of meaninglessness, righteousness in one's self interest, if only to forgive the nature of indulgence or guilt, are in the end merely a plateau to be crossed, an illness to be overcome and a lesson to their own meaning, which present as either a desert uncrossed by the heart of cowardice, or a plain of passage by the courageous who discover what lies beyond.

Perhaps I admit to the possibility of foolishness. Those who linger in that desert might proclaim as much with both fury and right within their own accord, but I find conscience allows me not to claim absolute my feelings of knowing. For only a fool believes himself to know anything beyond themselves with certainty, just as only a fool would ever delude their mind into believing that they have plumbed every depth of their own being... And yet if they have, what shallow and meager depths must they have found to begin with, in order to explore them each so thoroughly as one might claim to have traversed footstep on every patch of earth above the sea. It is in humble regard I acknowledge these feats as impossible for myself.

Yet I have come to not only accept these things, but to embrace the darkness and questioning in equal part to the lightness of being. Now I face this world in one final truth and embrace the adventure of death, not as an enemy or fear, but as another step along a path which has left fear at my back in the way that a student leaves behind his teachers in order to embark on new passages of life.

But in all the days and years of life, there is but one device which pains me to the point of bleakness, and that is the wretchedness of solitude without purpose. If I not find the solace of company in the heart of love, then give me please that function of purpose to these endless days.

To quote the words of her herself whom I loved so dearly, "We are unfashioned creatures, but half made up, if one wiser, better, dearer than ourselves – such a friend ought to be- do not lend his aid to perfectionate our weak and faulty natures. I once had a friend, the most noble of human creatures, and am entitled, therefore, to judge respecting friendship. You have hope, and the world before you, and have no cause for despair. But I – I have lost every thing and cannot begin life anew."

I urge of you, nay beg; Drain my blood. Dismember my body. Discover all of which you can by every device that gives me life, but do not insist that I live. Make me the Prometheus that I was once dreamed to become. Light symbolically my blood as torch and share it with the peoples of humankind. I have known this world at length in both it's beauty and malice... and I can no longer bear to suffer my inhabitance without my Mary, save for the hope that my passing in its action, may serve a greater good upon the earth, or that in those mysteries of death I should meet her once more, alongside all our loves past.

Do this for me please, and share this tale with those who would benefit, for I wish to be remembered as a man, not monster; Who in loving the potentials of mankind, would chance what might be achieved if given the opportunity to grow without death, explore and learn without fear or ending whether thru sickness or injury, that you may reach the heights of those promised dreams, and climb high toward those ambitious principles long proclaimed.

Do this for me Cassandra my descendant; Steven, my shining redemption of ambition untainted. Do this and remember me. My life, my story, love, hope, and lessons learned. Share them.

Recording ends.

EPILOGUE

"Adam 315" Was published April 1st, 2025, nearly a year after it's final interview. The public fascination was immediate, though unlucky in date to release, many suspected these stories to be a hoax. The worldwide scientific community debated, even when Adam's photos were released along with Steven's preliminary research and conclusions.

After one month however, officials within the American political sphere, granted Steven and his team the research funding and facilities to begin the studies of Adam's unique making, so that he might in fulfillment of his last wishes, truly provide those answers for which we all hoped.

Thru all of this, the three of us remained inseparable. Adam was the best man at my wedding to Steven, and we stayed with him in his home as our honeymoon. Then when the time came, we moved to a facility outside Atlanta where Adam, after saying his farewells and last thoughts, was sedated for the work to come.

Steven remained dedicated toward achieving all answers without Adam's death, and though this work was to remain incomplete due to circumstances later to take all of humanities affordable attentions, I would resume recording April 21st, 2026, to document the following.

Adam was sat partly upright, dressed in hospital gown and waking from anesthesia on a medical gurney. Steven and I stood by his feet while the watching the woman in front of him, brush the hair from his face with a gentle smile.

MS: I eat meat now.

AG: Mary?

Adam's eyes opened and he struggled to focus weakly.

MS: I read your telling and thought you should know... I eat meat now.

These words confirmed to Adam who was speaking to him and with excited efforts to rise from bed despite the drugs effects remaining, he could not raise his body enough to hug her. So he placed his hand over hers where she held his face, and tears streamed down his cheeks.

AG: You live?

MS: As do you it seems. I thought it first impossible, yet here you are... My love... I thought you lost in that fire. When your shouting stopped so suddenly, I believed you had perished and tore myself from the floor. I chased those men and killed them for their murder, yet when I came home once more you were gone. I believed as you of me, that your body had been consumed.

Mary cried also.

AG: Where did you go? Why did you not return to the farms?

MS: I chased the priests for days. After I'd killed them I could not face our dear neighbors in shame without you. I fled to South America where I have been these long years until reading your book and discovering your continued life.

AG: Claire and Percy would have notes.

MS: As do I. Yet you have honored them dear husband, far more than some might deserve.

I have missed you so... and our daughter... Survived in family here by these beautiful people... Oh Adam!

Mary at this point was overcome with tears and wrapped her arms forcefully around Adam, where she buried her head on his chest. Without words he looked toward us with the most grateful and humbled expression I think anyone has ever given in all human history, which may sound hyperbolic, but I assure I believe. We smiled in return before Adam returned his attention to Mary by pressing his lips to the top of her head with kisses while holding her close.

AG: Oh Mary you must tell me everything.

Recording concludes...

After these events Adam changed his mind about the absolute neccesity that his life come to an end for science. The study continued and we were moved along with Mary to a more secure location underground.

We worked in secret even after Titanfall.

The war and what came after it, diverted every attention elsewhere, and no more debate was had over Adam. The telling of our survival would become the history of

Adamstown and the first interspecies allliance .

Meanwhile "Adam 315", like Mary's "Frankenstein", before, would come to represent to us as Adam and Mary once phrased it, "only the beginnings".

The story will continue. Look for the "Stealing Fire" novels, by Dani Lebeaux.

...Coming soon...

Made in the USA
Columbia, SC
17 September 2023

22990564R00255